KEEP HER SAFE

ALSO BY K. A. TUCKER

Ten Tiny Breaths
One Tiny Lie
Four Seconds to Lose
Five Ways to Fall
In Her Wake
Burying Water
Becoming Rain
Chasing River
Surviving Ice
He Will Be My Ruin
Until It Fades

KEEP HER SAFE

A Novel

K.A. TUCKER

ATRIA BOOKS

New York London Toronto Sydney New Delhi

An Imprint of Simon & Schuster, Inc.
1230 Avenue of the Americas
New York, NY 10020

First Atria Books hardcover edition January 2018

Also available in an Atria hardcover edition.

Manufactured in the United States of America

10 9 8 7 6 5 4 3 2 1

The Library of Congress has cataloged the paperback original as follows:

Names: Tucker, K.A. (Kathleen A.)
Title: Keep her safe : a novel / K.A. Tucker.
Description: First Atria paperback edition. | New York : Atria Books, 2018.
Identifiers: LCCN 2017032787 (print) | LCCN 2017039112 (ebook) | ISBN 9781501133428 (eBook) | ISBN 9781501133404 (softcover) | ISBN 9781501149870 (hardcover)
Subjects: LCSH: Police corruption—Fiction. | Family secrets—Fiction. | BISAC: FICTION / Romance / Suspense. | FICTION / Suspense. | FICTION / Psychological. | GSAFD: Romantic suspense fiction.
Classification: LCC PR9199.4.T834 (ebook) | LCC PR9199.4.T834 K44 2018 (print) | DDC 813/.6—dc23
LC record available at https://lccn.loc.gov/2017032787

ISBN 978-1-5011-4987-0
ISBN 978-1-5011-3340-4 (pbk)
ISBN 978-1-5011-3342-8 (ebook)

For all the Abraham Wilkeses out there,
who risk their lives every day

KEEP HER SAFE

PROLOGUE

Corporal Jackie Marshall

June 1997

"There's gotta be a pound in each." Abe nudges the ziplock bag of marijuana with the tip of his pen. The kitchen table is shrouded in these bags, along with bundles of cash. I'm going to take a wild guess and say there's plenty more, hidden around this dive of an apartment.

I peer over at the guy we just busted, handcuffed and lying on his stomach, under another officer's watchful eye, waiting to be transported for booking. He's a scrawny nineteen-year-old with a temper. "Don't know about you, but I wouldn't be beatin' on my girlfriend if I had all these drugs in my house." His neighbors heard glass smashing and him making threats of death, so they called 9-1-1. He gave us cause to kick in the door when he uttered a string of racial slurs and then spat in Abe's face. That's how we found the bloodied blonde girl and *this*.

Now the paramedics are treating the gashes on her face, while we wait for Narcotics to swoop in.

Abe smooths his ebony-skinned hand over his cheek. "What do you think this is worth, anyway?"

"Depends how good it is. Ten grand? Maybe twenty?"

He lets out a low whistle. "I'm in the wrong business."

"You and me both. We bounced our mortgage payment last month." Blair told me we couldn't afford that house. I ought to have listened to him. But I also hadn't planned on getting pregnant when

I did. Not that I regret having Noah. I just expected to have earned a few stripes before I was elbow-deep in diapers and formula.

"Don't worry, you'll be making the big bucks soon enough, *Sergeant* Marshall," Abe mocks with a dimpled grin. He's been calling me that for months, ever since I passed my test and was put on the promotion list. "Just don't go forgetting about us beat cops when you start pinning those stars to your collar."

"You're ridiculous." I roll my eyes at him.

"Am I? You are one damn ambitious woman, Jackie, and my money's on you over half the clowns around here, present company included." He sighs. "My days won't be the same, though."

"I'm gonna miss being your partner, Abe." After seven years, there's no one else I trust more in the APD—and in life—than Abe Wilkes.

He lets out a derisive snort. "Don't worry, you'll see me plenty enough. Heck, Noah'll probably be at *my* house more than yours."

"Dina's managing alright, what with a baby of her own? Don't want Noah to be a burden on her."

Abe waves off my concern. "Dina'll steal that kid away from you if you're not watching. She *insisted*."

I can't be sure if it was Dina or Abe who offered to mind Noah while Blair and I work. I've never seen a grown man dote on a little boy as much as Abe dotes on mine. Even Blair doesn't pay that much attention, and Noah's his son. "That beautiful wife of yours is a blessing. I wish you'd have knocked her up and gotten married years ago. Would have saved me a ton on daycare bills."

Abe struggles to keep that booming chuckle of his at bay—it wouldn't be appropriate given current surroundings. "I'd say we're movin' plenty fast, don't you?"

Pregnant three months into dating and married at City Hall the week after finding out? I'd say so. "Your mom come around yet?" A good Christian woman like Abe's mother was less than pleased when she found out her twenty-eight-year-old son had knocked up an eighteen-year-old girl. An eighteen-year-old *white* girl. I've met

Carmel Wilkes. I don't believe she has an issue with Dina, per se; she's more worried about *other* people taking issue with Dina and Abe together, and the problems that may arise. As progressive as Austin is, there's still plenty of hate to go around when it comes to the color of a person's skin.

Abe shrugs. "Slowly but surely."

"I'll bet that gorgeous little Gracie is helping."

It's inevitable, the second anyone says his daughter's name, that Abe's face splits open with a wide grin. He's about to say something—probably tell another story about how cute she is—when our radios crackle with voices.

"The cavalry's here." I pat my stomach. "Good thing, too. I'm starving. Let's get this lowlife booked and then get some food."

"Hey . . ." Abe lowers his voice to a whisper. "I wonder, how honest do you think these narc guys are?"

"Honest enough. Why?"

His chocolate-brown eyes roll over the bundles of cash. "Wouldn't it be easy for one of those to go missing?"

It's a question you don't pose, especially not while you're in uniform and standing in front of a pile of drugs. "Pretty dang easy, I'll bet."

CHAPTER 1

Noah

April 2017
Austin, Texas

"Hello?"

A garbled string of code words over the police scanner carries down the darkened hallway, answering me.

My heart sinks.

She's still awake.

Kicking my dusty sneakers off, I drag myself all the way to the back of the house. "Hey, Mom," I offer as casually as possible, passing her hunched body at the kitchen table, a cigarette smoldering on the edge of a supper plate, a half-finished bottle of cheap whiskey sitting within her easy reach, her gun belt lying haphazardly next to it.

I don't know why I was hoping for something different tonight. I've been coming home to the same scene for weeks now.

"Where were y'all at tonight?" That Texan twang of hers is always heavier when she's been drinking.

I yank open the fridge door. "It's Wednesday."

She tilts rather than lifts her head and spies the basketball tucked under my arm. "Right. I can't keep up with you."

I *could* point out that there's not much to keep up with. I'm a creature of habit. If I'm not at work, then I'm with my friends, at the gym or doing laps at the pool, or tossing a ball around. I've been going to the same pickup courts every Wednesday night since I moved back to Texas to go to UT seven years ago.

I twist the cap off the carton of orange juice and lift it to my mouth instead. Wishing she'd berate me for not using a glass. That's what she used to do, back when she didn't beeline for her liquor cabinet the second she walked in the door from work. She'd also remind me not to dribble my ball in the house and to throw my sweat-soaked clothes through the hot cycle of the wash right away, so my room doesn't smell like a gym locker.

Now she doesn't even bother to change out of her uniform half the time.

As if to prove a point to myself, I let the ball hit the tile once . . . twice . . . seizing it against my hip after the third bounce, the hollow thud of leather against porcelain hanging in the air.

Waiting.

Hoping.

Nothing. Not a single complaint from her, as she sits there, her eyes half-shuttered, her cropped blonde hair unkempt, her mind preoccupied with something far beyond the oak table's wood grain that she stares at. She doesn't give a shit about basic manners anymore. These past few weeks, all she does is sit at the kitchen table and listen to the radio crackle with robbery reports and domestic assault calls and a dozen other nightly occurrences for the Austin Police Department.

Her police department, seeing as she's the chief. A female chief of police in one of the biggest cities in the United States. A monumental feat. She's held that position for two years.

And, up until recently, seemed to have held it well.

Coughing against the lingering stench of Marlboros, I slide open the window above the sink. Crisp spring air sails in. I never thought I'd say this, but I miss the smell of lemon Pledge and bleach.

"Don't forget to close it before you go to bed. Don't wanna get robbed," she mutters.

"We're not gonna get robbed." We live in Clarksville, a historic neighborhood and one of the nicest in a city that's generally considered to be safe and clean. I can't blame her for being cautious, though; she's been a cop for thirty years. She's seen society's underbelly. She probably knows things about our neighbors that would make me avert my eyes when passing them on the street. Still, even the worst parts of Austin are a playground next to typical city slums.

I frown as I peer down at the filthy sink. The stainless steel is spattered with black specks. "Did you *burn* something in here?"

"Just . . . trash."

I fish out a scrap of paper with perforations along one side. It looks like a page torn from a notepad. *April 16, 2003* is scrawled across it in writing that isn't my mother's.

"Biggest mistake of my life." She puffs on her cigarette, her words low and slurred. "I should have known Betsy wasn't the only one . . ."

"Who's Betsy?"

"Nobody anymore," she mutters, along with something indiscernible.

I fill a tall glass of water and set it down in front of her, using it as a distraction so I can drag the bottle of whiskey out of her reach.

She makes a play for it anyway, her movements slow and clumsy. "Give it on back to me, Noah. Right now, ya hear me?"

I shift to the other side of the table, screwing the cap on extra tight, though she could probably still open it. For a woman of her stature—five foot four and 130 pounds—she's all muscle. At least she *was* all muscle. Her lithe body has begun to deteriorate thanks to the daily liquid supper. "You've had enough for tonight."

"What do you know about *enough*? There ain't enough whiskey in the world for what I've done." She fumbles with the four silver stars pinned to her uniform's collar, looking ready to rip them off.

So it's going to be one of *those* nights. But who am I kidding? *Those* nights, when she starts in on this incoherent rambling, about not deserving to be chief, are more and more common lately. I miss the days when all she'd complain about was stupid laws and lack of department funding.

I sigh. "Come on, I'll help you upstairs."

"No," she growls, a stubborn frown setting across her forehead.

It's half past eleven. She's normally passed out by nine, so this is an unusually late night for her. Still, if she downs a few glasses of water and goes to bed, *maybe* she'll be ready for work by the morning, only a little worse for wear.

I fold my six-foot-two frame into the chair across from her. "Mom?"

"I'm fine . . ." she mumbles, her brow pinched with irritation as she fumbles with her pack of cigarettes.

I wish I could be angry with her. Instead, I'm sad and frustrated. I'm pretty sure I need help, but I have no idea who to turn to. I was eleven the last time she hit the bottle like this. She and Dad were still married, so he dealt with it. But Dad has wiped his hands of her. He's got a new wife and family and a meat-and-potatoes life in Seattle. He was never meant to be the husband of a cop, and especially not one as ambitious as my mother.

She'd skin me alive if I went to any of the guys I know from the APD about her drinking. There are too many people looking for a reason to get rid of a female chief. *This* would be a *good* reason.

I could go to Uncle Silas. He's the district attorney; he wouldn't want voters finding out that his sister the chief of police is a drunk. I should have gone to him already, but I hoped it was a phase, something she'd work out on her own.

Maybe with a little push from us, Mom can get sober again. She did it once before, years ago. Quit cold turkey. She's tough like that. She can beat this again.

If she wants to.

I turn down the volume on the police scanner. "Mom?"

Her eyes snap open. It takes her a moment to focus on me, but she finally does. "How was basketball?"

"They beat our asses."

"Who were you playing with?"

"Jenson, Craig. The usual crew."

"Jenson and Craig . . ." she mutters, her gaze trailing over my arms, long and cut from hours of lifting weights and swimming laps. And she smiles. It's sloppy, but I see the wistfulness behind the boozy mask. "You've become so strong and independent, Noah. And smart. *So* smart. You know I love you to bits, right?"

I nudge the glass of water forward. "Take a sip, Mom. Please."

She humors me by downing half the glass, only to then reach for her glass of whiskey and knock back the shot.

"What time do you have to be in to work tomorrow?" If I can catch her over her morning coffee, when she's sober and still feeling the pain of tonight, maybe I can start a serious conversation.

Maybe I can get through to her.

"You've grown into a good, honest man," she mutters, not answering me. "You're going to be fine."

"Here. Let me get you another glass of water." I fill up three more, lining them on the table in front of her. "Drink. Please."

With reluctance, she reaches for the first.

"I'm gonna grab a shower." Without the promise of more booze, she'll stagger upstairs and be passed out facedown in her uniform by the time I'm out, I'm betting. I dip down to grab the bottle from beneath the chair.

"He was a good, honest man, too," she mutters.

"You'll find someone else. You're still young." She does this when she's drunk, too—talks about Dad, about how it's her fault they divorced. Right after this, she's going to say that she's a terrible mother, because she abandoned me, let him take me to Seattle all those years ago. A boy needs his father, she believed.

"No, not your dad . . . Abe."

I freeze.

I haven't heard her say that name in years.

I ask cautiously, "*Abraham*, Abe?"

"Hmmm." She nods. Again, that wistful smile touches her lips. "You remember him, don't you?"

"Of course." He was the tall man with ebony skin and a wide smile who taught me how to dribble a ball. He was my mother's police partner for years, and one of her best friends for even longer.

Until he was killed by a cocaine dealer, only to be labeled a corrupt cop after his death. I was eleven when he died. I didn't understand what that meant, only that whatever Abraham Wilkes did was *bad.* It made statewide news and broadened an already perceptible racial divide within the community. It made Mom start drinking, and I'm pretty sure it broke apart our family.

"He was a *good* man." Her voice drifts off with her gaze, as her eyes begin to water. "He was a good, honest man."

I wander back toward the table. "I thought he was stealing and dealing drugs."

She chuckles as she takes another drag of her cigarette. It's a sad, empty sound. "That's what everyone thinks, because that's what they *made* them think. But *you* . . ." She pokes the air with her finger, her normally neat and trim fingernails chewed to the quick. "You need to know the truth. *I* need you to know that he was a good man and we are bad, bad people."

"Who's bad?" I'm desperate to pull the chair out and sit down across from her again, to listen to whatever it is she's trying to tell me. But I also don't think she realizes what she's divulging. And I don't want to give her pause to clue in and clam up.

She dumps her cigarette pack out on the table, scattering a half dozen cigarettes before finding one to light. "You know he broke Dina. Ran her and that beautiful little girl out of town. She was so young when Abe died. Gracie. He always smiled when he said her name." Mom smiles now too, reminiscing. "She has her mama's green eyes and Abraham's full lips and kinky curls. And her skin, it's this gorgeous color, like caramel, and—"

"Mom!" I snap, hoping to get her focus back. I vaguely remember Abe's kid—a cute girl with big eyes and wild hair—but I don't want to hear about her right now. "What are you talking about? Who did what?"

"It didn't start out that way. Or . . . I guess it did. But he made it sound *right.*"

"Who? Abe?"

Her head shakes back and forth lazily. "I don't deserve to be chief, but it was one heck of a carrot. Better than the stick. Abe . . . *he* got the stick. He couldn't be bought. He was just in the wrong place, at the wrong time. Because of me."

"You're not making sense."

Her jaw sets, and her eyes fix on a point behind my head. "What I let happen . . . I may as well have pulled the trigger." She barely has the cigarette lit when she mashes it into the pile of ashes. "I sold my soul is what I did, and there ain't no coming back from that."

"What—"

"'Course I should have known he'd be waiting like a wily fox in the thicket to use it against me."

"Who—"

"Just remember I meant to do good. And he *promised* me he didn't know her age. He *promised* he'd never do it again." She snorts. "I need you to know, Abe was a good man." A tear slips down her cheek, and her gaze locks on mine. "I tried to make it right. But I couldn't face her. After all this time, I couldn't face what I'd done to her. I'm a coward. Not a chief. A coward."

A shiver runs down my back. "Who are you talking about, Mom?"

She shakes her head. "She must hate her daddy. She don't know any better. But I *need* her to know. Tell Gracie he was a good man. You'll do that, right?"

I'm speechless, trying to decipher the meaning behind her jumbled words. "Mom . . . what are you trying to tell me?" It sounds a hell of a lot like a confession. But for what?

She opens her mouth to speak, but nothing comes out as she stares at me, her blue eyes—the same cornflower shade as mine—cast with a haunted shadow. I wait for her to explain herself.

Finally she flicks her lighter, letting the tiny flame dance for a moment before pulling her thumb away to extinguish it. "Go on to bed, and let sleeping dogs lie. They're less likely to bite." She chuckles. "He always liked that saying, every time I pushed him, every time I told him they were up to no good."

As if I could sleep after this. "Mom . . ."

"You remember Hal Fulcher?"

"Your lawyer?"

"Make sure you pay him a visit. Don't wait too long. They don't have much time."

What? Why?

"Go and grab that shower." She finishes the first glass of water, then chugs the second. I'm not going to get any coherent answers from her tonight. This conversation will have to continue in the morning, though I can't imagine how to start it.

I lean down to place a kiss on her forehead, and she reaches up, her palm cupping my stubbled jaw in an affectionate gesture. "I love you so much. Always remember that."

"Love you, too. And if you're not in bed by the time I'm done, I'll throw you over my shoulder." She knows it's not an idle threat. I've done it before.

She responds with hollow laughter, then turns up the dial on the police radio, her eyes beginning to shutter. Another five minutes and she'll be passed out, right there on the table.

The dispatcher's voice doesn't quite muffle her heavy sigh. "You're gonna be fine."

I peel off my clothes and throw them in a corner. I'll deal with them later. Just like I'll deal with the scruff covering my jaw. Or not. We're going to Rainey Street tomorrow night for drinks and Jenson's girlfriend is bringing her friend Dana, the one I hooked up with last week. I forgot to shave then, too, and she seemed to like it.

I simply stand under the hot stream of water for a moment, letting it rivulet over my skin, hoping it'll melt away the unease that's settled onto my shoulders. Mom was acting different tonight. Almost . . . crazy. The fact that she brought up Abe has thrown me for a loop. She took his death hard. That's when she started *really* drinking the first time.

And what the hell was all that talk of carrots and sticks and selling her soul?

I inhale the spicy scent of my shampoo as I scrub away at my scalp. Fucking dramatic drunken rambling. I can't imagine what my mother thinks she's guilty of. She's a highly decorated police chief. She's well respected in the community. She's smart and funny. When she's not drunk.

She's my *mom*.

The blast of a gunshot tears through the house.

CHAPTER 2

Noah

My uncle Silas walks with a limp.

I was five when I first recognized that he didn't walk like everyone else, when I mentioned his funny gait. He pulled me onto his knee and asked me if I knew what a ninja was. I laughed at him and held up my Raphael Ninja Turtle figurine. That's when he told me how he once fought a *real* ninja. He said he won, but in its last moments, the ninja gouged his leg with a blade. He rolled up his pant leg and showed me the five-inch scar to prove it.

Every time we visited, I would ask him to tell me the story again and he would, each version more detailed and far-fetched than the last. He told it so convincingly that I believed him, consuming every grand detail with a stupid grin on my face.

I got older. Soon, I was too big to be pulled onto his lap and too wise to buy into the tall tale. I'd still ask, though, with the smart-ass tone and that doubtful gaze of a boy growing into adolescence. But he'd hold fast to his story of the ninja's blade, capping it off with a wink.

I was nine when my mom finally told me the truth—that twelve-year-old Silas fell out of a tree while saving *her* from falling, and suffered a bad break that never set properly. My grandmother refused to let the doctors rebreak the bone, leaving her son with a mild limp.

Even though I had already figured out that the ninja story wasn't real, I remember feeling completely disenchanted. I guess that tiny flame of childhood hope for the impossible had still been burning, buried somewhere deep.

Now, I watch the silhouette of a man with a limp approach the front porch where I sit, his face obscured by the night and countless flashing lights that fill our cul-de-sac, and all I want is for him to tell me another story.

One where my mother is still alive.

Silas is fifty-seven and anything but an old man, yet he climbs the steps like one, his movements slow and wooden, his shoulders hunched, his hand on the wrought-iron rail to support him to the landing. I'm guessing he's stuck in the same surreal fog as I am.

He sounds out of breath by the time he reaches the landing. "I had my phone on silent. And Judy must have turned off the ringer to the house line while she was dusting today."

"It's okay." I tried calling his numbers three times each before the cops dispatched a car to his place.

He hovers near the front door.

"They might not let you inside," I warn him, my voice hollow. He's the district attorney for Travis County, but he's also the deceased's brother. What is the protocol in situations like this?

"I don't *want* to go inside." He fumbles absently with a set of keys inside his cardigan pocket. All he has on underneath is a white V-neck T-shirt, the kind you wear as an undershirt. The kind you pick out of the hamper at one in the morning, when the police have woken you to tell you that your little sister shot herself in the head.

I can't remember the last time I saw Silas looking so disheveled, but I'm not one to comment. Up until an hour ago I was wearing nothing but a blood-soaked towel hastily wrapped around my hips. My hair is still coated with shampoo suds.

Taking a deep breath, he mutters, "Give me a minute." And he disappears inside, leaving me to stare out at the chaos. They must have every available officer on site, the dead-end street filled with cruisers. Our neighbors are standing on their porches in various states of dress, watching quietly. At least we live in a secluded area, where there are only six houses' worth of people to witness this. The police barrier around the corner keeps the gawkers at a safe distance. Apparently there's a crowd over there.

Silas emerges two minutes later. Or maybe twenty minutes. His face is drawn and pale. He eases into the porch swing next to me, pausing for a moment to take in the dried blood covering my hands. I knew I shouldn't touch her, even as my fingers reached for her neck and her wrist, searching in vain for a pulse. "What the hell happened, Noah?"

All I can do is shake my head. The cops told me to stay put and not make calls or otherwise talk to anyone, but no one's stopping Silas from being here, so I guess he doesn't count.

"Noah . . ." he pushes.

"The kitchen window was open. Someone could have climbed in."

"Perhaps." I can tell Silas is saying that to appease me.

As fast as I flew down those stairs, no one would have had time to climb back out the window and reset the screen without my notice. Plus, why not use the door? But the doors were locked, and the alarm was set.

"Walk me through it."

"You're gonna be fine."

Those were her last words to me. *Jesus* . . . Those were her last words and I left her there.

Silas rests his hand on my knee, pulling me back from my guilt-laden thoughts.

I tell him what I told the emergency dispatcher and the cops—that I was upstairs for no more than twenty minutes. That I was in the shower when I heard the gunshot and I came down to find her facedown in a pool of blood at the kitchen table, the gun gripped in her hand.

"And before that?"

Before that . . . "She was into the whiskey."

"Just tonight?"

I hesitate, and then shake my head.

He takes a deep breath. "How long?"

"A few weeks." I lower my voice. "She was saying all kinds of crazy shit tonight, Silas."

"Oh?" He leans back, shifting closer to me. "Like what?"

"Like how she didn't deserve her job, and didn't earn it."

He pauses to consider that. "Too many bullheaded bastards telling her a woman doesn't belong as chief. Maybe it got to her head finally."

"I don't think that's it." I lower my voice even further, to a whisper. "She was talkin' about Abe tonight. She made it sound like he was set up. And like she was involved."

"She said that? Those exact words?"

"Not exactly, but—"

"She had nothing to do with that mess." He shakes his head decisively. "Nothing."

"She seems to think otherwise. *Seemed* to," I correct myself, softly.

"Believe me when I say this, Noah: that investigation was the most thorough I've seen. There were no two ways about it, that man was *guilty*." His eyes search mine. "Did she tell you why she thought otherwise?"

"She didn't give any details. But the way she was talking, she made it sound like she had a hand in it."

"Good Lord, Jackie," he mutters. His eyes rove over the crowd and the officers coming in and out. A few of them I recognize, but most I don't. "Did you tell APD any of that?"

"Not yet."

"Maybe I can convince them to wait until tomorrow for your statement."

"They said they needed it tonight. At least a preliminary one."

Silas makes a sound of agreement. "Can't blame them. She *was* the chief." He drums his fingers against his knee. "They need to hurry it up, though."

"I'm sure they'll take it as soon as they can." Mom's body is still cooling inside.

"Did she say anything else to you?"

"I don't . . ." I try hard to focus on our conversation but it's tough, in this fog. "Something about how it started off as being the right thing. And a wily fox, using something against her. Do you think she was being blackmailed?"

"She never told me. I'd think she would, don't you?"

I shrug. Because who knows what my mother would do, given what she *just did.*

Silas pauses. "Okay, here's what you're going to do." He leans in close to me, and I sense a plan coming into focus. That's Silas—you give him your problem, and he'll be formulating a solution within minutes. "They don't need to know what all was said," he mumbles, almost too low for even me to hear. "That's between you two. Your mom was a great cop and chief, and we don't need to give anyone ammunition to say otherwise. This is already going to be a hard pill to swallow for the city."

"But what am I supposed to tell the police? I can't lie, Silas."

"Did she ask you about your day?"

"Yeah."

"Tell them about that. You came home, talked for bit, and went upstairs. She was having a few drinks, but you didn't think anything of it. That's all true, right?"

"Right." Had the thought that she'd shoot herself crossed my mind, I would never have left her side.

"Then that's all you tell them. Whatever your mother was saying about Abe . . . she was drunk. She rambles when she's drunk. I'm sure it's not what it sounded like. It wouldn't be right to bring it up, not when she can't defend herself."

This isn't just my uncle telling me this. I'm getting the district attorney's seal of approval to keep my mother's crazy words to myself. Right or not, it's what I need to hear. I nod, and a flicker of relief sparks deep within this overwhelming void gripping me.

Silas and I fall into silence then, watching the parade of people stroll in and out with barely a glance in our direction.

". . . I don't know. When would be good?" Boyd steps out of the house, his radio in hand. I've known him since preschool and, while we've never been *best* friends, twenty-one years has earned us the right to call each other up at any time. Like the time he called me to ask if my mom would write him a letter of recommendation, when he was applying to the APD.

He was one of the first responders tonight.

The porch floor creaks under the weight of another man, following closely behind him. He's in plain clothes, but he must be a cop; otherwise they wouldn't have let him inside. "How 'bout next Wednesday, after our game?"

"Shit, does the season start next week? I'll have to see if I can make—"

"Officer, are you investigating your chief's death or planning out your social calendar? Tell Towle that *District Attorney* Silas Reid wants to get his *nephew* out of here *immediately*," Silas interrupts in a loud, annoyed voice.

Boyd turns to look at me with a grim expression. No cop with half a brain would want to get on the DA's bad side, and Boyd's no idiot. "Yes, sir. We're waiting for . . ." My attention drifts from whatever excuse he's giving Silas to the other guy, whose dark gaze has settled on me. His expression is blank and yet menacing. It could just be his deep-set eyes and steep forehead, the steepest I've ever seen. The combination makes him look like a mean son of a bitch.

"Noah?"

Silas's voice snaps me out of my daze. Boyd is standing in front of me, his notepad and pen out, sympathy on his face. "He'll take your preliminary statement and then we can deal with the rest tomorrow." Silas gives me a reassuring smile. "Are you ready?"

Am I ready to tell half-truths? "Yes, sir."

Of course Mom wouldn't have had anything to do with Abe's death.

And no one needs to know she said otherwise.

CHAPTER 3

Grace

Tucson, Arizona

I toss a baby carrot to the sandy ground. "Don't say I never shared."

Cyclops dives and devours it in one fell swoop, unbothered by the gritty coating. I'm not surprised. He'll eat anything he can fit into his yappy mouth. I've caught him trotting by with a rat tail dangling from his jaws more than once.

"Now go on." It's pointless; the mangy dog can smell the chicken taquitos I tucked away in my purse. He won't be leaving my heels anytime soon. Persistence is how he's survived this long. He doesn't have an owner to feed him; he follows the trailer park's inhabitants, hoping someone will pity him enough to throw him scraps. Usually that someone is me.

I remember the day he showed up, limping from an infected cut on his hind paw, a chunk of his ear freshly torn out, long since missing his left eye. I had one hell of a time holding him down to clean and wrap that foot of his. That was three years ago, and he keeps coming back.

Like many of the people who find their way to the Hollow.

I stroll along the laneway, ignoring him. It's two in the afternoon and Sleepy Hollow Trailer Park is practically a ghost town, as usual. Most everyone's either sleeping off their midnight shift or out working a long day for shitty pay, so they can come back to *this*.

I pass the Cortezes'. There are six people living in that trailer. It has a sheet of plywood covering a window because Mr. Cortez smashed it with his fist in a fit of rage last month and he doesn't have the money to replace it yet. Management won't say anything. Five hundred a month in rent doesn't buy you much around here, besides a roof that leaks during monsoon season. The park runs out of water at least three times a week, and the smell of sewage lingers in the air more days than not.

It looks like nobody's home there, and I say a quick prayer of thanks for that because if the Cortezes are home, then no one's getting *any* sleep. I was up at five for my shift at QuikTrip and I'm desperate for a nap before I have to bust my ass serving tables at Aunt Chilada's tonight.

Next to the Cortez family is the Sims trailer, where Kendrick Sims, his sister, her boyfriend, and their seven-year-old son live. While his sister and boyfriend work honest jobs, Kendrick has been in and out of prison more times than I can count. Currently he spends his days hanging around their yard, shaking a lot of hands, and disappearing around corners. Everyone knows he's dealing drugs.

He lingers by the chain-link fence now, leering at me. But he won't come sniffing around here. He tried eight years ago, when he waylaid me along the lane one night and started telling me how I should date him because he's black and my daddy must have been black for me to look the way I do, and that he would teach me all that I need to know about my heritage. He was nineteen.

I was twelve.

No one has ever accused me of having a dull tongue. As scared shitless as I was, I let him have it before running home and digging out my mom's switchblade from beneath her mattress. I carry it in my purse to this day.

Next to the Simses is the Alves family. Vilma Alves waves from her spot in the crimson velvet armchair that sits outside her front door. It's her throne; no one dares touch it. Her son brought it home years ago, a treasure from the curbside. It's remained in that exact place, rain or shine. Mostly shine in Tucson.

"*¡Buenas tardes!*" she calls out in her reedy voice.

"*Hola.*" I offer her a smile as I always do, because she's ninety years old and she's dropped off homemade enchiladas and mole at our door on many occasions, when she knew things were especially rough for me.

She scowls at Cyclops, shooing him away with a wave of her hand and a hiss of, "*¡Rabia!*"

I peer down at the scrappy mutt—part terrier, part Chihuahua, all parts annoying—and smirk. "He's not foaming at the mouth yet."

She shrugs reluctantly. I'm not sure which is worse—my Spanish or her English. We always muddle past the language barrier, though.

"*Hasta luego.*" With a lazy wave, I make to move on.

"*Un hombre visitó a tu mamá.*"

While my Spanish might be terrible, I know what that means. Or, more importantly, I know what it *means* when a man visits my mother while I'm at work.

My stomach tightens. "How long ago? Time?" I tap my watchless wrist.

"*A las diez.*"

Ten. Four hours ago.

I gaze out over the rectangular box ahead, the two-bedroom 1960s mobile unit that served as a childhood home to my mother and was left to Mom when my gran passed a few years back. I shouldn't be surprised. I'm long past buying my mother's empty promises and then screaming at her with anger and fear every time she breaks them. That was the teenaged, hopeful version of me.

The stupid one.

Nodding solemnly at Vilma for her warning, I offer a soft "*gracias.*" I struggle between rushing and prolonging these last twenty steps to my front door, knowing that one of these days I'm going to open it and find a corpse waiting inside. I haven't figured out if this twisted knot in my gut is because I'm dreading or have already accepted that outcome.

Probably both.

Cyclops's ear-piercing bark distracts me momentarily. He knows it's his last chance and he's peering up at me with that one soulful eye.

"Rich foods aren't good for you." I toss another carrot his way. He gobbles it up and then scampers off under the Alves trailer after Mrs. Hubbard's tabby cat.

"You're welcome," I grumble, stealing a carrot for myself, though my appetite has all but disappeared. I stare at our mangled front door for a moment, mentally itemizing all of its various cuts and bruises—a size-twelve boot dent where Mr. Cortez tried to kick it in because he was drunk and thought his wife had changed the locks on him; a notch in the frame where thieves tried to pry it open; the streaks of black spray paint where neighborhood punks redecorated.

Holding my breath, I climb the concrete steps and slide my key into the lock.

I open the door.

A cloud of cigarette smoke overwhelms me, making me cringe in disgust. Yet, I try to focus on my relief.

If she's smoking, then she's alive. Though the air is thick enough to choke the life out of a person. "Why didn't you turn on the air-conditioning?" I scold, stepping into the stuffy, dark interior. It's 95 degrees out, thanks to this spring heat wave.

"It's broken," comes the languid response.

"It can't be. I just bought it!" Marching over to the window, I adjust the dials and check the plug, then smack it for good measure. But she's right; it has stopped working. And that delivery guy from Aunt Chilada's whom I bought it off promised it was in mint condition! "Ugh!" I kick the front door wide open.

Mom squints against the sunlight. She's exactly where I left her this morning on the couch. Only then she was snoring softly, and now her eyes are red-rimmed and glassy, and she's sliding her hand out from beneath the cushions, where she stuck her needle and spoon. As if she can hide them from me.

I used to go searching for her stashes, back when it was vodka and weed and prescription painkillers. Back when I believed I could stop her from using. It's surprising how many places there are to hide drugs in this nine-hundred-square-foot tin box. But I'd find them and then I'd flush them down the drain or the toilet, because if she couldn't afford to buy more, then she wouldn't be able to use, right?

I learned the hard way that she's too far gone to go without. She'll just find other ways to pay.

So I started leaving cash in a kitchen drawer. Not a lot, but enough. We don't talk about it. I leave it there, and when I come home it's gone and she's high. But I didn't have extra cash to leave this week because I had to buy this shitty air-conditioning unit that doesn't work.

My stomach curls at the thought of what she must have done for today's hit.

"If that mangy dog shows up . . ." Mom grumbles, unmoving.

"Cyclops doesn't want to be here." *Neither do I.* But I'm trapped. In this trailer, in this park.

In this life.

The only reason I haven't walked out that door and not looked back is because she'll be on the street or in the morgue within a week if I abandon her.

I struggle to quell my resentment as I set my purse on the dining table and unwrap the taquitos. "Here. Eat. They're chicken." Ernie, my manager at QuikTrip, lets staff take the ones that have sat under the warmer for too long to sell.

"Already did." She waves the food away, her eyes glued on the old tube TV in the corner and one of her daytime soaps. I'll bet she couldn't tell me what the show is called. And she's lying about eating. She lives off of melted cheese sandwiches and, when she does remember to eat, I come home to a counter of bread crumbs and torn-apart slices of bread, and a fire-conducive layer of processed cheese in the toaster oven. Today, the countertop is exactly as I left it after cleaning up last night.

Mom has always been thin but she's a waif now, her dependence on hard drugs gripping her, leeching away fat and muscle, leaving nothing but sallow skin and bones, stringy mud-colored hair, and hollow cheeks where a striking face once resided.

I'm not going to fight with her about eating though, because you can't reason with a heroin addict and that's what my mother has become.

"I'm gonna get some sleep. Don't burn the place down," I say between mouthfuls, moving toward my bedroom. At least there's a fan in there, and I know enough to tuck towels under the door to keep the stench of smoke from overwhelming me.

"Jackie Marshall's dead."

That stops me in my tracks. "What?" I would have thought she'd lead with that news.

Mom uses her hand to mimic a gun and points her index finger at her temple. "She put a bullet in her own head. So they say, anyway."

Jackie Marshall. My father's old police partner and one of his best friends. The woman who turned her back on us when we needed her. The woman my mother is convinced had something to do with framing him almost fourteen years ago.

Apparently I knew her, back when we lived in Austin, in a nice bungalow with a picket fence surrounding it. In a past life. That life ended when I was six, and I don't remember much from it. Shadows of faces, glimmers of smiles. The echo of a child's giggle as a man tossed her in the air, before that man stopped coming home.

That old life paved the way for my new one, where I remember a lot of hurt, a lot of tears. And a lot of hatred toward the Austin Police Department and a woman named Jackie Marshall.

"Where did you hear that?" We're in Tucson, two sprawling states over, and we severed ties when we left, even changing our surname to Richards, my mother's maiden name.

"It's all over the news." She struggles to hold her phone out for me.

My mother let go of reality a long time ago, and yet Texas still has a bitter hold on her. She couldn't tell you who the governor of Arizona is, but she trolls the Texas news pages like a conspiracy theorist during her lucid moments, keeping tabs for the sake of keeping tabs. Since she stumbled on the news story that Jackie Marshall had been named chief of the Austin Police Department two years ago, that vicious obsession has grown.

So has her drug addiction.

I'm surprised she's kept up with her scrutiny lately, given how bad she's getting.

"*Austin's Top Cop Commits Suicide.*" I scan the news article from this morning, cringing at the gruesome details. Mom prefers the tabloid newspapers to the reputable ones. She says there's less political bullshit and riskier truth. They also care little for people's privacy, it would seem. "Her son found her." Noah Marshall. Mom says I knew him, too. I vaguely remember a boy, not that I'd be able to pick him out of a lineup.

"What kind of mother does that to their own kid?" she asks.

"A sick one." I could make a strong pot-and-kettle comment, seeing as I've had to rush *my* mother to the hospital twice for OD'ing, but now's not the time. "It says she couldn't handle the pressure of the job."

"I'll tell you what she couldn't handle . . ." Mom's head more lolls than turns, and she settles haunting, bloodshot eyes on me. "The guilt. The festering kind, that eats you up from the inside out after you've betrayed someone."

Someone like my father.

"Told you. All these years of lying. Of pretending . . . There it is . . . the proof." Mom's gaze is once again glued to the TV. "*Chief* Marshall . . . It's all caught up to you, hasn't it."

"Where's the proof?" This isn't proof. That's the problem—Mom has *never* once given me a shred of evidence that Jackie or anyone else on the police force framed my father. She just believes it down to her core, because she loved him that much, because she can't accept the alternative.

When it first happened, she told me that he'd had an accident and wouldn't be coming home. That's what I believed, up until I was ten and at the library working on a school project. Curious, I searched his name on the computer. That's when I saw the articles.

The headlines.

The truth.

I ran home, crying, and confronted her. She told me not to read that crap, that it was all lies, that my daddy was innocent.

Again, I bought her story, because what else does a girl do when her mother tells her these kinds of things? I *wanted* to believe that my father wasn't a corrupt drug-dealing cop who got tangled up with criminals.

Then I got older, wiser. I asked questions my mom couldn't answer. I watched her mental health deteriorate as she embraced her denial full-heartedly. And I accepted that what I want to believe doesn't matter, because everyone else has gone on living their lives while Mom is stuck in the past. Along with me, in this hellhole, unless I figure a way out.

I've long since come to terms with reality: that the evidence pointed to a corrupt cop who got what he deserved. That my father was *not* the good man she swears he was. That he didn't give a damn about me or this little family of three, and he deserves my hatred for what he's done to us, for what has become of my mother, thanks to his greed.

And now Jackie Marshall has to go and kill herself. It's fodder for my mother's delusions. As if Austin's chief of police would be so twisted up with guilt fourteen years later that suddenly she couldn't take it anymore.

I'd be an idiot to believe that her death has *anything* to do with us.

I scan the rest of the article out of curiosity. There's plenty about her fast-tracked career through the ranks to assistant chief, then chief. Jackie Marshall was a "highly motivated" police officer, according to this. Stalwart, focused, career-driven; determined to succeed.

So how does a woman like they're describing rise through the ranks and then fall apart when she gets to the top?

Near the end, I find mention of her corrupt ex-partner, Abraham Wilkes. To this day, my stomach still clenches—with anger, with humiliation, with pain—when I see that name. I guess even the woman they eventually made chief of police couldn't fully separate herself from the scandal.

"There's nothing about a suicide letter," I note.

"You think they'd let a suicide letter get out?" Mom snorts. "Come on, Grace. I've taught you to be smarter than that." She fumbles for a cigarette, lights it. "God only knows what she would have admitted to in there. They'll bury it in the official report, like they buried your father. Use some bullshit excuse, find some loophole. Freedom of Information Act, my ass. That's the way that world works. They made me stay quiet and so I did. But, *I* know what she helped do."

"Who made you stay quiet?" I ask the question, though I know I'll never get an answer. I never have.

"They'll get what's coming to them one day." Her fingers fumble with the charm on her necklace, her thumb running along the edge of the heart—half of a heart, to be specific.

The other half is six feet underground, deteriorating along with my father's bones.

I can handle being near my mother when she's high for only so long, and I've reached my limit. Plus, the stench of her cigarettes is churning my stomach. Setting her phone down, I quietly head for my room. I shed my shorts and work shirt and dive into my twin bed, the mattress lumpy from age. If I turn the fan on high and lie still, flat on my back, the heat is almost bearable. *Maybe* I'll fall asleep.

So . . . Jackie Marshall killed herself last night.

Does it matter? Should I give it a second's thought?

My dad's still a corrupt cop who got shot while dealing drugs.

My mom's still a heroin junkie with one foot in her grave.

And I'm still their by-product, stuck here, in this shitty life.

No, Jackie Marshall being dead doesn't change a single, damn thing for me.

CHAPTER 4

Austin Police Department
Commander Jackie Marshall

April 16, 2003

"Whoever said rank earned you the right to laze around don't know nothin' from nothin'," I mutter, sucking back a gulp of burnt coffee, hoping the caffeine will give me a third wind, now that my second has long since passed. I've been on my feet and dealing with crap since seven this morning; it's almost eleven at night.

"Go home and let the men handle this," Mantis sneers. He's an odd-looking man, with his sloped forehead and beady eyes; not a man that a woman would fall for on looks alone. Although he has a certain bravado that some might love.

I sure as hell don't. But I tolerate him because I don't have much choice.

And the fact that he's talking to me—a commander, who grossly outranks him—with such disrespect tells me he knows it.

"Canning asked me to come down and check on things," I say through another sip, studying the cruisers parked at various angles across the street, their lights blaring. A wiry white guy with thick glasses and messy blond hair sits in the back of one. "Do we have enough to put this asshole away?"

"He's got a meth lab in his house, Marshall. What do *you* think?"

"Just making sure you boys dot all your *i*'s. Wouldn't want his defense finding a loophole that puts him back on the street."

"If he ends up back on the street, it's because the DA screwed up." He emphasizes *DA* like *I'm* the DA. It's not the first time I've caught the brunt of these snipes, and my brother hasn't even been elected yet. It's enough that Silas is running in the next election for the coveted spot.

"Make sure there're no fuck-ups, Mantis. And that's coming straight from Canning."

"Relax. We've got this one in the bag." Mantis chuckles, that deep, scratchy timbre of his voice making it sound sinister. "He's the type to sing like a canary to save his own ass. We'll get a few names out of him. This is a real score for us."

"I guess you'll be practicing your pose for this week's photo op, then?" Mantis has been in the newspapers more times than anyone cares to look at his face as of late. But Canning wants the public to know the APD is fighting the fight against drugs, and the best way to do that is through the media.

"Go home and sleep. You look awful, Marshall."

He's trying to get under my skin, as usual. "Go home and take a shower. You *smell* awful. Have some sympathy for the poor hooker you hire after shift." He's been wearing that same cheap grocery-store brand of cologne for as long as I've known him.

My phone rings then, interrupting whatever lewd retort Mantis was going to throw back at me.

CHAPTER 5

Noah

April 2017

I shift in the wingback chair, again, looking for a more comfortable position. There isn't one. These chairs are designed to get rid of people and quick. That a lawyer chose them for his office is counterintuitive to me. You'd think he'd want to keep his clients lounging longer, so he could rack up billable hours.

"Given everything is going to you, this will be straightforward," Hal Fulcher explains from across the desk as he scans the summary of Mom's finances and I stare at the pink mole on his balding head. "She's got a small credit-card debt . . . a car payment . . . but that's it. We'll get this year's taxes filed, but I don't expect any surprises. There's a 401(k); that's a good chunk of coin. And her life insurance policy will pay out, too. That'll help with the funeral bills, so that's great news. A lot of them don't pay out if . . ." A frown flickers across his forehead. "Well, it depends on manner of death."

I clear the painful lump from my throat. "My uncle already sorted all that out with the funeral home." I'm so glad I have Silas to help me. I don't know that I could handle this on my own. He's good at getting what he wants out of people. He may be a lawyer, but he's also a politician. "So, this will work at the bank?" I wave the document that states I'm my mother's executor. I don't know the first fucking thing about being an executor.

"They shouldn't give you any issues. Bank statements say there's about twenty grand in her account. Should be enough to pay the bills for a few months. Have you decided what you want to do with the house?"

"I'll probably sell it." My parents sunk every penny they had when they bought it twenty-six years ago, a year before I was born.

"Maybe you don't want to rush into that. Property value around Austin is skyrocketing."

"That's what Silas said." He figures that the quaint, old house, on a quiet street backing onto a park, minutes away from the river, could go for close to a million. A year from now? Even more. Besides, it has fresh blood on its walls. It'll take time for wary buyers to look past that. If I put it on the market now, I'd be dealing with people looking to cash in on my tragedy and throw me lowball offers. Fuck that. And them.

"You might want to listen to him. Are you staying there?"

I shake my head. "I've been crashing at my buddy's place." Jenson rents a small two-bedroom bungalow with Craig a couple blocks away from Sixth Street—Austin's big entertainment district. Easy walking distance, which means their place is the before-and-after go-to spot from Wednesday to Sunday.

For the first few days after Mom died, they kept things quiet, but it's back to the status quo—me falling asleep on their lumpy sectional, surrounded by people jeering at each other while sucking back beer and playing video games. But I can't complain; it's better than being alone, and it's definitely better than staying at home.

I can't see myself living there again. Ever.

"Make sure someone is checking in at the house regularly. You don't want it looking abandoned. That's when places get robbed."

"Yes, sir. We have a security system."

"Are your mother's guns there?"

"Yes, sir." My born-and-bred Southern manners have crept back into my daily life. I lost them for a time, living in Seattle, where people just don't say "sir" and "ma'am."

"They're in a safe?"

"Yes, sir." It took two days of searching, but Silas finally found the combination in one of her files.

"I can help transfer ownership over to you. May as well add them to your collection. You don't want to be selling those."

"Right." I scan the wall behind him, at the array of mounted animal trophies quietly gazing down over us with their glass eyes. The thought that I don't actually *have* a gun collection wouldn't even have crossed Hal's mind. Had I not moved to Seattle with my father during my impressionable teenage years, maybe I would. Mom had insisted I start carrying four years ago, during a rash of muggings, so I do have a Glock locked away in a gun box under my passenger seat whenever I'm driving. I don't need or want more.

I guess I should keep the Colt Python, though. More out of nostalgia than anything else. That's the one Mom taught me to fire with when I was eight.

"And let me know what you decide about the house. You can sell it as part of the estate, or we can transfer the title over to you and you can do what you want with it down the road." He puts his pen down. "Aside from that, we're in good shape to get this all settled quickly. You're going to be set for a few years."

"Is that all?" I move to stand. Sitting in this office, talking about my financial windfall because my mom committed suicide, is the last thing I want to be doing.

Hal holds a finger up. "There's one more thing." Clearing his throat, he reaches into his desk drawer and pulls out a white letter envelope. "She asked me to give this to you."

The air in the room has suddenly grown thick.

I stare at the envelope, my heart hammering in my chest as all kinds of questions crowd my mind. I manage to force out the most important one. "What is it?"

"I don't know. She dropped it off the afternoon before she passed."

The afternoon before she passed.

I glare at it with renewed understanding, the sight of my name printed across the front in Mom's tidy handwriting weakening my knees.

This is why she mentioned Hal Fulcher's name the night she killed herself. Not because she had been getting her affairs in order.

The hell if Hal doesn't know what that letter is. Or at least suspect. And the somber look on his face says he *strongly* suspects.

He holds it out for me, but I'm frozen. There's only one thing that envelope could hold.

Answers.

"I don't want it," I mutter, even though I *do* want it. I *need* it. I just don't know if I can handle it. "What does it say?"

"She didn't tell me to open it; she told me to hand it directly to *you* and to make sure you were alone when I did it." His outstretched arm falls to rest on his desk. "Listen, I don't hold envelopes for clients unless it's a documented part of the will. This was a personal favor."

"Why'd you do it, then?"

"Because your mom was the chief of police," he says matter-of-factly, but adds in a softer tone, "and a friend."

I shouldn't be surprised that she'd leave this with Hal Fulcher. Mom was convinced that he was the only honest lawyer in existence—aside from Silas, of course. Plus, she'd never want such a private letter entered into evidence for all of her subordinates and colleagues—and God knows who else—to see. "Do I have to report it?"

"I'm not a criminal lawyer, so I can't advise you on that. But . . . if this were me and my mother was the chief, and what's in that envelope is what I think it is, then I'd consider if anyone else needs to see it. That's not legal advice, though."

The APD and the insurance company are convinced of suicide. The DA's office reviewed the police report and are comfortable with the findings. The media sure as hell is. They've had a field day with this, everything from the somber albeit lean accounting from the respectable papers to the crude, almost barbaric retelling from the *Texas Inquirer*, a tabloid paper who must have stellar contacts in the department because it released details the police were trying to suppress. "Blown brains" made it into their piece. So did mention of Abe.

Would I want to submit this letter to the police, so it could end up on the front page of a newspaper? Hell no.

And it's not like I'd be hiding crime scene evidence.

I eye the envelope, my name and the words *Confidential. Open this in private* scrawled across it. "What *exactly* did she say when she dropped it off?"

"That you'd be by to pick it up soon, and that it was important I give it directly to you. It was important that *you* opened it." He stares at me for a long moment, like he can hear what I'm *really* asking. "There were no signs that I could see, Noah. She was her usual self. I did *not* see this coming."

We didn't see this coming. We're so shocked. If I had a nickel . . . Of course, no one else saw Jackie Marshall at night, behind closed doors, drunk and rambling nonsensically. Only I did.

And I still didn't see this coming.

With a shaky hand, I finally accept the envelope and turn to leave.

"Noah?" When I lift my head, he simply offers me a nod.

I leave his office quietly. There's nothing left to say. You can offer your condolences only so many times. Three seemed to be the magic number for the majority of people, as far as my mother is concerned—once at first contact, the second time as they greeted me at her closed-casket funeral, and the third as they said their farewells at the cemetery before continuing on with their life.

It doesn't matter how many times I hear it, though.

It's been eight days since I leapt down the stairs at the sound of a gunshot, shampoo suds in my hair and a towel hastily wrapped around my waist, only to find my mother's lifeless body.

That's eight days of shaming myself for not putting her gun out of easy reach, for not forcing her upstairs to bed before taking my shower. Eight days of blaming myself for not doing something about her drinking sooner. Eight days of kicking myself for not understanding what she meant when she said that I was going to be "fine."

"Fine" after she held a gun to her temple and pulled the trigger. That's eight days for this festering guilt to build. Now it sits squarely on my chest, and it's impossible to shake off, no matter how many people are "sorry for my loss."

All that guilt coupled with a healthy dose of anger as I try to wrap my mind around how she'd go and do this. *Why* she'd do it. To herself.

To me.

And now I have those answers sitting between my fingertips.

Maybe.

I wait until I'm in my Cherokee before I dare look down at the envelope. I weigh my ability to handle reading my mother's suicide letter while sitting in the parking lot of Fulcher & Associates under the shade of a blooming apple tree for a good ten minutes.

And then I set it on the passenger seat, unopened, and crank my engine.

I don't notice the navy sedan parked on the street until I've pulled into the driveway and am stepping out of my SUV.

"Noah Marshall?" A blond guy in his early thirties, clad in cargo pants and a casual golf shirt, approaches me, his black-haired companion trailing close behind.

"Yes, sir." I can tell before they've flashed their golden badges that they're law enforcement, but the moment I see the eagle I grow wary. Why is the FBI here?

"I'm Special Agent Klein; my colleague is Special Agent Tareen. We have a few questions for you."

"About?"

"Jackie Marshall."

This is not good. I wish Silas were here.

His gaze drifts over the house. "Mind if we come inside?"

The last thing I want to be doing is answering the FBI's questions about my mother, only steps from where she killed herself. I fold my arms across my chest, hopefully making it clear that I have no plans on inviting them into the house. "What do y'all wanna know?"

The two guys share a glance behind dark sunglasses.

"We're sorry for your loss," the other agent, Tareen, offers coolly. A formality, nothing more.

"Did she ever talk about work?"

"Like what?"

"Like cases, or trouble she was having with officers . . . anything like that." Agent Klein grips a pen and notepad in his hand, poised to take notes.

"No."

"Any internal investigations that may have left her unsettled?"

"She never talked about cases with me, internal or otherwise." That, I can answer honestly.

"Did your mother ever mention anyone by the name of Dwayne Mantis?"

I frown. The name sounds familiar, but I can't place it. "No. Who is he?"

"The night she died, she spoke to you not long before. Is that correct?" Tareen asks, ignoring my question.

I clear my voice. "Yes, sir. Briefly. The police have my statement."

"Yes. We've read it," Klein says.

Unease slides down my back. If they've already read it, why are they asking? What does it say? Did Boyd make note of how I couldn't stop my hands from fidgeting? That my recounting of the night seemed light, or that I seemed to be stumbling over my words?

Boyd asked me three times if I was sure she hadn't said anything else. It was as if he knew I was lying.

I've been dreading the day when someone asks me about all the words hidden behind those pauses and caught in those stumbles, all the things I didn't share.

I press my lips together and wait quietly, a trick my mother taught me when you're in a situation you don't want to be in. Too often, people feel the need to break awkward silences with words. You end up saying too much, showing cards you'd rather keep concealed.

Stay quiet and let the awkwardness stand. Eventually, someone will break. Don't let it be you.

Unfortunately, these two play this game well.

The silence lingers on until I can't handle it. "If there's nothing else . . ." I take steps toward my door.

"Did your mother talk about Abraham Wilkes?" I can feel Tareen's eyes dissecting me from behind those sunglasses.

I wonder if they noticed my misstep, just now. "Abe?" I force a casual tone; meanwhile, inside I'm screaming. What do they know about Abe? "No."

"Nothing at all? About his death . . ."

"No."

"Have you had contact with his family?"

"He broke Dina. Ran her and that beautiful little girl out of town."

"I haven't seen or talked to anyone in the Wilkes family since shortly after Abe died." At Abe's funeral, to be precise. It was the last time I saw them.

"Thank you for your time," Tareen says abruptly, turning to leave.

But Klein isn't finished. "Did she leave anything for you?"

Besides the note in my back pocket? Thank God they can't see my heart hammering through my chest. "Like what?"

Klein shrugs nonchalantly, though there's nothing nonchalant about his question. "Like . . . anything."

If I tell him about the note, I'll have to show it to him, and there's no way I'm letting on that I have it until after I've had a chance to face it alone. "A fridge full of food that's gone bad," I mumble dumbly. I remember seeing a stack of empty Trader Joe's bags in the kitchen the day before. Who goes grocery shopping the day before they plan on killing themselves?

Klein's lip twitches and I can't tell if that's the beginnings of a smile or a sneer. He produces a business card from out of nowhere, holding it out for me to take. "If you think of anything, give us a call."

Before arriving, I was dreading stepping inside this house. Now I can't unlock the door fast enough, feeling the gaze of the two FBI agents on my back long after I've closed the door behind me.

In the spring, this backyard was her happy place.

There was a time when I'd come home from class and find her perched in her lounge chair under the shade of a tree, a sweet tea in one hand and a book in the other. Seemingly at peace. When she'd notice me, she'd smile and lay her book open-faced on her lap. She'd point out the latest flowers that were peeking out from the dirt and then chuckle when I rolled my eyes at her, because I don't know the first thing about plants.

Now I sit in her chair, under this tree with the fragrant purple flowers, and I try to recall their name. Did she write this note while sitting under this tree? Was she sober when she wrote it?

My fingers tremble as I hold the envelope. What if she admits to whatever was causing her so much guilt? What if she spells out what she meant when she said she sold her soul? I'd have to tell someone. It's one thing to leave out the cryptic ramblings of a suicidal drunken woman from my statement, but not to go to the police with a handwritten confession?

I can't bury that.

And yet I can't shake her comment that someone was waiting for the perfect time to use something against her. Silas maintains that she would have told him about being blackmailed, but he's the DA and he's as straight and law-abiding as they come. The man has never had so much as a speeding ticket. If she did something to deserve that blackmail—something that made her a *bad, bad person,* as she claimed—I can't see her running to him. She wouldn't want to put him in that position.

The envelope is thin, so whatever she had to get off her chest must be to the point. That was my mom, though.

Taking a deep breath, I tear the corner of the seal.

"Noah?"

Uncle Silas's voice startles me. I look over to find him standing in the kitchen window. The same window Mom reminded me to lock that night. The police investigation concluded that there was no evidence of anyone slipping in through there, or anywhere, and no signs of a struggle. The only evidence they found was the gunpowder residue on her hand.

Tucking the envelope in my back pocket, I make my way around the pool and through the French doors. "Hey."

He turns to offer me a weary smile as he leafs through the stack of mail I left on the counter, unopened. The sun's rays highlight the dark circles under his eyes. They're only mildly better than when I last saw him a few days ago. He's taken his sister's untimely death hard. Couple that with the fact that he's been working at least sixty hours a week, and he could use a few days' worth of sleep.

"You seemed intense out there. What were you doing?" He glances at my empty hand, and I know he saw the envelope.

If I tell him about the suicide note, he'll convince me it's best to read it right here, right now. I *will* tell him about it—I'll show it to him—once I've had a chance to deal with it in private. "Just . . . opening a bill and I guess I got lost in thought."

He nods to himself. "I've been doing that a lot lately, too."

I almost don't want to tell him. "The feds were here."

His hands freeze mid-shuffle. "What'd they want?"

"They asked me if Mom had said anything about Abe."

"And what'd you tell them?" he asks carefully.

"I said no."

He sighs with relief.

At least he can feel relief in all this. Me? I feel like the concrete block already sitting on my chest has gained a hundred pounds in one afternoon.

"Why is the FBI asking *me* about Abe? Did you tell anyone about that night?"

"No. I have no idea, Noah."

The more I dwell on it, the more unsettled I feel. "And you're sure there's no way that what my mom said could be true."

"I've never been more sure of anything in my life." Silas's voice rings with confidence, and yet a worried frown crosses his forehead. "Did they ask you about anything else?"

"They asked about problems with officers at work. And then they mentioned some guy."

"Who?"

"Dwayne Mantis?"

There's a delay before his eyebrows spike, which makes me think he's not entirely surprised by that name.

"You know him?"

"*Of* him. He runs the Internal Affairs division. He was here the night your mom died. He was the one talking to the officer who took your statement."

I frown, vaguely recalling the surly-looking man with the sloped forehead standing on the porch. *That* was Dwayne Mantis?

"Your mother and Mantis knew each other well."

"What do you mean 'well'? They weren't dating, were they?" As far as I know, she hadn't dated anyone since the divorce. She'd been too wrapped up in her career, and claimed it was too hard to meet men outside work. I brought up online dating once, and she laughed it off, asking how a person in her position could even think about doing that. Plus, she'd seen horrible results of blind dates in her field of work.

"No." Silas chuckles. "From what I recall, Jackie wasn't too fond of him. Said he was bullheaded and manipulative."

And now the feds are asking *me* what I know about him. And Abe.

"Could he have been giving my mom problems?" The feds don't walk around throwing out names for the hell of it. It must be part of an investigation. And Silas is the DA, which means he hears things.

His delay in responding tells me he's heard something. "Silas?"

He sighs. "There were allegations made around IA investigators falsifying evidence to clear police officers. Mantis was said to be a part of it."

"What came of that?"

He shrugs. "They were investigated and cleared."

"Could the FBI be looking into it?"

"Maybe. They must be looking into something to do with Mantis. What, though, I can't say."

I hesitate. "But there's no investigation into my mom, right?"

"Not that I'm aware of, but you don't hold a position like chief without eyes always being on you, wondering what you do or don't know about what's going on in your department." He pauses. "Did you let them in the house?"

"No."

"Good. Don't, not without a warrant. And if they show up with one, I guess we'll have our answer." He collects the stack of unopened bills for me.

A troubling thought crosses my mind. "But if they're investigating Mantis, then why ask about Abe? Are they reopening Abe's case?" Is that what got Mom so unsettled in the first place?

"I don't see why they would. There isn't any evidence to speak of."

I frown. "What do you mean?"

Silas picks up a pen, only to toss it across the counter. "The department was changing over their computer system in evidence storage and there was an error. Several cases were accidentally marked for disposal instead of retention. Abe's was one of them."

Holy shit. "So, there's *nothing* left?"

"Nothing useful. The crime scene photos, the 9-1-1 call, the canvassing notes . . . they're all gone. I mean, we could track down soft copies of reports. And of course there's the final internal investigation report submitted to the chief. There's got to be a copy of that stored somewhere . . ."

"When did this happen?"

"Twelve years ago?" His brow furrows. "No, thirteen. It was my first year as DA and I had to let five guilty criminals go free. I was furious."

My body sinks back against the wall. A year after Abe dies, all evidence from his case is destroyed. How is that possible? I mean, I know *how* it's possible. It wouldn't be the first time I'd heard of evidence accidentally being incinerated. It happens more than any police department wants to admit.

And sometimes guilty people walk free because of it.

But will an innocent man remain guilty because of it this time around?

Something still doesn't make sense. "Then why would the feds be asking about Abe's death, if they have nothing to go off?" I ponder out loud.

Unless they found new evidence.

Silas looks as perplexed as I feel. "Did Jackie say anything to you about the FBI that night?"

"No, not that I understood, anyway." And I've spent the last week jotting down every incoherent ramble of hers that I could remember. I've spent hours studying each line, hoping this elusive "he" that she kept referring to will reveal himself.

Could "he" be this Dwayne Mantis? Is Mantis the wily fox in the thicket?

Silas watches me. "What's on your mind?"

"Nothing, it's just . . . Mom used to say that having the FBI breathing down her neck would be the worst pressure."

"Noah, your mother killed herself because she was sick. Not because the FBI was asking questions."

But what if those questions had to do with Abe? Something that would implicate her in his death?

"What I let happen . . . I may as well have pulled the trigger."

What did my mother do?

Silence falls over us.

Silas's voice softens when he offers, "Sorry I couldn't make it to Fulcher's. Court took longer than expected. How'd it go?"

"Alright. I'll go to the bank tomorrow to settle her bills."

"There's enough money?"

"Sounds like it."

"Good. If not, let me know and I'll cover it until the estate pays out. Everything is as we expected? No surprise liens or anything?"

Here's my second chance to come clean about the suicide note.

I grit my teeth and shake my head.

He nods to himself. "Still couch-surfing at Jenson's place?"

Mention of the couch reminds me of the kink in my neck, and I reach up to rub against it. "Yeah. Not sure how much longer I'm gonna do that."

"You know, Judy's itching to empty out Becca's room for you."

"Thanks. I might take you up on that." Between my cousins and their kids flying in, and Silas hosting the luncheon after the funeral, his house was bursting with people in the days after Mom's death. It was too much for me to handle.

"Talked to your dad lately?"

"A couple nights ago."

"And?"

"And he wants me to move back to Seattle to live with them. They finished that apartment in their walkout, and he said he'd rent it to me for a few months."

"He'd *rent* it to you?" Silas rolls his eyes. "I shouldn't be surprised. Blair always did have short arms and deep pockets."

It's no secret he thinks my dad is a cheap son of a bitch, and I can't argue with him on that one. My mom paid for all my flights home to Austin to visit her. And it's thanks to her that I'm not saddled with a crippling student loan. The guy has never owned a new car, not because he can't afford one but because he doesn't want to pay the premium that comes with driving it off the lot. He hasn't taken an out-of-state vacation since moving to Seattle, convincing his urban wife that she should love camping because the price is right.

Then again, I have to remember that he also has my stepsisters—twelve- and ten-year-old girls—to raise on a single income.

"He said he'd give me a bargain price."

Silas seems to ponder that. "I wouldn't be able to hold your job for you. We're stretched beyond capacity as it is."

"I'd never ask you to do that." Being an investigative analyst at the District Attorney's office when your uncle is the district attorney has its advantages. I haven't stepped foot inside the office since Mom died and haven't received so much as a text from my manager about when I need to come back.

I can almost see the wheels churning inside Silas's head. "I have connections at the Seattle DA's office."

"Is there a state where you *don't* have connections?"

He chuckles. "I could make a few calls . . . see what's open up there. These jobs are tough to come by, though. I don't even know if Washington employs IAs. A lot of states don't. You sure you'd want to start over somewhere else though?"

"I don't know." Do I even *want* to work in another DA's office? I took this job because Silas offered it to me, and Silas can sell a wild Vegas weekend to a devout nun. I'd just finished five years of college—a bachelor's degree followed by my MBA—and had no clue what I wanted to do with my life. That was two years ago, and not much has changed.

My job isn't exactly thrilling. It's digging through phone records and social media accounts, and hunting down and organizing case data for court. It's tedious, mind-numbing work with brief moments of heart-pounding excitement when you discover a detail that's relevant to a case. I do whatever the ADAs ask me to. I'm basically their slave.

"You're making a real name for yourself here, son. Maxwell and Rolans are losing their minds without you. And Cory mentioned a raise and a promotion. I'd hate to see you throw that all away before you give yourself time to come to terms with everything."

Maxwell and Rolans are two of the ADAs I support. A bunch of jokers, but they're good at their jobs. And I can't complain about Cory, though I think she wants to promote me to another group so she doesn't have the top boss's nephew reporting in to her.

Silas rests his elbows against the counter. "You could apply to law school. I told you, I can make a few calls and put in a good word."

"You don't need to do that."

"You're right, I don't. But you'd make one helluva lawyer if that's the way you wanted to go. I'd hate to see it wasted." Silas has been pushing me toward law school for years.

I sigh. Too many decisions to make. "How long before I need to be back?"

"Take as long as you need. The work will get done. Your mental health is more important. I mean . . ." He gestures to the wooden chair—painted a buttery yellow—that they hauled my mother from. "Case in point."

That's the unofficial media byline: Jackie Marshall Couldn't Handle the Pressures of Being Austin's Top Cop So She Killed Herself. There's no proof to back it up, but if enough people whisper the same speculations, eventually it becomes fact.

Silas shifts to lean his back against the counter, his focus on the kitchen table. "You'd never know by looking at it, would you?"

"No." Not since guys from the APD showed up off shift to clean up the bits of my mother's brain matter so I wouldn't have to. But there's no way they can scrub the horrific memories from my mind. Every time my gaze wanders over there, all I see is a pool of blood.

That prickly lump that's been lodged in my throat flares with the thought.

Silas reaches for the bottle of whiskey on the counter, a deep frown furrowing his brow. It's the one I confiscated from her that night. I found it in my room when I came back for clothes the other day. I'm torn between dumping it down the sink and cracking it open. "You should have told me about her drinking sooner. If I'd known, I could have—" He cuts himself off abruptly, his jaw clenching tight. "That came out wrong. This isn't on you, Noah."

And yet I feel like it's *all* on me. All I want to do is forget everything about that night. Everything she said about Abraham Wilkes.

Let it stay buried, six feet under the ground, while she rests in peace, her name untainted.

It's not that easy, though.

Especially now that I may be one letter away from learning everything she *didn't* say.

"Come for supper. We're having guests tonight. Your aunt's making her pot roast."

"Sure. Maybe."

He levels me with a look. "You've been saying that all week."

"How about tomorrow?" Making conversation with Silas and Judy sounds exhausting, let alone one of Silas's friends.

Silas grabs his keys from the counter and hooks an arm around my shoulders. "I won't take no for an answer this time. Judy will have it on the table by seven. We can eat a nice meal together."

The thing with Silas is he won't leave until he gets what he wants. Plus, I've barely eaten a full meal in a week. My jeans are starting to feel loose.

And my aunt is a fantastic cook.

"She's going to be so happy to see you." He gives my back an affectionate pat. "This is just what you need."

I force a smile.

CHAPTER 6

Noah

I'm catching up on sports highlights in the family room when Judy's delicate hand settles on my shoulder. "Would you mind helping me with the table, Noah? I'm so terribly behind."

"Yes, ma'am." I pull myself off the couch. Not that I would ever deny help to anyone, but it's impossible to refuse Judy's lilting Southern accent and motherly smile. She may be the sweetest woman alive.

Silas and Judy have lived in this big, old white colonial outside of Austin for as long as I can remember. We'd drive out on weekends when I was young and spend our days hanging out on one of the three covered porches, or running through the sprinklers in the expansive yard. Coming here is like entering a time warp—instead of renovating to modernize, they've poured money into the place to hold on to its historical charm, plastering the rooms with busy wallpaper and moldings, refinishing the old plank wood floors until they shine, and hanging antique chandeliers.

As much as I dread the idea of making small talk with strangers, it feels good to be here. Familiar. Plus, dinner with people who don't know me may be exactly what I need. "Thanks for letting me crash your party," I tell Judy.

"You know you're always welcome here, my darling." She reaches up to give my cheek an affectionate pat. "Silas has an early morning meeting, so our meal will be served shortly after they arrive. I hope you brought your appetite."

I rub my stomach. "I'm starved." I'm not, but telling Judy that would only make her worry. "Are we eating in the dining room?"

"Yes, of course. The dishes are stacked on the buffet. We need five settings. Salad forks on the outside."

"Yes, ma'am." Everything about my aunt is proper, right down to the table settings when company comes. I'm grossly underdressed in my T-shirt and jeans and she's the type to gently reprimand me about that, but tonight she hasn't said a word. I guess I've earned a pass.

The doorbell rings as I'm Googling "wineglasses and placement" because I know Judy will come in and quietly fix it all if I don't do it right. Moments later, Silas's loud voice carries down the hall. "Retirement's treating you well, I see."

A man chuckles. "Can't complain."

"And yet he does complain about being bored, *daily*," a woman says, earning a round of laughter.

"How was Italy?"

"Just lovely! We'll be going back, soon."

"*You'll* be going back. This old fart's had enough of trains and planes. Let me rock in my chair in peace."

His voice sounds familiar, but I can't place it.

"You'll have to tell us about it over supper. Judy's already pricing out tickets to Tuscany for the fall."

"She must know that she can't get you away from your office for more than twenty-four hours?"

"Well, she's darn determined this time." The hardwood floors in the hallway creak.

"Thank you for the invitation," the woman says. "I was in the midst of figuring out what to make for tonight when George mentioned it this morning. Saves me from having to cook!"

I frown. Silas invited this couple over for dinner just this morning? That's unlike my aunt and uncle. They're normally reserving space in their calendars two months in advance.

"Come. Let's have a drink in the parlor."

I chuckle. My cousin, Emma, would be rolling her eyes if she heard him. Judy is desperate to live in nineteenth-century England, and has decorated their living room with stiff furniture and china figurines and floor-to-ceiling bookcases that house leather-bound volumes. It's one of those rooms that's used only when company comes and is not at all comfortable.

I finish setting the table and then wander in, to find Silas midpour from a crystal decanter. His idea of a pre-supper cocktail is Kentucky bourbon. "There you are! Noah, do you remember George?"

"Hi." I offer my hand in greeting, but can't help the frown as I study the portly man with the gray beard because he *does* look familiar. I just can't place where I've seen him.

"Well, look at you!" He seizes my hand in a firm grasp. "To think I last saw you when you were a gangly boy."

"And if we don't get food into him soon, he's going to turn into one again," Silas mutters, passing a drink to the man.

The way they're talking, I feel like an ass for not knowing who this guy is. "It's been a while," I say casually.

George's round belly jiggles with his laughter. "You don't have the first damn clue who I am, do you, son?"

"George, really!" his wife, a petite brunette with a round face, a glass of sweet tea already in hand, scolds.

"No offense taken. You probably only saw me in uniform and it *has* been a while. I'm George Canning. I was chief for some time."

"For twenty years," Silas pipes in, clinking glasses with him in a toast. "And he was so dang good at it, he's getting his own life-sized monument downtown this June."

"Yes, hopefully a *trimmer* version." He emphasizes the word with a pat against his gut.

Silas adds, "Your mother knew George well."

George clears his throat and with the act, all amusement vanishes. "Dolores and I were on our way to Italy for a wedding when we heard the news. It was a shock to all of us."

I simply nod, not trusting my voice with this prickly ball sitting inside my throat. So much for mindless conversation with people who don't know anything about me.

———

"Noah!" Silas nods his head toward his office entrance.

"I should get going home." Two hours of listening to the women babble about Italian food and grandchildren, and the men debate about Republicans and Democrats, is my limit. Thankfully, the one thing everyone stayed far away from during supper was talk of Jackie Marshall.

"Nonsense." He hooks an arm around my shoulder and pulls me into the traditional man cave of dark leather, mahogany furniture, and heavy drapery. George has already found his spot in a chair in front of the wide-open French doors, a lighter held against the cigar in his mouth.

Silas sees my brows pop and laughs. "Your aunt may reign over the roost, but I get the final say in my little coop." He thrusts a glass of amber liquid into my hand. "Join us."

I hate hard liquor—more now than before—but when Silas offers, you don't refuse. "Yes, sir. Thank you."

"That Jackie raised you right, I can see that." George lifts his foot to push a chair out for me with his polished shoe. "The kids these days . . . My grandkids misplace their manners more than those godforsaken electronics they're attached to."

"She's a stickler for some things. *Was* a stickler." A fresh wave of numbness washes over me before I have to feel the full impact of that simple correction.

George's heavy sigh fills the room. "I still don't know what to say. I never would have seen that comin' in a million years."

"No one did." My standard three-word line. Pretty sure I've started saying it in my sleep.

"Silas mentioned that she had a bit of an issue with . . ." He tilts his glass in the air.

"Near the end," I admit reluctantly.

"Bad?"

"Bad enough."

"I reckon so." He shakes his head. "She'd be far from the only one to get caught up in the drink. She and the boys could tie one on, back in the good ol' days. Still . . . I can't make heads or tails of it." Sweet smoke fills my nostrils as he puffs on his cigar. "She was smart as a whip, that one, and driven to succeed. Loyal . . . honest . . . Integrity like I've never seen."

I can't help but drop my gaze, afraid that he'll see the doubt in my eyes.

"I wish I could say the same for the rest of the force and your blue wall of silence," Silas mutters. "It's no wonder the public doesn't trust the police."

"Now don't get all riled up with that hogwash," George warns through another puff.

But Silas is never one to back down. While the two of them bicker over police politics, I hide behind the terrible burn of this bourbon, picking through my mother's final words. It's funny . . . I can still smell the acrid stench of her Marlboros, can hear the crackling buzz of the radio, can see her lifeless body hunched over the table, but the most important part of that night—all the seemingly nonsensical rambling—is swimming loose in my mind, testing my memory.

I do know that she spoke of honesty that night, of Abe being a good, honest man and, if I were to read between the lines, *not* guilty of what he had been accused of. So what exactly is the truth? The version I've believed for the past fourteen years? Or what might have been a deeply hidden confession that forced itself to the surface in her final moments?

Silas's cell phone rings. He checks his screen and sighs. "I've got to take this. Maybe while I'm gone, you can talk my nephew into staying in Austin. The DA's office can't afford to lose him."

"Stay with a bunch of liars and crooks? You're two sandwiches short of a picnic if you think I'm gonna help you with that," George hollers after Silas as he ducks out the door. "Heck, if I'm convincin' you of anything, it'd be to apply for the academy. If you're half as determined as your mother was, Austin PD would be lucky to have you."

"Yes, sir."

His eyes narrow, studying me. "That ain't something you're interested in, though, is it?"

"No, sir." I grew up thinking I was going to be a cop. After I finished my stint in the NBA, of course. But when it came time to make those big life decisions, the last thing I wanted to do was apply to the police academy. I had too many bad associations with it already.

"Oh, to have your whole life ahead of you . . ." he says wistfully. "I didn't have no choice but to retire, heart issues and all. Both the doc and the wife insisted it was time. But you know, Jackie'd call me almost every week, askin' for advice. It was nice; made me feel like I was still of some real value. And she'd talk about you, plenty. She was so proud of you. Of the man you've become." He pauses. "You two were close, weren't you?"

"She's the reason I applied to UT." I wanted to come home.

His forehead furrows with his frown. "And she never gave you any clue, hey? Just out of the blue up and did that? No warning at all?"

"I mean, she said things, but I didn't think anything of it at the time." All those nights of drinking, mumbling to herself about making better choices . . . how did I not take it more seriously? "She told me she wasn't good enough to be chief." That seems innocent enough to admit.

He snorts. "That there's the biggest load of bull crap I've ever heard. She was one of the best damn officers I've ever seen, and believe you me, I saw a lot over my forty-odd years on the job. I was groomin' her to take over my spot. She should have had it when I was forced out, but that spineless city manager Coates put Poole in. Took me a few years of meddlin' to get both of them out, and your mother in there. But she knew the job of chief inside and out long before she ever accepted it."

I'd love to take his high praise at face value.

"What's the matter? You look bothered."

I smooth my expression. "No, nothing. It's good to talk to someone who knew her well."

George takes a long puff of his cigar. "My oldest son, Wyatt, was a police officer. He came home one day and said, 'Dad, they gave me a female partner. Can't you do somethin'?' I said, 'Sure I can, son. I can move you to the graveyard shift of the drunk tank, if I hear you sayin' another word about having a woman partner.' Just three shifts later, Wyatt found himself starin' down the barrel of a pistol at a routine traffic stop. This guy was all cracked out on somethin', ranting and raving, with two little kids in the backseat. He wasn't goin' anywhere with the police. It was that female partner—your mother—who talked him down from pullin' the trigger. Her and her level head. She never panicked, not once. Didn't even raise her voice while dealin' with him, from what I hear. Cool as a cucumber. I knew right then and there that I had a good one. I kept a close eye on her after that. Mentored her some."

"I thought Abe was her first partner." He's all I remember.

"No, sir-ee. Jackie and Wyatt were partnered for three years." George peers into his drink, his mood suddenly somber. "Then Wyatt got caught in the middle of two gangbangers on some drug-turf-war issue. He was mindin' his own business, walkin' out of a corner store. Bullet hit his throat. He died right there on the sidewalk. That's when she got paired up with Abraham Wilkes. And, well, we *all* know how that turned out."

"He was a good, honest man."

"We are bad, bad people."

George shakes his head while I struggle to ignore the way my stomach tightens. "Lord knows I'll never lose that name. One cop goes rogue and I'm left scrubbing filthy fingerprints off the whole dang department for *years*. Forget that I spent years before that all up in everyone's asses with more task forces than anyone else in the state of Texas, trying to rid this city of the kind of drug runners who killed my son."

I hesitate. "My mom never talked about Abe after he died. She wouldn't answer my questions." I don't want to sound too eager, but I'm desperate to know what George Canning knows. Did my mom tell him what she admitted to me?

"I remember her sayin' something about you havin' a rough go of it afterward. She didn't know what to tell you." George studies me for a long moment. "What was he, again? Your baseball coach? Or was it football?"

"Basketball."

"Right." George pauses. "You still have questions about him? Because if you do . . ." The chair creaks as he leans back. "I'm all ears."

I should say no. I should pretend that what Abraham Wilkes was or wasn't doesn't matter to me after all these years. My mother's cloudy confession might be safer that way. But the truth is it has mattered to me, since long before the night my mother died.

Abe wasn't *just* the guy who taught me how to dribble a ball like a pro. And he may have been my basketball coach for five years, but he was never just my coach.

Every time I scored in a game, no one cheered louder than Abe.

My dad didn't come to most of my games. He said it was because of work, but Abe was a cop on shift work, and he managed to work his schedule so he could coach my team.

Abe taught us how to lose with grace, and to treat all players with respect. Two or three times a year we'd volunteer as a team at a soup kitchen. Other times we'd come out and run drills with young kids from low-income areas. All this was a mandatory requirement for being on his team. More mandatory than playing in the actual games.

I was eleven the first time I kissed a girl. Her name was Jamie, and Abe was the only person I told. He patted me on the back with a knowing smile.

Then he took me for a drive through one of the rougher parts of Austin, slowing past a community center ripe with teenaged girls pushing around baby strollers. Even though schoolyard gossip had already taught me the basics, I got "the talk" from Abe. The one where he stared me down with those penetrating chocolate-brown eyes and told me if I got a girl pregnant and the thought of walking away from my responsibility even crossed my mind for a second, he'd beat my ass because I'm better than that.

Abe was like a father and a big brother and the man I wanted to be when I grew up, all rolled into one.

Yeah, Abe's death left a lasting impression on me.

The void was gaping.

And the betrayal I felt from this father-figure, this moral god . . . it was crippling. At first, I didn't believe what the news was saying; I couldn't. How could someone so focused on doing the right thing do something so wrong?

But my mother didn't defend him, didn't discredit what the newspapers were saying. Didn't deny it. She just drank and let her marriage and our family fall apart.

Before long, it became easier to believe everyone. To believe that Abe was guilty, as much as I didn't want to.

There's not a lot that's worse than finding your mother dead in your kitchen with a gun in her hand. But having that happen on the same night she alludes to having something to do with the death of your childhood idol . . .

Now the one person who would have seen *all* the evidence against Abe is offering to give me answers.

George leans over. "Boy, you're as nervous as a long-tailed cat in a room full of rocking chairs. What gives?"

After forty years on the police force, it's not a wonder he can see right through me. "I still have a hard time believing he did it," I finally admit.

George presses his lips together. "What do you remember?"

"Just what was in the news." Over the past few days, I've spent hours reading old articles online to refresh my memory, unable to shake my mother's words.

Abe died in a sketchy motel, along with another guy. Two bags—one of drugs, one of cash—sat on the bed between them. In the beginning, the only statement the police would release was the one confirming that a police officer and a man known to police were found dead, and that they were investigating. The media got hold of Abe's name quickly, though, along with the details about the crime scene and the fact that Abe was alone and not on duty at the time. They also learned that the "man known to police" was Luis Hernandez, a drug dealer released six months prior. One thing led to another, and soon the public was screaming that the APD was trying to cover up a crooked cop.

George stares hard at his drink for a moment, his lips twisted in thought, before taking a sip. "Did you know that Austin is now the eleventh-largest city in the nation, and one of the fastest growing?"

"I read that somewhere." Or maybe Silas told me, right after he said not to sell the house.

"It was less than half of what it is today back then, but we all saw it coming. This population explosion. And yet so many people still have a hard time seeing how it's changing. They expect us—the mayor, the police department, your uncle, all of us—to keep it the same.

"Everyone wants to continue living in their happy little bubble. They want to drink their fancy lattes and go to their music festivals and restaurants and 'keep Austin weird.' Sure, we look like a fairy-tale city next to Houston or Dallas or San Antonio. But make no mistake, there's crime here and it is damn ugly. I mean, for God's sake, we're some two hundred and thirty miles from the Mexican border, where they're funneling through a million pounds of marijuana and who the hell knows how many tons of cocaine every single damn year!" George's face is turning red with anger. He takes a few breaths to calm himself.

"We started noticing a big problem with the drugs coming into Austin. Our patrol divisions were stumbling on it all over the place; they couldn't keep up. I knew I had to take the bull by the horns before Austin turned into another Laredo."

That's being a little bit dramatic, given that Laredo borders Mexico, but I can appreciate his point. Like he said, we are only a couple hundred miles away—and some days, the distance feels even shorter.

"So I assigned four officers to a narcotics field unit. Their job was simple—to hit the streets and bust as many dealers as possible. Big, small, didn't matter. Uncover the stash houses and labs, seize everything. Shut 'em down. Don't let them get comfortable in my city.

"And son, let me tell you, these guys were *good*. They were dogged, churning through tips, securing informants. They were sniffin' out dealers like bloodhounds." Canning chuckles. "That's what I called them—my hounds. Dumbest thing Poole coulda done when he took over for me after my heart attack was shut them down. Budget cuts, my ass.

"Anyway . . . they caught wind of a patrol officer who was emptying the pockets of dealers he'd come across on routine calls and reselling at a discount. They didn't have a name. All they knew was this guy was of African descent." He stares into his drink. "Not long after, Abraham Wilkes turns up dead in a motel room with Hernandez. Wasn't too hard to connect the dots."

"What do you think happened the night Abe died?"

"Who knows? Maybe Hernandez wanted more drugs for less money. Maybe he didn't know Wilkes was a cop and panicked when he found out. Maybe Wilkes threatened him with somethin'. These guys . . . they're lowlife criminals; some of them are dumb as dirt. There ain't no rationalizing with them." He takes another long puff of his cigar. "But it was all cut and dry what was goin' on in there—a gym bag full of a bit of this, a bit of that . . . a brown paper bag with piles of twenties. No sensible explanation for why Wilkes would be in that seedy motel that night. Still, I hoped for another reason, for my own sake as much as the department's.

"But the evidence against Abe quickly piled on. We traced a call from Hernandez to him earlier that night. We found cash and drugs stashed away in his house, taped to the back of furniture, in the vents, under the mattress. We were able to link the drugs to batches checked in to the evidence room, from busts he'd been at over the last month." He shakes his head. "It's a damn shame that he lost his way like that."

The steady tick of the old grandfather clock is the only sound in Silas's study for a long moment, as I take in all that Canning has told me. It makes no sense when it's laid out next to what my mother said. But, then again, she was drunk and in a poor state of mind. Still, I'm confused. "So, how was my mom involved in all this?"

George frowns. "Jackie? She wasn't involved. I put together an investigative team with my very best people, but she didn't have nothin' to do with that. I never would have allowed that, what with her being close friends with him—partners, too—for years. She didn't want to believe it, but the evidence was impossible to ignore. That was a hard pill for her to swallow."

She washed that hard pill down with plenty of booze. "What about his family?"

George clucks. "It was just his mother, and the only thing she was ever gonna accept was a report that said Abe Wilkes was framed and murdered. She wanted a lie. She refused to believe the truth, even when it was finally there in front of them, in bold black ink." He shakes his head. "And his wife, well, she up and took off with the kid. I guess she decided that all would come out in due time. Hell, she probably already knew what was comin'. She was his wife, after all. If there was extra money under their mattress, I have to think she'd have noticed it while she was tuckin' in the sheets. Probably turned a blind eye. Given where she came from, it wouldn't surprise me one bit."

Where she came from? The Dina I remember was pretty and gentle and slight. She spoke softly. She wore floral dresses and baked chocolate-chip cookies and delivered her husband bottles of beer at barbecues, with a kiss. She was everything my mother wasn't.

"What happened to her?"

"Started her life over elsewhere, I reckon. Can't say I blame her. Being the wife of a cop who got himself into selling drugs won't earn you no prize at the county fair, that's for damn sure. As I recall, she didn't even bother comin' back to ask for the report once we released it." His brow tightens. "It's odd, don't you think? Wouldn't she want to see it, for closure?"

"Unless she already knew he was guilty."

"Exactly." George levels me with a somber look. "And unfortunately, Abraham Wilkes *was* as guilty as they come. Of course, we can't try a dead man, but any jury would have seen it for what it was."

"Seen what for what it was?" Silas asks, stepping back in.

"Jackie's old partner, Abraham Wilkes."

Silas's eyes dart to mine, and I see the warning question in them: Did I tell George what my mom said?

I give him the slightest shake of my head, and I can see him exhale. He reaches for his drink. "Some people can't help but abuse the authority they're given."

"Jackie sure didn't. To one helluva cop." George toasts the air. "And one of the hardest-working people I ever met. Not like this blister here, who don't show up 'til the work's done." He nods toward Silas, flashing a smile to go along with the gentle ribbing.

Silas clanks glasses with him.

It finally dawns on me that this last-minute supper was Silas pulling his puppet strings. I can see what he's trying to do—discredit my mother's drunken rambling and give me something else to believe.

Manipulative, yes, but I appreciate it, because it's given me the courage to face whatever sits folded in my back pocket. In fact, I'm now desperate to read what my mother had to say. I set my barely touched glass down on the desk.

"That's good bourbon!" Silas scolds.

"I have to drive."

"Right. Of course. So you're going to pack up your things this weekend? Judy will have your room ready for you by Saturday."

"Yes, sir. Thank you." Silas made a compelling case before George Canning and his wife arrived. I should move in with them rent-free—I'll get home-cooked meals and can commute into work every day with Silas. I'll borrow against the house's equity and have the kitchen renovated. Give it a different feel, so my skin doesn't crawl every time I walk in.

When the renos are done, I can either move back into the house and rent the two extra bedrooms out to my friends, or rent the entire house out for enough income to pay bills and a mortgage on a second property. Yup, Silas has made easy sense of my life for the next few years. I'm not sure if I'm sold on it—maybe I should start over fresh in Seattle, or somewhere completely new—but the thought of leaving behind everything I know isn't appealing, either.

Plus, there's no escaping what happened. My mother killed herself, no matter where I live.

"Chief Canning, it was great to meet you. Again." I offer him my hand.

He stands and takes it, chuckling. "It's just good ol' George now. And if you ever need anything, give me a holler. Or better yet, come on out to my ranch for a visit. Anytime. The door's always open. I'm out near McDade, the only Canning in the book."

With a polite nod, I duck out.

The second my engine is running, I reach into my pocket for the envelope.

An odd mix of relief and disappointment hits when I see the single scrap of paper inside.

It's not a suicide letter, after all.

It's a diagram of the kitchen pantry, and what looks to be a removable panel in the floor beneath one of the shelving units, along with three words in her messy scrawl:

Open it alone.

My eyes roam over the long, narrow room, pausing on the thousand-pound green metallic Browning safe sitting in the corner, tucked away among the shelves of canned tomatoes and potatoes, bolted to the floor.

That safe is built to hold twenty-nine firearms, but Mom had only four personal guns registered to her: a Glock, a Colt Python, a Remington shotgun for the rare occasion that she had to play politics in the old boys' club and go duck hunting, and my grandfather's Hawken rifle—a family heirloom. They're all present and accounted for, along with a healthy supply of ammo, and there's plenty of room left in there.

So why the need for this hidden compartment under a shelf?

I set to shifting cans of food to the other shelves until the metal rack is empty, and I'm able to drag it away from the wall. It's not heavy but the space is tight, making it difficult to maneuver.

I study her sketch, and then the floor. On first glance, there's no obvious panel. Not until I crouch down and shine the flashlight on the worn wood do I see the seams.

It takes a few minutes with a butter knife before I manage to pry the covering off, revealing a compartment about two by one feet in size, and stuffed with a black nylon gym bag.

How long has this secret hiding place been here?

Pushing that question aside, I fish out the bag and yank open the zipper.

And my heart starts racing.

"Holy shit."

I couldn't even hazard a guess as to how much cash is in here, but it's a lot more than I've ever seen, and it definitely wasn't included in Mom's list of assets that Hal reviewed earlier.

Pulling out one wad, I fan through it. A lot of twenties, but also everything from fives to hundreds. I must have a grand in my hand, and there's plenty more. What the hell was Mom doing with this much money, and why would she hide it under the floorboards?

That's not all there is.

Tucked in with all the cash is a tan leather gun holster. I frown as I fish it out, running my fingers over the black stitching along the seams. I've seen this holster before, but I can't remember where or when.

Not until I flip it over do I see the letters embroidered on the other side.

A.W.

A sour taste fills my mouth.

Who else would this belong to, besides Abraham Wilkes?

Why does my mother have Abe's gun holster hidden with a bunch of cash beneath the floorboards?

I notice a slip of paper mixed in with the bundles of money. I fish that out and unfold it, an ill feeling firmly settled in my gut.

Gracie needs this money. Make sure she gets it asap. Don't ask questions, Noah. Trust me, you don't want the answers.

Below it is an address in Tucson, Arizona.

There are no explanations.

No apologies.

Nothing that might give me any sense of closure, any relief. In fact, it does the exact opposite.

A mixture of anger and resentment burns deep inside. Maybe she thought that the last "I love you" would carry me through this more than anything she could have written down?

She had no plans of explaining herself, of exposing her demons.

"I'm a coward."

That's what she said. She said she couldn't face Gracie, that she wanted to make it right but couldn't. Is that what this money is supposed to do? Make it right?

Where the hell did you get this money from, Mom? And why did you have Abe's gun holster?

How much is in here, anyway?

Stretching my legs out, I dump the money onto the floor in front of me and begin counting, pulling apart the bundles and creating small piles for every thousand. And then every five thousand.

Until there are piles of bills all around me totaling ninety-eight thousand dollars.

I fall back against the wall, my mind churning. What was my mother expecting me to do? Hand-deliver this gym bag full of cash to the daughter of her late police partner? Because hand-delivering this much money is the *only* way Gracie will get it. And she also doesn't want anyone knowing that I'm doing it, including Silas. That's why she didn't put it in the safe. She knew her brother. She knew he'd be in the thick of things and find it.

That she wouldn't want him—the district attorney—knowing about this money leaves my stomach in knots. Mom made good money—over two hundred thousand a year as chief, and a solid salary as assistant chief for all those years before that, too. But to pay off the house and most of my tuition *and* still have all this cash? It doesn't seem possible on a single woman's salary.

So where did this money come from? Why is Abe's gun holster stowed away with it?

And why does she want Gracie Wilkes to have it?

Why not Abe's wife, Dina?

I rack my brain, trying to remember everything she said about Abe's family the night she died. But all I keep coming back to is how she wanted his daughter to know that he was a good man.

And then another thought occurs to me: if the feds *are* investigating my mom and they show up on my doorstep with a warrant, the last thing I want them finding is this.

"Fuck." I pull out my phone and Google the distance. It's a twelve-hour drive to Tucson, and I have no choice; I have to drive. I can't get through airport security with this much money on me.

Twelve hours.

Twenty-four hours, there and back.

It's Thursday night. If I leave now and drive straight, I can be there early afternoon, catch some sleep, and be back by Saturday night.

My foot begins tapping with nervous energy. Maybe this isn't such a bad idea. It's a chance to get away. And what the hell else am I going to do between now and then anyway?

How do I explain this to Abe's daughter, though? Won't she be suspicious? I'm not about to repeat what my mother claimed that night. It's like Silas said—it wouldn't be right, casting blame on my mom. She's not here to explain herself. Plus, everything George told me about Abe was damning.

He sounds as guilty as he was made out to be.

Just like Mom said *they* wanted it to appear.

Fuck.

Feds waiting outside my house to question me about Abe and Dwayne Mantis. Now, this giant bag of money that my mom has obviously been hiding shows up, meant for the daughter of the ex-partner she basically said was framed.

And Abe's gun holster.

Silas is wrong—there's definitely *something* going on here. Something that my mother had to be involved in.

CHAPTER 7

Austin Police Department
Commander Jackie Marshall
April 16, 2003

I stay three cars back as I tail the older-model black Mercedes, hoping the guy driving hasn't spotted my unmarked sedan.

Who knows what the girl told him. *If* she told him anything. Most times these girls stay quiet, having learned the hard way that complications with a john earn them fists and threats from their pimp, regardless of whose fault it is. And it wasn't her fault. It wasn't the anonymous caller's fault, either. That person did the right thing by requesting a welfare check on that hotel room.

But did I do the right thing? Even with the chilly night air, I brush a bead of sweat from my forehead. It goes with the nauseating flutters churning inside my gut. I'm a jumble of anxiety, anger, and regret.

Up ahead, the Mercedes makes a right after the freeway underpass. I slow down a touch before following and turn into the parking lot of a seedy motel, the bulbs in the green neon sign above flickering intermittently. I haven't been to this exact motel, but I've been to plenty like it—desolate spots on the outskirts of town, quiet except for the hum of cars on the nearby highway, their sign advertising plenty of options except the one most visitors are interested in: the hourly room rental.

I back into a spot among several cars—hidden but within prime view of the Mercedes—and flip my visor down to shield my face. I quietly watch as a short white male climbs out of the driver's seat, the number eighteen tattooed to the back of his neck marking his gang affiliation.

The passenger door opens and out she comes, her red heels clicking across the paved walkway, her shoulders hunched as he leads her into one of the rooms. He reaches for her, his hand like a vise around her slender arm.

Just before she disappears inside, she glances back, her long blonde hair flitting about with the sudden turn. Her face is filled with sheer hopelessness.

And I swear, she looks right at me.

It's a sucker punch to the chest.

I let my eyes wander to the picture of Noah I keep tucked in my visor. That boy is sweeter than honey and smart as a whip. So generous, too. How he turned out the way he did is a mystery to me. It's not on account of his father, that's for damn sure. Blair is as tight as a wet boot and as exciting as a mashed-potato sandwich. Why I didn't listen to my mama when she tried talking me out of marrying him . . .

Abe. That's the reason Noah is who he is.

Good ol' Abraham Wilkes. You can hang your hat on that man. He's taught Noah to be the fine young man that he's becoming.

The tightness in my chest grows as I flip the visor up, hiding my boy's smiling face, his inquisitive eyes.

Would Noah understand why I did what I did tonight, if he ever found out?

Probably not. Most people wouldn't.

I'm guessing Abe never will.

With a heavy sigh, I climb out of my car and walk toward the room, flicking my spent cigarette to the pavement.

CHAPTER 8

Noah

Tucson, Arizona

"In one mile you will arrive at your destination."

"Good job for getting me here, Sally." I let the last drops of my coffee hit my tongue and then I chuck the empty Styrofoam cup to the passenger-side floor, where it joins the others. The caffeine stopped doing the trick around El Paso, and I had to pull over in a Waffle House parking lot to crash for a few hours. I guess the lack of sleep over the past week finally caught up with me.

Now it's pure adrenaline that's keeping me going. As if having ninety-eight grand in cash sitting in a gym bag on my backseat isn't enough to stress me out, I'm about to hand it all to a girl who is basically a stranger, without any explanation, because I don't have an explanation to give.

Will Gracie Wilkes even remember Mom or me? Doubt it. The papers didn't say how old she was when Abe died, just that she was young. I'm guessing five or six? The only thing I remember from when I was five was the day I shat my pants at recess.

Add fourteen years and that would make her nineteen, maybe twenty. What will this Gracie do when a strange guy shows up at her home and hands her a pile of money? How many questions will she have for me?

"In two hundred and fifty feet, you will have arrived at your destination," Sally chirps.

I'm on the outskirts of Tucson. A vast expanse of sand and tall, leggy cacti stretches out to my left, all the way to the mountain range in the distance. It's a lot greener here than I imagined, and yet plenty different from Texas or Seattle, or anywhere else I've been.

A sign ahead of me on the right sways in the light breeze—a metal plaque hanging haphazardly by one chain, rust eating away at the edges. Sleepy Hollow Trailer Park. Named after the street it's on, obviously.

So Gracie Wilkes lives in a trailer park.

The only trailer park I've ever been to was the one on Lake Chelan—outside Seattle—that my friend and his family went to every summer. We'd stay for two weeks, playing tennis and swimming, making out with girls by the bonfire after the parents went to bed.

"You have arrived at your destination."

I guess not all trailer parks are created equal.

I turn into the main entrance. Rows of mobile units line either side of the lane. They're all a little different in color and size, but equally dented, stained, and surrounded by junk. Some have chain-link fences to give the illusion of having a yard, but those "yards" are filled with old furniture, scraps of metal, and corroded cars. One even has a toilet sitting outside the front step.

It's close to two p.m. and empty of people, and yet I feel plenty of eyes on me as I roll through in my black Jeep Grand Cherokee—fresh off the lot only three months ago—at five miles per hour, searching in vain for unit 212. It's a game, because nothing is consistent. Some doors display their number in brass, others are scribbled in black marker on pieces of wood and hung on fences. Another has a cardboard sign taped to the streetlight.

These people are dirt poor; there's no two ways about it. That means Abe's daughter is dirt poor. I guess that answers one question for me—this girl is going to take the money and run without a second glance at me.

But how did they end up here? Dina must not be alive.

If she is . . .

The Dina Wilkes I remember wouldn't be caught dead in a place like this, let alone let her daughter live here.

A woman as old as Moses sits in a ratty chair on her front porch, watching me intently. I lower my window, and a waft of hot, dry air and dust invades my cool air-conditioned interior. "Afternoon, ma'am. Can you please tell me where 212 is?"

Her eyes narrow. "*Vete a la chingada.*"

Spanish. Shit. My Spanish sucks.

"Uh . . . *Lo siento . . . Número* 212?"

"*Come mierda!*" Leaning over, she spits on the ground next to her.

Yeah . . . it doesn't sound like she's going to help me. I give the truck a little bit of gas and keep rolling forward. A small white sign with the number 212 neatly written hangs from the fence post ahead of me. I glance back at the old lady—Gracie's next-door neighbor, I now realize—to find her glaring at me. I wonder if she's suspicious of everyone who comes through here, or just the corn-fed Texas boy with the nice ride.

Killing the engine, I reach for the gym bag.

And then second-guess that move.

Is getting out of my car with a pile of cash safe? Checking my rearview mirror, I spot a gangly man leaning against a fence and watching me, looking all kinds of shady. I can't tell if he's just curious or if he's looking for an opportunity. I outweigh him by at least forty pounds and I can hold my own if I have to, but I'm guessing people who survive around here don't rely on physical strength to protect themselves.

Just in case . . .

I punch the code into my portable safe and fish out my Glock.

As much as I'd feel safer with it on me, I don't know that showing up at Gracie's door with a gun is going to comfort either of us. Plus, I didn't bring a holster—I left Abe's where I found it, under the floor—and I didn't even look up the carry laws for Arizona, too eager to hit the road.

Still, I want it easily accessible, should I need it in a rush.

Tucking it into the gym bag with the money, I leave both on the backseat. I step out of my SUV, locking the doors behind me.

A mangy mutt strolls past, making me falter a step. I've never seen a dog look so rough. It's missing an eye and a chunk out of its floppy ear. Its dull brown matted fur looks like a soiled shag rug from the seventies. Still, it has a light trot to its step as it passes me, that one eye narrowed as if warning me away from the twitching rat within its jaws. I can't help but grimace.

With a quick glance around me—creeper is still creeping, and the old lady is still rocking and staring, but at least not spitting—I climb the steps to the old trailer. Taking a deep breath, I knock on the door.

And wait.

No one answers. There's no sound of footfalls, but I can hear the television through the cracked window. Maybe they left it on to make people think someone's home? No, I can't see people who live in a place like this bothering to take that kind of precaution.

Plus I smell the faint waft of a grilled cheese sandwich coming from inside. Someone's definitely home.

I knock again.

Still no answer.

"Gracie?" I call out.

Nothing.

What do I do? I can't sit around here, not with that old woman burning holes in my back. I guess I could find a hotel to chill for a few hours. Get some sleep and a shower. Come back later, when she feels like answering. She had better answer. I need to get rid of this money and move on.

"What'd you want with them?"

It's the fence lurker, strolling over like he doesn't have a care in the world. His white T-shirt clings to his body, colored with streaks of dirt, the pits stained yellow. I'd say it hasn't seen a washing machine in weeks, if ever.

Them. So Gracie doesn't live alone. Is she with a boyfriend? A friend? Does she have a kid already? What does she look like? I had a lot of hours to kill during my drive last night, and I spent some of them wondering if I'd recognize her.

I turn to face this guy dead-on, keeping my stance casual and my voice relaxed. "I'm a friend of the family."

His calculating gaze drifts over me from head to toe and then shifts to my Cherokee. "I ain't seen you 'round here before, *friend*."

I don't like this guy, and it has nothing to do with him living in this dump. He has bad news written all over him, like if I were lying in the gutter, he'd ask me how hurt I am so he'd know how hard I'd fight when he went through my pockets. I'm regretting not tucking my gun into my pants. At least he's not carrying, from what I can see.

I decide to keep playing it cool. "That's because I've never been here before. Do you know if anyone's home?"

He pauses as if to consider my question, his mouth twisting up as he sucks on his teeth. "Dina's 'round."

So she *does* live here after all. I don't trust this guy at my back, so I stay facing him as I knock again. After ten seconds and no answer, I say, "She must be asleep."

"Yeah, maybe." He smirks, like that's somehow funny.

That settles that. I'll have to come back later.

I'm a second away from heading to my SUV when a female yells, "Hey, you! On my steps!" I can tell she's pissed before I even spot her charging toward me.

Her striking face tight with anger.

Her haunting pale green eyes locked on me.

A switchblade open and gripped in her fist.

CHAPTER 9

Grace

I pulled my knife from my purse the second I rounded the bend and saw the shiny SUV parked outside our trailer.

I'm going to catch one of the assholes who's been enabling my mother's heroin addiction red-handed. *Finally*.

"Let me guess, you're doing it so you can pay for college?" I march past the black Jeep Cherokee, giving the quarter panel a swift kick with my heel. "And why the fuck are *you* here?" I sneer at Sims but don't give him a chance to answer, walking right up to the steps. This guy's big. Huge next to me, and built. But I'm banking on the fact that he grew up in a Stepford Wife subdivision with a basketball net out front and parents who think weed is the devil's device, and he doesn't know what to do with a crazy chick charging him with a knife.

By the wide-eyed look he's giving me, I'm right. "What's the matter? Poor little rich kid didn't learn how to earn an easy living so he decides to sell smack?"

"Whoa." He holds up his hands, his gaze shifting between me and the blade. "I don't know what you think—"

"Come near my mother again and I will gut you like a fish," I hiss, holding the knife inches away from his stomach for impact. "Get the hell off my steps!"

"Okay . . . I'm going. Can you give me room to get by?" he says slowly, calmly.

I take a few steps back, and he edges past me, his key ring dangling from his finger. Ready to fill this park with dust clouds as he speeds away in his fancy ride.

Wait a minute . . . "Why am I letting you go?" I step forward, waving the knife in front of his face, forcing the guy back until he's pressed against his hood. "I should call the cops on you."

Panic flickers in his bright blue eyes. "You don't want to do that."

"Actually I do. That's one less dealer to help my mother get high. They'll *love* you in prison." I pull my phone from the back of my shorts. "I hope your mommy's ready to send you tubs of Vaseline in your care package."

"I'm not a drug dealer!" he exclaims, irritation flaring in his voice. If I didn't know better, I'd believe him. But only Mom's dealers come to our door these days. There was a time when child protective services would make random stops, but that ended when I turned eighteen and they could officially not give a damn about me.

"What do you think, Sims?" If anyone can sniff out another dealer, it'd be him.

"He told me he was a friend." Sims steps forward until he's inches away from the guy, taking on a menacing stance.

"I've never seen this guy before in my life." I'd remember. Six-foot-two-ish, square jaw, sandy brown hair in that perfectly messy style. He also has that "I've got money" vibe, even in a faded black T-shirt and dark blue jeans. Not what I'd expect my mother's heroin dealer to look like. And honestly, not the kind of guy I'd expect to come sniffing around a strung-out, haggard thirty-nine-year-old woman. If he were looking for blow jobs as payment, I'm guessing he'd have no issues getting it from the pretty blonde cokeheads on campus.

"Look, I don't want trouble." He's doing his best to ignore Sims, who's shifting his weight from foot to foot, ready to pounce. "I was coming to drop something off. No one answered the door, so I was going to leave and come back later." I detect a slight accent, though I can't place it.

"What d'you wanna give her?" Sims's gaze drops to the guy's pockets, looking for this "thing."

The bastard will just as easily steal it as give it to me. This is the point where my drug-dealing neighbor is no longer useful to me here. In fact, he's making me angrier. "Go back to your pen, Sims. I'm sure someone'll be coming around for a dime bag soon enough."

Taking two steps, Sims turns that menacing gaze toward me, his nostrils flaring. "You know, you're awful mouthy for a little girl needing help."

"Do I look like I need help?" I wave the blade at him. "You think I'm stupid? You're not here to help me. You're looking for an opportunity. And what're you gonna do to me, anyway, huh?"

"You've always been a bitch," Sims mumbles, taking a step closer to me, puffing out his lanky chest.

The guy adjusts his stance, looking ready to grab Sims and throw him to the ground.

"Relax, Rich Boy, Sims here is all talk. Plus he's on probation and if he lays a hand on me, he's going straight to jail for a *long* time. Isn't that right?" I need to stop egging Sims on. I'm banking on him being smart enough to walk away, but I already know he's an idiot.

Before I can find out how big an idiot, Vilma's shouting pulls all our attention away. "*¡La casa se está quemando!*" I look to where she's pointing, to the smoke curling from the kitchen window.

Oh hell. Mom's finally gone and done it.

Shoving Sims out of the way, I snap my blade closed and toss it into my purse with one hand while I fumble with my keys using the other. "Mom!" I unlock the door and throw it open, bracing myself. A plume of dark smoke rolls out above me and sails upward.

The kitchen is on fire. No surprise, the toaster oven is the source, angry flames spouting from it, igniting the threadbare curtains that dangle by the window. They go up in a rush, doubling the size of the fire as the flames reach for the cupboards and the walls.

I dive for the fire extinguisher, my heart pounding in my ears. "How do I even use this thing!" I shriek, panicked.

A strong hand yanks it from my grip. The guy I just held at knifepoint pulls the pin and aims the nozzle toward the toaster oven.

White foam shoots out toward the flames. He seems to know what he's doing and I don't have time to wonder why the hell he's helping. I turn my focus on Mom, sprawled out on the couch, one arm and one leg dangling off the edge.

As still as the dead.

I dive for her, shoving the coffee table out of the way to make room. Trying to ignore the chaos behind me, I press my ear against her mouth to check for breathing.

I feel nothing.

My feet pound against the floor as I run to my room, for the hollowed-out book where I hid the doses of Narcan and next to it, the breathing mask. The last time she OD'd, the doctor set me up with a course and sent me home with this stuff for *when* I needed it next.

I fumble to collect the pieces, my heart hammering in my chest.

I've been gone maybe thirty seconds, and yet when I return, it's an entirely different scene. Flames crawl along the walls and ceiling of the kitchen, the intense heat from the blaze causing me to flinch as I step over the spent extinguisher that lies on the floor.

The guy is holding mom's lifeless body in his arms. "It's too late. Come on!"

Shit. This means firefighters and maybe police . . . I lunge for the used syringe, snapping the needle off the end. I toss the syringe into the heart of the fire.

"Forget that!" The guy grabs hold of my arm and tugs me out the door with him, forcing me down the stairs. I chase after him as he marches past where Vilma stands, phone in hand, spouting a bunch of Spanish words that I *do* understand, like *ambulancia* and *fuego*. She must have called 9-1-1.

"Put her down!" I grab the guy's arm, his skin hot, his muscles tense under my mom's weight, and wave the Narcan in front of him. "I need to give her this *right now*."

He finally relents, setting her down on the dirt laneway, though I can tell he doesn't like doing it.

I rip the cap off the nasal spray applicator and the tube. Steps I memorized but have never actually executed in real life. My hands are shaking as I shove the glass cartridge into the applicator and twist it into place.

"Come on . . ." Holding her floppy head up, I spray half into one nostril, and then half into the other, hoping I haven't messed it up and put too much in one and not enough in the other. I set the breathing mask over her mouth and lean down to blow into it.

"You're doing it too fast."

I try to slow down.

"Here, let me." Strong hands clamp over my biceps and pull me to the side. Normally, my fists would be flailing—a natural reaction to anyone manhandling me—but right now I'm thankful for the help. He's the only one who's offering any.

He drops to his knees, sealing his mouth over the tube to blow into it. He pauses, then blows into it again before shifting his gaze to her withered chest. With a slight shake of his head, he goes back to the mask, repeating the rhythmic pace.

"If she doesn't start breathing on her own after three to five minutes, I have to give her another dose," I explain, wringing my hands as I watch him, desperate to hear sirens. The fire station is around the corner.

Not close enough, I accept as I glance over my shoulder to see the angry flames dancing inside, eagerly charring every last, sad possession we have.

Unfastening his watch with smooth precision, he hands it to me. "It's been about a minute."

I take the watch without a word.

After another glance at her chest and a pause, he warns softly, "You might want to get the other one ready."

I dig it out of my pocket and kneel beside him, my fists balled up tight.

"Your place isn't well marked. You should head down the road to wave them in."

"They'll follow the smoke. Besides, they already know where we live."

His eyes, the color of an Arizona summer sky at mid-morning, flash to me quickly before refocusing on his task, and I catch the pity in them. But he says nothing, continuing to administer breaths as I watch the second hand make its laps, waiting for her to wake up.

Fighting to keep the tears from letting loose as I take in her bluish-tinged lips and fingernails. "Hang in there, Mom—help is coming," I whisper. It's not help that's coming, though. It's just a Band-Aid until next time.

The fire department is the first to sail in, the paramedics on their heels.

And the next minutes are a surreal flurry of firemen trying to save our home, of EMTs giving Mom another dose of Narcan, their standard questions bringing an unsettling sense of déjà vu, because I've been here before.

"What did she take?"

"I don't know."

"But you gave her Narcan . . ."

"Maybe heroin."

"Anything else?"

"I don't know."

"When?"

"I don't know."

"How much did she take?"

"Too much, obviously."

The crowd of curious onlookers stands nearby, watching the spectacle but offering no help, no "Come on, we'll get you to the hospital," as I watch the ambulance speed away, whatever energy I had drained.

Is this the last time?

How many more times can she handle?

How many more times can *I* handle?

I'm so tired.

"Did they tell you where they're taking her?"

His deep voice startles me. For a moment, I actually forgot the guy was here. "St. Bart's." That's where they always take her.

"We should follow them, then."

"*We?*" I turn to regard him. He's shifting from foot to foot, keys already dangling in hand, looking ready to bolt. I can't blame him. "I'll find my own way." That's probably what he's waiting to hear.

"Come on. I'll drive you."

"Why?" It's a loaded question. Why is he offering to drive me? Why is he even here? Why did he help me? "What do you want from me?" Everyone wants something.

He heaves a sigh. "Just . . . come on. Please." He punctuates that plea with a hand floating so close to the small of my back that I can feel the heat without his touch. I tense automatically.

This guy's a complete stranger, but surrounded by people I've known for years, he's the only one who reached for the fire extinguisher, who carried my mom out, who helped me try to keep her from dying. So instead of walking the three miles to the hospital, I climb into the passenger seat of his Cherokee.

The guy hastily grabs a lined sheet of paper from the dashboard, folding and tucking it into his back pocket, but not before I catch the word *Tucson* and my zip code scrawled across it. Then, without warning, he leans over the console, his long, muscular arm reaching to my feet to collect the pile of empty coffee cups. "Sorry. It was a long drive," he mumbles.

I fold my arms around my ketchup-red QuikTrip work shirt, acutely aware of every time his forearm brushes against my bare leg. My gut tells me he's being polite by cleaning up the trash. That he's not taking advantage of the opportunity to touch me. And that reminds me that I haven't thanked him.

"You didn't have to do what you did," I whisper. Not exactly a thanks, but I'm still wary of this guy.

"Yeah, I did." He twists in his seat to stuff the coffee cups into a plastic bag in the backseat, a waft of burnt wood and melted plastic catching my nostrils. His clothes reek of it. Mine must, too.

Starting the engine by pressing a button—I've never been in a car that can do that—he guns it, creating a cloud of dust as he passes Sims, a quiet mutter of "fuckhead" slipping from his lips.

Despite the dire situation, I struggle to hide my smile.

"Right or left?"

"Left." His earlier words finally catch up to me. "You said long drive. From where?"

"Austin."

My heart skips a beat. "Texas?"

"Yes, ma'am."

An odd sense of familiarity washes over me. I clear my throat, hoping to dispel the huskiness I can feel growing in my voice. "I didn't catch your name."

There's a moment's hesitation, before he says, "It's Noah Marshall."

CHAPTER 10

Noah

"You have to wake it up," a man in standard-issue hospital-green scrubs says on his way past, pausing long enough to smack his palm against the vending machine. A hair-raising metal-against-metal sound kicks in and then, a few seconds later, a steady stream of brown sludge begins trickling out.

"Thank you, sir."

"Don't thank me. After you taste it, you'll want to make a right turn out of the parking lot and drive to the nearest Waffle House." His chuckles trail him down the dimly lit hall as I wait for the paper cup to fill.

If this coffee matches this hospital, I'll be taking him up on that advice.

I can't put my finger on what it is about the emergency room that bothers me. Is it the unwelcoming waiting-room chairs—the color of canned peas and as comfortable as a plank of wood—or the dim lighting that screams of cutting overhead costs, or the dove-gray tile floor that can't hide the thin layer of dust coating it?

Or maybe it has nothing to do with the hospital's lackluster décor and everything to do with being here with Abe Wilkes's daughter, waiting to hear if her junkie mom managed to kill herself this time around. After fighting a kitchen fire that ended up burning down their home.

I don't know how I saw today going, but it definitely wasn't like this.

The vending machine takes forever to dispense my order, so I use the time to study Gracie from afar, tucked away in the corner, her smooth, caramel-colored legs crossed at the ankles, those hands that brandished a knife to my stomach mere hours ago now folded daintily in her lap, her profile a stone mask as she stares out the window.

She hasn't spoken to me since the car ride, except to give directions and numbly agree to my offer of coffee. Given what she just went through, I've respected her silence, keeping quiet as I trailed her through the emergency-room doors.

But now I need to know more. Specifically, how the hell did Abe's family end up living like this—and did my mother know about it?

She must have. Her note said Gracie *needs* this money.

Holding two cups filled with the lukewarm tar-like substance, I make my way over to the corner.

She's on the phone. "I can't make it into work tonight . . . No . . . My mom is in the hospital . . . Still waiting to hear . . ."

She's wearing a red polo shirt with a label that says *QuikTrip* and she told the paramedics that she was at work all morning, so either she was supposed to pull two shifts today or she has two jobs.

When she hangs up, I hold out her coffee for her. "I forgot to ask you what you wanted in it."

She stares blankly at it for a moment. "That's fine."

I set the cup down on the small table between us, emptying my pockets of all the cream and sugar I scooped up. "You might need the sugar anyway." The adrenaline that's kept me going is waning. I fall into the seat kitty-corner to her, stretching my long, tired legs out.

She glares at them. "Do you have something against personal space?"

"No, ma'am." I adjust myself so I'm angled away from her. And remind myself that she *did* just come home to find her mother overdosed and her shitty-ass trailer on fire, so she's entitled to her foul mood.

Uncomfortable silence hangs between us.

"Where'd you learn about rescue breathing?" she finally asks, her voice softer, almost conciliatory.

"CPR training. I got my lifeguard certification in high school." I unconsciously slide my hand up my arm, thinking that I haven't been in a pool since my mom died. Or on the courts. Or at the gym.

Her eyes trail the movement. "Let me guess—you sat in a chair at the beach, watching girls in bikinis all summer. Must have been rough."

I guess knowing I'm not her mother's heroin dealer hasn't changed her unflattering opinion of me much. "Rich Boy." That's what she called me earlier. True, I've never wanted for much, but I hardly grew up "rich."

I force a grin. "More like, I taught four-year-olds how to swim in a pool that they definitely peed in."

Her face doesn't so much as hint at a smile, the humor lost. I sense her wanting to say more, but she stops herself with a sip of coffee. "Ugh . . ." She winces and sets the cup back on the table, glaring at it like it's laced with arsenic. "Glad I never gave that machine a dime the last time I was here."

"When was that?" I ask as casually as possible. She had mentioned that the paramedics knew where they lived. Her mom's an addict. This clearly isn't the first time Dina has overdosed.

"Two months ago. And five months before that." She studies her fingernails for a long moment, perhaps deciding how much she wants to divulge to me, a stranger. "I go to work, and she makes a few calls. Sees which of her dealers are around. Sometimes she goes to them. Sometimes they'll swing by our trailer with it. I never actually see who they are; I just see the aftermath. She takes a little bit more each time, until it's too much."

She says it calmly, but now I understand why she freaked out when she saw me on her steps. "I'm sorry. It can't be easy, finding your mother like that." Though I'd take it over how I found *my* mother. A sharp pang fills my chest and I lean forward to rest my forearms on my knees, my focus on the dusty shoe prints covering the floor. "So, what happens now?" *Assuming she makes it.* The paramedics administered another dose of Narcan when they arrived, trying to pull her back from the edge of a cliff she may have already slipped off.

"If she survives, they'll help her detox. She'll check herself out too early and promise to go to one of those free shitty rehab programs. She'll go to one or two meetings and decide that it's not for her, that she can do this on her own. She'll stay clean for a few days. And then she'll go out and pick up a bottle of vodka, and polish it off in one sitting. Once that's not enough, she'll start pumping crap into her veins again. Then, one day, I'll come home and find her unconscious. Or dead." She snorts, but it's a poor attempt to distract from the fact that her eyes are welling. "Then again, we don't have a home now, so . . ."

It seems Gracie has already accepted the fact that her mother is going to die soon. It's just a question of when.

"I'm sorry you have to deal with this." There are so many other questions I want to ask, like when did this start, and why? But I know why. Because the beautiful, loving woman who swung Abe's girl in her arms had her life turned upside down. That woman I carried out of that trailer today? That frail, wasted-away, greasy-haired human with track marks up her arm? That's not the same person.

Gracie's piercing gaze weighs on me, silently assessing me, before she quietly admits, "I know who you are."

My stomach dips at her admission. "How?"

"My mother . . . she told me about Austin and my dad. And your mom. She—" She stops abruptly, gritting her teeth.

It stirs unease in me. "What did she say about my mom?" I can't keep the edge from my voice. What might Dina know?

Gracie's throat bobs with her swallow. "I knew you, before."

That's not what she was going to say, but I'll go with it. For now. "Yeah. You did."

"I don't remember," she mumbles, more to herself.

"You were young." A little girl, with bows in her hair.

But Gracie's no little girl anymore.

For the first time since I saw her storming up the road toward me, hatred burning in her eyes, I finally have a chance to *really* take all of her in, up close—the wild mane of golden brown hair that frames her face, the curls like soft springs jutting out in all directions; her perfect, dainty nose; the defining emerald-green rim that makes the icy mint-green filling of her irises pop that much more; a set of full, soft pink lips that stretch wide across her caramel-colored face.

I've never met anyone who looks quite like her.

I must have been staring at her for too long, because she starts to fidget, tugging at the hem of her shirt, then crossing her arms over her chest. "What's in there?" She nods toward my gym bag.

I instinctively pull it closer to my side. The Glock is back in my portable safe. I let Gracie go ahead of me so I could lock it up, because walking into a hospital with a gun is definitely not a smart move. But there's no way I'm letting this money out of my sight. "Just my stuff."

She eyes it suspiciously. "You have something to give me. That's why you came."

I hesitate. "Yeah. But it'll have to wait."

"Why?"

"Because it's not something I can give you right here."

Her gaze narrows, and I'm beginning to think that whatever trust I earned by helping her earlier has already dwindled.

I'm saved from more uncomfortable questions when a male calls out, "Grace Richards." Not Wilkes, I note. She's on her feet and moving toward the desk where a man wearing a salmon-colored shirt and a stethoscope around his neck waits for her. I follow closely. She glances over her shoulder at me once, spearing me with a strange expression, but she doesn't send me away.

Dina is going to make it. The Narcan worked, reversing the deadly effects of the heroin she injected. They're running additional tests to determine if the drug was mixed with something else that could cause organ damage or other complications.

A heavy sigh of relief sails from Gracie's lips. "So what now? The usual?"

The doctor offers her a sympathetic smile. "We don't have a bed available in our rehab program today. I can get her in as a regular inpatient to help her detox. We'll start her on Subutex and switch her over to Suboxone once she's stable. That would be best given her history."

"Great. Thanks."

"None of it is going to be enough for her," he says gently. "Have you looked into those programs that we talked about?" Obviously this isn't the first time he himself has treated Dina.

She gives him a flat look. "We live in a trailer park."

"And you're sure there are no family members who could help with the cost?"

"Yeah, I'm sure." Her icy tone leaves no invitation for more questions about that.

"Okay, Grace. I'm just trying to help." He pauses. "You know, some people are able to get the services they need while serving time."

She bows her head and remains silent. Seeing as Gracie had the focus to destroy the syringe her mom used to shoot up even with the trailer burning down around her, I don't think she's willing to consider jail as an option for her mother.

"Do you want to see her?"

She shakes her head.

His answering look is one of sympathy. "Then go home and come back tomorrow during visiting hours. I'm sure seeing you, even for a few minutes, would help her through the worst of it."

"She burned down our trailer today."

"Jesus." The doctor sighs with defeat. "Let's wait a few days to tell her about that." His gaze flickers to me, and I instantly see the question in them.

I'll take care of her, I mouth. Because I have a feeling that saying it out loud would earn me a verbal flaying.

With a slight nod, the doctor pats her on the shoulder, repeating, "Try and get some rest."

She watches him as he disappears behind doors and then abruptly spins on her heels and wanders back toward the waiting area to sink into the same chair, a lost look in her eyes. "I should have left that syringe there. I shouldn't cover for her," she mumbles.

"Do you think they would have found it?"

"Probably not, unless I handed it to the cops myself. But he's right. Jail is better than the alternative."

Dead. I have to agree.

"You seriously have no family out here?"

"Nope."

"Does your dad's family know what's going on with her?" I never met them, but I have to believe Abe's family was decent.

She studies her short, plain fingernails for a long moment. "My father's parents are both dead. There's no one else."

For the first time since I found this money, I'm actually happy to have it. I couldn't be giving it to her at a better time. I just have to figure out exactly *how* to give it to her, and it's not going to be in the hospital waiting room.

The sound of her stomach growling gives me an idea.

"I was thinking of grabbing a burger. Do you want to come with me?"

"I'm not hungry." Her face remains stony, even as she gives me a sideways glance.

"Well, *I* am. And tired. And filthy." I can't wait to wash the stench of smoke off me.

She leans back until her head is resting against the wall. She folds her arms over her chest and closes her eyes.

This is not going to be simple, but she seems smart enough to listen to reason. "Look, you heard the doctor—you should get some sleep."

"That's exactly what I'm trying to do. If you'd stop talking . . ." she mutters.

As if the girl who carries a switchblade around in her purse will fall asleep surrounded by a bunch of strangers in a waiting room. "There's a motel down the street, about a mile. I'm gonna grab a room for the night. Why don't you come with me?"

Now she cracks an eyelid, to give me a scathing look. "You think because your mom and my dad knew each other fourteen years ago that

I'm going to follow you to *your motel* room?" She snorts, like it's the most absurd idea ever. I guess under normal circumstances, it would be.

"I don't . . . That's not . . ." I sigh, the implication behind her words thick. I can't help but let out a soft chuckle. The thought of getting laid right now is laughable. "I'm trying to help you. And I'll get you your own room, seeing as I don't trust that you won't stab me in my sleep."

"No one's ever just trying to help. So tell me what you want or leave me the hell alone."

I rub the spot between my eyes where my head is beginning to pound. There's not going to be any dancing around this with her. "My mother died last week, and she left something for you."

Wariness flickers across her face. "What is it?"

"Something that could . . . change things for you."

"What is it?" she pushes.

"I can't say here." I hold her gaze.

"Does it have to do with my dad?"

I hesitate. "It might." *Ninety-eight thousand dollars in cash that my mom went out of her way to hide and insisted it go to Gracie?* My gut says it has *everything* to do with Abe.

It's clear that the topic of her father is a touchy one for her, even after all these years. "Let's go find a place to stay and get some food, and then we can talk."

She sits up, looking ready to follow me out. But I see the moment she decides against it, the moment when her shoulders sag and her body sinks back into her chair and that ongoing fire that's been simmering inside her fades out. "You know what? I'm tired of this. So no . . . unless you've got something that's going to prove that my father wasn't some drug-dealing scumbag who ruined our lives, then I don't want whatever it is, because it's not going to change anything for me." Her slender, lithe frame suddenly seems so small, so . . . beaten down. Physically, she's still young and vibrant.

Beautiful.

But she's got a haunted gaze in her eyes, the kind you get when life has disappointed you over and over again, when you've seen and suffered.

"He was a good man."

"I need her to know."

My stomach tightens as my mother's voice fills my head, reminding me that it's not just money that she wanted to give Abe's daughter. She wanted to fix *this*. To give Gracie peace of mind. A coat of polish for the tarnished memory of her father.

A chance to know a different truth.

But how the hell do I give her that without telling her everything that I know, everything Silas made me swear to keep to myself, to protect my mother's name?

I don't think I can.

But I *can* give her ninety-eight thousand dollars, if I get her somewhere more private. Someplace where she can't cause a scene and bring the cops around.

"Look, I just drove twelve hours across two states to see you. I know you didn't ask me to, but I'm here. I haven't done *anything* today to make you think that I'm a bad guy, or that I'd hurt you, have I?"

"No, but—"

"You don't want to sit in this crappy hospital waiting room all night, starving and tired. So *please*, Gracie. Trust me. Just this once." I've been told that I'm hard to resist when I resort to begging. I don't usually use these powers—I do have some dignity—but if there ever was a time to pull out all the stops, this is it.

Her wary gaze shifts to the gym bag, then back to me.

Finally, she stands, tugging at the bottoms of her shorts to adjust them. "No one calls me Gracie." I hear the pained warning behind it. And I can guess why.

That's what Abe called her.

"I'm sorry . . . *Grace*."

Grabbing her purse, she starts walking toward the door, mumbling, "Pizza is better."

I sigh with relief. "Pizza it is."

She does a quick scan of her clothes, which are as dirty as mine. "And can we stop at a store on the way?"

"Anything you want."

"Are you always so agreeable?"

"Yes, ma'am. I try to be."

She exhales a shaky breath and presses her lips together. I can't miss the hint of anticipation flickering in her eyes or the faint air of hopefulness that lifts her shoulders.

She *does* want whatever my mother left for her and, despite her obvious skepticism, she *is* hoping it's something that will change her life.

A bag of money will do that, but I'm not sure it's what she's looking for, especially if she starts jumping to conclusions about why it should go to her in the first place.

Who am I kidding?

This girl is going to kill me.

CHAPTER 11

Officer Abraham Wilkes

April 17, 2003

Noah answers the door, those innocent blue eyes instantly dulling the simmering rage that still burns inside me from last night.

I check my watch. "Why aren't you in school?" I intentionally waited until I thought he'd be gone.

"Got an orthodontist appointment in half an hour." The sullen look on his face tells me the news isn't good. "They're gonna tell me that I need braces."

"You're not surprised, are you?" Jackie's been bitching for years about how much money she'd have to fork over to fix those crooked front teeth of his, because our benefits won't cover all of it.

"No, sir. It's just—" His prepubescent voice cracks, and he clears it. "It's gonna suck."

I ruffle the top of his head, his sandy-brown hair as soft to the touch as it was when he was knee high. "Would you rather go through life like *this*?" I gesture at the gap between my two front teeth.

Noah grins. "That's not so bad."

"Says who?" I chuckle, remembering those awkward teenage years when I pursed my lips together to keep myself from smiling wide. "Don't you worry. You'll be thankin' your lucky stars later, when all the girls are chasing you." Noah's going to be one heck of a handsome man when he grows up. I try to keep my voice neutral when I ask, "Listen, your mom around?"

"Out back."

"Why don't you hang in front here for a few minutes and practice that jump shot. I need to talk to your mom alone. It's about work." I don't want Noah anywhere near where he can overhear. He doesn't need to be the wiser.

"Yes, sir." Noah leans over to grab his basketball, which is resting on the floor next to the door and within easy reach, as always.

"Good boy." I ruffle his hair once more as I pass by him.

I find Jackie in the backyard, cutting back dead branches that the winter left behind. I've always found it to be a contradictory passion of hers. I'd never peg her to be the type to fuss over pretty, girly things, too busy fussing over collecting career stripes. If there's one thing everyone can agree on about Jackie Marshall, it's that she has her sights set high in the police force.

She sees me coming and casts away the handful of debris, wariness filling her face. Her bag-lined eyes drift behind me to the patio door. Checking for Noah, no doubt.

Whatever calm that boy incited in me quickly vanishes, as thoughts of last night resurface with a vengeance.

"What do you want me to say? That I'm sorry? Because I am. You shouldn't have been there. None of that should have happened." She's choosing her words carefully, her lips twisting as if she's tasting something bitter in her mouth.

"But it did happen!" I lower my voice, knowing it'll carry far around this peaceful neighborhood, especially at this time of morning. "Where is she?" I enunciate each word as calmly as I can.

Jackie hesitates. "She doesn't want to be found, Abe."

"Bullshit. I saw the look on her face."

"And I heard the words coming out of her mouth when she told me she wasn't going anywhere with me." She stoops to collect a loose branch, avoiding my hard gaze.

Which tells me that there's either more to the story or she's altogether lying, because when Jackie Marshall's telling you how it is, she could stare down paint until it peels right off the wall.

"You should have gotten her out of there anyway. Hell, *I* should never have listened to you in the first place! You manipulated me!" I can't *believe* I let her pull rank. I can't *believe* I trusted her.

God, what would Dina think if she knew!

"What was I supposed to do, Abe? What would you have done in my position?"

"The right thing!"

Jackie whips the pair of shears she's gripping tight at the ground. The sharp end spears the dirt. "Well, no one's arguin' that you're a better person than most, Abe. You deserve a goddamn medal, just for being born."

"I don't need a medal. What I need to do is find Betsy, and you've made sure that's gonna be next to impossible." I've never hurt a woman and I never will, but dammit, my fingers around Jackie's neck would feel satisfying right about now, even just for a second.

"I'm sorry, Abe. I was stuck between a rock and a hard place. I just didn't see any other choice."

"You mean another choice that would benefit you." I shake my head. "As far as you and I go? We're done. Got it?" I spin on my heels, needing to get the hell out of here before I *really* lose my temper.

"Try The Lucky Nine," she calls out, reluctance in her voice.

"What?"

"The Lucky Nine. It's out by the highway. I told you I'd follow her and I did. That's where she went."

"And that's where you left her. A *fifteen-year-old* girl."

At least Jackie has the decency to look ashamed.

CHAPTER 12

Grace

"You'll be in rooms 240 and 241. They share an adjoining door," the bubbly front-desk receptionist says with a smile. I'm sure she smiles at every customer, but I doubt like *that.* Like she wants to hop over the desk and throw her giggly self at Noah.

I shouldn't be surprised. He's tall and built and, now that I don't think he's one of the skeevy guys pumping my mother full of heroin, I can appreciate his angular jaw and his full mouth, and every other detail that makes it hard not to stare at him. He doesn't fit the preppy-rich-boy image that I accused him of, but he definitely does have the well-put-together thing going for him.

And if I had to guess, this girl—with her fluttering fake eyelashes and French-tipped nails and skin as smooth and creamy as a porcelain doll—is exactly his type.

Either oblivious or used to the attention, Noah merely offers her a "thanks" as he slides his credit card into his wallet, his arms naturally flexing with the movement. I didn't think he was serious about getting me my own room, but I plan on leaving as soon as I have my hands on whatever he has for me anyway.

"Is there anything else I can help you with?" the clerk asks, tucking a strand of her silky blonde hair behind her ear.

My stomach decides that's the best time to growl, loud enough to echo through the empty lobby.

Noah grins. "Is there a good pizza place nearby?"

Front Desk Flirt's eyes light up as if he's asked her out to dinner.

"Enzo's. It's cash-and-pick-up only, but I promise you, it's so worth it. Here's their info." She hands him a flyer.

"Thank you, ma'am."

He turns to regard me, and grins.

"What?"

"I was wondering if you knew how to smile." His eyes drop to graze my lips. "Looks like you do."

I *am* smiling. And blushing, from the way he's looking at me. "That's because your Texas is showing." He'd dropped more than a few "yes, sirs" and "no, ma'ams" at the hospital, and for the paramedics. Apparently my dad used to say things like that all the time. Mom said it was one of the first things that made her fall in love with him.

Now I can see why. It's charming, especially coming out of Noah's mouth.

He reaches down to collect his bags, the grin firmly in place. "I'll try harder to hide my Texas."

I bite my tongue before "don't" slips out and follow him out the door, my eye on that gym bag, which he hasn't let out of his sight.

Whatever Jackie Marshall wanted me to have, it must be in there.

I follow him past the pool that fills the center of the courtyard, with two floors of rooms overlooking it, wishing I had a bathing suit. I can't remember the last time I swam. I was lucky that I had enough cash to pick up a cheap pair of shorts, a T-shirt, and underwear, along with laundry detergent. Hopefully I can get the smell of smoke out of my work shirt before tomorrow's shift. I'll have to swing by the trailer after to see about salvaging clothes. And then . . .

My stomach tightens with the reality that I have no place to go after tonight.

"I'm sure the rooms are nothing great, but it'll be safe and clean. Here, you take this one." He hands me a key card. "I'm gonna drop my stuff off and run out to grab that pizza. What do you want on it?"

"Whatever it is you came here to give me."

He smiles, but it's not with the same ease as earlier, in the lobby. "Too bland."

"I'm serious."

His jaw muscles tighten. "You need to eat."

"You're stalling. Why?"

He passes his room key over the lock. "So . . . what do you want on it? Mushrooms? Green peppers? Bacon?"

I glare at him, but I get the feeling that my stubbornness isn't going to persuade him.

"Come on, Gracie. *Grace.*" He pleads gently. The way his deep voice slides softly over my name, the way his blue eyes weigh on me . . .

The bastard used that to sway me at the hospital, too.

I sigh. I guess I can wait twenty minutes. "Crispy bacon," I admit reluctantly.

"Pepperoni?"

"Who *doesn't* put pepperoni on their pizza?"

He shrugs. "Crazy people?"

"Exactly. *I'm* not crazy. Are *you* crazy?"

He shakes his head, and amusement dances over his face again. "I'll knock on your door when I'm back." With that, he disappears into his room.

I sigh at the feel of the fresh, cool air as I step through my door. It's a newer hotel, decorated in soft whites and grays, with a rich charcoal padded headboard and black-and-white patterned bedding that contrasts with the crisp white sheets. The bathroom is bright, with white subway tiles in the shower and a lemon-yellow curtain.

Despite everything, an unexpected wave of giddiness washes over me.

This may be "nothing great" by Noah's standards, but it's the nicest place I've ever stayed at. Sure, I had friends with normal families, who lived in normal houses, and who invited me for sleepovers. But for tonight, this place is all *mine*, and I can't think of anything I need more than a quiet space to try and deal with today's turn of events.

Dropping my purse on the dresser, I head for the shower.

A soft knock sounds on the adjoining room door. Twisting the towel around my wet hair and piling it on top of my head, I unlock the deadbolt and open it. The delicious scent of bacon and cheese hits me.

"She wasn't lying. This *is* amazing," Noah announces between mouthfuls, sucking a glob of tomato sauce off his thumb as he backs up to let me in. His room is an exact replica of mine, only in reverse. He pulls a handful of clothes from his backpack. "I'll be out in five. Eat as much as you want."

I watch him as he heads into the bathroom, sliding the pocket door shut behind him. And then I do a quick scan. The gym bag is nowhere in plain sight, which means he hid it. There aren't *that* many places to hide a gym bag in a hotel room.

Maybe the dresser?

My hand is inches from the knob when the door slides open and Noah pokes his head out. I smoothly divert for the pizza, tearing a slice free.

"Forgot to tell you, there's Coke and beer in the fridge."

"'kay. Thanks." He must think I'm twenty-one. Or, more likely, he doesn't care. He also either thinks I'm not the type to raid his room while he's thirty feet away in a shower or that I'm not clever enough to find his hiding spot.

When you've grown up scouring your trailer for your mother's drug stash, you know a thing or two about playing hide-and-seek. Noah's in for a rude awakening.

The shower starts running. I want to be sure that he's not going to pop back out to catch me red-handed, so I occupy myself with my slice and a can of beer, accepting that I'm both famished and thirsty. I hardly ever drink—watching my mother's dependence on drugs and alcohol has given me an unpleasant perspective—but I need something to take the edge off.

A minute later, I get the signal I'm waiting for—the sound of curtain rings dragging over a metal rod.

I go straight for the dresser, yanking all four drawers open. Empty. Next, I throw open the closet door. Nothing but extra pillows and a small safe that sits open. I move over to the nightstand drawer, even though I already know it's too small to hold anything but a Bible.

There's nothing under the bed, either.

And nothing tucked behind the curtains.

"Dammit . . ." I survey the room again. This should be easy, but maybe he's smarter than I think he is and he left that gym bag in his car. Why else would he trust me in here alone? He'd have to be an idiot to—

The mattress.

It's been shifted down slightly, just enough to see that it's not lined up with the box spring.

Adrenaline pulses through my veins as I dive for the headboard, sticking my hand into the unknown. My fingers graze the nylon material and I smile with nervous satisfaction. The mattress is heavy and it takes full-body effort to push it, and then serious tugging on the strap.

But finally I pull the bag free.

And unfasten the zipper.

Whatever anticipation I felt gives way to pure shock. "Oh my God."

The bag's full of money.

So much fucking money.

What is Noah doing with *all this money*?

I drop down onto the edge of the bed. Is *this* what Jackie Marshall wanted me to have? A bag full of cash? My hands shake as I fan through wads of it.

There's only one explanation that I can come up with for him showing up here with this a week after she died, and for being so evasive about it.

It's drug money.

Was this Dad's cut from whatever he and Jackie Marshall had going on? Did she feel some twisted sense of duty to pass it on to me? Fourteen years later, after she's dead and no longer has to answer questions?

Noah must know my father's story. And he did say whatever he had to give me might have something to do with my dad.

How much does Noah know, anyway?

I squeeze my eyes shut and take a few deep breaths. For the second time today, my temper rears its ugly head, and that's never good. I don't think straight when I'm this angry. I do things like wave knives at strangers on my doorstep and antagonize slimy drug dealers. I need to calm down.

But when I open my eyes and see all that money at my fingertips, my rage only flares hotter. And mixed in with it is a healthy dose of pain and disappointment.

Somewhere, deep inside, I held the tiniest sliver of hope that my mother isn't delusional, that the police had it all wrong about my dad.

I glare at the bathroom door, imagining Noah behind it.

That coward. This is why he was stalling.

He was afraid of how I'd react.

CHAPTER 13

Noah

I hold my breath as the stench of smoke intensifies. Hot water and a handful of shampoo will fix that.

At least Gracie seems more agreeable now than she was earlier. It must have been the shower and food. That always makes me feel better.

Or maybe she's finally accepted that I'm not the asshole she thinks I am. I could be stressing myself out about the money for no reason. She's homeless and, I'm assuming, broke. This money is going to solve her problems. She can rent a decent apartment, get her mom into a rehab program that might actually help her to stay clean.

Hell, I may get to see another one of those genuine, unrestrained smiles across that pretty face of hers.

I'm thinking about that when the shower curtain flies open. I turn to find Gracie standing there, the gym bag held open within her shaking hands.

That pretty face is brimming with shock and rage.

"Is *this* what you came to give me?" she hisses, her voice barely audible above the stream of water.

Shit. "I'll explain everything." Of course she snooped. She doesn't have a trusting bone in her body. And here I thought I hid the bag well, but clearly I'm not smart enough for her. I should have handed her the entire pizza box and sent her back into her room. And I definitely should have locked the bathroom door. Generally if a girl is barging in while I'm in the shower, it's not to yell at me.

"I don't want a dime of this fucking money!" Her teeth are clenched and I can see the muscles working in her jaw. At least she's not waving her knife this time.

My hands fall from where they were rubbing shampoo through my hair to a surrendering position. "Just . . . let me explain before you make any decisions."

"You *lied* to me!"

What? "How did I lie? I didn't tell you anything!"

She whips the bag to the floor and then folds her arms over her chest, her voice turning snippy. "Fine. *Explain.*"

"Can I have a minute?" I'm far past the point of trying to hide myself, so all I can do is stand there like a fool.

The rage in her eyes dims the moment they drop from my face. Even with her caramel complexion, I see the flush of color. It's as if she's only now realizing that I'm naked. Grabbing a towel from the rack above the toilet, she throws it at me. "Hurry up," she snaps, spinning on her heels and marching out, leaving the gym bag where it landed.

"Dammit," I mutter under my breath, my forehead falling hard against the tile.

She's never going to believe me now.

"There's a lot left." I hold out the box, my feeble attempt at a peace offering as I pass through the adjoining doorway. At least she left the door to her room open.

"I'm good, thanks." Gracie is perched on the edge of her bed, her fingers nimbly weaving her hair into a braid. It's twice as long wet as it is dry.

At least she isn't glaring at me like I pulled the trigger on her father anymore. She won't even look at me, her focus locked on the wall across from her.

I tear off two slices for myself and then toss the box on the dresser. After more than a week with no appetite, I suddenly can't seem to fill this nagging hunger. Maybe my body is finally saying enough is enough. That, and I've been offered a distraction from my own problems in the form of Gracie's.

I grab a beer, along with a second one because I noticed the can on her nightstand. I still don't know how old she is but given what she's been through, telling her she's too young to have a few drinks would be stupid on my part.

Setting it on her end table, I opt to take the chair directly across from her instead of sitting on her bed.

The gym bag full of cash makes a thudding sound as I drop it to the floor by my feet.

Then I wait quietly for her to say something, because the hell if I know how to approach this, and she's impossible to read.

"I'm sorry about earlier," she finally offers, her eyes flickering to me, skittering over my body before snapping back to the wall. Color crawls up her neck. "I have a hard time keeping my temper in check."

"It's okay."

"I don't think things through; I jump to conclusions and then I act."

"Don't worry about it."

"I was angry with you and I just . . . I wasn't trying to . . ." She's stumbling over her words.

I didn't expect this reaction, and it's all I can do to press my lips together to hide my smile. I'll gladly let her barge into my shower and scream at me if it means I get this softer, docile version afterward. "Yeah, I've noticed the anger issues."

Awkward silence hangs in the room once again, broken momentarily by the crack of my beer can.

I guess it's my turn. "I'm sorry. I didn't know how to tell you about *that*." I gesture toward the bag. "I found it last night with a note, asking that I give it to you. Here, see for yourself." I fish the sheet of paper out from my pocket and hand it to her to read.

She sets her jaw but, after a long pause, I get a small nod of acceptance. "I knew about your mother already," she admits quietly, taking a sip of her own beer as her penetrating eyes land heavily on me. "That she died. And *how* she died."

Her words stir a sharp pang in my chest. "How?" I ask, clearing my voice against the sudden gruffness that comes whenever the topic lands on my mother's suicide.

"On the news."

"But you live in Tucson." Why the hell would my mother's death get coverage here?

"My mom has an unhealthy obsession with Texas. Especially anything to do with the Austin Police Department." She stretches out on her bed with her back against the headboard and her long, shapely legs crossed at the ankles. She looks like she's getting settled in for a long night of talking. "She says someone there framed my dad. She'll swear up and down that he would never sell drugs."

Exactly what my mother alluded to.

Dina must know something. But would she have told Gracie?

I do my best to feign ignorance, and hope that Gracie can't sense the tension coursing through my limbs. "It would be hard to accept that about someone you loved and trusted." I hesitate. "Why does she think that he was framed?"

"Because she's a crazy, cracked-out woman? I don't know." Gracie snaps off the tab on her beer can and tosses it haphazardly toward the trash can in the corner. "But it's ruined her life. And mine."

Either Gracie's an A-list actress or Dina hasn't told her anything. "Do you believe he did it?"

"I didn't. And then I did." Her gaze shifts to the bag of money, her throat bobbing with a hard swallow. "And now you've shown up here with *that*, and no explanation. So, I'm thinking that he's guilty of *something*." She seems to consider her next words for a long moment. "My mom talks about Jackie a lot."

"Oh yeah?" I take a big sip of my beer and then coolly ask, "What does she say?" I can already tell I'm not going to like it.

Gracie picks at a piece of thread on the bedcover. "That she was part of my father's setup."

"We are bad, bad people."

I push my mother's voice out of my head. "Does she have proof?"

Gracie's head shake brings me an odd sense of relief.

"Why did you leave Texas?"

"The neighborhood turned on us. That's what she told me, anyway; I don't remember, but she said people watched our every move, glared when we walked by. Neighbors who'd had us over for dinner before wouldn't even say hello. Some yelled at her. I remember that happening once or twice." Her face tightens with a cute little frown. "I didn't understand why they'd be so mean to us because my dad had an accident at work. That's what my mom told me happened: that he had an 'accident' and he wouldn't be coming home again.

"Then one night, someone threw a brick through the window. So she packed us up and we left for Arizona." The sadness in Gracie's voice has quickly changed to bitterness.

I guess having a neighborhood turn on you might make you up and move. Maybe overnight. *Maybe*. But according to Canning, Dina never came back, never even asked to see the police report. Why?

"Why accuse my mother of being a part of it?" Is she simply a heartbroken widow turned junkie? Or is there more to this part of the story? There must be, because why else did my mother have Abe's gun holster hidden under our floorboards?

What does Dina know?

Gracie responds with a shrug, but there's nothing nonchalant about it. She's still suspicious, still calculating in her gaze as she studies me. "My dad and your mom were best friends and partners for years. Even after your mother got promoted. But then my dad died, and she cut us off. She stopped answering my mom's phone calls."

"She wouldn't do that."

"Why would my mother lie?" Gracie's piercing eyes settle on me. "It seems odd, doesn't it? They were partners and friends for *years*, and then she just turned her back on us. For *fourteen years*. And now you show up with *this*." She gestures to the bag. "Why?"

Why, indeed? I focus on the beer in my hand as I try to recall those first few weeks, those months, after Abe died. We went to the funeral, that I remember. Dina simply stood there, a husk of a woman, her eyes puffy but no tears shed—as if she'd already drained herself of the ability. Tucked in next to her, a sullen little Gracie, her gaze wide as her eyes roved the crowd of faces around her.

We left soon after. I don't remember attending a reception. All I remember is Silas and my mother sitting in the backyard, my uncle speaking quietly while repeatedly topping up the glass in my mother's hand. My mother . . . all she did was stare into the depths of the pool and empty her glass over and over again.

She went back to work a few days later. And that's when I started staying home alone. She said I was old enough, that there was no need for me to go to Dina and Abe's after school anymore. At the time, I was more thankful than anything. I figured she was doing it so I wouldn't have to walk through Abe's front door every day and remember that he was dead.

But if what Gracie is saying is true . . .

If my mother believed Abe was such a good man, why would she cut Dina and her little girl off like that?

I don't have an answer for Gracie—or myself—so I divert. "We didn't exactly have it easy after he died, either. My mom started drinking and my parents divorced. I moved to Seattle to live with my dad."

"Yeah, I've heard Seattle is rough. Was your trailer park like the Hollow?" She doesn't hide her scorn.

"You're right. I'm sorry." I'm an ass.

She shrugs. "You didn't have anything to do with it."

And yet I can't help but feel responsibility here.

She pauses. "What do *you* think? You're older than me. You must remember him, right? Do you think my dad was guilty?"

"He was a good man."

"I need her to know."

My mother's words are a constant thrum. Why can't I bring myself to give voice to them? "I don't know." I chug half the can of beer so I can gather my thoughts. Based on what George and Silas said, the case is firmly closed, the evidence irrefutable. Would knowing what my mother mumbled—drunk, and moments before she decided to take her own life—help Gracie and Dina? I'm not sure I believe her, and it doesn't feel right to repeat it. It could hurt them more. It would definitely hurt the memory of my mom.

Let sleeping dogs lie.

How many times will I have to tell myself that before this guilt lifts from my chest?

The weight of that green-eyed gaze on me is suffocating. I need off this topic. "The Hollow. Sounds like a horror movie."

It's delayed, but Gracie's face finally cracks with a smirk. "Even the cops call it that. Suits it, doesn't it?"

Of all the places to run to . . . "How'd you end up there, anyway?"

"That's where my mom grew up."

"No shit."

Gracie reaches for the fresh can of beer I left on her nightstand and cracks it open. "It wasn't bad when she was a kid. But then the owner sold it to people who don't give a rat's ass about anything but getting their monthly fees. It all went to hell after that."

"So Dina moved from Tucson to Austin . . . and back to Tucson." Trailer-park girl to stylish Texan wife, to heroin junkie. I'm struggling to reconcile my memories of Abe's Dina with the Dina I carried out of a burning trailer earlier today.

"To the same trailer." Tension tightens her jaw. "The one she burned to the ground making her cheese melt sandwiches."

"At least you don't have to go back to that life. You can start over somewhere new. Somewhere with good people."

"My mom's a heroin addict, Noah. 'Good people' don't want her kind around."

"Then get her the help she needs. You can do that now."

She nods slowly. "Why?"

"Why get her the help?"

"No. Why did Jackie want me to have all that money?"

Good question. "I don't know why, or where it came from. She asked me to bring it to you, and so I did."

"*After* she died." Gracie's lips purse. "'Don't ask questions. You don't want the answers.' That's what the note said, right?"

"If it can help you, take it." I'm not going to sit here and brainstorm all the terrible ways that APD could have fucked Abe over fourteen years ago, because they could include my mother. I need to get through this conversation, wave goodbye to Gracie and her big bag of money, and move on.

She turns her focus to the ceiling, her deep inhale drawing my attention to the way her black tank top stretches across her chest, hugging her curves. I quickly drop my gaze.

Definitely not a little girl anymore. And if she weren't who she is, if she were some girl I spotted at the gym or the bar . . . a hundred bucks says I wouldn't be able to keep my eyes off her for a hot second. But she *is* Abe's daughter, and that reality is a cold shower for those thoughts.

"How did Jackie know where to find me?"

I shrug.

"It wouldn't be that hard," she answers for herself.

"Not if this address is listed in your mom's records." The bigger question for me is, was Mom keeping tabs on Abe's family all these years? Watching Dina's downward spiral? Or had she tracked them down recently? Did she foresee the situation Gracie would find herself in today? Probably.

It makes sense, though, that she would want to give the money to Gracie and not Dina. You can't give a bag of cash to an addict.

So yeah, Mom definitely knew how far they'd fallen.

Had I not been there, I hate to think what might have happened. Gracie would be curled up in a ball in that hospital waiting area. She'd have nowhere to live.

Then again, had Gracie not found me on her doorstep, she might have walked through that door sooner, might have turned off the toaster oven before it had a chance to catch flame.

Either way, Dina would have overdosed on heroin.

I nudge the gym bag with my foot, pushing it toward her a few inches. "This money couldn't have come at a better time then."

"How much is in there?"

Ten thousand. Twenty. What's an amount that sounds reasonable? What could I tell her to make it easier to accept this, at least until I'm long gone? I could lie and tell her I didn't count it, but who in their right mind would have driven across two states without counting it?

"Ninety-eight thousand."

"Holy shit," she whispers, a gasp slipping through her lips before she covers her mouth with her hand. At least ten heartbeats pass before her face twists with skepticism. "Why didn't you keep it?"

"Because my mom asked me to give it to you."

She rolls her eyes. "That wouldn't stop most people."

"*Some* people, no." I *could* have kept it. I *could* have given it away to charity, anonymously. I *could* have taken it to the police.

I'm not going to say that all those scenarios didn't run through my mind on the drive here, as I wondered if I was doing the right thing. But, somewhere along that dark, open highway, I came to accept a simple truth. "She didn't write me a letter. She didn't give me an explanation, or an apology. She knew she was going to kill herself and she didn't want to tell me why." I swallow against that prickly lump in my throat. "The only thing she *did* do was leave that pile of money and that note. So I figure it must have been important to her that you get this."

More important than telling her son she was sorry.

I glance Gracie's way to find her watching me intently, sympathy in her gaze. Maybe she doesn't hate me, after all.

"What would you do if a stranger showed up at your doorstep with a bag of money for you and no explanation besides 'don't ask'? Would you take it?"

"If I were in your situation, with no home and a mother who's one injection away from never waking up, I'd take that money and never look back."

Her face pinches. "Even if it's here because of something immoral? Hell, illegal?"

She has way too heavy of a conscience for a piss-poor girl with no place to live. But I like that about her. It means that despite growing up with a junkie mom and the ghost of a corrupt cop father, somewhere along the way she picked up a sense of integrity.

This is one of those times, though, when you have to take what's in front of you and not ask questions. She's smart enough to see that. Maybe all she needs is permission. "What do you think would happen to this money if I gave it to the police?" Besides stir up questions I don't want to answer. "They'd use it for their department. Buy a new SUV, maybe office equipment. They'd have no issues spending it on their overhead. So why shouldn't you use it? You deserve a chance to start over."

It's a long while before her head bobs in an almost imperceptible nod. She's going to take the money. She's not stupid.

"Are you going to be okay?"

She brushes my concern away with an unconvincing, "Yeah. Of course."

"Listen, I'm gonna grab a few hours of sleep before I have to drive home tomorrow." I haul my weary body out of the chair, tossing my napkins and cans in the trash can beside the small desk. I'm ready for today to be over.

I make it all the way to the adjoining door, my palm on the handle. Almost home free.

And then Gracie asks the one thing I hoped she wouldn't.

"Did your mom ever talk to you about what happened to my dad?"

My shoulders sag. I don't owe her anything, and yet I hate lying to her about this.

"She said something, didn't she?"

Take the money and run, Gracie. Forget about the past.

The bed creaks behind me. I'm half-expecting to feel the sharp edge of her blade poking into my flesh, but instead cool fingers settle on my forearm in a gentle way I didn't think her capable of. "What did she tell you about my dad?"

Another long pause and then her touch slips away. "He was guilty, wasn't he?" Her voice cracks and when I gather the nerve to turn around and face her, she's blinking away tears. "It doesn't matter. I already knew he was. This doesn't change anything."

I can't handle the sight of any girl crying. But for some reason, it's worse with Gracie. Before I can stop myself, I reach for a tear slipping down her cheek, brushing it away with the pad of my thumb.

She turns away with the slightest flinch, and I let my hand drop. I've noticed that about her—she recoils anytime anyone goes near her. The only time she didn't was when she was brandishing her knife against that piece-of-shit Sims guy.

"You're right, it doesn't. Take the money and move on with your life."

"It's just . . ." Her jaw tightens. "My mother never did drugs before; she didn't even drink. What he did? That's what turned her into *this*. He ruined our lives, and she will swear that he's innocent, right to her last breath, and I can't stand—" Those full lips press into a tight line. "I hate him so much for it."

Dammit. I can't let her believe this. "She didn't say that he was guilty, Gracie."

She peers up at me from behind a thick fringe of lashes, the eight-inch-or-so height difference forcing her head back to meet my eyes. "What did she say?"

"Not much, after he died. And then near the end, she was drinking a lot." I sigh. "But she said that your dad was a good man."

"Right. Who was *also* a drug dealer?" A skeptical frown furrows her brow.

"That's all I know." I start for my side of the suite, hoping she's not going to follow. She doesn't move a muscle, a dazed look filling her face. "The money is yours, Gracie. A decorated police officer and chief of the Austin Police Department, and an old friend of the family, left it for you, to help you through a hard time, and that's all you need to know." That sounds like something Silas would tell me to say. "I'm going to shut this door. Knock if you need anything." I've already seen what this girl is capable of when she's angry. I don't want to wake up to a blade against my nuts after she's been stewing in bed for three hours and decides that what I've told her isn't good enough.

My body sinks with relief the moment the latch clicks. Hoping that she doesn't knock, that she doesn't want a rehash of the night my mom died in hopes of finding clues. Reasons for the money, and for my mother's words.

I peel my clothes off and slide under the cool, crisp covers, waiting for that feeling of relief and accomplishment to hit me. I've done what my mother asked of me. Gracie has her money, and I've told her that Abe was a good man. She's going to be okay.

And yet a suffocating weight still bears down on my chest.

CHAPTER 14

Grace

I'm woken from a dead sleep by my phone.

"Uh-huh?" My greeting comes out more like a sigh.

"Grace Richards?" a woman asks, low voices buzzing in the background.

"Yeah?"

"Dr. Coppa wanted me to let you know that a bed became available in our rehab facility this morning, so we've moved your mother. She's doing well, and she'd like to see you. Visiting hours will begin shortly."

I doubt everyone gets personal calls like this from the hospital, but I also doubt everyone has a doctor bending over time and time again for them. I'm aware that I have Dr. Coppa's full pity. "Okay. Thanks. I'll be there . . ." I glance at the clock to see that it's already ten thirty a.m. ". . . soon."

It's a good thing I called in sick for this morning's shift. Dealing with gas station customers is the last thing I can face right now, as I try to pull my life back together and make sense of Noah's surprise visit.

The low hum of a TV sportscaster's voice carries through the wall between his room and mine. He's probably packing up, eager to get on the road for that long drive back to Austin.

Thoughts of him getting dressed make me groan into my pillow. I'm mortified about barging in on him in the shower last night. Granted, he should have locked the door, but that's no excuse. And then he stood there, not swearing or yelling at me to get the hell out. Instead, trying to calm *me* down.

My cheeks flush at that awkward moment, firmly emblazoned in my memory.

It's not like Noah's the first naked guy I've ever seen. I had boyfriends in high school. Plus, living in the Hollow, where drunken disorderliness goes hand in hand with public indecency, I've come across more than one asshole who gets a kick out of a midday stroll in the flesh. It's always the sweaty ones, too, with their bellies permanently swollen from hard liquor and tufts of hair growing in places where tufts of hair shouldn't be growing.

And then, there's the time I finished my English exam an hour early and came home to find my mom on her knees in front of some scrawny guy, his pants pooling around his ankles, a ziplock bag of Oxy pills dangling from his fingers like bait.

I've seen my fair share of naked men, but none of them have looked anything like Noah. Every inch of him is sculpted in golden muscle, and the tan line that sits low around his hips proves that he has no qualms about showing off that broad chest.

And to top it all off, he was covered in soap suds, water dripping from every—

A soft knock comes from our adjoining door, startling my thoughts. I drag myself out of bed and do a quick mirror check to confirm that my hair is a wild mess. My mom always told me how lucky I am to have inherited her silky, soft texture and Dad's curls. I wonder when I'll agree with her on that, because most days it seems more of a nightmare than anything resembling luck. Going to bed with it damp does awful things, but the hotel's hair dryer didn't have a diffuser, no surprise. So I was forced to braid it and cross my fingers.

By the halo of frizz around my face, I'm thinking that wasn't the best move either.

Doing my best to smooth it down with my fingers, I finally give up, throw on the clothes I bought yesterday, and then open the adjoining door.

Noah has his back to me, giving me a brief opportunity to admire the way his soft gray T-shirt clings around his muscular arms and shoulders and his dark jeans sit low on his hips. He's busy stuffing his toiletries bag into his backpack. "How'd you sleep?"

"Fine." When he glances over at me, I notice the circles under his eyes.

"Better than you, from the looks of it."

He chuckles. "Yeah. I need at least a week to catch up on all the sleep I've missed lately." He swallows hard.

I mentally kick myself. His mother just shot herself and here he is, helping me deal with *my* shit. "I'm sorry about your mom." Regardless of what my mom believes Jackie did, Noah had no hand in it.

He offers me a sad smile and nods, but it doesn't mask the flash of pain in his eyes.

"Hey, you should find a safe place to keep that money, like the bank."

"Right." But not my bank account. There'd be red flags waving above my head the moment I passed ninety-eight thousand dollars over the counter.

"Checkout here is at eleven, but they'll take cash payment, if you want to stay a few more nights. You know, until you find a place to live. I'll let them keep my credit card on file so they don't give you any hassle."

Another check in the "nice guy" column.

"I could rack up your bill with room service."

"They don't have room service here."

I struggle to keep my expression smooth. "Fine, then. *Porn*."

A deep dimple forms in his cheek. He reaches down to fasten his belt, flashing his taut belly. "I'm sure they have that. But I just drove twelve hours to give you almost a hundred grand that I *could* have kept for myself. Something tells me you'd feel a bit guilty."

He's right, I would.

His forearm cords under the weight of his backpack. With his free hand, he scribbles something on the hotel notepad and tears the sheet off. He holds it out to me. "Here. You should have my number."

"Why?"

He sighs. "I don't know why, Gracie. Why *not*?"

I bite back the urge to correct my name. I don't mind it so much, coming from him. And he's right—he could have kept that money. Instead, he drove across two states, saved my mother, tried to save my home, and gave me a place to stay, all in addition to handing over enough money to fix our problems. And what have I done besides wave a knife at him, accuse him of being a heroin dealer, scream at him while he was naked and vulnerable, and generally act like a royal bitch?

Despite all that, I don't want him to leave. It's been nice, not being alone to deal with everything.

Setting the paper on the dresser, he peers at the door. "I really should . . ."

He really should get the hell away from me and Tucson, is what he's thinking.

"Yeah. I have to head over to the hospital."

His features soften. "Do you need a ride?"

"No, I'm going to sort out this room first."

"And then what?"

"I don't know. I'll figure it out. I always do."

"Okay." He slides on a pair of aviator-style sunglasses. I feel his friendly blue eyes studying me from behind the mirrored lenses, and I instinctively cross my arms over my chest, though I doubt Noah's into ogling poor, homeless girls with drug addict moms.

"So, I guess this is it?" Are we supposed to hug?

His face tenses. "Take care of yourself. You've got the money to find your mom a good rehab center. Make her go."

I chuckle half-heartedly. "It's not that easy."

"I know, but right now, you still have a chance. You have to take it before it's gone. Don't make the same mistake I did."

I quietly watch his back as he takes smooth, measured strides all the way to the door, my stomach churning the entire time.

His hand rests on the handle for two . . . three . . . four seconds.

"You know what?" He tosses his bag to the floor. "I'm not ready to drive another twelve hours just yet."

An unexpected sigh of relief escapes my lips.

"How about I stick around. I can help you get things sorted." His hands are in the air in a sign of surrender, as I'm opening my mouth to argue that I don't need help. "I know you can handle yourself fine, but . . ."

"But what?"

He slides his sunglasses off and I see his earnest gaze. "I'm not in any rush to get back home."

I press my lips together, hoping he can't sense my sudden and pathetic giddiness. "How long are you going to stay?"

He shrugs. "A few days? Until you're settled somewhere new."

So basically, I'm going to spend the weekend with Jackie Marshall's son. "My mother can't know you're here. You'll remind her of my dad."

He frowns. "How is that not a good thing?"

"She's weak."

"She's been through a lot."

"Strong people don't pick up and run because of a brick through their window. They don't start taking heavy drugs and leaving their child to fend for herself. She's a weak person. She can't handle facing the past like that." God knows what it would do to her mental state, as fragile as it already is.

His full lips twist in thought. "Then don't introduce me as Noah right away. Tell her my name is—"

"She'd take one look at those blue eyes of yours and know exactly who you are. I mean—" I cut myself off as heat touches my cheeks. I've basically just admitted to him that I've been admiring his eyes.

His jaw tightens and he stares at me with intensity. "She was like a second mother to me. I'd like to talk to her again."

He doesn't get it.

"Dina Wilkes is dead. *This* Dina . . . she can't handle it."

He slides a palm through his hair, sending it into disarray. "Fine. I'll wait outside the hospital for you." His gaze skitters over me briefly. "Let me talk to the front desk while you get ready and then we can grab breakfast on our way over." He waits for my nod and then heads out the door, leaving me to wonder why he's staying.

Because, as nice as Noah is, my gut says there's something he's not telling me.

"I didn't mean to take so much. I don't know why I keep doing this." A tear trickles down her cheek.

"Because you're a heroin addict, Mom." We're long past sugarcoating reality. All the same, it hurts to watch her flinch as I say it bluntly. Not as much as it hurts to see her lying in a hospital bed, her hair stringy and matted with bits of dried vomit. The nurse gave her a sponge bath but until she's strong enough to use the shower, she's stuck like this.

There are other things, though, that won't be fixed with a simple shower. She used to have a nice, creamy complexion. Now, her cheeks are sunken in, and her skin tone is sallow and marked with splotches. That pretty smile she flashed in pictures is now distorted by swollen gums from lack of care. It's only a matter of time before her teeth begin to rot. And the track marks along her arm . . . will those ever go away?

So, no. I won't sugarcoat this for her.

"That was the last time. I swear. I'm done with this." She squeezes her eyes shut as if she's in pain. She probably is. It's been about twenty-four hours since her last hit and, while the meds will help abate the withdrawal symptoms, they won't stop them entirely. The nausea is especially hard on her.

The first time she was in here, I stayed with her as much as I was allowed, through the cold sweats, the vomiting, the emotional whirlwind. I thought living through that would have been enough for her to never touch drugs again.

Clearly, I was wrong.

"I should go. You need to rest."

She gives me a weak smile. "You go home and take care of things there. I'll be out of here in a few days and then that's it. I'll stay clean; I'll get a job. We'll be fine. Everything will be fine."

I wasn't going to say a word—detoxing is hard enough—but the unintentional lies spewing from her mouth make my rage flare. I can't bite my tongue fast enough. "We don't have a home, Mom. You burned it down."

"What? What are you talking about?" She grapples with her memory, her brow furrowing.

"You put one of your cheese sandwiches in the toaster oven to cook and then decided to take a hit."

"I don't remember . . ."

"Of course you don't." How many neurons has she fried in her brain by continually poisoning it? What can she even remember about anything?

"I wouldn't do that."

And yet you did. "The trailer went up fast. We tried to put it out with the fire extinguisher."

"And I was inside?" My words finally seem to be sinking in.

"I got home from work in time to get you out." There's no way I'm telling her who carried her out.

"How bad is it?"

"I'm guessing everything's gone."

It's a long, slow moment of dull shock as I stand there, quietly watching her try to process that truth. And then her eyes widen with panic and her hands fly to her throat. "*Everything?*" She whispers, the words strangled, her face going even more pale. "What about the closet?"

"I don't know," I say slowly. *Shit.* I completely forgot about the closet—about the few things she managed to whisk away with us when we ran from Austin. A handmade quilt from my great-grandmother, my first pair of tiny, pink cowboy boots, the menu from dinner the first night my parents went out, a shoe box brimming with photos.

Back when she wasn't a full-fledged junkie, she used to drift off each night with a picture of my dad resting on her pillow.

Suddenly, Mom's fumbling with her sheets to push them off. She struggles to climb out of bed.

"What are you doing?"

"I need to go. I need to see if—"

"Mom!" I pin her down by her forearms. "You're in detox. You can't leave!"

"I *need* to get the box!"

"*I'll* go."

Her head's shaking back and forth furtively as she writhes against my grip. "No, you can't. You don't know . . ."

"You need to stay here. Look at you! You can barely stand!"

Tears well in her eyes. "It's all I have left."

"I'll leave now and go straight over to the Hollow. If it survived the fire, I'll bring it back. Just tell me which box it is."

"The *only* one that matters!" My mother's brow furrows deeply with distress. She wrings her trembling hands, fumbling with her bare finger where her wedding ring *should* be. She traded the simple gold band for a few Oxy pills years ago. She was high when she made that swap, and hysterical when she sobered up and realized her terrible mistake.

That ended up being a turning point for her. For the worse.

"It was in the closet?"

"Yes! I mean, no. I mean . . ." She hesitates, as if she doesn't want to tell me. "The floor, there's a hole in it. Pull the carpet up and you'll find it. Bring it to me. Just . . . bring it."

My suspicion flares. "If you think I'm going to bring you drugs—"

"It's not drugs! It's not. It's . . . paperwork. You know—your birth certificate, stuff like that." She swallows hard. "Everything that's important to me. Promise me you'll bring it to me and you won't open it?"

It's got to be more than paperwork. "Okay. If it survived the fire, I'll bring it."

"It's a metal box. It was your father's. It's all I have to . . ." Her breathing is ragged. She's exhausted herself.

"Okay. I'm going now."

"You'll come back after? You'll bring the box with you?"

"Sure."

She curls up into a ball and runs her palm against her cheeks to wipe away her tears. I still remember glimmers of the old her—the real her, I'd like to think—when she lived by the "smile, even when you're crying inside" motto. She has her hospital room to herself for the moment, at least.

"Get some sleep."

"Okay." A long pause. "Where did you stay last night, anyway?"

I was wondering if she'd even ask. "At a friend's. I'll be fine." I have a bag full of money to help solve the housing problem, if I can bring myself to ignore my conscience and use it. A bag of money from a woman who she believes helped frame my father.

I don't know what's true. The money alone could paint a convincing story where Dad's hands are as dirty as they say. But then there's what Jackie Marshall told Noah. That my dad was a good man.

I lay in bed last night, trying to come up with a reasonable explanation for the money. A reason why Jackie Marshall would send her son. And tell him to not ask questions.

What did she even know about us? Did she know that Mom has had one foot in her grave for years now? That this money would change our lives?

Why would she care to help *now*? Why this secret parting gift after her death?

So many questions that lead down so many dark paths.

I'm beginning to think Jackie said more to Noah. Something he doesn't *want* to tell me.

My mother's voice cuts into my suspicion-laced thoughts. "This place is horrible, Grace. I hate it here."

"You have nowhere else to go. So focus on getting better."

Her despondent gaze drifts over the dull green wall across from her. "That manager. What's his name . . ." Her face furrows as she struggles with her thoughts. "The manager at the Hollow."

"Manny?"

"Yes. He'll have a unit available to rent. They let people move in the same day. You know them. They don't care." Her eyes are shutting, the lids heavy. "Go see him."

"Why? You think we're going back to the Hollow?"

"Just until I can get a job. You believe me, right? That this is it? This is the last time? I promise it is, Grace."

That promise was broken before she uttered the words. I grit my teeth to keep from snapping at her. It's like I've hit repeat. We've been here before. It'll be the same old pattern, slightly varied by a unit number. She's looking for an easy, quiet hole to crawl into. Going back to the Hollow would be a death sentence for her at this point. If Noah hadn't shown up when he did, we'd have no other choice.

But he *did* show up, and we *do* have a choice.

I push down my bubbling anger. "Here—I picked up a toothbrush and comb, and pair of pajamas for you." I set the plastic bag down on her bed for her. "I should go, before whatever's left is gone. You know how it is." There are plenty of scavengers, looking to clean up on someone else's tragedy.

She winces. "Can you ask the nurse to give me another dose? It's been hours since I had one. They've forgotten about me."

"Sure." I study her frail, emaciated body for another long moment, and then I leave her room, checking my phone for messages from Noah. None. He and the bag of cash are sitting in the parking lot. Now I understand why he was so attached to it. It's unnerving, having that much money on us, waiting for some scumbag like Sims to take it away.

I head for the nurses' desk. "Hi, I'm Dina Richards's daughter. She's in Room 538 and she asked for more Subutex."

The nurse scans her records with a frown. "We just gave her a dose. She'll have to wait."

They forgot about her, my ass. "How long?"

"Three hours." She gives me a sympathetic smile, which I return in kind, because the nurses are the ones who will be dealing with Mom's tantrums until then.

She watches me linger for a moment before asking, "Is there anything else I can help you with?"

Mom won't stay clean a week outside these walls without serious help. I need to make a decision. One that will change both our lives. Noah's words from last night echo in my mind, as the pain of regret I saw in his eyes twists my stomach.

If I don't take this chance—if I wait any longer—it'll be too late.

But first, I need to find out what's in that box that has my mom so unnerved.

CHAPTER 15

Officer Abraham Wilkes

April 20, 2003

"Have you seen her?"

"You don't need her when you can have me, brown sugar." The woman laughs—a practiced sound—as she reaches for my chest, her long, painted fingernails dragging along the cotton of my T-shirt. The color of those claws matches the red lipstick on her lips—and accidently, on her teeth. I'm guessing she's around twenty, though her pale skin is weathered enough, and her eyes are hard enough, to suggest a decade older. Years of working the streets have been as kind to her as one could expect.

I take a step back, and hold the picture steady in front of me. "This girl. Have you seen her?"

She shrugs, her gaze never touching the photograph.

With a sigh, I pull a twenty-dollar bill out of my pocket, for motivation. I've made three trips to a bank machine these last four days with all the "motivating" I've been doing around Austin's dive motels and on the streets.

So far, no luck.

The prostitute snatches the bill right out of my hand and lazily scans the picture. "She's a pretty little thing. And young."

"And she has a family who misses her. Have you seen her?"

"Nah, she don't look familiar. How long she been gone?"

"About a year."

The woman shakes her head and tsks. "Wouldn't bother if I was you. That girl's already lost." She steps away, her attention shifting to a passerby, looking for her next target. It's Easter Sunday; business might be slow for hookers today, but I'm no expert.

"If you do see her, could you please give this to her?" I hand the woman my business card.

The prostitute's face hardens. "You a cop? 'Cause I ain't done nothin' wrong. This here is entrapment! You bribed me with that money and—"

"Thank you for your time, ma'am." I give her what I hope is an assuring smile. I'd win my twenty bucks back if I bet that she's going to toss that card into the trash the second I turn around.

I head for my car, exhausted, wanting desperately to be with my Gracie. I can imagine her, sitting up in bed, her innocent gaze locked on her doorway, *Where the Wild Things Are* resting on her lap. Eagerly waiting for me to come home so I can read to her using my gruff voice.

But I can't give up now.

Not when I'm so close to finding Betsy.

CHAPTER 16

Noah

I should have left.

I should leave now.

I should drop off Gracie, grab my shit at the motel, and go.

I keep telling myself that, even as the brakes on my SUV come to a squeaky stop in front of the charred remains of Gracie's home. From the outside, it actually doesn't look too bad, but I already know the inside is a different story.

That mangy one-eyed dog from yesterday scurries out from beneath a trailer and runs to Gracie as she climbs out, wagging its tail with excitement. Its matted fur is even dirtier than yesterday—if that's possible.

"You've been in my house, haven't you," she scolds. "Here. This should keep you busy for a while." Reaching into her purse, she retrieves the strip of beef jerky she grabbed at the gas station on the way here and tosses it to him. He catches it midair, and then hunkers down to begin chewing.

Eyeing me with that same shifty gaze.

"He's yours?"

"Cyclops isn't anyone's. I just feed him sometimes." When she looks up to see the wariness on my face, she snorts. "What?"

"Nothing."

She folds her arms over her chest, taking on a haughty stance. "What's wrong? Is he not the right pedigree for you? Not pretty enough? Let me guess: you had a golden retriever named Cooper growing up."

His name was Jake, actually. But I'm not going to admit that because I'd only be proving whatever point she's making about me. Instead I lift the sleeve of my T-shirt to show her the silver scars on the ball of my shoulder. "I was attacked by a stray at a playground when I was four. Needed fifteen stitches to close up the bite marks and rabies shots, just in case. So I'm not exactly comfortable around them."

Gracie presses her lips together, that self-righteousness in her gaze softening. "Cyclops has never bitten anyone."

"That you know of. And he had a rat in his mouth yesterday. Rats carry disease."

"So do squirrels and mice. He eats those, too. And lizards. Once, a snake, but only the head. He didn't much care for it."

I don't know a single girl whose face wouldn't pale a few shades at this conversation, but it doesn't seem to faze her. Meanwhile, my stomach is churning.

"I'm sure he'd love a big house with a yard and two bowls of food set down for him every day, but that's not the hand that was dealt to him. He does what he needs to survive. You don't need to look at him like that. Just because one stray bit you doesn't mean every one will." As if to make a point, she reaches down to pet him, her eyes locked on me. Daring me to sneer.

I get the feeling this has nothing to do with accepting a mangy dog.

"*¡El perro te va a extrañar!*" The old woman who called the ambulance breaks our silent showdown, setting her watering can on a step and settling into that ratty chair.

"What'd she say?"

"No idea," Gracie mutters, offering a wave.

The woman shakes her head with frustration. "He miss!" She gestures toward the dog.

"*Sí, sí*. That's because I'm the only one who feeds him." Gracie taps her lips with her fingertips.

The woman's attention shifts to me. "*Quién es*?"

"A friend."

She makes a clucking sound and then, almost begrudgingly, nods.

I return the gesture in kind. "Better reception than yesterday."

"She thought you were a drug dealer yesterday."

"I see that. *Now*."

"*¿Tu mamá?*" the woman asks.

"She's good. She'll be in rehab for a while."

"*Rehabilitación*?"

Gracie nods. "*Gracias* for calling 9-1-1."

She waves a hand at the burned-down trailer, then over her shoulder toward hers. "*Mi casa casi se incendió.*"

"That would have been bad," Gracie agrees. When she sees the questioning look on my face, she explains, "I think she said she was worried the fire would spread to her home."

"And that's the *only* reason she called for help?" What kind of people are these? I noticed that everyone stood around and watched yesterday, never offering assistance.

Gracie lowers her voice, though I doubt the woman understands much. "Vilma seems cold, but it's all an act. You can't be soft around here. I mean, look who her other neighbor is." She nods toward the trailer on the far side. "Sims would sell his own sister if it earned him twenty bucks."

"Funny, I thought you two were best friends."

She rolls her eyes. "Sims is everything that's wrong with this world. You think he would have helped me carry my mother out yesterday? Hell no. He was running in the opposite direction at the first sign of smoke. If you hadn't been here . . ." She lets her words drift and then her jaw tenses.

She hasn't said a word about what happened yesterday, or last night. She's barely said a word about the money. She hasn't given me details about her visit with her mother. I drove her to the hospital and waited in the parking lot. When she came out twenty minutes later, she simply ordered me to drive here. No explanation.

"I'm glad I was there. And I'm glad your neighbor was keeping an eye on things."

Gracie smirks. “She doesn’t like my mother, but she’s always liked me.”

“Must be because you’re so damn sweet.” It slips out before I can help it.

Gracie throws a glare my way, but when she turns her attention back to the trailer, a ghost of a smile touches her lips. There’s a sense of humor in there. I’ve seen glimpses, buried beneath that prickly exterior. A necessity when living in a place like this, it seems.

“*Un hombre vino y me preguntó.*” Vilma shrugs. “*Pensé que era la policía.*”

“Did she say that a cop came by?” I ask. I remember that much from Spanish class.

“She said ‘maybe.’ I guess he wasn’t in uniform?”

“*Javier bloqueó la puerta para usted.*” She points toward the giant piece of plywood blocking the gaping hole where the front door used to be.

“Tell him *gracias*.”

“Tell who ‘*gracias*’?”

“Her son. He put that wood up to try and keep people out.”

I trail her up the stairs with a frown. “Why would people want to come into a burned-out trailer?”

“There’s always something to steal. Wiring . . . copper pipes . . .” Her slender arms strain against the weight of the plywood board.

“Here, let me.”

“I can do it.” She resists my help, refusing to let go even as I tower behind her, grabbing the sides and dragging the plywood to the side, my chest rubbing against her slender back in the process.

“Are you always so stubborn?”

I wait for a snippy comment in return but she ignores me, slipping through the gaping doorway into the mess beyond.

The air reeks of wet soot. Chunks of charred drywall, wood, and insulation litter the floor and gaping holes in the ceiling allow the sun in to cast an unflattering spotlight on the little that’s left—drab brown paneling along the walls, a tacky gold picture frame, bits of a sodden couch. The carpet beneath my feet is matted and damp from all the water used to fight the fire. It reminds me of that dirty stray outside.

"I don't remember it looking so shitty," Gracie murmurs. "I guess being in that hotel spoiled me . . . See?" She points out fingerprints around the old tube television. "Someone's already been in here. Probably hoping to find money or my mom's drug stash." She snorts. "Joke's on them."

She sifts debris this way and that with her sneaker. "My nan must be rolling in her grave as we speak. She never had much, but this trailer was hers and she kept it clean and tidy."

"When did she die?"

"Five years ago. Heart attack. Living here wasn't so bad back then, even though I slept on the couch. Mom wasn't into the heavy stuff." She smiles wistfully. "Nan would tiptoe around in the kitchen on the weekend and whip up a batch of pancakes. I'd wake up to the smell of them. And we'd sit around the kitchen table and play card games and dominoes for hours, with game shows in the background. Nan loved her game shows." Gracie heads for the far corner of the trailer—the one farthest from the kitchen, where the damage isn't as bad—and leans over to inspect the scattered contents of what I assume are Dina's purse and wallet.

And I can't help but admire the shape of Gracie's thighs in those shorts.

What the fuck is wrong with me?

I give my head a shake. "What about your grandfather?"

"My mom's father wasn't in their lives. My nan lived with this guy—Brian—for years, but they split up before we moved here."

She shoves everything into the purse and collects it, tucking it under her arm. "I need to check the bedrooms."

I follow Grace down the hallway, maneuvering past dangling ceiling tiles and insulation. "Should we be in here?"

"Who's going to stop us?" She curses softly, brushing at a sooty streak against her new T-shirt.

"No, I mean it's probably a hazard."

"You can go outside if you're afraid."

I heave a sigh to let her know that I'm annoyed. "What do you need in here, anyway? Doesn't look like there's much to save."

She enters the first bedroom, which is in only marginally better shape than the kitchen and living room. Scraps of paper are strewn all over the floor and burnt cardboard shoe boxes have been cast aside. The thieves have been rooting around in here, too.

Gracie steps over the heaps of trash, heading for the nightstand to collect a square book from the floor. She attempts to flip the cover open, but it falls apart within her grasp. I hear her hiss "dammit" under her breath. "Their wedding album." She tosses the book to the bed, a look of dismay twisting her features. "And those were all her pictures. They're all gone. Every last one."

It takes me a moment to realize that the scraps of paper littering the carpet are photographs. *Were* photographs.

She moves for the closet. And pauses. "You shouldn't leave the money alone out there."

"I can bring it in and—"

"I left a list of rehab centers on your dash. The nurse marked off the best ones. Call them to see which ones are taking people right away."

I sigh with relief. She's going to use the money. *Good.* "So your mom has agreed?"

"Let me worry about that. You call. From outside."

A dismissal if I've ever heard one. "Holler if you need me."

"I thought dry heat was supposed to be easier to manage."

The old woman, Vilma, raises an eyebrow.

"Hot." I fan myself with the rehab list, beads of sweat beginning to form at the back of my neck. I told Gracie I'd be within earshot, but I'm regretting that now. She's been in there for a good twenty minutes, banging away at something metal-sounding, and I'm baking under a hot desert sun on these concrete steps.

I get nothing but a hard stare in return as Vilma rocks herself back and forth in her chair, her left foot doing all the work. So, I go back to reading up on Desert Oaks. It's the only rehab center marked that has an immediate opening. They can take Dina as early as tomorrow.

I told them we'd take the spot.

With a sigh of accomplishment, I slide my phone into my pocket and look up.

The old woman is still staring at me.

So is the dog.

"Fuck," I mutter, averting my gaze. Any minute now, tumbleweeds are going to roll by and the twang of a harmonica will carry through the corridor of trailers, like an old western face-off. This place is desolate. Black squiggles of graffiti, boarded-up windows, dented trash bins, rusted chain-link fences that half hang from their frames, keeping nothing and no one out. Occasionally, someone will pass by on their bike or on foot, their somber expressions and suspicious eyes reminding me that I don't belong here.

At least that Sims guy is nowhere to be seen.

My phone rings and Silas's name shows up on the screen. I answer it without thinking, happy for the distraction. "Hey."

"Judy's got your room ready."

Shit. I'm supposed to be moving there today. "Would y'all mind terribly if I bring my things over during the week?"

"I suppose not. When?"

"I'm not exactly sure."

"What's going on, Noah? Have you changed your mind? Because she spent hours—"

"No, I haven't, I swear. I'm just out of town right now."

There's a pause, and I can picture Silas's frown. "You never said anything about going away this weekend. Where are you?"

"Arizona. It was last-minute."

"Oh? Friends out there?"

"Yeah, I guess. Sort of." I was hoping to be back home before anyone noticed I was gone. "I'll fill you in when I see you."

I hear the heavy creak of his office chair. "Oh, this sounds like something I'd rather hear now."

There's that tone of his, the one that says he knows I'm hiding something. *He always knows.*

I sigh. "I came to meet Abe's daughter."

Silence hangs. "Why would you do that?"

This *is* Silas, I remind myself. I can trust him.

Except Mom obviously didn't want Silas knowing about this money either. She didn't want her law-abiding, straight-laced big brother knowing what she was involved in.

"Noah!"

Fuck me. "Mom left money, with a note and Gracie's address, asking me to bring it to her."

"Money."

"Yes, sir. Money."

There's another long pause. "How much are we talking about here?"

I hesitate. "Enough to raise eyebrows."

"You should have talked to me about this first."

"Why? So you could talk me out of coming here? She *asked* me to do it, Silas." I peel myself off the steps and wander away from the trailer, glancing over my shoulder to make sure Gracie isn't standing there. "And they need it. You should see how they're living." I quietly tell him about the fire and Dina overdosing.

"Good lord," he mutters. "How is the girl handling this?"

"Better than you'd expect. She's tough."

"And what did you tell her?"

"Nothing. Just that Mom left it for her."

"But you didn't say anything about what Jackie said that night, did you?"

"No." At least, not all of it.

"That's for the best, Noah."

Silas is still in denial. I wish I could be, too. "But why leave the money for Gracie and Dina then, if she didn't have something to feel guilty about?"

"I imagine she felt sorry for how their lives turned out."

"Then why not include it as part of the will?" It's like she didn't want a record of it anywhere.

"Hmm . . ." I can almost see his brow furrowing as he considers that. "It would have taken months to get to her. It sounds like Dina didn't have that much time. Had your mother taken any trips to Arizona lately?"

"I don't know." We could go days without actually seeing each other, communicating only through texts. She could easily have hopped in her BMW and driven the twelve hours.

"I tried to make it right. But I couldn't face her. After all this time, I couldn't face what I'd done to her."

What if she was talking about coming here and seeing Dina?

"From what I remember, Abe's wife didn't take too kindly to Jackie or anyone from the APD after his death. Maybe Jackie thought she would have refused it. I don't know, Noah. But leaving money for her old partner's family isn't evidence of anything except your mother's generous heart."

And maybe a guilty conscience.

Silas's excuse doesn't explain the gun holster I also found. But that news is for another time, not over the phone, two states away.

Cyclops's head suddenly jolts up. A low growl rumbles from his chest, and then he's charging toward me. I freeze, ready to punt him at the first sign of teeth. But he scampers past me, hiding beneath an overturned wheelbarrow, as a white van rounds the corner, the words *Animal Control* painted across the side.

"Smart little bastard."

"Excuse me?" The shock in Silas's voice has me chuckling.

"Not you. This stray dog."

"Stray dog?"

"With one eye. Damn ugly thing."

"Remember that one that bit you?"

I roll my eyes. "*Vaguely.*" The shift in conversation seems to have defused the tension.

Silas sighs. "So, no idea when you'll be back?"

"We're likely putting Dina in rehab tomorrow. I don't want to leave Gracie alone to do it." And I got the feeling earlier, when I told her I'd stay, that she was relieved. Though, she's impossible to read.

"And Gracie? Where will she stay?"

"I got her a room in a motel."

"I hope it's nicer than that trailer park."

"Yeah, it's decent enough." Anything's better than this place. "It's called Cactus Inn or something like that. Everything around here is named after a cactus or a desert. Anyway, she has enough money to get herself an apartment."

"Good. How'd she turn out? I remember thinking she'd grow up to be a real looker."

"You weren't wrong." Even scowling, Gracie turns heads.

"Hmm . . ." The sound is laced with insinuation.

"It's not like that." Frankly, I'm not sure if she even likes me as a human being.

He chuckles. "Okay. Call me when you're back in town. I'll be tied up in court and interviewing for a secretary all week but Judy will be home, ready to welcome you with open arms."

"God, you're *still* interviewing? You need to just pick someone already!" Silas fired his last secretary *months* ago, and has been struggling to survive on his own since.

"I'm too damn picky," he admits reluctantly.

"Yes, sir. You are."

"And Noah? You're doing the right thing, by helping them move on. It's what your mother wanted."

"See you soon."

The Animal Control van rolls along the sandy lane, keeping pace with the man who walks alongside it. He's carrying a long pole with a noose-like rope hanging from the end in one hand.

"We got a call about a rabid dog wandering through here?" he hollers to Vilma.

She shrugs.

"*Perro*?"

She retorts with something in Spanish that I have no hope in hell of understanding, but by her sharp tone, it isn't pleasant.

Shaking his head, the guy dismisses her and keeps walking toward me. "Seen a rabid dog? It's beige and scruffy, fifteen pounds. One eye." Somehow he keeps the toothpick that hangs from the corner of his mouth in place as he talks.

"Rabid dog?"

He smirks. "You know . . . a dog with rabies."

Dickhead. "I saw him. He's not rabid, though." Diseased, likely.

His gaze roves over the various trailers, his disgust plain as day. "Yeah well, I'm tired of coming to this dump every time that woman calls us. We're catching this asshole today, and my report is gonna say he tried to bite me, and neither him or me are ever comin' back here again." He pats the dart gun that hangs from his hip for impact. "Which way did he go?"

I don't know who keeps calling Animal Control, but I'm suddenly rooting for Gracie's one-eyed dog. I point down the laneway, in the opposite direction. "He was bookin' it, so y'all probably won't catch up to him."

"Oh, we'll get him." He nods toward the trailer. "What happened here?"

"It burned down."

"How?"

I smile wide. "You know . . . a fire."

Spearing me with a glare, he and the white van set off down the road, his eyes scanning the shadows, grumbling under his breath.

"*Se metió en una pelea con el gato de la señora Hubbard de Nuevo*," Vilma calls out.

All I caught from that is "cat" and a woman named "Hubbard."

She nods toward the upturned wheelbarrow, where I can make out Cyclops's front paws peeking out beneath it. "You take," Vilma hisses, pointing to my SUV. "*You take.*"

"What?" A bark of laughter escapes me.

She waves toward the wheelbarrow urgently. "You take!"

"I can't. *No puedo*. We're staying in a motel." I saw a guest leaving her room with a Maltese on a leash, so it must be a pet-friendly place, but Cyclops doesn't exactly fit in the "pet" category. And what the hell am I going to do with a rat-carrying one-eyed dog? In the backseat of my nice, new SUV no less?

"Gracie's *perro*!"

"He's no one's *perro*."

She snorts. "*Idiota. ¡Si note llevas el perro ahorra ella nunca te perdonará!*"

"I'm sorry, ma'am. I don't know what you're saying." Except for the *idiota* part. I'm clear on that.

She struggles to climb out of her chair and down the steps, looking ready to topple over as she hobbles to her fence. "*Ellos lo matarán!*" She makes a throat-cutting gesture and then hisses, "*Ese perro es todo lo que tiene.*" Her wrinkled old hands press against her chest. "Gracie love."

I groan. Maybe I should go and warn Gracie. I check the path. The guy has stopped to talk to a gray-haired woman four doors down, out watering a planter. With a shaky hand, she points back my way. She's probably telling him that Cyclops was just here, gnawing on a bone beside my truck.

If it's not one thing with Gracie, it's another. I feel like I've been in danger every turn since meeting her. Granted, a fire and a knife to my stomach are a hell of a lot more serious than a fifteen-pound dog, but acknowledging that doesn't settle my nerves.

"Okay, okay." I head over to the back and pop open my tailgate. As soon as the guy's not looking, I whisper halfheartedly, "Come on, get in!" and cross my fingers that the dog stays put and I can say I tried.

Cyclops darts out from his hiding spot and leaps in without trouble. *Awesome*.

"Stay back here," I order, shutting the gate.

I look over in time to see Vilma's smile of satisfaction. She wanders back to her chair to resume her watch.

CHAPTER 17

Grace

I ignore the voices outside, focusing on the melted tip of the screwdriver as I bring down the hammer for what feels like the hundredth time.

The flimsy lock remains intact. "Dammit!" I toss the tools to the side and simply glare at the small, gunmetal-gray box I found beneath sodden, charred memories and a layer of old carpet, next to a baby milk snake. Exactly where my mom said it would be hiding. It's about eight inches long by four inches wide, and secured by a small padlock.

I've never seen it before.

And there is no way in hell I'm going to hand this over to her without finding out what's in it first.

Luckily, my grandma's old metal tools withstood the fire, though the plastic handles are distorted. That's okay; I can grip the hammer well enough. Brushing the springs of hair off my forehead, I line up the flat metal end and swing, this time putting real force behind it.

The lock falls to the floor with a dull thud.

Satisfaction fills me as I pry open the box with my sooty hands, my stomach tight with anticipation.

CHAPTER 18

Noah

"Come on." I tap the steering wheel with my fingers at a furious tempo, my gaze darting between the trailer, the laneway, and my rear-view mirror. Cyclops has made himself comfortable in my backseat, his tail thumping rhythmically, dozens of dirty footprints all over the leather. The smell of his hot, rank breath and filthy fur makes my nose crinkle.

Toothpick Guy smacks the side of the Animal Control van and begins marching back toward us, his free hand hovering over his dart gun, hard determination splayed all over his face.

"What trouble are you gonna get me into now, Gracie?" I murmur under my breath, cranking my engine and tapping the horn with my fist in warning, hoping she hears it. Does this guy have jurisdiction over an attempted dog rescue?

To my relief, Gracie appears in the doorway then, a box tucked under her arm. She's covered in soot. It streaks her arms, her shirt, and her cheeks.

She's beautiful.

I pull up closer and she climbs into the passenger side. Cyclops barks excitedly, as if announcing, "Hey, I'm here!" She eyes him, and then me, but doesn't say a word, her stony face revealing nothing. This girl would be a proficient poker player.

I do a quick three-point turn and speed away, leaving nothing but a dust cloud for that nut job to shoot. "Some lady called Animal Control."

"Mrs. Hubbard. Cyclops keeps trying to kill her cat." She pauses. "Why'd you take him?"

"Your neighbor insisted. She was worried you'd be upset if they got him."

Gracie lets out a derisive snort. "That cat pees on Vilma's tomato plants. She just wants Cyclops to live another day so he'll finally do away with it."

"So, should I leave him here to—"

"No." The answer comes quick enough to tell me that Vilma was right, and it's not just about saving the tomato plants. But Gracie won't admit to caring.

A metal box sits on her lap, covered in soot. "What's that?"

"A box."

I roll my eyes. She's about as delightful as that Animal Control guy. "What's *in* it?"

"Did you call those rehabs?" She smoothly diverts.

"Desert Oaks can take her in tomorrow, but you need to call them to confirm."

She points to the street ahead. "Turn here. We're going back to the hospital."

I make a sharp right, sending Cyclops tumbling against the backseat. I grimace, picturing the scratched leather from his nails.

Just like the fresh, silvery gouges along the side of that box, where a lock might have hung.

Now I know what that metal-clanking sound was.

Silence lingers the few minutes it takes to reach St. Bart's, Gracie's mind elsewhere, deep in thought.

Finally, I try again. "So . . . anything important in there?"

"Important enough to hide under the trailer and never tell me about it," she mutters. After a pause, she asks, "Are you sure your mother didn't tell you where that money came from?"

"You saw the note she left me." I frown. "Why? What did you find?"

"The truth, maybe? And things I can't make sense of."

The truth.

The truth about what? Abe? My mom?

About what my mom might have done to Abe?

There's an odd note in Gracie's voice. She seems *too* calm for a girl who has a hard time controlling her anger, which makes me believe this isn't about my mother specifically.

Still, my heart begins pounding hard against my chest wall. "Maybe if you told me, we could make sense of it together."

"Doubt it."

"You know, I work for the District Attorney's office. I spend a lot of time trying to make sense of things for cases. I'm pretty good at it."

"And humble."

I pull into the hospital parking lot. "It's worth a shot. Come on, Gracie. Let's see it."

I assume she's going to blow me off with another snide remark, but finally she flips open the latch. The hinge creaks as the lid falls back. "She made me promise not to open this. But she's a drug addict. I can't trust her."

"You thought there were drugs in there?"

"Or something else she'd want to hide from me." She swallows hard. "She doesn't get to keep secrets. Not if she's going to get better."

"That's probably the right call." I offer her what I hope is an understanding smile, as I wonder how different my mother was from Dina, in her last days. It was a different drug, a different coping mechanism, but in the end . . . what if she hadn't been clinging so tightly to her own secrets? Would she have had a chance? "So, what'd you find?"

"Birth certificates. My dad's death certificate. A few pictures and a copy of a newspaper clipping. Nothing earth-shattering, as far as I can tell."

I ease into a parking spot. "Show me."

She searches her shirt for a clean spot, only to rub her sooty hands on it. Carefully, she collects the various papers and hands them to me, our fingertips grazing in the process. It's impossible for me not to be hyperaware of her.

There's a photograph of the three of them. Abe's arms are full—Gracie in one, her eyes round like saucers, while his other one wraps around Dina's waist, pulling her in tight to him. Gracie and Dina are wearing matching blue dresses and cowboy boots, and wide grins.

"You were cute back then."

"I still am."

"You still are," I agree with a smile. "This is at the Houston Rodeo." The sea of people holding corn dogs and beers behind them confirms it.

Gracie studies the picture with an unreadable gaze. A stray curl falls across her face, and I fight the urge to shift it off her forehead. "I don't remember."

"Of course you don't. Look how small you were."

She turns to me, her eyes filled with sadness. "No, I mean I don't remember him. I've heard a life's worth of memories *about* him from my mom. I remember him *existing*, but I can't see him, or hear him." Her brow furrows deeply. "I can't remember a single conversation we had."

As painful as facing the reality of my mom's death is, at least I have twenty-five years of memories, both good and bad, to keep me going. Hell, I could recall a dozen things about Abe with the snap of my fingers. And that Gracie can't say the same is a damn travesty.

"He had this booming laugh," I say, studying the picture. Abe looks exactly how I remember him—tall and broad-chested, his arms ripped from working out, his wide, white smile taking up half his face, the gap between his front teeth only adding to his charm. "He'd laugh and people would stop and stare, but then their faces couldn't help but crack. He could make the most miserable person smile, just by laughing."

I feel her heavy gaze on me as I shuffle through the pictures.

I struggle to keep my face calm as I take in the photograph of Abe in shorts and a T-shirt, crouching on a driveway with his arm around me. I'm young—six or seven, young enough to be wearing Velcro-strapped running shoes. And I'm leaning into him, holding up my first basketball trophy with both hands, a proud grin on my lips.

That trophy still sits on my shelf in my room. I smile as I recall the day I accidentally knocked it with my elbow and broke it. Abe was over at the time, and he saw me trudging down the stairs, carrying the pieces, on my way to chuck it in the trash. He took it from me and fixed it, and then made me promise never to throw it out. He said that it was my first trophy and no matter how old I was, it would always be the most special.

"That's you, isn't it?" Gracie asks softly.

I nod. My hair is a lot darker now than it was back then, but there's no mistaking my blue eyes. "Your dad loved basketball. He was my coach for years."

"My mom said he tried to teach me, but all I wanted to do was ride him like a bull. He was going to enter me into some weird sheep-riding competition at the rodeo."

"Mutton Bustin'." I chuckle. "Holy shit, I remember you doing that." A frizzy-haired, wide-eyed Gracie climbing onto Abe's back, giggling madly as he crawled around an all fours and she held on tight.

She nods at the pictures. "You must have spent a lot of time with him."

Hours, every week. For years.

I swallow the lump and keep flipping.

There's a picture of Abe and six guys standing side by side on a basketball court, their hair matted with sweat. When I see the face of the man on Abe's right—the one with a sloped forehead and deep-set eyes, whose arm hangs lazily over Abe's shoulder—a chill of recognition runs down my spine.

It's Dwayne Mantis.

I don't recognize the others, but maybe I've met them; men change so much with age. Mantis hasn't, though. Even with less hair and an extra twenty or so pounds, he's impossible to mistake. That gleam in his eyes is just as menacing. The only thing that softens his look is the fact that he's standing next to Abe, whose smile stretches across his face.

So, Abe and Dwayne Mantis were friends. Or, at least, they knew each other. They obviously played on a team together. "It's probably the police league basketball team."

"That would make sense." She hands me a photocopy of an article, torn from a newspaper. It's from April 23, 2003. "That's the same guy, isn't it?" She points out Mantis in the picture of four cops standing proud over a pile of small white parcels.

"Looks like it." The picture is grainy, but there's no mistaking that forehead. I quickly scan the bylines. It's a major drug bust by Austin's notorious drug squad at an Austin motel called The Lucky Nine.

The pieces begin clicking together.

These must be the "hounds" that George Canning was raving about.

Dwayne Mantis was one of his hounds.

Mantis, who now heads the Internal Affairs department of the APD, a department that was recently investigated for falsifying evidence to clear police officers, according to Silas.

Mantis, who is likely being investigated by the feds.

Someone marked up the original article, circling the line listing the drugs seized—three kilos of cocaine, marijuana, and meth—along with four guns. And below it, added notes in tidy scrawl.

Harvey Maxwell.

I frown. That's *Maxwell*, the ADA I work with. Why did someone write his name down on here?

Below his name is a more concerning note.

$98K.

"Holy shit," slips out.

"Don't tell me that's a coincidence, Noah. You just brought me a bag of ninety-eight thousand dollars. A hundred? I'd believe that was a coincidence. Not *ninety-eight thousand dollars*." She jabs the article with her finger, where the date of the bust is clearly printed. "Not when this was ten days before my dad died, *at the same motel* where he died."

She's right to be suspicious.

Should I tell Gracie about Mantis?

And why did Dina have this hidden under the trailer?

And how did *my mother* end up with this money?

Gracie's gaze drifts over the parking lot, watching a woman and a small child head toward the hospital, a bouquet of pink carnations in the woman's grip. "I've always wondered if there was something my mother wasn't telling me."

Exactly what I'm wondering, too.

I notice a crinkled, worn picture in the box that looks like it's been passed through a hundred sets of hands. It's of a young, fresh-faced Dina, posing in front of the typical blue backdrop of a school picture. "You two have the same eyes," I note absently.

"Oh, right, and then there's *that*," Gracie scoffs. "Do you see that heart-half charm on her necklace?"

"Yeah?"

"She told me that my dad gave that to her."

"So?"

"She didn't meet my dad until she was seventeen."

"And she can't be more than twelve or thirteen here," I say, catching on.

"Exactly." Gracie shakes her head "Why lie about a stupid necklace?"

"Maybe she got mixed up?"

"Maybe." She doesn't sound at all convinced.

"I find the best way to get information is to . . ." I flip the picture over to check the back, and my voice drifts as I see the name scrawled across the top right corner in blue ink.

Betsy, 2002.

"Is to . . .?" Gracie prompts.

"Ask questions," I mutter absently, struggling to make sense of the pieces. My mother said the name Betsy that night. Why is it written on a picture of Dina? Does Dina have another name? What was it my mom said when I asked her who Betsy was? Something about her biggest regret, or—

"What the hell!"

Gracie's panicked voice grabs my attention, even though my mind is swimming in all these bits of new information. Her gaze is locked on the sidewalk near the hospital entrance, where Dina rushes along in the pair of light blue pajamas that Gracie brought to her earlier, her arms hugging her frail body, casting furtive glances this way and that.

Looking every bit the escapee that she is.

"Stay here." Gracie, her clothes and face and legs streaked with soot, climbs out of my Cherokee and goes charging toward her mother.

CHAPTER 19

Officer Abraham Wilkes

April 21, 2003

"I've noticed you around here these past few days, talkin' to folks." The man smooths his calloused hand over the ice-maker, frowning at the dent. The tool belt strapped around his wiry hips tells me he's some sort of maintenance man for The Lucky Nine.

"Yes, sir. I'm looking for a girl." With no luck, after five days of searching, before and after shifts, on my days off. Here, and every other motel, and on the streets. I'm beginning to think Jackie was telling the truth and Betsy doesn't want to be found. "You spend a lot of time around here?"

"Every damn day." The man shakes his head, muttering about fools as he rubs a motor-grease-coated finger over the vending machine next to the ice-maker, where someone tagged it with black spray paint. "If my mama caught me doing this, she'd tan my hide."

I grin at him. "Our mamas sound about the same." His skin is a touch darker than mine. He must be in his early fifties, and on the too-thin side, the jutting bones around his neck peeking out from beneath the loose collar of his wrinkly work shirt. I'd peg him as an uncomplicated, hardworking man. One of those guys who start their day at the same time without need for an alarm, who sit down to the same three simple meals delivered from a can or a frozen-food box, who buy new pants and shoes only when the current ones are beyond repair.

"Maybe we should have the two of them stand guard for the next time those hoodlums decide to bust this open."

"That a common problem?"

"Almost every week, lately. Vending machine company tells me *I'm* the one who has to pay for it."

"Hardly sounds fair."

"*Fair* ain't a word I'd bother using around here. But don't you worry. I'll catch them, all right. They wanna be stealing money, let them try and steal it from my pockets. We'll see how that goes."

"You be careful. I don't want to be reading a story about you in the news. It's best to call the police."

The man guffaws. "If the police come out this way, it won't be for vending machine vandals."

I believe him. I've stopped by The Lucky Nine every day. It's always the same—people darting from car to room to car, their heads down. Not wanting to be seen. Few linger around the poorly lit exterior of the three long rectangular buildings that make up this place. The ones who do, I'd keep a close eye on. I don't doubt they're up to no good, and it's worse than stealing soda and small change. "Tell you what, you give me a call next time something happens and I'll make sure someone pays a visit out here." I hand him my business card.

He tips his head to peer at me, his wise brown eyes surveying my jeans and T-shirt. "So, who you lookin' for?"

I hold up the picture.

He studies it long and hard—more intently than anyone else I've shown it to, as if he truly wants to help me—and then nods. "She hasn't been here in almost a week."

My heart skips a beat. "You know her?"

"Don't *know* her. Seen her. Pretty little thing. She was staying over in A Block." He nods to the building across from us.

"When did she leave?"

"Like I said, haven't seen her in a week. Girls come and go around here. A lot. Never know, she might be back around."

"Would you do me a kindness and call me if you see her again?"

He takes his time, leaning over to pick up his toolbox. "Who's she to you?"

My stomach clenches with that gnawing guilt I can't shake. "Someone I should have looked out for a long time ago."

CHAPTER 20

Grace

"What the hell are you doing out of your room, Mom?"

"Grace! Oh, thank God. I was going to walk home." She peers at me through wild eyes. Not the same wild eyes I've seen countless times before, when every thought, every action, every need is trained on her next high.

This is different.

It's worse.

"It would take you an hour to walk there, and you look ready to collapse!" She's hunched over, her arms folded around her chest, her face a deathly shade of pale. "Besides, there's nothing to go back to, remember?"

She reaches out to seize my wrist. "Did you get the box?"

"Yeah. But—"

"Okay. Good. We need to get out of here." She begins tugging at my arm. For a woman as frail as she is, she has more strength than I'd expect. Whether it's adrenaline or fear or plain madness that's fueling this, I can't say, but I'm forced to grab hold of her forearm with my free hand to keep her put.

"No. *You* need to get back to your hospital room. Dr. Coppa is not going to keep helping us if you pull this shit!"

"He came to my room!" she hisses, scanning the parking lot again.

"Of course he did! He's your doctor!"

"No, not him. *Him!*"

"Who?"

"This cop. I've never seen him before, but . . ." Her face scrunches up with her frantic head shake. "But I know it was *him*!"

The police? Is that what this is about? Vilma did say that some man—maybe a cop—came by the trailer park. To do what, exactly, I don't know because I didn't see any caution tape. "Did he say anything about arresting you?" I ask as calmly as I can.

"Arresting me . . ." A nervous laugh escapes her. "If only."

"What does that mean?"

"After all these years, they're still *watching*." Drops of sweat trail down the side of her face.

Jesus. "Did you get your dose?" Given how crazy she's acting, she must be overdue.

"Don't you patronize me, Grace. I know what I sound like, but there are things you don't understand."

Such as what's in that box?

Again, she casts a furtive look around. "I can't stay here."

"And where are you gonna go? Back to our burnt-out trailer? *In your pajamas?*" The cops would have picked her up in minutes. Maybe that'd be for the best.

Heavy footfalls sound behind me and Mom's eyes widen.

"Is everything okay?" Noah asks smoothly.

Dammit. I grit my teeth to keep from snapping. "It's fine. I told you to stay in the car." Mom's already a loose cannon. The last person she needs to see is Jackie Marshall's son.

"Who is this, Grace?" Despite the shameful things she has done for a high, during these brief post-overdose interludes when she's convinced herself she can stay clean, she's embarrassed about her addiction. She doesn't want anyone to know.

"A friend. *Mike*." I shoot him a warning glare. She hasn't seen Noah since he was a gangly eleven-year-old. There's nothing left to recognize, besides his striking blue eyes, which are hidden behind his aviators. "Why don't you wait for me in the car. I'll be there as soon as I get her back inside."

"I'm not going back inside. I have to leave. It's not safe here."

"I can help." Noah reaches for her and she flinches away. He lifts his hands in a sign of surrender.

People are starting to look. Soon, someone will come and intervene, and it'll upset her even more. "This is *my* problem. *I'll* handle this." I plead with him, "Just go. *Please.*"

The muscles in his jaw tense. "I'm sorry, Gracie. But no. I'm not going anywhere."

He slides off his sunglasses.

CHAPTER 21

Noah

Gracie said the Dina Wilkes I knew is dead, but I don't buy it.

I can't.

Because I've already lost so much—first Abe, then my mom. And while happier recollections of this frail, terrified woman may have been pushed to the recesses of my mind for years, she still exists there, in my fondest childhood memories, humming a soft tune as she picks through ripe cherries to make Abe's favorite pie; brushing my tears away as she blows against the scrape on my knee; ruffling my hair with a loving pat as she walks by.

In many ways, she was a second mother to me, my own mother often too preoccupied with her career.

Yesterday, Dina was a lifeless body on a couch that I had to save. Seeing her conscious, her green eyes—not quite as vibrant as Gracie's but pretty nonetheless—staring up at me, brings all those childhood memories rushing back.

But those eyes are filled with fear and mistrust. With pain and suffering. With fourteen years of knowing *something* about what happened to Abe and not telling a soul—not even her daughter—because I'll be damned if that box I just went through doesn't have *everything* to do with Abe's death.

I came to Tucson, telling myself it was to drop off a bag of money. Trying to convince myself that my mother was caught in some confused, suicidal fog, nothing more. But deep down I think I always knew I'd never be able to let these questions around Abe's death go, no matter what Silas or Canning is convinced happened that night.

My mother held on to a secret that ended up killing her.

A fate Dina will share, if I allow it. And then won't her death be partly on my hands, too?

I look down at the woman, hoping she's not too far gone, that she'll see the little boy she gave so much love to. "You don't have to deal with this alone, anymore, Dina."

"Oh, my God." Her knees buckle.

I dive for her, my hands gripping her emaciated body beneath her arms before she folds to the pavement.

Shock fills her face as her gaze flickers over my features. "Noah, is that you? You're . . ." Cool fingers graze my arms, trying to squeeze but lacking the strength needed.

"It's me." A lump swells in my throat.

"You're here."

"I am."

A light gasp sails from her chapped lips. "Are you here to keep me quiet? I won't say a word, I swear!"

What? "Dina, it's *me*, Noah. I'm here to *help* you."

"He showed up yesterday," Gracie admits, her jaw clenched tightly, her eyes shining with resigned anger. "He's the one who carried you out of the trailer."

Tears stream down Dina's cheeks as she reaches up to paw at my cheek, her fingers scratching against the stubble. "You look so much like her." By the pained expression in her face, I can't tell if that's good or bad.

How could my mom let Dina get like this?

I have to squeeze my eyes shut against the flash of rage that stirs inside me. When I open them, she's still staring at me, almost in awe.

"What did she tell you, Noah? About Abe. She knew what happened, didn't she?" Desperation fills her face as she pleads with me, to hear what I suspect she already knows.

I hesitate.

For fourteen years, Abe was nothing more than a memory. A life lesson. Someone who taught me so much good, and then, through his alleged actions, so much bad.

And now I'm holding back the one thing I desperately wanted someone to tell me all those years ago: that Abe might be innocent.

"Noah. *Please.*"

"Abe was set up. He was made to look guilty." *Jesus. There, I said it. I can't take it back.* I exhale deeply, my breath ragged.

"What?" Gracie's face pales. She couldn't look more shocked had I slapped her across the face. "You said . . . You lied to me?"

Dina grabs my shoulders, pulling my attention back to her. "Jackie must have said something, if they're coming after me again. What did she say?"

"*Who's* coming after you again?"

Her lips press together, and she glances around. "It wasn't him. But . . . it was him," she whispers.

"*Who*, Dina?"

Another glance around. "Why is he coming after me again, Noah? All the way out here? I *told* him I didn't have the video."

"No one's coming after you," I say as gently as I can, hoping it will calm her growing agitation, even as I try and process her rambling words.

A man was looking for a video, and he thought Dina might have it?

What's on this video? Something that someone didn't want seen?

By the way she's reacting, I'm going to take a wild guess and say the person looking for it wasn't too casual about it the first time around.

Did *Abe* have this video? Was what was on it serious enough to get him killed?

"I'm not going back in that room." Dina's limp hair swings as she shakes her head furtively. "I'm a sitting duck in there. I'm telling you it was him. He wants—"

"Okay. Let's get you somewhere comfortable and safe, where we can talk. We can figure this out, together."

"No, I can't tell you. He said if I talked about it with anyone again—"

"No one's going to do anything to you, Dina." I grip her hands within mine. "You're not alone in this anymore."

That seems to calm her a touch.

I scoop her up as gently as I can and start moving for my Cherokee. She's so small, a collection of bony limbs within my arms.

"Noah!" Gracie hisses, grabbing onto my arm, her nails digging into my bicep. "She can't leave. Look at her! She'll be hunting down a hit by tonight without her meds."

"Then find that doctor and get what you need." I keep walking.

"You have no idea what you're dealing with here."

"You're right, I don't. But trust me, neither do you." I unlock and open the back door, and settle Dina in. She startles at the one-eyed dog perched next to her. "Sit tight. The motel is five minutes away." Shutting the door, I head for the driver's side, intent on getting out of here and dealing with Gracie's explosive anger in the privacy of our rooms.

But Gracie shoves me against the back of my SUV with surprising strength. "You don't get to swoop in, lie to me, and then take control!" Her small fists slam against my chest.

"Not *here*, Gracie."

"Yes, *here*, Noah. I want the truth!" she hisses.

"I don't know what the truth is. Honest."

"You obviously know a hell of a lot of *something* that you're not telling me!" Her eyes shine as she fights against her tears. She's furious with me, and I don't think picking her up and tossing her into the passenger seat will work.

"Okay, fine." I drop my voice to a whisper. "The night my mom killed herself, she was blind drunk and rambling all kinds of nonsense about how someone set up Abe and about how he was a good man and she needed *you* to know that."

"Why wouldn't you tell me that when I asked?"

"Because I don't know what's true and I didn't want to get your hopes up. Besides, there's nothing we can do about it."

"Who says?"

"My uncle, who's also the district attorney."

"Well, good! If he's the DA then he can make the police reexamine the evidence, right?"

"That's the problem; there isn't any evidence to reexamine!" I quickly explain the incineration mishap.

By the time I'm done, tears of anger are streaming down her cheeks. I reach up to brush them away, but she jerks her head out of reach.

"I'm sorry. I thought it might do more harm than good, telling you."

With rough strokes, she rubs her tears away. She backs away from me. "I'll go and see what Dr. Coppa will give us, if anything." Her voice has turned steely, a mask for the simmering rage hiding beneath.

And the hurt.

I watch her march for the hospital doors, feeling the chasm between us widen. Getting her to trust me at all again will be an impossible feat. I can't worry about that right now, though.

I need to focus on finding out what Dina knows.

CHAPTER 22

Grace

Noah's SUV bounces over the speed bumps into the motel's parking lot, jostling me in my seat. "I'll see if there's an extra charge to bring him in. You should carry him to your room, though."

"Does he look like a dog that lets people carry him?" I snap. I haven't said a word to Noah since I climbed into the passenger seat, my mind too busy replaying all of his words, trying to pick out fact from fiction. What else hasn't he shared with me? What other lies might he have told?

He sighs. "He can't run loose around here. He'll freak people out, and we don't need to be looking for a new motel."

"Did she force that dog on you?" my mom asks from the backseat. She hasn't spoken much either, whether it's from the shock of Noah, the nausea that's likely overwhelming her, or the thick, choking tension swirling around us, I can't be sure.

"No, ma'am, but your neighbor did. The dog catchers were hunting him."

"Vilma?"

"Yes, ma'am. And I have a soft spot for the elderly, so I couldn't say no."

"Of course you do." There's rare delight in her voice. It's not a wonder; Noah is oozing Texas charm. I would have thought it would agitate her, but now I see she's smiling. And she's so much calmer than she was when I found her in front of the hospital.

Cyclops lets out an excited bark.

"Actually, Noah was talking about adopting him. He *loves* strays."

I meant it to unsettle him, but Noah only chuckles.

"Meet you up there in a few." He nods to the black duffel bag. "Can I carry that for you?"

"I've got it." I'm guessing he slid the metal box in with the money.

I watch his long strides and his lean, strong body as he heads for the main lobby, wondering if he's going to grab his things and bolt. No . . . Noah's not the type to run.

And neither am I.

I ease out of the passenger seat, covered in soot for the second day in a row, a bag of pills in hand. Dr. Coppa was alarmed that my mom didn't last even a day in rehab. After I told him we had lined up Desert Oaks—with financial help from "a friend"—he made me call them and confirm her spot for tomorrow morning before he'd give me enough medication to get her through until then. It's a lie, of course. I can't use that money, now that I have a good idea where it came from.

Still, we can manage the worst of her withdrawal symptoms, at least for tonight.

But what about the rest of it? I asked the nurses about this police officer who supposedly visited. They were adamant that no one—especially the police—visited Dina Richards this afternoon. They even checked the visitor logs in front of me.

So that means she's either lying or delusional.

Or the hospital is lying.

Or someone snuck in to scare her into running, and Noah is right—I have no idea what we're dealing with here.

"Don't make me regret this," I warn Cyclops as I release him from my grip inside the motel room. Surprisingly, he let me carry him to the second floor. His nose hits the ground in an instant and he runs off to sniff out every corner of the room. And, hopefully, not urinate in them.

Mom's drowsy gaze drifts over the bed, the TV, and the curtains, her eyes tightening against the light. Whatever bit of energy she mustered to run from her hospital bed is long gone. A sheen of sweat coats her pale forehead. "Is this where you stayed last night?"

"Yeah."

Her fingers smooth over the duvet cover. "With Noah?"

"He's in the room next door."

"I'm glad to see Jackie raised him right, at least." She eases herself onto the bed gingerly, as if the frame might not be stable enough to hold her hundred-pound frame. "It's nice here. Quiet."

"Here. Drink some water."

She accepts the bottle from me with a shaky hand. "They brought this woman into the wing, after you left. She was hysterical."

"Probably her first overdose." The first time in a long time that woman has had to face her demons sober, and that must hurt more than all the physical withdrawal symptoms, combined. I know because I went through the same thing with Mom, her first time in the hospital after OD'ing. I could hear her wails down the hall.

Only now I have to wonder exactly what those demons calling out to her have been saying.

Fourteen years.

It's been fourteen years since I wrapped my arms around my dad's broad shoulders, since he kissed me good night.

Fourteen years since he was shot and killed, and labeled a criminal.

Fourteen years since my life was turned upside down.

And here we are, my entire life turned upside down *again* in the span of twenty-four hours.

As much as I want to interrogate her about . . . well, *everything* . . . I can tell she's minutes away from throwing up if she doesn't lie down. I toss my purse to the dresser, realizing that every last possession I have is in there. "Get some rest."

"Where's the box?"

"It's safe."

She folds herself into bed. "Bring it to me. Please."

Something in her voice stops me from dismissing her. I fish it out of the duffel bag and set it on the nightstand beside her, careful not to let her catch a glimpse of the money.

She gazes at it for a long moment. "You opened it."

"Of course I did."

I expect her anger to flare, for her to yell at me. The look of resignation on her face takes me by surprise, even as weary as she is.

"Is this stuff about Dad?"

"Everything is about him. It always has been." Her voice is barely a whisper as she flips open the lid and rifles through it. "And now I have so little left. Just this box. And you." She lifts the picture of Noah and Dad on the driveway, her thumb sliding over Noah's face. "And him." She smiles sadly. "Do you remember Noah?"

"Not really."

"He was a good boy." The wistful smile touching her lips slips away. "When I lost your dad, I lost Noah too." Slowly, she places the picture back inside. She closes the lid. "I wondered if he'd come looking for us."

"Jackie gave him our address. She sent him here."

"He had nothing to do with what happened to your father." She closes her eyes. "Don't be so hard on him. He must be hurting a lot."

She's singing a different tune from the day she told me Jackie Marshall died, strung out and incapable of showing the smallest amount of compassion, even for the son who found his mother dead in their kitchen.

"I know what you think of me, Grace. But maybe when I explain it all, it'll help you understand this . . . Me . . ." Her words start to drift. Probably the anti-nausea medication she took on the way here. It always knocks her out when she's this weak. "Maybe you won't hate me so much."

"I don't *hate* you." A lump forms in my throat. "But I can't do this anymore. I can't walk through our front door *every* day, wondering if it's going to be the day I finally find my mother dead. Do you know what that does to a person?"

Silent tears meet my words.

Minutes later, she's fast asleep.

And I'm left with a thousand questions.

I open the adjoining door and find Noah's side already open. He's sitting in a chair, his legs splayed, his frown shifting from the sheet of paper in his hand to Cyclops, who's sniffing through the backpack in the corner. "How is she?" Genuine concern fills his voice, and it pulls at my heart despite my fiercest attempts to keep my anger fueled.

"Asleep."

"She wasn't looking good back there." His gaze skates over me from head to toe. I know I'm covered in soot and I should shower.

But first, I need answers.

"Tell me everything, Noah. *Everything.*"

"She said Betsy's name?"

Noah nods solemnly. "I think it had something to do with the papers she burned in the sink. There was a piece left, with a date. April *something*, 2003. I can't remember which date exactly, but it wasn't too far off the day Abe died."

I guess we'll file that under "suspicious things Jackie Marshall was hiding." The list is growing. "But why is 'Betsy, 2002' written on the back of my mom's school picture, then?"

"I don't think that's your mother."

"That's impossible. Look at her." I hold up the picture for emphasis.

"People write names and dates on the back of school pictures to keep track. Your mother was in her midtwenties in 2002. That girl is way too young to be her."

I stare at the youthful face, comparing it to my memories of my mom before all the drugs started ravaging her, aging her terribly. Same eyes, same color hair, same jaw structure. Her nose looks daintier and her cheeks are fuller, but that's not unheard of for a girl that age. "Then who is she?"

"I'm hoping Dina can tell us that." Noah drops his gaze to his hands. I note the way his shoulders sag, as if burdened by an enormous weight. Have they always been like this, and I hadn't noticed, too wrapped up in my own turmoil? "Did she say anything about the box while you were in there with her? About what was in it?"

"Nothing useful, but she'll be awake soon. She can't sleep for long stretches when she's detoxing."

He sighs, setting the copy of the newspaper article on the bed beside him. "I'll see if I can track down anything about this bust when I get back to Austin. Harvey Maxwell is an ADA at my uncle's office."

"And you think he'll tell you the truth, if he did something shady?"

"There's got to be a good explanation for this." Noah's forehead wrinkles with worry.

More like he's praying for a good explanation. He likes this Maxwell guy.

"You mean a good explanation, like there must be a good answer for why your mom had my dad's gun holster?"

Noah bows his head.

He's not at fault here, I remind myself. "When are you going back?" I ask with a softer tone.

"I don't know. Soon."

Despite Noah's lies and evasiveness, disappointment pricks me. I push it away as I study the picture of the man with the sloped forehead and squinty eyes, who Noah recognized but didn't tell me.

I wonder how long he would have kept that to himself, had my mother not run from the hospital today.

Noah fumbles with the leather band around his wrist. "I'll run out and grab a pizza for us, and some soup for Dina."

I snort. "Good luck getting her to eat."

"We have to try. And food for *him*, I guess." He scowls at Cyclops, who has made himself comfortable on Noah's bed and is busy gnawing at an itch on his back leg. The bedspread is covered in sooty paw prints.

I sigh. "Come on. I need your help, before you go anywhere."

"With what?"

"Something you're not going to like . . ."

Noah frowns at the half-full tub of warm water. "Shouldn't we be using dog shampoo?"

"Do you have any?"

"I can buy some."

"No point adding extra stops. You need to be here when my mom wakes up. We'll only get a small window of time where she'll feel up to talking." I grab one of the towels off the rack. "Hold him down for me."

With a heavy sigh, Noah reaches over his head and pulls his T-shirt off, tossing it on the counter.

Leaving me staring at his bare chest. "What *the hell* are you doing? I said hold him down, not get *in* with him!"

"You think he's gonna be calm about this? That shirt is all I have left."

"Fine, whatever." I peel my eyes away, feeling my face burn as I recall a naked Noah in this very spot yesterday. "Cy, come here!" I whistle.

The mangy dog trots into the bathroom, oblivious.

"I hope Vilma was wrong about the rabies," I mutter, lifting him in.

With a soft curse, Noah kneels beside me and seizes Cyclops's wiry body. Cyclops lets out a low growl as he squirms, and Noah's arms cord with tension.

"Quiet. Unless you want to go back to the Hollow alone," I warn in a sharp voice.

As wild as the dog is, Cyclops stops growling, as if he understands.

The combination of water and soap releases a putrid smell of soot, wet dog, and things we're probably better off not identifying. "Oh, God."

"Yeah," Noah agrees with a grimace.

I try not to breathe through my nose, shifting my gaze away. It skates to Noah's bare shoulder beside me, to the thin silver lines decorating the muscular contours. How a dog Cyclops's size could fit its jaws around that shoulder is hard to believe, but I've now seen how scrawny Noah was when he was little.

And yet Noah's here to help me, unhappy, but with barely a complaint.

"Thank you."

"If the little asshole is gonna make my bed his, then I don't have much choice, do I?"

"Thank you, for getting him out of there." I feel like I've been saying those two words to Noah a lot lately, and yet not nearly enough.

His eyes land on mine. They're all the more striking up close, a kaleidoscope of blues that draw me in like a cool pool on a blistering-hot day. "Your neighbor makes me nervous, too. She basically forced me."

"The ninety-year-old shrunken woman who might break with a strong wind and doesn't speak English *forced* you? How exactly did that go down?"

His mouth curves into a playful smirk. "She's persuasive."

"I'll bet." I picture Vilma going head-to-head with a guy Noah's size and can't help but chuckle at the mental image. "Anyway . . . He would have been a goner if they had caught him. So, thanks."

Noah's gaze drifts to my lips. "I figured that would bother you." His voice is softer, deeper, and it stirs something inside me.

"Yeah, it would have." It would have *more than* bothered me. If Noah had sat there and let it happen, I doubt I would have forgiven him, regardless of his childhood stray trauma.

Cyclops starts squirming.

"He is one filthy animal." Noah's nose crinkles at the blackened water as he holds on tight.

"This is probably his first bath . . . ever." I laugh as I scrub the dog's neck and back, unable to avoid Noah's hands. Quietly reveling in the feel of them beneath my own. "Here—I need to rinse him." I pull the plug and get the handheld sprayer.

Noah manages to hold him down for another ten seconds before he snarls and twists his body to snap at Noah's wrist. With a curse, Noah scrambles away, falling onto his back. Allowing Cyclops to leap out of the tub, knocking me over in his mad, soaking-wet dash out of the bathroom.

I lose my balance and tumble on top of a sprawled-out Noah.

"Well, that was fun," he mutters, his head falling back to thump against the tile.

"Did he get you?" I'm hyperaware of how smooth and hot Noah's bare skin feels against my hands as he inspects his wrist.

"He didn't break my skin. It was a warning . . ." He sighs. "I swear to God, Gracie. It's never-ending with you, isn't it?"

I don't know why, but that makes me burst out laughing—a deep sound rising from my belly, until my whole body is shaking. I should be peeling myself off him but I can't move—I'm laughing too hard.

He peers up at me, an unreadable expression on his face.

"What?" My heart starts pounding in my chest.

"Nothing, I just . . ." His words drift, and I can see that he's changed his mind about what he was going to say. "I was trying to decide who's dirtier now—you or your stray dog."

I elbow him in the ribs as I roll off.

"You have to eat, Mom." I set the container of chicken broth on the nightstand next to her.

She dismisses it with a pinched nose. "Everything is making me nauseous. Even that pizza . . ." She has some color in her face again, at least, but I know that she's not exaggerating. At least she's in that happy lull, though, after the harshest of the drug's effects have worn off, but before the heroin withdrawal symptoms come back with a vengeance.

Noah's immediately on his feet and closing the door to his adjoining room, where the offending smell permeates the air. "Gracie's right. You need to put something besides all this medication into your body. That's why you have no energy."

She offers him a weak smile as he returns to sit on the edge of the bed beside her. "You still call her Gracie."

He collects the bowl and spoon. "It's all I know."

"Abe called her that. Gracie . . . or Gracie May . . ."

Slowly, Noah slips a spoon's worth of soup into her mouth. "I remember watching you feed her like this."

She swallows with only a slight grimace. "Do you really?"

His mouth twists into a boyish grin. "I'd make faces at her, and she'd get so excited she'd slap your hand away."

"Her food would end up all over the wall. Drove me bananas." Mom begins to laugh, the rare sound bringing a prickle to my throat. "I never had the heart to scold you for that."

He slips another mouthful of soup into her. And another, and another, like some doting son, as they reminisce about summer barbecues in the backyard, and games we used to play, and how my dad used to keel over from laughing when I'd dance around in nothing but a diaper, my hips swaying and my arms waving above my head. I quietly listen and watch.

But talk of my dad also brings the tension slithering back into the room, like a snake coiling around its prey, squeezing tighter and tighter until I'm unable to focus on anything else.

My mom feels it too; I can see it in her pained eyes as she studies Noah's face, who sits quietly, biting his bottom lip. Waiting, as if he's suddenly afraid to push her.

I'm not. I've been waiting *years* for proof of her quiet accusations. "Tell us what you've been hiding. Now, while you can handle it." How long before her attention wanes, before she's more focused on keeping down her soup than letting loose skeletons she's been so adept at hiding? Ten minutes? Half an hour?

Her eyes fall to her lap, where her hands are entwined tightly. "I don't even know where to start."

I flip open the metal box and pull out the first mystery. The picture of my mom that might not be a picture of my mom. I hand it to her.

She smiles weakly as she studies it. "That's probably a good place to start."

My mother gathers her thoughts, as scattered as they may be. I have to keep reminding myself that she's far from well, even if she's lucid.

"The first time I introduced Abe to your nan was when I was six months pregnant with you. She insisted that we make the trip from Texas to Arizona. She and Brian wanted to meet him before you were born."

Mom says I met my mom's stepdad, but I was too young to remember. Nan kicked him out a year before we moved out to Tucson. But I heard enough of Nan's offhand unflattering comments to figure out that they hadn't parted on good terms.

"So we drove here for Christmas. She insisted we stay in the trailer. All of us—Abe and I in one room, your nan and Brian in the other . . ." She drags a finger along the picture. "And Betsy, on the couch."

Noah was right.

"Betsy is my little sister. Well, half-sister," she corrects. "Nan had her with Brian when I was ten."

My mouth drops open. "Why haven't I met her? Or even heard of her?"

"You did meet her. We came back to Tucson for a visit when you were three."

I pause to digest this shocking new information. It's hard enough imagining your parent as a person who had an entire life—an identity—before you came into the picture. But when that identity includes a sister you've never heard of . . . "What happened to her? Did she leave with Brian?"

My mother swallows hard, then shakes her head.

The alternative hits me. "She died."

"I don't know. Maybe she *is* dead by now." My mom studies the picture for another long moment. "Betsy was fourteen when she ran away. Nan phoned us in hysterics, the goodbye letter in her hand. Your dad hopped in his car and drove through the night to go looking for her. He grilled her friends and found out that she'd been seeing this older guy. He was buying her clothes and things, making all kinds of promises for a better life.

"Abe looked for days, but she was gone. He figured she was picked up that same night and taken out of the city right away. That's how those things work. Steal 'em young and in the night."

"*Those things*? What things?"

"Human trafficking. They bring in young girls from broken homes and force them into prostitution. Betsy was stolen, and sold." Mom's voice cracks with emotion.

Oh my God. "And you never heard from her again?"

Another solemn head shake, my mom's eyes glazing over with the threat of tears. "Abe felt responsible for what happened to Betsy. He convinced himself that he should have seen the signs. He didn't like Brian right from the second he met him. I figured it was because Brian had a thing or two to say about me marrying a black man. Abe said it wasn't that. My stepfather was an ignorant fool, and he expected as much from him. He couldn't peg exactly why, but Brian rubbed him the wrong way, and your daddy could find the good in most anybody. That's why we stopped coming here—"

"Wait a minute, what do you mean, 'he should have seen the signs'?" I interrupt.

Mom pauses. "Brian was abusing Betsy. Touching her and stuff."

My stomach drops. "In *our* trailer? In *my room*?" I feel my face twist with disgust. "And Nan didn't know?"

"That's the thing . . . Betsy tried to tell her, but she wouldn't listen."

"Bullshit." How could my nan—my sweet grandma who made me pancakes on weekends and smothered me with hugs—ignore that?

"Gracie, you have to remember, I grew up in that trailer, too. And I had never come to her so much as suggesting something like that was happening to me. In her mind, it didn't make sense. And Betsy was a wild kid. She was getting into all kinds of trouble—shoplifting, neighborhood mischief, that sort of thing. She and Brian were butting heads all the time, so your nan assumed Betsy was lying, that she was being an uncontrollable teenager.

"It wasn't until Betsy ran that she confronted Brian. And he admitted to it. Nan kicked him out, but it was too late. Betsy was gone. Nan never forgave herself. When I phoned her to ask if we could move in, she packed up everything to do with Betsy."

"And you both went on like she never existed." I can't help the accusation in my tone.

My mom's fingers fumble with the charm dangling from her necklace. "Believe me, neither of us ever forgot about Betsy. But Nan couldn't handle you asking her questions. She'd have to lie because she couldn't handle telling you the truth." After one last look, she passes the picture back to Noah, who hands it to me.

I study Betsy's—my aunt's—face. "I thought this was you."

Mom smiles sadly. "We're both spitting images of your nan when she was young. People called us twins, ten years apart."

"And the necklace she's wearing . . ."

"I sent Betsy that half for her tenth birthday. Told her I'd always wear the other half. It wasn't anything fancy, just this cheap metal. Thank God, or I would have traded it for a high, I'm sure."

Noah, who has sat and listened quietly through this, asks with a thoughtful look, "Did Abe ever say anything to you about seeing Betsy in Austin?"

"In Austin?" She frowns. "No. Why?"

He tells her about the night Jackie killed herself, and how Jackie mentioned Betsy. Mom's left with an equally perplexed look.

"The morning after Abe died, I found that picture of Betsy in the top drawer of the desk. I thought it was strange that it was there. It's the picture Nan gave to Abe, to show around Tucson, right after she'd run. I had put it away, in a box of photos in the closet."

"And he never said anything to you about seeing her again? Maybe while working? Are you sure?" I can't help the doubt in my voice. Would she even remember at this point?

"Your father never talked about work with me. He didn't want to bring that into our house or our marriage. But he would have told me about seeing Betsy in Austin. Wouldn't he?" Even as she says that, I can almost see her mind clawing at her memories, first with a shadow of doubt, and then with a touch of realization.

"What is it, Dina?" Noah asks, seeing the same.

"He started working *a lot* of overtime in those last couple weeks. Or at least that's what he told me. APD said he wasn't clocking in extra hours for them. That it was a cover he'd been using to lie to me, to be out at all hours with prostitutes and drug dealers. I could never make sense of that. I figured the department was covering up something, because I knew he was *not* selling drugs, no matter what they accused him of, but I couldn't figure out why he'd lie to *me,* and why he'd be at that seedy motel. For a while I started to wonder if maybe he was cheating on me. But that wasn't Abe. If you knew him, you'd know he just didn't have that in him."

"But what if he had reason to believe Betsy was in Austin? What if he was looking for her?" Noah finishes.

My mother gasps, as if everything suddenly makes sense.

"But why wouldn't my dad tell her that he'd seen Betsy?" I ask.

"If he was going around looking for her for weeks, then that means he couldn't find her. Maybe he didn't want to get your hopes up?" Noah offers, looking toward my mother.

"It would make sense. That whole year . . . it was hard on me." My mom's voice cracks.

Despite my anger, my chest pangs with sympathy for her. While I giggled and rode my father's back and demanded attention like any normal child, I was oblivious to my mother's silent pain.

"And if Abe was looking for Betsy, that could explain why he was at that motel," Noah says.

I hold up the picture. "Then why didn't he take this with him?"

Noah stares at Betsy's face, considering my question. Finally, he says, "Maybe he thought he didn't need it."

"Because he was convinced she was there?"

"He got a call that night," my mom recalls. "We were sitting on the couch, watching TV. It was late. He answered, and then told me he had to go out for a bit. Something for work. I wasn't happy, but I knew that it must be important if Abe was leaving me at that hour. He seemed in a rush."

"And then?"

"That was the last time I saw him alive."

"Did you tell the police this?"

She nods, her mouth twisting with bitterness. "They said the call came from the phone found on that dead drug dealer who was in the room with Abe. That he called Abe to meet up for a drug exchange. It just . . . it never made sense. Nothing about that night ever made sense to me. When Abe left, he took his Colt .45 with him. I know because I watched him take it out of his safe and check the bullets, and then slide it into the holster I gave him for his birthday, the one with his initials on it. But the police said Abe had been found with a stolen gun on him. I told the police about the Colt .45. They said they'd make note of it."

I look to Noah, only to see his subtle head shake. *Don't mention the gun holster*, he's saying.

Anger begins to burn in my mother's eyes. "Why was Jackie talking about Betsy that night?"

"I don't know. I swear, Dina. I don't." Noah's head is in his hands, as if the weight of listening to this is too much. Or maybe he's as overwhelmed by all the new questions swirling as I am. Then he looks back up. "What about this video you mentioned earlier? You said someone was looking for it? Who?"

"Yes." Mom turns to me, her gaze full of both fear and resignation. "The man who held a knife to my throat and threatened to take Grace if I didn't give it to him."

CHAPTER 23

Noah

By the time Dina has finished describing the night she woke up to find a masked man standing over her bed, holding a knife to her neck while her six-year-old daughter slept peacefully one room away, Gracie's face has taken on a sickly pale color.

"So you didn't have the video that he was looking for?"

She shakes her head. "But I'm pretty sure I know what it was about. A few nights before Abe died, I came into the office and he was watching something on the computer. It was a video taken in a parking lot, and there were police surrounding a guy."

"APD?" I ask.

"I'm not sure. They were shouting at him and their guns were pointed. That's all I saw. Abe shut it off when he realized I was there. He said it was some YouTube video, but I could tell he was lying. His face . . ." She frowns. "It was this weird mix. As if he was angry, but also ecstatic. I didn't think any more of it, until that morning after he died and I found that newspaper clipping in the office. The one with the notes Abe made."

"This is Abe's handwriting?" I study the scrawl—all caps, with slanted ligature strokes, the tops of the letter *T*'s exaggerated.

Dina nods. "I thought it was strange, that it had happened at the same motel Abe died in, The Lucky Nine. But I still hadn't connected it with the video. Not until the day I drove over there. I needed to see if I could, I don't know, *feel* him there . . ." Her voice cracks. "I saw the flashing green neon sign. That's when I remembered."

"Did you check his computer for this video?"

"The police had already taken the computer when they searched the house, but I mentioned it to them. I gave them the original newspaper clipping, too. They said they'd look into it. And then that very same night, the guy showed up. He kept insisting that I give him the video, all while holding that knife to my neck." Her fingertip skates over a tiny scar.

"He was trying to scare you to see if you had it," I say.

"He did that, alright. I didn't know what to tell him. I couldn't even think up a lie. He kept threatening me, first with the knife, and then with Grace. He said he'd take her away and let"—Dina's voice wobbles, cracks—"men do horrible things to her. I could barely get out a word, I was shaking so bad. I was scared that Grace would wake up and come in. I don't know how long he was there. It felt like hours. He told me that the police report would say Abe was guilty of dealing drugs and nothing I told anyone would change that, but that if I said a word to anyone about his visit or about the video, he'd come back to take Grace away from me. He promised that I'd never see her alive again. That's when I knew it all had to be connected—the video of that bust at the motel. And Abe dying.

"So, I packed through the night, stuffed everything I could fit into our car, filled the garage with trash bags of personal things we couldn't take. Then I got Grace and drove away. Left the house for the bank to repossess it. The way I saw it, our lives in Texas were already over. The man holding a knife to my neck and threatening my daughter was making sure I knew it."

"And this video?"

"I waited, hoping the police might uncover something on Abe's computer." Dina gives a weak head shake, her energy visibly draining, her eyes darting to the bottle of medication on the table. "And then, just like he promised, they released the official findings, and Abe was labeled a corrupt cop who got himself killed in a drug deal gone wrong."

Turns out Dina knew *far* more than she'd ever let on to her daughter. "Any guesses about who the guy was?"

Another head shake. "But, I got the feeling he was a cop and that he knew Abe. The way he used his name . . . you know, in that familiar way. It was odd. He seemed so confident about how the investigation was going to go. As if he had some say in it."

The fact that the guy showed up the night after Dina went to the police with talk of this video makes me think she could be right.

"And you think the guy in your hospital room today is connected to him?"

She gulps back water, a light sheen forming over her forehead, her skin tone sickly. I don't know how much longer we can press her for information. "I haven't seen or heard from anyone since we left Austin. And then, all of a sudden, I open my eyes today and a man is standing over my bed. He flashed a badge. At first, I thought I was being arrested."

"What did he look like?"

"Blond hair. No . . . brown hair? Tall?" She frowns. "I think he was tall."

"Was he in uniform?"

"Yes . . . I mean, no. I don't think so?"

"That's okay. What exactly did he say?"

Again, I see her searching through her thoughts, struggling. "He asked if I'd been talking to anyone from Texas lately about Abe. He asked me if I remembered how Abe died. And then he asked me when I saw you last, Grace. And where you were, I think. I can't remember his *exact* words. I was so scared. I begged him to leave you alone. I swore up and down that I hadn't said anything to anyone." Her brow furrows. "And then he . . . disappeared. He was there one second, and gone the next. That's when I got up and ran out of there."

Gracie hasn't said a word in all of this, simply sitting and listening, her fists balled in her lap.

Dina's glassy eyes shift to her. "I'm sorry, Grace. I couldn't tell you. I couldn't bear the thought of you being afraid that someone might show up and steal you away, hurt you terribly. It was bad enough that *I* was terrified. Constantly. And then you got older and I . . ." She sighs. "It wouldn't have changed anything, you knowing that part of it."

"It would have changed *everything*!" Gracie bursts out. "I would have known that my dad was innocent! I wouldn't have spent so many years hating him for ruining our lives!"

"And then you would have had to live with what I know, and believe me, it's not any better. Knowing who your father was, *how good* he was and what someone did to him, what they got away with . . ."

Gracie's anger flares. "No one's getting away with this!"

"They already have."

"That's because you didn't do anything! You should have gone to the police, or the newspapers, or . . . I don't know . . . the mayor's office! You should have told everyone about the guy in your room and about the drug bust that Dad must have had some doubts about. There are *so* many things you should have done instead of pumping drugs into your body and hiding in this deep, dark hole a thousand miles away for all these years!" Gracie blinks away tears.

"I was so scared for you. I couldn't bear the thought of losing you. Especially not like that. Knowing Betsy was out there was bad enough." Dina's voice cracks with a sob.

"I'm not Betsy. And I'm not letting some asshole scare me into silence."

"*This* is why I've never told you. You're so much like your father. So stubborn. I needed to protect you from that."

"You call *this* protecting me?" Gracie flings an accusing hand toward the pills by Dina's bedside. Dina flinches. "I don't need your version of protection. Besides, I'm not six years old anymore." Gracie storms through the entryway to the adjoining room, pushing my door until it is nearly closed.

I offer Dina a reassuring smile. "She'll come around once she cools down." Maybe. I can't say if the revelation of these secrets has shrunk or expanded the chasm that exists between them.

All these years of living with this . . . The fact that Dina managed to keep it buried, even in her drug-induced fog, seems impossible. But maybe it's only because of that fog that she was able to. "Why didn't you go to my mother with this?"

"Jackie?" Dina hesitates. "Your mother wanted nothing to do with us. I went by your house and she wouldn't even let me inside. All she said was that it didn't look good for Abe and she didn't want to be pulled into the scandal. She seemed more focused on her own reputation and what damage it might cause to have an ex-partner—a friend—who everyone was saying looked as dirty as a sewer rat."

I'm already shaking my head. It echoes what Gracie told me yesterday, but it doesn't make sense.

"I was there, Noah," Dina says softly. "She said the words to me. I wasn't high when she said them. Besides . . . she and Abe were already at odds when he died."

"What? You mean they were fighting?"

"I mean, he'd cut her out of his life. Something happened between them not long before that. I don't know what; he wouldn't say."

I frown. "But . . . Abe came over the same day that he died." He said he'd try to get tickets to a Spurs game.

"Abe wouldn't let what was going on between the two of them affect you."

"I don't get it."

"But don't you?" Dina's eyes soften.

"I sold my soul for what I did and there ain't no coming back from that."

Did my mom's treatment of Dina have more to do with a guilty conscience than concern over her own reputation?

Dina reaches with a feeble hand for a pill bottle but struggles with the cap, her complexion tinged a sickly green.

I gently slip it from her weak grasp and open it for her. But it's a long moment before I'm able to meet her eyes. "I'm sorry."

"None of this is your fault, Noah."

No. But it is my mother's. And I've been protecting her.

Dina sets the pill on the nightstand and pulls herself out of bed. "Go to Grace. She trusts you." She stumbles toward the bathroom, using the wall to catch her balance.

"Are you sure I can't . . ."

The bathroom's pocket door slides shut and a moment later, I hear her start to heave. Saliva pools in my mouth at the sound, and I'm forced to go to my room before I follow suit.

I find Gracie struggling to get the collar I bought earlier around Cyclops's neck. Surprisingly, Cyclops is sitting still. But Gracie's hands are trembling.

"I'll take him out for a walk," I offer. "Your mom will probably need you in a minute."

"I'm going to Austin with you," Gracie blurts out in response.

"For what?" I ask, though I already know the answer.

"To prove that my dad's innocent."

"Just like that?"

She holds her chin up stubbornly. "Yeah, just like that."

Gracie's smart enough to know how ridiculous that sounds. "Based on what?"

"What do you mean, based on what?" she snaps. "My mom should have told the police about the guy in her room! If she'd told them, maybe the real guilty people would have been caught!"

I push the door shut, hoping to spare Dina from her daughter's sharp tongue. "You can't walk into the police station and demand a fourteen-year-old case be reopened based on what a heroin addict told you."

"So you don't believe her?"

"I do believe her, but—"

"Why the hell would a cop show up in her hospital room *in Arizona* all of a sudden, and start asking questions about a guy who died fourteen years ago, if not to cover up a murder?"

I drop my voice to a whisper. "Come on, Gracie . . . Do you *really* think a cop showed up in her room today? Think about it; you heard her back there. She couldn't remember what he looked like, or if he was even in uniform. She was asleep, pumped full of medication. The nurses didn't see anyone . . . And you're right. Why now, right after my mom died?"

Gracie won't admit it, but I see it in her eyes: she considered that Dina might have been delusional, too.

"Look, I believe her about what happened in your house that night. But nobody else will."

She stops fussing with Cyclops's collar and grabs the copy of the news clipping. "We have this! *And* a bag of ninety-eight thousand dollars! And my father's gun holster!"

"The money isn't going to prove anything."

"Yes, it will!" She sputters, "Fingerprints!"

"Yeah, *mine*."

Gracie's not to be swayed, though. "We have a suspicious timeline—a drug bust that my dad observed on video and had a newspaper clipping about and ten days later, he's dead, in the same motel where that bust happened—and then some guy is breaking into our house, threatening my mom about a video. How can you call that 'nothing'?"

"Fine. It's something."

"And if someone could break in to threaten my mother, who says it was the first time? The same guy could have also planted the money and drugs that the cops found!"

Maybe. But . . . "None of this is enough, Gracie."

"Then we *find* enough!" Her voice has risen, and Cyclops bolts from the bed, eyeing her warily. "We find Betsy. If she was in Austin at that time, then she's his alibi for all those other nights. Maybe she knows something."

"Do you know what kinds of things happen to those girls?" I don't want to come right out and say it, but the chances of finding Betsy alive—fourteen years later—are not good.

"I'm not going to sit in Tucson and do *nothing*."

"And you can't go to Austin and stomp around, waving your knife and accusing people of framing your dad."

"Not people, Noah. Cops. Or *a* cop."

"Even more reason not to!"

She pauses to study the newspaper clipping. "I'll bet that Mantis guy stole money or drugs from this bust, and my dad found out about it, and that's why Mantis killed him."

"We can't prove that. We don't even have the original case evidence."

"Yeah, that's convenient, don't you think?" Her tone is dripping with sarcasm. "Plus, I heard what my mom said—that Jackie and my dad were 'at odds.' Why? What did Jackie do? Why would she not care about what happened to him—or us—after he died? Why would she be so quick to believe he was dealing drugs when anyone who knew him knew there was no way it could be true? Huh?" Her eyes narrow as she fires off accusation-laced questions. "There's only one reason I can think of. Guilt over something she did, or something that someone else did that she knew about and kept quiet. I'll bet she knew my father had been set up right from the start!"

I collect the collar from the bed. Surprisingly, Cyclops comes to me unbidden. I focus my attention on fastening the thin leather strap and hooking the end of the leash, all while trying to come up with a suitable response. "You know what? Maybe my mother is guilty of something. And maybe that money is the only way she knew how to make it right."

I give the leash a light tug and Cyclops hops off the bed, looking as ready to get out of this suffocating motel room as I am.

But Gracie's not ready to let me leave yet. "When I was eleven, thugs robbed the convenience store down the street where Nan bought her cigarettes. They shot the nice man behind the counter three times and he died. His name was Ahmed. He had a mole above his right eye and he always threw in a candy and a wink for me when he handed my nan her change. He had been working there for six months when it happened. For *three* years, every time I went into that store, I'd ask if the police had caught the killer. I hated that this person was running free, that Ahmed didn't get the justice he deserved." Gracie stands there with her arms folded, watching me.

"Why are you telling me this?"

"Because he was just Ahmed—the nice man who I saw two to three times a week, who gave me candy. He wasn't the man who played basketball with me in his driveway, who coached my team, whose wife cared for me almost every day. He wasn't a part of my life. But my dad was a part of yours—a big part. How can you *not* be furious? How can you *not* be fighting to make the people responsible for his death pay?"

"Because what if one of those people is my mother?" My voice cracks with emotion.

Sympathy flickers in her eyes, but it quickly vanishes. "My dad deserves to have his name cleared. What exactly does *she* deserve?"

Part of me is desperate to know the answer to that.

The other part hopes I never find out.

I march out the door, Cyclops on my heels.

CHAPTER 24

Officer Abraham Wilkes

April 23 , 2003

"How's your Coke machine doing, Isaac?"

"Nobody messin' with it yet. Maybe having you loiter around the parking lot has helped scare 'em away." The Lucky Nine's maintenance man rests his forearm on the hood of my car. "Still no luck findin' that girl?"

I grimace. "And no leads." Every time my phone rings with an unknown number, my heart races. I've gotten a few calls, but they've led nowhere. Gutsy hookers, thinking they can bait me into coming to their rooms. I'm not going to track them down and arrest them. Not much else to do except tell them not to call again and hang up.

Isaac's gaze drifts aimlessly over the lot. "I can tell she's important to you."

"She's my wife's sister," I admit, something I don't tell anyone when I'm canvassing. But Isaac seems trustworthy enough.

"I've been keepin' an eye out."

"I appreciate that. But I'm beginning to wonder if I'm talking in the wind. I've got a little girl at home, crying herself to sleep every night because she wants her daddy home." And a wife that I'm lying to, because I can't explain how I lost Betsy in the first place. It's bad enough that I won't ever forgive myself for it; I can't bear what Dina might think. It's best she doesn't know about my run-in with Betsy until I can bring her sister home. Then . . . I'll admit the truth and pay the consequences.

If I find her.

"What's your girl's name?"

"Gracie." I smile wide. "Gracie May. She's six and stubborn as a mule. She wouldn't understand this, even if I did tell her."

"But she will one day, and she'll love you for it." He says it with such certainty.

"Hope you're right," I murmur as I watch a bronze Chevy coast into the parking lot. It pulls into a spot almost directly across from me, right in front of the vending machine. The driver, a thin white guy with a shaved head and ink marking his throat, climbs out, seemingly in a hurry, his eyes casting furtively back toward the parking lot entrance where a dark SUV races in.

I recognize the vehicle, even before it comes to a halt and the men hop out, the reflective police decal on their bulletproof vests gleaming in their headlights as they round the truck, guns drawn and pointed. Dwayne Mantis is in the lead, the same stony look on his face no matter where he is. He was always a cocky son of a bitch, but he's become even more so since Chief Canning created this special task force against drugs in Austin and tapped Mantis to lead it. I guess he has something to be cocky about, given the DA's office has put more dealers away in the last six months than the previous two years, thanks to him and his team. And, if it keeps Austin's streets and schools clean for Gracie, then I'll accept his inflated ego with a smile and a thanks.

Mantis and the others surround the driver of the other car with purpose. He looks like a cornered animal.

"Isaac, you should go on about your business," I murmur.

I don't have to warn the maintenance man twice. He's gone in a flash, leaving me to watch what I'm guessing is an impending drug bust from the privacy of my car.

The driver has his hands up and is arguing with Mantis, telling him he knows his rights and the police have no cause to harass him, that he's done nothing wrong.

"Then you don't mind popping the trunk for me?" Mantis says with feigned casualness.

"There's nothing in there. It's empty."

"We received a tip that says different."

"That's a lie. You have no cause!"

Mantis nods toward Stapley, who reaches into the car and hits the release.

Mantis's stern face splits with a wicked grin.

"That's not mine! You planted it there!" the guy exclaims before spinning on his heels, looking intent to run. Two of the cops cut him off. They have him pinned against the hood of the car and in handcuffs in seconds.

"What do we have here . . . coke, meth . . . Jesus, this might earn us a commendation! Hope you don't like freedom, because you're not gonna see it again for a *long* time," Mantis says jovially. He shakes his head to himself, but he's enjoying every second of this. "Read him his rights."

As the fourth officer begins reciting words I could say in my sleep, Mantis reaches into the trunk. When his hand reappears, it's with a wad of money. He glances over at Stapley and then, barely missing a beat, he grabs a black duffel bag and tosses it through the open window of the SUV.

CHAPTER 25

Noah

"Good boy," I whisper, giving Cyclops a scratch behind his ear as he settles by the park bench. I sigh heavily, my mind a chaotic mess of puzzle pieces with no picture to guide me.

Gracie's right—we can't use that money. Not yet, anyway. I have enough savings to cover Dina's first month of rehab. It'll wipe me out completely, but I have a giant inheritance coming my way. Hopefully, Fulcher can speed up—

"Rough night?" a voice calls out into the quiet night, cutting into my thoughts and unsettling Cyclops.

It's a familiar voice, and yet I can't place it. Not until the park bench sinks and I look over to find Special Agent Klein sitting beside me.

"Shhh . . ." I warn Cyclops, tightening my grip on his leash, even as panic swirls inside me. What is the FBI doing here? "Don't you belong in Texas?" I ask coolly.

"I belong wherever my case takes me," Klein retorts just as evenly.

I glance around for his dark-haired partner.

"Agent Tareen stayed behind, to follow up on a few other leads," Klein explains as if able to read my mind.

"Leads for what?"

Ignoring me, Klein reaches a hand out toward Cyclops.

"I wouldn't do that if I were you," I warn as a deep growl resonates from the small dog's chest.

Klein pulls back. And frowns. "He's missing an eye."

How observant. I bite my tongue. Antagonizing the feds will do me no good.

Klein leans forward, resting his elbows on his knees. "He yours?"

"A friend's."

"Is that what Grace Wilkes is? A friend?" He says it so casually.

Klein found me in Tucson. I shouldn't be surprised that he knows who I came to see. And yet my stomach tightens with anxiety, hearing him say her name.

I give Cyclops's head another pat and avoid answering his question.

"Two days ago, you told me that you haven't seen or talked to anyone in the Wilkes family since Abraham Wilkes died. But here you are, in Tucson, with his wife and his daughter. You even rented her a hotel room."

I want to ask him how he knows, but I can already guess. He flashed his badge at that bubbly blonde receptionist. "So?"

"So, why are you here?"

I lean back, trying to give off the same air of indifference. "To see Dina and Gracie."

A smirk dances across Klein's face before he smooths his expression. "I went by the Sleepy Hollow Trailer Park today, right before going to visit Dina Wilkes at the hospital, and—"

"*You* were at the hospital today?"

"Yeah."

"You went to her *room*?"

Klein pauses to regard me, curiously. "I wanted to ask her a few questions. Why?"

I heave a sigh of relief. The man with the badge . . . Dina's not delusional after all. The man in her room wasn't some ghost from fourteen years ago, looking to silence her. "You scared the shit out of her."

"Why would she be scared of talking to me?"

"She thought you were someone else."

"Who is she afraid of?"

"I'm not sure, but . . ." I hesitate. "She doesn't think her husband's death was an accident."

Klein doesn't appear at all shocked by that. "And what do you know about Abraham Wilkes's death?"

"Do you make it a habit of talking to hospital patients without signing in at the desk?" I say instead.

"There was no one at the desk to sign in with. Security is rather lacking there, wouldn't you say?"

"I noticed." Dina, in pajamas and barely upright, managed to dart out, undetected.

There's another long pause, and I suspect Klein is weighing his next words like a move on a chessboard. "I came here to talk to Dina Wilkes about her husband's death. Imagine my surprise when I found out that *you* carried her out of the burning trailer. It's interesting . . ."

"How is that interesting? What should I have done, left her there to die?"

"The fire was yesterday, in the early afternoon. It's twelve hours to Tucson from Austin if you drive, and you drove. I saw your Jeep Cherokee over there, in the lot. Now, I've never been good at telling time, but if we stopped by your place in Austin around . . . what was it, four in the afternoon on Thursday? You would have had to leave for Tucson that same night." He mock frowns. "Did you decide all of a sudden to drive two states over and see the Wilkes family, whom you've had no contact with for fourteen years, after our little talk?"

Shit. I force a shrug. "I wanted to get away."

"Did your mother tell you to come and see Dina and Grace Wilkes on the night she died?"

"No."

"You sure?"

"Tell Gracie he was a good man. You'll do that, right?"

I heave a sigh to mask my panic. "Am I under some sort of federal investigation, Agent Klein? Because if I am, I'm entitled to have an attorney present."

"No. Not yet, anyway." He reaches into his pocket to pull out his phone. "I want to play something for you. It's short. Do you mind listening?"

"Go ahead," I mutter, my curiosity getting the better of me.

He holds his phone up in the air.

"*Ten fourteen p.m., Wednesday, April fifth, 2017 . . .*" the automated recording chirps into the still night, the time and date setting the hairs down the back of my spine on end. "Agent Klein! Since you're so hell-bent on arrestin' somebody, I've got a name for you," a woman says, her Texas drawl thick, her words slurred, her tone bitter.

My vision blurs with dizziness as I'm instantly transported back to that terrible night.

"You need to look into Abraham Wilkes's death. Everything about what happened to him was a lie. He was set up because he saw Dwayne Mantis steal money in a drug bust and he was gonna nail him for it. I don't know exactly how Mantis did it, but I *know* he killed Abe. Look into him. Look into how Dwayne Mantis *murdered* a good man." The call ends abruptly.

"That's your mother, isn't it?"

I'm sure I don't have to answer; my ghostly white face must say it all and Klein is watching me closely.

There's no mistaking it. That was Jackie Marshall.

"You could have warned me," I manage to get out, my voice hoarse, my heart pounding in my ears. I could punch this dickhead for ambushing me.

"So you could prepare a lie?"

"Why would I lie?"

"I'm not sure yet. The same reason I don't know why you lied to the police in your statement." Klein focuses his attention on twisting the metal ring around his pinky finger, but I know he's acutely aware of my every twitch.

I should tell him everything. Unload this burden off my chest. Let the FBI do something with it. Something I surely can't. That's sounding better and better. But first I need to talk to Silas. He's always been my voice of reason. And this affects him, too.

A thought strikes me. If my mother was directing Klein toward Mantis, it's because he wasn't after him in the first place. "Who are you trying to arrest?"

Klein shrugs noncommittally. "Another case. Another criminal your mother could have helped put away, but didn't. She has a real problem with seeking justice, doesn't she? Not exactly a good quality for a police chief."

FBI agent or not, I'm not about to sit here and listen to him trash-talk my dead mother. "Sounds like you should be busy going after this Mantis guy. Don't let me stop you." I stand, giving Cyclops's leash a small tug toward the motel's entrance.

"What did you need to give Gracie Wilkes?" Klein calls out.

My feet falter. "What are you talking about?"

"Her neighbor said you came to give her something."

Sims, that piece of shit. "Some old family pictures."

"You drove twelve hours to give old family pictures to her? You sure about that?"

His tone puts me on edge. It's like he already knows about the money.

"Have a good night, Klein."

"So, if I were to go into that motel room, I wouldn't find anything suspicious at all?"

A bag of ninety-eight thousand dollars that is too coincidentally the same amount written on that news clip to be at all coincidental.

But, most importantly, he'd find Gracie, and then she'd quickly realize that I left out the part about the feds coming to see me the other day. It was fully intentional on my part, and—probably—the wrong decision, but I already know Gracie enough to know she'd hold me at knifepoint until I gave her Klein's business card. She'd have no issue telling him *everything*, including her own suspicions about my mother.

"You'd find a sick woman who needs her rest. I think you've already scared her enough for one day, don't you?"

He pauses, as if to consider that. "When will you be back in Austin?"

"As soon as I help Gracie get Dina into a rehab program and find a new place to live."

Klein eases himself off the bench to stand next to me, and I sense his mood shifting. "Lying to a police officer in a statement carries a maximum of six months in prison. That's a criminal record, Noah. But you know all this, working in the DA's office. Then again, I'm guessing your uncle would do what he needs to do to make the charges go away."

I swallow. "Have a safe trip back."

"Of course, he'd have a hard time doing that, what with all the media attention around you being a homicide suspect—"

Homicide? I'm unable to keep my cool anymore. "What the hell are you talking about?"

"So who put you up to it? Who wanted Jackie out of the picture?"

I feel my face twist up as I struggle to grasp his meaning. Because he can't be saying what I *think* he's saying . . .

"Jackie was so drunk, I'll bet she didn't even see you coming until the gun was—"

My fist connects with Klein's mouth, needing the vile words to stop. "I did not kill my mother!" I force out through gritted teeth.

I did, however, just punch an FBI agent in the face and, dammit, if he didn't have cause to arrest me before, he does now. *Smart bastard.*

Klein tests his lip with the back of his hand. It comes back with blood. Oddly enough, though, he doesn't look at all surprised, and he hasn't made a move for his cuffs. "I know how to push your buttons, don't I?" He produces a business card from his back pocket. "Here . . . in case you *lost* my other one. You've got forty-eight hours to sort out things with Dina Wilkes, and then I expect you to contact me and tell me everything you know. After that, when I show up on your doorstep, it'll be a lot less pleasant than this talk. For you, and for anyone who's hiding information from me."

I numbly take the card.

With one last sharp look, Klein strolls away, ducking into a dark-colored sedan.

I exhale a lung's worth of air slowly. Is this what my mom meant when she talked about having the feds breathing down her neck being the worst pressure?

Because I get it now.

I peek into the adjoining room. Gracie is curled up in the chair, her head resting on the armrest. Fast asleep.

I breathe a sigh of relief.

Dina offers me a weak smile and beckons me in with a limp wave of her hand.

"Do you need anything?" I whisper.

"No. Thank you, Noah."

The wrappers from the oyster crackers that came with the broth sit empty on her nightstand. "Good. You ate." I move to collect them.

"Noah! What'd you do to your hand?"

I stretch my fingers out in front of me, studying my reddened knuckles. I haven't punched a guy since high school; it was some punk who was picking on a disabled kid out in the parking lot. I feel only marginally bad about hitting Klein, mostly because the guy didn't have warning. He definitely deserved it, though. "Banged it. It's nothing."

I toss the trash into the bin in the corner, feeling Dina's gaze on me the entire way.

"Abe always said that if we didn't end up having a son of our own, he'd be just as happy having you around. He loved you *so* much."

A lump swells in my throat. I nod, unable to come up with a suitable response.

"When do you think you'll be leaving to go back to Texas?"

"Tomorrow morning. I need to talk to my uncle." And find out what Maxwell was doing fourteen years ago that would explain why Abe jotted his name down on that news clipping.

And I need to do that all before my forty-eight hours are up.

"Silas . . ." A weak smile touches Dina's face. "He's the district attorney now. How's he doing?"

"Good, all things considered. He'll be running for District Court judge in the next election and he's basically a shoo-in."

"I thought about going to him. Telling him about the intruder. But then I realized that no matter what I did, it wasn't going to bring Abe back, but it could mean losing Gracie, too. That man . . . it's been fourteen years and I still feel his hand around my throat when I close my eyes."

My gaze skates over the needle marks in her forearm. Gracie called Dina weak. But is she? Because some could argue that she's one hell of a strong lady, to bite her tongue all these years to protect her daughter. And maybe biting her tongue turned her into *this*.

She twists her wrist to hide the marks. "I'm glad you have Silas."

"And I'm glad she has you." I nod toward Gracie.

"For whatever that's worth." Dina takes in a deep, almost exaggerated breath. "I can't explain this feeling. It's like . . . I'm finally feeling sun against my face again, after so long."

"That's because you've been alone in all this. But you're not anymore."

Tears well in her eyes. "If anything happens to her—" Her voice cracks. With effort, she rolls her head to settle her gaze on her peacefully sleeping daughter for a long moment. Gracie's features look so soft in slumber, almost childish. I never noticed her thick fringe of dark lashes before, too busy mesmerized by her penetrating gaze.

"Abe and I never had it easy. It seemed like for every person who accepted us, there were two looking at us with disapproval. Because of Abe's skin color. Or mine. Or our skin colors, together. I remember rocking Grace as a baby, holding her in my arms, worrying about what her life would be like. How people might treat her. How they might punish *her* because I fell in love with her father. Seems like the least of our problems, doesn't it?" Her hard swallow fills the room. "She grew up to be so beautiful. And strong."

"Yes, ma'am." I look down as I agree with Dina, afraid that she'll see the thoughts I've been having about Gracie these past two days. "And she needs you, alive and clean."

Dina chuckles softly. "That girl hasn't needed me for years."

"She does. She always will, no matter what she says. That's why we're taking you to a rehab center tomorrow morning. It's a great place. Dr. Coppa recommended it."

"We can't afford—"

"I have money. My mother left it for me."

"No, I can't—"

"You *have* to, Dina. Do it for Gracie. And for Abe. Imagine what he'd say if he saw you like this."

She falters over whatever rejection she was going to throw out, and finally, sighs with resignation. "You know she's not going to let this go, don't you?"

"Yes, ma'am. She's already told me she's coming back to Texas with me."

"Did you tell her no?"

I chuckle. "Is there such a thing as telling Gracie 'no'?"

"You've figured her out already. She'll find her way there whether it's with you or in the back of a Dumpster."

"Yes, ma'am. She's the most stubborn girl I've ever met," I agree.

"Takes after her daddy. I wish he got to see her grow up. He'd be so proud." Dina blinks away tears. "If she goes, I'd rather it be with you. I'd feel a lot better about that."

"You focus on getting better and I'll make sure she doesn't do something too bullheaded." Easier said than done. Gracie's as subtle as a pickup truck barreling through your front door.

Dina nods. "Keep her safe, will you? For Abe."

"No one's going to come after her, Dina. She doesn't know anything."

"Neither did I. Not really."

"I won't let anything happen to her," I promise. It was easy for a masked man to terrorize a broken-hearted Dina fourteen years ago, using threats against her little girl to scare her into silence. But Gracie's not a little girl anymore, and something tells me she won't be as easy to scare away as Dina was.

The real question, though, is whether Gracie is going to give someone a reason to try.

CHAPTER 26

Grace

Saguaro cacti stand like quiet sentries on either side of us as we pass through the stately gates of the Desert Oaks rehab center.

I try to decipher my mom's steely face in the window's reflection as she takes in her new home. It's nothing too clinical, nothing too urban. Nothing that will make her feel like she's being incarcerated.

What is it that I see in those eyes now? I've always thought I could read her like a book. But that hasn't been the case after all, not entirely. Because buried deep down were secrets she was too afraid to share. Was it paralyzing fear or was it the pain of knowing that her husband had been murdered and framed for corruption that turned her into this shell of a woman?

Fourteen years of this secret, festering inside her.

What if it has festered too long? What if she has no real chance for recovery?

Noah pulls up to the curb in front of the sand-colored one-story building. "I've already made the first payment," he tells me in a hushed voice.

I frown. "What? When?" Because the bag of cash—that bag of dirty money that we fought over last night, that we shouldn't be using but what other choice do we have?—is sitting in the back, untouched.

He slides out of his seat and shuts his door, not answering me. I watch him from the rearview mirror as he pops the back and grabs the small suitcase full of clothes and toiletries I ran out to buy for her earlier this morning. "Stay, buddy." He gives Cyclops a rough pat on his head before shutting the door and heading for the main entrance.

What has he been up to? Besides making sure everything falls into place, that is.

Mom didn't put up a fight this morning when Noah announced that we were bringing her here. She simply nodded. But I caught the wordless look pass between the two of them. Noah must have said something to convince her during those few hours I drifted off last night. Her little golden boy, coming to her rescue.

Yet another thank-you that I owe to him.

Mom sighs. "So I guess this is it for a while?"

"You'll like it here. It's a female-only center. You'll share a unit with five women. But you'll have your own bedroom, so you have space to escape to when you need it. There are male security officers, but you won't see much of them. Security is tight." As tranquil as the place looks, they make an intensive effort to keep the people needing help in and the people causing the harm in their lives out. She'll be hard-pressed to find a heroin dealer with the balls to show up.

If she has a chance anywhere, it's here.

"They have a pool and a gym, plenty of yoga and meditation sessions. You'll have daily individual therapy sessions and healthy meals. It has a high success rate. And who knows? Maybe you'll make a friend." God knows she could use one.

I catch her gaze in the side-view mirror, drifting to Noah, who's busy chatting up the security lady by the door. "Every time I look at his face, I see Jackie." A long pause. "What he's doing for me. For us . . ."

"He's trying to make up for what his mother did." I open the door and climb out.

Mom follows, smoothing the front of the white blouse I bought for her over her slender hips. She looks far from healthy, but a shower and fresh clothes are definitely an improvement. "Don't stir up trouble in Texas."

"I'll be fine. We're just going to try and get answers, that's all.

And hopefully the police report. Noah has good connections. Plus he's smart." And I have no idea if he's going to argue about taking me to Texas, because we've barely said two words to each other since last night. "Maybe we can find Betsy, at the very least." It'd be nice to have more family.

"I don't know, Grace. Fourteen years and she never came home. If she's even alive, she might not remember who she was. Or maybe she doesn't want to remember, with all they would have done to her . . ." Her voice drifts. She reaches around her neck to unfasten the chain and slips it into my palm. "Maybe this will help jog her memory."

I accept it quietly. "We should get you checked in."

"Okay. Well . . . take care of yourself." She reaches for me.

I instinctively take a step back, putting myself out of reach. We're a long way from hugs.

With a small nod of understanding, she turns and heads for the main entrance, patting Noah's arm as she passes by.

I move to follow her in but Noah grabs my wrist, the heat from his hand searing my skin. "She needs to know you think she can do this," he whispers, leaning in close. So close, the minty scent of his gum kisses my senses.

"I *don't* think she can do this."

Pleading blue eyes stare down at me. "You *need* to. For your own sake, as much as hers."

"You don't know her like I do." He hasn't been let down by her, time and time again. Still, for Noah, I find myself wanting to pretend. "Don't leave without me." I shake off his grip and march through the doors.

I step outside and exhale with relief.

Noah's leaning against the side of his SUV, his feet crossed at the ankles, trying to convince a leashed Cyclops to sit for a treat.

And here I was, sure I'd find Cyclops and my things sitting with security, and him gone the second he had the opportunity to ditch me.

I saunter over and mimic his stance. "So, how long until she runs out, screaming at the top of her lungs?"

He chuckles. "I don't think she'll do that."

"They told me you phoned this morning and paid for the first week with your credit card? And you promised to wire the rest tomorrow, after the bank opens?"

He slides on his sunglasses but says nothing. I know why he did it—because whether he wants to admit it or not, he knows that money is dirty.

Which means he's using his own money to pay for my mom's rehab. One part of me wants to refuse the help; the other wants to throw my arms around his neck. But we have important things to discuss.

"We should get going, then. I'll drive the first stretch, seeing as you didn't get much sleep last night."

Noah chews the inside of his cheek and I ready myself for a battle.

"Are you even allowed to drive?"

"Who's gonna stop me?"

He raises an eyebrow.

"I have my license, if that's what you mean."

After another long moment, and with a reluctant sigh, he dangles his keys in the air in front of me.

"What'd you do to your hand, anyway?" I noticed his bruised knuckles this morning, as he was loading the bags.

"Nothing important." He sets the keys into the palm of my hand, the heat of his fingertips both comforting and thrilling against my skin, making me forget about bruised knuckles and heroin-addicted mothers for a split second.

"Ready?"

This is it. I'm going back to Texas.

Either I'm going to find a bunch of roads that lead to nothing but dead ends—the person or people behind my father's murder having covered their tracks so well that no amount of digging will uncover them—or I'm going to find the truth.

All I'm certain of is that someone out there killed my dad and got away with it.

Until now.

"I'm ready."

CHAPTER 27

Noah

Shit. I turn the volume down on the radio so I can grovel properly. "I'm sorry. I forgot."

"You forgot about courtside at a Spurs game?" Jenson can't hide the disbelief in his voice. I don't blame him. They're my favorite team and he won tickets for today's game against the Rockets.

"I've been . . . preoccupied." An eighteen-wheeler blasts its horn at another car as it speeds past.

"Where the hell are you, anyway? I haven't seen or talked to you since Thursday."

"Right now? At a gas station in New Mexico." In my rearview mirror is an annoyed Gracie trying to coax Cyclops into peeing. I should have told her to take him near a sign; he's partial to those. "I had some things to take care of for my mom."

"For her will?"

"Nah."

He waits a beat for me to elaborate before he starts pressuring. "Dude, what's with all the cloak-and-dagger? It's me."

I sigh. Jenson's good at keeping his mouth shut. "You remember my old basketball coach? The one who was shot in a drug deal?"

"Sounds familiar."

"His daughter lives in Tucson. My mom left something for her, and I had to bring it to her in person. Plus I figured it'd be good to get away for a bit."

"You could have told me."

"Sorry, man. It was last minute."

"Alright. Well, I guess I'm taking Craig with me. See you tonight?"

"Actually, I'm gonna crash at home."

"Noah . . . you know you shouldn't be sitting in that house alone."

"I won't be. Gracie's coming back to Texas for a while and she needed a place to stay, so she's staying there too."

"Oh yeah?" A pause. "What's she like?"

"She's a firecracker, is what she is." It would have been so much less complicated for me had I left her in Tucson.

"As hot as one, too?"

I chuckle. "It's not like that."

"So . . . she's hot, then." I can hear the grin in his voice. "How hot? Scale of one to your-hand-is-getting-sore."

"Don't be a dick."

"Come on . . ."

I grin. "She's hot as hell. She's got this wild, curly hair, and these green eyes. And a body—"

The passenger door behind me opens, startling me.

"What about her body?" Jenson presses.

"I've gotta go."

"You'll be at tomorrow's pickup game, right?"

"Probably not." I hang up before he has a chance to bust my balls.

Cyclops jumps up onto the backseat, his tail wagging as he peers at me through his one eye.

"He's getting used to his leash." Gracie gives his head a scratch.

"He's a whole new dog." His once matted fur is soft and fluffy and almost inviting to touch.

I watch her round the hood of my Jeep. Maybe she didn't hear me talking to Jenson.

"Are you sure you can drive?" she asks as she climbs in. "That *five-hour* nap may not have been enough for you."

I smile at her sarcasm. "I feel great. You should grab a few hours, too."

"This body doesn't need it."

I crank the engine and take a few extra seconds to check my side-view mirror, waiting for my cheeks to cool.

She heard me talking to Jenson alright.

A twelve-hour road trip with any one person can feel like an eternity, especially when you're driving hundreds of miles through uncivilized desert and forced to either talk or listen to a static-filled country-music radio station.

And yet hundreds of miles with Gracie hasn't been painful at all. Maybe that's because we've taken turns being unconscious through most of it.

It's only now that we're attempting conversation.

"This is a whole lot of nothing," Gracie murmurs, taking in the strip of gas stations as we make our way through *another* sleepy town.

"It's not the most exciting drive."

She groans and stretches her legs out on the dashboard. "Forget the drive. I don't know how anyone could live out here. What do you do with your time besides sleep and drink?" She nods at a derelict-looking Mexican restaurant. "And eat tacos."

Each time we pass a streetlight, it casts a glow over her shapely bare legs. "Not much," I agree, stealing a glance every chance I get.

"I won't miss serving queso and chips, that's for sure."

"How'd you leave the job situation, by the way?"

"I told them I'm going out of town."

"And?" Sometimes getting Gracie to answer questions is like pulling teeth. I can't tell if it's because she can't be bothered to talk about herself, or she doesn't trust me with personal information, or her head is too wrapped up in other thoughts.

"They said to come by and see them when I'm back in Tucson. If they haven't filled my spot, then it's mine." She snorts. "So much for being a highly valued employee. QuikTrip even gave me a raise last month. A whole fifteen cents more per hour."

I whistle mockingly. "I'm sure you'll find something new easily enough."

"Yeah, I'm not worried. I mean, there are Aunt Chilada's everywhere. Did you know my mom worked at one in Austin? Wouldn't that be funny? If I decided to stay in Texas and worked at the same one?"

Gracie, staying in Texas? What would make her want to do that? Especially with everything that happened to her father. Though I can see why she doesn't hold much love for Tucson, either.

"How did Dina end up in Texas, anyway?"

"She took off for Austin with a friend when she was seventeen. She had these grand plans of marrying into a Texas oil family. You know, get far away from her trailer-trash childhood. Anyway, my dad pulled her over for speeding one day. She cried and told him that they'd fire her if she was late to work again. She promised she'd never speed again if he let her go. It actually worked. He let her go with a warning.

"That same night, he showed up at the restaurant after his shift and asked to sit in her section. He wanted to make sure she hadn't been fired. They got to talking and . . . by the end of her shift, she knew he was the one. She got pregnant with me three months later, and they got married straightaway."

"That's a great story."

"Yeah." She picks at a thread on her shirt. "When I was little, my mom would hold me in her arms at night and tell me all kinds of great stories about him. Those were the good old days, when I thought he'd died in an accident."

Meanwhile Dina buried the dark, scary truths deep inside, until they began rotting away at her.

We pass a highway road sign for Austin.

"Only two more hours, right?" Gracie asks, and I swear I hear a tremor in her voice.

I navigate the familiar streets, a conflicting sense of emptiness and relief building as I turn into our neighborhood, and then into our quiet cul-de-sac. *My* quiet cul-de-sac soon. It's strange to say that.

"Home sweet home."

Gracie's gaze rolls over my darkened house, which by comparison to what she came from is a palace. "It's nice."

I turn off the engine and rest my hands on my lap for a moment, staring at the covered front porch. I wonder if I'll ever be able to look at it again without seeing yellow police tape around it.

From the backseat, Cyclops gets to his feet, having spent most of the ride belly up and snoring like a lap dog. "So there are a couple of neighborhood cats around here . . ."

"He's never actually killed a cat, as far as I know." Gracie sees the look on my face and huffs. "I'll keep him on the leash."

"He can run free in the backyard, as long as he doesn't dig under the fence." I slide out of the driver's seat and stretch my sore legs. I collect our bags from the back.

"I'm capable of carrying my own bag." Gracie holds her hand out.

I put on an extra-heavy Texas drawl to mock her. "Not in Texas you aren't, little lady." That earns me an eye roll, but also a ghost of a smile. She doesn't argue further, trailing me along the stone path, her shoes dragging. I can't tell if that's due to weariness or reluctance.

"My mom said our house in Austin was nice."

"You had a deep backyard," I confirm, my keys jangling in the quiet night. "And a big-ass Texas state flag—"

"Hanging from the porch. He hung it before they even stepped inside, the day the Realtor gave them the keys. He was so proud to be a Texan. She took it with us when we moved." Gracie adds in a softer voice, "It's gone now."

I sense the melancholy slipping in and I'm desperate to chase it away. "He had a basketball net on the garage door. That's where I learned how to play. And there was this one day, I was dribbling the ball out there after school and the neighbors called the cops for a noise complaint. Your dad showed up with his partner, and then my mom showed up, along with another cruiser of cops. They all started playing in the driveway, in their uniforms." I smile at the memory. "Three on three. Even my mom, who couldn't dribble a ball to save her life."

"Did the neighbors ever complain again?"

"If they did, I never heard about it. Abe told me to keep on playing because it meant I was staying out of trouble." Every once in a while I still hear his booming voice, telling me to keep my eyes up, to dribble low, to use my body to block.

I climb the front steps to the porch and unlock the door. I step aside so she can let Cyclops off his leash. He takes off through the house as I disarm the alarm system, his nose to the tile. "Go ahead, make yourself at home," I say mockingly, but to be honest, it's nice to have a dog in the house again. Mom and I had talked about getting another dog when I moved back, but neither of us could commit to the kind of schedule it would need.

I wonder what he smells. The forty or so boots and shoes that have traipsed through here in the last few weeks? The bleach mixture used to scour the kitchen and remove the blood?

Or maybe it's the faint scent of lilac—my mother's favorite—from the plug-in air fresheners. It still lingers, even weeks after the oil has burned up.

A strange silence settles over us as Gracie's eyes travel down the long hall toward the kitchen, her arms folding tightly as if she feels a chill. "Does it feel weird being here, after . . . ?" She drifts off.

"I can't stand being here," I answer honestly. "Being in the kitchen is the worst, especially at night. I've only been back three times since she died."

Gracie bites her bottom lip. "So if I hadn't come, where would you have stayed?"

"I was supposed to move to my uncle Silas's this week." He's going to have a thing or two to say about me bringing Gracie back with me. I'm not looking forward to that conversation. Then again, I'm sure he'll be easily distracted when I tell him about Klein.

"So I messed up your plans."

"Not at all. Follow me." I show her to her room upstairs, setting her bag inside the door. "The guest bathroom is there." I nod to the bedroom opposite hers. "And that's mine."

She eyes my door, but doesn't say anything.

"I'm gonna crash. Do you need anything?"

"A glass of water."

I open my mouth to offer to get it for her, even though I'd rather run headfirst into a wall than go into that kitchen right now.

"It's okay. I can get it for myself. Remember? Independent woman."

"Right." I watch her descend the stairs with slow, measured steps.

But I don't have the guts to follow her.

Mom kept meticulous records—paperwork filed neatly, spending tracked thoroughly.

How thoroughly, though, I wonder, as I've just spent two hours sifting through the tall filing cabinet in her office.

Did she account for *all* her money?

Will there be something in these folders that explains the ninety-eight thousand dollars that she left to Gracie? Something that proves it *isn't* tied to that drug bust?

If there is, I haven't found it. All I've found are tax returns that look legitimate and three years of her personal spending records that match her salary on the police force.

"You couldn't sleep either?" Grace's voice cuts into the eerie silence, startling me enough that I jump. "Sorry." She leans against the door frame, her smooth legs crossing at the ankles, her arms crossing at her chest. Her shorts and tank top leave just enough to the imagination. Even at three a.m., my blood begins to race.

It doesn't help that I can feel her intense gaze drag over my body.

Had I known she was going to show up, I would have thrown on pants over my boxer briefs.

I smoothly slide Klein's business cards into the top drawer. I'll tell her about him *after* I talk to Silas. "I thought I'd do a few quick online searches for your aunt. Get those out of the way." The same rudimentary steps I take when I'm searching for people in my job. I hit up Google, all the major social media sites, a few people-search databases. Two Betsy Richardses and two dozen Elizabeth Richardses turned up, but nothing promising yet.

She nods toward the file folder in my hand marked *Visa*, a knowing smile touching her lips. "You're still holding out hope about that money, aren't you?"

"I was just looking for . . . I don't know what I was looking for." I sigh, flipping it open. Every month reads mostly the same—weekly grocery shopping, gas, maintenance on her BMW, stops at local restaurants to grab lunches. Mom paid for everything on her card. She liked to collect points for that big trip she talked about taking one day. Where to, she couldn't decide.

A line item catches my notice.

A charge at a gas station in El Paso.

I keep scrolling through the statement—from two months ago—to find a hotel charge in Tucson.

"What is it?" Gracie asks, stepping farther into the room.

"Did your mother mention my mom coming to see her?"

Gracie frowns in thought. "No."

"You sure? Maybe when she was high and you assumed she was making up things?"

"*I* wasn't the one who was high." Understanding passes over Gracie's face. "Your mom came to Tucson, didn't she?"

"For one night, back in February." The same weekend that Jenson and I flew to Colorado Springs to go snowboarding.

"Why didn't she give us the money then?"

"I tried to make it right. But I couldn't even face her. I couldn't face what I'd done to her; what I'd made her become."

"Because she was a coward," I whisper, sliding the bill back where it was and shutting the filing cabinet. So far, everything she said that last night, though seemingly incoherent, ties to the truth.

Based on her call to Klein, my mother knew Mantis killed Abe and she did nothing about it. The question is, why? If I figure that out, then maybe I can distract the feds from wondering why I lied to the police in the first place. Maybe I can keep my mother's name—and her own admissions of guilt—out of this. But in order to do that, I need information.

Tomorrow . . . I've had enough truth for today. "Let's go to bed."

Gracie's eyebrow lifts with surprise, making me replay my choice of words and then cringe, as I brace myself for the sharp-tongued rejection I've come to expect from her.

"Good night, Noah." She disappears down the hall, into her room.

I shake my head, the smile slipping out despite the somber mood. "'Night, Gracie."

CHAPTER 28

Officer Abraham Wilkes

April 24, 2003

"Mike!" I clasp hands with the officer sitting behind the desk. "Where have you been all summer, besides *not* on the court?"

"In hell." He gestures to the brace around his knee, frustration filling his round face.

"Still?" Mike Rhoades tore his MCL chasing down punks who'd robbed a convenience store months ago and, it appears, is still on light administrative duty.

"It was this place or answering phones. Either way . . . great for the waistline." He pats his growing stomach to emphasize his sarcasm.

"So? How is it down here?" I rattle the fence partition that surrounds the desk. It's part of the evidence room's security measures.

He shrugs, then offers a wan smile. "They let me out to see daylight every once in a while."

"Damn, man. Hope you're back on the road soon."

"You and me both. Definitely before they upgrade this computer system. I don't want anything to do with that mess." He sees that I've come empty-handed. "So what are you doing down here?"

I glance over my shoulder to make sure no one's behind me. "You know that big bust over at The Lucky Nine the other night?"

"Who doesn't? Canning wants to give Mantis a commendation for that one."

"Yeah, I heard." I hesitate. "Can you tell me what was logged in for evidence?"

His bushy eyebrow pops up, making me think that I'm overstepping our long-standing friendship.

"Or, at least, how much cash came in with the drugs?"

"Who's asking?"

"I am."

After a long pause, Mike shifts his attention to his computer and begins tapping the keys. I wait quietly, watching his gaze as it scrolls down the screen.

His head shakes slightly. "No cash. A shit-ton of drugs, four guns . . . no cash." His green eyes flicker to me. "Why?"

"Just a hunch."

More like a glaring understanding about how Canning's prize-winning hounds are operating.

CHAPTER 29

Grace

Cyclops growls at the strange bird caw.

I scratch behind his ear to settle him, and he relaxes against my side once again. "I know, buddy. Weird, right?" I snuck out to the back porch to huddle in this wicker chair and watch the sunrise half an hour ago and in that time we've listened to ten of the bluish-black crows singing back and forth to each other, Cyclops's mangled ear twitching this way and that.

Otherwise, it's been peacefully quiet out here, giving me a chance to gather my thoughts with a view of Jackie Marshall's backyard, an urban oasis of large trees and border gardens surrounding a kidney-shaped pool, and a gate in the fence to a park beyond. It's paradise.

What would my life have been like, had my father not died? Would I have grown up in a quiet suburb with gardens and trees?

I've often wondered that through the years.

"Who were you, *really,* Jackie Marshall?" I whisper into the morning quiet.

Everything is so meticulous. The gardens are cared for and bursting with spring blooms; the pool is crystal clear, the stone around it pristine. Inside is a house full of order, a palette of beige, creams, and coral, everything from the clean-line furniture to the knick-knacks flowing seamlessly. Cookbooks sit in neat stacks on shelves, the spines barely cracked. Cute "hearth and home" signs hang from hooks on the wall, welcoming family and friends. It all makes me conjure a version of the blonde Texan woman who doesn't leave the house without a pristinely made face and a stylish outfit, who offers sweet tea to every guest before they have a chance to cross the door's threshold, who hums while she putters in the kitchen, her apron on to protect her clothes.

And she raised Noah, who, by any standards, is the most decent guy I've ever met.

But Jackie Marshall was also the chief of police and an abuser of whiskey.

And had a giant bag of money for her dead partner's daughter but didn't have the guts to deliver it herself.

And she blew her brains out on the other side of this French door, with her son upstairs.

As far as I know, I've never been in a house where someone committed suicide. I wonder if the hairs on my neck would have stood on end when I stepped in that kitchen last night had I not known for a fact that's where Jackie died. I was happy to fill a glass of water and get the hell back to my room, unsettled by the eerie silence.

I hear someone—I assume Noah—shifting around in the kitchen. Just the idea of seeing him stirs nerves in my stomach. I heard what he said about me to his friend over the phone yesterday. But what does it mean? More importantly, what do I *want* it to mean?

This is Noah. *Jackie Marshall's* son . . .

Noah is his own person. He's not Jackie.

But he wants to protect her—a woman who, at the very least, knew my father had been set up and never did anything about it. How do I get past that?

I do like Noah, though. More with each passing day.

But I've never been that girl who loves too much, too fast, too soon. That girl gets hurt too much, too fast, too soon.

So, I stay in my chair, sipping the last of my coffee and enjoying the sun cresting over a tall maple tree, not rushing in like some lovestruck dimwit.

It's the smell of sizzling bacon that finally lures me through the doors.

But it's the view that stops me in my tracks.

Noah's standing in front of the stove, dressed in a pair of dark-wash jeans and a white T-shirt, the cotton stretched over his broad shoulders, his hair slightly damp from a shower. "Ow!" He flinches and steps away, brushing a bubble of grease from his sinewy forearm.

"You need an apron."

He glances over his shoulder, giving my body a quick once-over. He does that a lot. Not in a leery way. In a way that makes my heart pound. "Oh, hey. There isn't much food, but there's bacon. I know you love that."

"Here. Let me." I slip the fork from his hand, our fingertips grazing, the scent of his soap overtaking the food smells, stirring my blood.

"What time did you get up?"

"Too early. Cy needed to go out."

He drops two slices of bread into the toaster. "Did you get a coffee?"

"Yeah. After I spent twenty minutes trying to figure out how to use *that*." I give the high-tech machine a dirty look.

Noah checks his watch. "Alright. I locked up the cash in the safe. I'll be back in a bit."

"Uh . . ." I frown, and gesture at the stove.

"I was making that for you."

Of course you were. I stifle my groan. Mom said my dad was like that, bringing her coffee in bed, making her breakfast. Is that a Texas thing? Or a nice-guy thing?

Or can he not handle being in this kitchen for another second?

In any case, I see what he's trying to do. "You're not leaving me here while you go talk to Harvey Maxwell."

"I'll be back soon, I promise. And I'll grab groceries on the way."

"I'm going with you."

"He's a good guy—"

"Let's find out how he was connected to my father before you go throwing around the 'good guy' label, okay? Harvey Maxwell might be the mastermind."

Noah chuckles. "Trust me, he's not. I have to do this on my own."

"So you can protect more people for what they might have helped do to my father?"

Noah averts his gaze to the floor, and I feel a twinge of guilt. I need to remember the difficult position he's in when I lash out at him.

"This is about my father, so we're in this together, *all the way*."

"It's just . . . my mother said something that night, about it being safer not to ask questions. And I promised your mother I'd keep you safe."

"Did you happen to notice where I've been living for the past fourteen years?" I can't help the sharpness in my voice. "I don't need you protecting me. I can take care of myself."

The doorbell rings then, interrupting our argument, which is far from over.

I check the stove clock with a frown. "It's seven thirty in the morning. Who would come to your door this early?"

It rings again, three times in quick succession, and Noah groans.

CHAPTER 30

Noah

"Three . . . two . . ." I count down quietly, my hand on the knob, " . . . and let the ball-busting begin."

"As if I'd let you bail on me." Jenson's dressed in his usual shorts and T-shirt. He's even got his basketball tucked under his arm, ready to go.

"I can't today. I've got a lot to do."

"I'll bet." He gives me a knowing look.

"I told you, it's not like that."

He holds up his hands in surrender. "All right! Me and Candace are hooking up later. You should come out. Dana was asking about you."

"Nah, I'm good." It sounds bad, but I haven't thought about Candace's friend for weeks.

"Why not?" Jenson's face is full of mock innocence. "It's a guaranteed lay, and God knows you could use one."

I grit my teeth and glance over my shoulder. Jenson has a booming voice, the kind that carries down a hallway and right to a girl's ears.

My move gives him the perfect chance to shove his way past me, muttering, "Knew it," as he stalks down the hall to the kitchen. He stops at the doorway and takes in Gracie.

Her back is to him as she butters fresh toast, her slender arm flexing. "Hello, Noah's loud friend," she says without turning.

"Hello, girl cooking in Noah's kitchen," Jenson responds with a wide smirk, his eyes trailing downward, stalling on her little cotton shorts. She may have one of the most perfect asses I've ever seen and my friend is admiring it.

Gracie uses a fork to pile strips of bacon onto her plate. "Do you always stare?"

"I don't know. I've never met a girl that can keep Marshall from playing ball. I'm not sure you're real."

"I can come over and punch you, if that'll make you a believer."

Jenson laughs. He thinks this is a game. He thinks she's joking. I think she still has that knife in her purse.

With a sigh of exasperation, she finally turns around to size Jenson up with her cool mint-green eyes, her wild, curly hair a sexy halo around her perfect face.

His grin only widens. "Hi, I'm Jenson."

"Hi, Jenson. I'm sorry Noah won't come out and play with you today."

"Oh, he will. For at least five minutes, unless he wants me to start telling the hot girl in his kitchen all kinds of mortifying stories. Like this one time . . ."

With her plate in her hand, Gracie strolls over to the French door to allow Cyclops in.

Jenson's face twists up, suitably distracted. "What the fuck is that?"

"Noah's new dog. Isn't he cute?"

"No, he's not even ugly cute. He's plain ugly."

"I'm going to change. Don't you dare leave without me, Noah." With one last warning glare my way, she heads up the stairs, Jenson's gaze on her the entire way.

He lets out a soft whistle. "Firecracker is right."

I sigh. Why did I think she'd let me get away with ducking out on her?

"Sounds like you've got a few minutes to kill." Jenson spins the ball on the tip of his finger.

I could use his ear. Grabbing the ball from his hands, I head toward the front door, happy to be out of that kitchen. "Five minutes. But don't piss off my neighbors."

"So she's the reason I haven't seen you since Thursday?"

Jenson bounces the ball at a steady, slow rhythm. The sound isn't too bad, but the dirty look I got from Mr. Stiles, as he left his seat on his front porch to read his newspaper inside, tells me it's a nuisance all the same.

Jenson's been my best friend since the first grade. He's also like a dog on a bone when he wants something. "Yeah, but it's not what you think."

"For the record, I call bullshit. But if you're telling the truth, then you're an idiot." Jenson's arms go up and the ball sails over my head and through the basketball net. It bounces back, and no sooner has he grabbed it than he throws it to me. I automatically reach for it, dribble and shoot, the action as unconscious for me as breathing is.

"She didn't come here because of me."

"What's she doing here, then?"

"It's a long story." Where the hell do I even start?

The front door creaks open and out comes Gracie, dressed in jean shorts and a white T-shirt, her hair still a wild frame around her fresh face. She doesn't wear makeup, I've noticed. She doesn't need to.

"Eat, Noah." She holds up a sandwich, wrapped in a napkin.

"Marry this girl or I will," Jenson moans, following with a fake-out and spin, tossing the ball clean into the net again. "Hey Gracie, you wanna play?"

"Nope," Gracie mumbles between a mouthful.

"Come on. Don't be afraid. I'll go easy on you."

She settles onto the back bumper of my Cherokee. "I hate basketball."

Jenson dribbles past me, muttering, "Cut bait. It'll never work between you two."

I shake my head, giving Gracie an apologetic smile. She responds with an indifferent shrug, her gaze doing a lightning-quick scan of my chest.

"So, why are you here?" Jenson asks with zero ounces of tact, the ball smoothly sailing through the net again.

She gives me a high-browed stare that says, *You tell him what you want him to hear.*

"Like I said, it's a long story."

The problem with Jenson is, he may act like a beer-guzzling goof, but he's a smart son of a bitch whose brain is usually working a mile a minute. "Noah said Jackie left something for you?"

Gracie chews and calmly studies him the way she once studied me, with complete mistrust.

Finally, I offer, "Money, to help out."

"Really . . ." He stops dribbling and closes in, dropping his voice. "Is that why you guys are acting cagey?"

Gracie and I share a glance.

"Dude . . . *Come on.*" He throws his hands out.

"My mom said some things before she died that made it sound like Gracie's dad wasn't selling or stealing drugs."

My Cherokee sinks as Jenson leans down against the rear bumper beside Gracie. "What, like someone pinned it on him?"

"She wasn't exactly clear, but yeah." I hesitate. "And there may have been cops involved. At least one." I walk him through what we know of Mantis, and the Lucky Nine drug bust, and what Dina told us. And, while I haven't come clean with Gracie about my mother's phone call to Klein yet, I throw out the idea that *maybe* Abe was killed because he saw cops stealing money at a bust and *maybe* one of those cops was Mantis.

Because maybe Jenson can make better sense of this than I can.

He absently rotates the basketball within his grasp. "Ninety-eight thousand dollars."

"Exactly."

He lets out a whistle. "So you're gonna talk to this Maxwell guy, right?"

"That's where I was heading before you showed up."

"Where *we* were heading," Gracie corrects sharply.

"And you don't wanna go to the APD with this?"

I give him a knowing look. "Mantis runs Internal Affairs."

"That shouldn't stop you. Most of them are honorable cops who'd risk their lives for complete strangers any day of the week. Don't let a few corrupt pieces of shit stop you from trusting them."

Corrupt pieces of shit like my mom, maybe.

I feel Gracie's eyes on my profile and tension slides into my shoulders. "We'll see what Maxwell knows and go from there."

"You're probably better off going to the feds anyway. You must have an in with them, through your job?"

I avert my gaze. I have an in all right, thanks to the asshole stalking me. By my watch, if Klein was serious, then I have another sixteen hours before he comes knocking again. I'm not even as worried about that as I am about what Gracie's going to say when she finds out I'm still keeping things from her.

Jenson nods slowly, his mind working. "The cops didn't find the video." He says it so matter-of-factly.

I frown. "Why do you say that?"

"Logic. Gracie's mom tells the cops about this video and then suddenly a guy—who she thinks is a cop—comes looking for it. That makes me think someone working on the case tipped him off. And if this guy came to look for it—"

"The police didn't find it on the computer." I finally catch on to Jenson's thinking. "It had to be an external file. A memory stick or something. Wait, did they even have memory sticks fourteen years ago?"

"Good question. I honestly don't know how people survived back then, without all—"

"Why wouldn't they have found this memory stick—or whatever—when they searched the house?" Gracie, always quick to poke holes in theories, interrupts.

"Because it wasn't in the house," Jenson says, simply. "Abe must have known how valuable it was. Maybe he'd already been threatened. You need to find this video."

"No problem. Just find a video that my dad hid fourteen years ago," Gracie mutters sarcastically.

"He must have given it to someone he trusted."

"He didn't give it to my mom," Gracie says. "And he and Jackie were at odds, so it's not likely he gave it to her."

"I didn't find anything that even remotely resembles a video file in the safe, or in that floor compartment," I add. "So, who's left?"

Jenson shrugs. And then he says, almost as an afterthought, "Not that a video of cops lifting money would be any good now, anyway."

Gracie glares at him. "Why the hell not?"

"The statute of limitations would have run out years ago. But it could prove motive to something bigger," Jenson quickly adds, looking ready to hold up his hands in surrender against her scathing look.

"Like what?"

"Like motive for murder. And there's no statute of limitations on that."

Jenson's right, as usual. That doesn't bring me much comfort, though. We'll probably have better luck finding Betsy than we will this video.

Could she be somehow tied to it?

So many questions.

But talking to Jenson has helped. "Thanks, man."

His phone chirps. "Listen, I've gotta go. Candace needs a ride to school."

"Little sister?" Gracie asks.

"Girlfriend. She's in her first year at UT."

"He likes 'em young." I smirk, taking a bite of my sandwich.

"I'm not the only one from the looks of it," Jenson throws back, not missing a beat. "You know, we should all go out while you're in town. I think you'd like her."

"Like a double date? How fun!" Gracie exclaims with a wide,

fake grin. She hauls herself up, the bubbly façade vanishing. "We should get going. I'll get Cyclops."

"We can't bring a dog to the DA's office."

"We'll leave him in your car. It's cool enough."

"So he can finish destroying the leather? No, we're leaving him in the yard."

"Fine," she mutters, marching inside.

I snatch the ball from Jenson's hands and dribble for the net.

He's on his feet and stealing it off me without effort, mainly because I let him. He dekes and edges around me, sinking the ball. "So, when are you gonna put the moves on the firecracker?"

"Kind of busy trying to solve a cover-up and murder at the moment." But that's Jenson—always looking for a way to get laid, no matter the situation.

"Right . . ." Jenson begins strutting around me with folded, flapping arms, making chicken sounds.

CHAPTER 31

Officer Abraham Wilkes

April 24, 2003

"Better luck next time!" Mantis hollers from the door of the men's changing room, grinning widely as he strolls in. "Not a bad game, Wilkes." He raises his hand to deliver a fist-bump.

Normally I'd respond by reminding him how many points I scored, which is always triple what he earned, at minimum. Today, I stay quiet, hesitating a few beats before finally meeting his knuckles.

If he notices my reluctance, he doesn't let on.

I bide my time, waiting until the last two guys are gone, leaving us alone in the room. "Saw the news on the big bust."

"Fucking awesome haul, right?" He yanks off his jersey. The guy is a human tank—stocky legs and a thick pad of muscle around his torso, impossible to knock down. "We got a good tip."

"Strange, though, that you didn't find money, isn't it? Where there's drugs, there's cash, I thought."

Mantis rifles through his locker for a few beats. "He was moving his stash and decided he needed to get a little action on the way. What can I say—the guy's as dumb as a prairie dog."

"So, he didn't have a duffel bag of money in his trunk?"

That sloped forehead of his looks all the more menacing as a deep frown forms across it. "What are you gettin' at, Wilkes?"

"Just that I was at the Lucky Nine motel that night."

He snorts, then rubs his nostrils furiously. The word is he's broken it so many times, his sense of smell doesn't work. That's the only excuse anyone can come up with for how much cheap cologne he doses himself with every day. “What, Dina not giving you enough at home?”

I bite my tongue against the urge to cuss him out for mentioning my wife’s name. “I was looking for someone. But that’s beside the point. I was there, sittin’ in my car and watchin’ the *whole* show go down. Surprised you didn’t notice me.”

Mantis throws a towel around his waist to cover his nakedness. “Then you know that guy is right where he deserves to be.”

“And the money? Is that right where it deserves to be?” *Under your mattress?*

He chuckles softly, but there’s an edge to the sound. “You’re mistaken. There was no cash in the trunk.”

“That’s not what I saw.”

“Good luck proving that.”

Cocky bastard. I grab my backpack and march out before I do something I’ll regret, like hit the guy.

I have my answer.

CHAPTER 32

Noah

"That last hair I was nurturing?" Rolans points to his shiny, bald head. "Gone, since you left us. But don't worry, we've got a shit-ton of mind-numbing work, piling up for you. Best of three on who gets him first." He's poised for a round of rock-paper-scissors with Maxwell, standing next to him.

Despite my purpose for being here, I can't help but chuckle. When Silas first suggested I apply for a job at the DA's office, I figured it'd be all stiff lawyers and miserable government workers who hate their lives and their jobs. It's far from that. These two may be pushing their midforties, but they act like a couple of frat boys.

It *does* feel comforting to be here. Even my cramped cubicle doesn't look so mundane. Someone has tidied it and set a Twix candy bar by my keyboard. Cory, my manager, likely. She knows I love them.

If only I could sit down in my chair and go back to the way things were.

"I'm actually not here to work."

Maxwell is subdued as he shakes my hand, the guarded look on his face telling me he remembers why I've been gone in the first place. "You just missed Silas. He left for court five minutes ago." His gaze settles on Gracie, forcing me to make quick introductions.

"Actually, Maxwell, I'm here to talk to you, too."

"Me?" He looks genuinely surprised.

I swallow against my growing anxiety. How exactly is the right way to bring this up? "Yes, sir. It's about a—"

"Forget something?" Rolans's voice booms, cutting me off. I turn to find Silas making his way toward us, his limp more noticeable than usual, his face looking gaunt.

"A file." Silas's gray eyes—lined with deep, dark bags—are locked on me. "Noah . . . you're back."

"Yes, sir. I got home late last night."

His gaze shifts behind me and my stomach instantly tightens. "Silas, this is Gracie. I mean, Grace."

"I had a feeling it was . . ." He holds out a weathered hand. "Goodness, you have grown a lot since I saw you last."

"It's definitely been a while," Gracie says warily, and I know she's picking through her memories, trying to place him as she accepts the greeting.

"I hope my nephew is showing you around town?"

"If the DA's office counts as sightseeing?"

"Knowing him, it probably does." Silas chuckles. To anyone else, it sounds normal. But I can hear the strain. "Noah, can I see you in my office for a moment?"

"But, I thought you had court—"

"Maxwell, would you show Grace to the staff lounge? I'm sure she'd love a coffee or a cold drink."

Shit. The last thing I want to do is leave Gracie alone with Maxwell, given her tendency to be, well, her. "I'll be there in a minute." I shoot her a warning look—one that I hope says to keep quiet until I get there.

She spears me with one of her own—I'm not sure what it means—before she lets Maxwell lead her away.

"So?" Silas leads me into his office and shuts the door. "Good trip to Tucson?"

"For what it was."

"How's Dina? Did you get her settled?"

"Yes, sir. In a good place."

"I'm glad," he says through a sip of his coffee as he rounds his desk. "And you've made a new friend?"

"It's not like that."

"I hope it's *exactly* like that, Noah. Why else did you bring Abe's daughter back to Austin with you?" Silas doesn't have to yell to let me know he's disappointed in me for not listening to him, and even though I have good reason, I *hate* disappointing him.

Where do I even start? "Dina knows things, Silas. About Abe and what really happened."

"Dina is a drug addict."

"She is, but—"

"You can't trust what she thinks she remembers from fourteen years ago. Her brains have been scrambled."

"No, Silas. I mean, yes, maybe. But if you heard what happened to her, you'd know there's a lot more going on here."

"For God's sake!" He pinches the bridge of his nose. "I went down this road fourteen years ago and let me tell you, it leads to nothing but pain and suffering. It killed Carmel Wilkes! Day by day, ate her up until her body said enough! And Dina Wilkes?" He waves a hand as if nothing more needs to be said. "Hell, even your mother was never the same again. Look . . . I know you want to believe this, Noah, but you can't do this to yourself. You can't do this to that poor girl out there. She has been through enough!"

"But what if there's evidence—"

"I *saw all* the evidence myself! I lost days of sleep, scouring over every piece, looking for *anything* that could point to another explanation. Abraham Wilkes was guilty, guilty, guilty!" He punctuates each "guilty" with a finger-jab to his desk.

"Or you only know what they wanted you to know!" I match his raised voice as I parrot my mother's words. "Silas, Mom called the feds the night she killed herself. She told them that it was all a lie and that Dwayne Mantis killed Abe!"

"How . . . how do you know that?" Unease fills Silas's face.

"Because the damn feds were in Tucson, looking to talk to Dina, and they found me. I heard the voice message. It was *her*, Silas."

"She was drunk and suicidal. She didn't—"

"Abe had a video that someone didn't want getting out."

He pauses, and I swear, his face pales two shades. "A video?"

"Yes. Of a police bust."

He checks his watch. "Okay, start talking, and fast."

Silas eyes the decanter of scotch he keeps in the corner of his bookshelf. For a minute, he looks ready to pour himself a glass. "I always figured Dina up and ran in the night like that because she knew Abe was guilty."

Relief overwhelms me. My uncle hasn't dismissed it as crazy talk by an addict. Yet. "Whoever did this ruined her life. And Gracie's."

"And Dina couldn't tell you *anything* about this man who broke into her house?"

"No. Other than that he was scary. And she has no idea where this video went. But I was talking to Jenson and—"

"You've told your *friends* about this?" His face twists with horror. "Are you insane?"

"Jenson's not going to say anything. And listen! If this guy who threatened her was a cop, or had an in with the cops, then the video must not have turned up from the search. Dina told them about it, so they would have been looking for it, right?"

"There was no video file entered into evidence from the search," he confirms.

"That means it's still out there."

"Fourteen years later?" His expression is grim as he turns away from me to stare listlessly out the window. "I'm guessing it's long gone."

"What are we going to do, Silas?"

"What *can* we do? We have none of the original case evidence, no video, and nothing except the claims of the heroin-addict wife and the incoherent ramblings of a suicidal, drunk woman. Where did you find this money and gun holster, by the way? It wasn't in the safe."

I tell him about Fulcher and the secret compartment in the pantry.

"A five-thousand-dollar gun safe and she's burrowing under the floorboards like a damn gopher." He shakes his head, then sighs. "I'm not about to hang your mother out to dry. She's not here to defend herself if some of this lands on her."

"Neither is Abe."

He points a finger in warning. "She did not do this to him, Noah."

"Then why does she have a bag full of money that has to be from a drug bust *and* Abe's gun holster—which Dina swears Abe left with on the night he died? She *knew* there had been a setup and she didn't do anything about it! And the only reason for that is because she had something to do with it." It's time I stop denying that reality, time that I stop protecting her. Gracie is right—Abe deserves better from me. And my mother . . . well, maybe she deserves whatever comes with the truth.

Silas takes a deep breath, his own agitation having risen. "Maybe she only found out recently. Maybe someone threatened her, had something on her. Or maybe she had to accept that knowing something and being able to prove it are two entirely different things. I have no idea, Noah, but I won't risk moving a guilty label off one innocent dead person, only to stick it onto another innocent dead person, especially given that the latter is my sister. And that's exactly what will happen here. How do we know the person responsible for Abe's death didn't hand her that bag of money and that gun holster?"

"We don't, but—"

"Corruption, followed by murder and a cover-up in the APD? Do you know what this would do to the department's reputation if it got out? We can't throw these kinds of accusations around, based on speculation."

"This isn't speculation! Mom knew about it!"

"But she couldn't prove it; she said so herself. 'I don't know how he did it.' You can't put Mantis's feet to the fire based on that, when your own mother is the one with evidence against her!" He snorts derisively. "And here we are, about to give Canning his own monument in part for the wins that Mantis himself delivered."

"So it's better to let people go on thinking Abe was guilty? All because of some stupid statue?"

"George Canning put his heart and soul into this city. The job damn near killed him! I don't want all the good he did getting tarnished, any more than I want your mother's name dragged through the mud."

His words from last week trigger a thought. I hesitate for only a second before I ask, "What if Canning knew about it?"

Silas glares at me. "George Canning is a good and honorable man. He would have hung Mantis by his trunk of a neck in a city square had Mantis jeopardized those busts with a case of sticky fingers and Canning found out. Don't you even suggest something different." He rubs furiously at his eyes. "I have to think about this. Give me time, Noah. Stop talking to other people about it and give me some damn time." Silas is cursing. He curses only when he's rattled.

"Well, I only have the day before Agent Klein comes at me again." I tell him about the threat of a homicide investigation.

By the time I'm done, he's staring at me with a gaping jaw. "You *punched* an FBI agent?"

"You had to be there . . ." I mutter, feeling my cheeks flare with shame.

Silas shakes his head. "He was trying to scare you. He could never make a case against you. Not for homicide, anyway. But don't say another word to him until he's formally hauled you in for questioning and you have a good lawyer."

We sit in defeated silence. There's no quick thinking this time, no formulating a plan. Silas seems as lost as I feel.

"What am I supposed to tell Gracie?"

"Nothing. I warned you not to say anything in the first place."

"I hadn't planned on it. Things just got out of hand, quickly. And she's not going to back down until her father's name is cleared."

"Well, she had better learn patience because *if* this is true, and Mantis killed Abe to protect himself from being busted for corruption . . . what do you think he'll do to avoid getting nailed with murder?"

A chill runs down my spine. "Gracie doesn't have anything on him."

"Let's make sure he doesn't think otherwise, because word gets around, fast. So go, show Grace around the city, take her shopping, hang out by your pool . . . do *whatever* a twenty-five-year-old guy needs to do to keep a pretty girl occupied on things that pretty girls *should* be occupied with."

I want to tell him that Gracie's not the type to throw on a bikini and lie out in the sun to get away from her troubles. But I simply nod.

He frowns. "What were you two coming here for, anyway? You knew I had court this morning."

In my rush to tell Silas everything, I realize that I forgot to mention Maxwell's connection. But something tells me that Silas will forbid me from stepping within a hundred feet of his ADA. And if I can't talk to Maxwell, then I'm stuck wondering, and thinking the worst about yet another person in my life. I'd rather plead forgiveness than ask permission as far as Maxwell goes. "I wanted to check the database for arrest records for Betsy, if you don't mind," I say instead. "It'd be good for both Dina and Gracie if we could find her. And it'll keep Gracie occupied."

"Go on ahead." He glances at the clock on the wall. "Listen, I have to *run* to court to fight a case I actually *do* have evidence for." He ushers me out of his office, pulling the door shut behind him.

"We'll talk soon."

"Yes, sir."

I watch him hobble away, messenger bag hanging from one hand, an apple in the other.

His shoulders slumped as if by a great weight.

CHAPTER 33

Grace

"So, where y'all from?" Maxwell asks with his thick Texas croon. Awful stereotype or not, I can't help but picture him going home to trade in his poorly fitting suit for a pair of dusty cowboy boots and a wide-brimmed hat.

"Originally from here, but I moved to Arizona."

"You known Marshall a while then?" He pours himself a cup from the fresh pot of coffee, his shaggy black hair falling across his forehead messily.

It's taking everything in me not to blurt out who I am and demand answers about why my father scribbled this guy's name on a newspaper clipping fourteen years ago. "You could say that."

"When'd you two start dating?"

"We're not dating." I take my time, sipping at my can of Coke as my eyes roam the small staff lounge. It's nothing fancy—a common area along the west side of the building, overlooking the parking lot, with small café-style tables and chairs scattered throughout and a cherry-red kitchenette along another wall.

A tall, lanky guy strolls in then, mug in hand, to distract Maxwell. "Did I hear something percolating?"

"In your five years here, have you *ever* made a pot of coffee?" Maxwell shakes his head, but he's smiling when he turns to me. "Darlin', why don't you just grab a seat anywhere."

I bite my tongue about the "darlin'" and find an empty chair that puts my back to them and occupy myself with my phone. No calls from the rehab center to tell me that my mom escaped yet. That's a good sign.

"You done with those depositions yet?" Maxwell asks.

"When am I supposed to do those?" the other guy whines. "I've been reviewing surveillance video feed for Rolans since yesterday. My eyes are starting to bleed."

"Best of three says who you work for today."

I glance over my shoulder in time to see them with their hands out in front of them, making hand signs for rock-paper-scissors. "You've got to be kidding me," I mumble under my breath. This Maxwell guy isn't exactly the mastermind criminal I was envisioning.

"Tell Rolans he's shit outta luck! I'll check in on you soon." Maxwell wanders over to me, chuckling as he sits his bulky body down across from me. "Gracie, right?"

"Grace."

"So, tell me . . ." He lowers his voice and it's like that boisterous bubble around him has been popped by a needle. "How's Noah doin', really?"

"His mother shot herself, so . . ." I'd say Noah is holding up miraculously well, but I don't have a comparison point.

"Right." His brow furrows deeply. "Did you know Jackie?"

"A long time ago."

He dumps two packs of sugar into his coffee and I watch him stir, much like any typical man—rushed, the metal spoon clanging noisily against the porcelain sides.

"Were y'all neighbors?"

"No. My dad and Jackie were partners a long time ago."

"So your daddy's a cop! Is he workin' out of Arizona?"

A segue, if I ever did hear one. "He died fourteen years ago. He was shot by a drug dealer, here in Austin." I take a sip of my Coke, watching Maxwell's large gray-blue eyes as they skate over my face. I sense a glimmer of recognition there.

"What'd you say his name was?"

Noah can't get mad at me for answering a simple question. "Abraham Wilkes."

I get another intimidating, bulgy-eyed look. I'll bet he uses those in court with great success. And then Maxwell leans back in his chair, muttering a "no shit" under his breath as he tests his coffee.

"Did you know him?"

"Know him? No. I talked to him once, though."

"What about?" I ask as innocently as I'm capable, hiding my cringe as he adds another sugar to his coffee.

"A case. He had evidence he thought would help me." He takes a long sip, and a part of me thinks he's weighing his words, deciding what he should tell me. "I started out as a public defender, and I ended up on this case where this guy got busted with a trunk full of drugs. He was goin' away for a *long* time."

My heart starts racing. "When was this?"

He frowns. "It would have been . . . '03? Yeah, that's right. Spring of '03. I remember because I was picking up my wife's engagement ring from the jewelry shop when Wilkes called. I proposed to her over Easter brunch. You should have seen her face when she opened the plastic egg that I—"

"Do you remember what the case was about?" I interrupt.

"Darlin', I remember *every* detail about it, it was so bizarre."

"And what'd my dad have for you?"

"Well, that's a story and a half. I suppose I can tell you, seeing as my guy won't be minding anymore. The way it went was the defendant swore up and down that he had a pile of cash in the trunk and that the cops stole it when they busted him outside this dive motel. I told him no one's gonna buy what he's sellin'. But, days later, lo and behold, I get a call from an APD cop—your dad—who tells me that he was there that night and he saw the whole thing shake down, and he had a video to prove it. He was ready to testify for my client against another officer."

Something like giddiness fills my chest. "Who was the officer?"

"Don't matter, does it?" He takes a sip of his coffee.

I'd love to push that it *does* matter, and that he has to give me a name, but I don't want to give Maxwell a reason to grow suspicious and stop talking. "Did you see the video?"

"That's the thing. Your dad died before I even had a chance to meet him in person. Needless to say, his testimony never made it to court."

Despite my attempt to remain calm and innocent, my anger flares. "And you didn't think it was *at all* strange that he was shot *right after* telling you he wanted to out a cop for corruption?"

"Honestly? The fact that he was gonna torpedo a slam-dunk drug bust seemed more strange. I mean, the defendant was guilty, there's no two ways about it. And once your dad testified, his career in the APD would be as good as done and my guy might actually get out, and go on sellin' drugs. Wilkes knew that. I couldn't figure out why he'd do it."

"You mean other than being an honest cop who wanted to do the right thing?"

"Well, yeah, sure . . . *I guess*. But that wasn't the case here." I glare at him and he quickly adds, "It was pretty obvious that your dad was doin' one of his drug connections a favor. A retaliatory thing. That's how all those gangs work."

"*Pretty obvious?* Do you argue your court cases on 'pretty obvious'?" I bite back the sharpness in my tone. I can't blame Maxwell for thinking that my dad was lying to him. Why shouldn't he think that? Someone went out of his way to make my dad look like the criminal.

And it sounds like there was one cop who stood to benefit from that.

Maxwell slaps the table once as he stands. "Well! These criminals aren't gonna put themselves behind bars."

"What happened to that drug dealer, anyway?"

Maxwell lets out a disgusted snort. "Oh, that idiot went to jail. There was no getting around a trunk full of drugs. 'Course, I threatened the prosecutor with leaking the story to the press. I mean, it'd never stick, but if the public heard that the cops walked away with a hundred grand in drug money, it'd sure tarnish our police department's shiny reputation."

I let out a mock whistle, even as dots keep connecting before my eyes. "A hundred grand?"

"Just shy of it, if I recall correctly. Anyway, it was a dirty trick on my part, but Silas fell for it."

"Wait . . . *Silas?*"

"Yes, ma'am. He was the prosecutor. And he was so impressed with my bluffing game that he offered me this job. Which is good, 'cause I'm better off putting the guilty guys away than I am letting them go free. Worked out for everyone."

For everyone but my father. I struggle to keep my voice even. "Did you tell Silas about this video?"

He chuckles. "Not straightaway. You don't show your whole bag of tricks off the bat. I went in with 'irrefutable evidence.'" He uses his fingers to air-quote. "Not until he agreed to knock off five years did I fess up about your dad claiming to have video proof of the defendant's claims."

My gaze wanders down the hall, toward where I know Noah and his uncle sit behind closed doors. Is Silas admitting all of this to him? Is he telling him that he knew about both the drug bust and the video?

And if Silas knew, why didn't he do anything about it?

"So this drug dealer . . . he's still in prison?" I need to talk to him.

"Nah, he ended up getting knifed to death by a rival gang inside a few years in." Maxwell is so casual about it. "Some turf war. As far as I see it, he got what he deserved."

And his stolen cash ended up going to a poor girl from a Tucson trailer park, it would seem.

There's no doubt in my mind that Jackie Marshall knew where that money came from, and if my dad died because of that bag of money, I could see how she'd want it to go to us, as some twisted form of compensation.

But it doesn't explain why she had the money in the first place.

Noah appears from around the corner then. Just in time. Maxwell has confirmed everything, and then some. "Hey." His blue eyes drift over me on their way to Maxwell and I catch the heaviness of his thoughts in that gaze. "Thanks for keeping Gracie company."

"You kidding? She's a doll."

I roll my eyes.

Maxwell turns to leave, and then stops. "Wait . . . You needed to talk to me about something?"

"He'll have to catch up with you later. We have an appointment," I answer for Noah, earning his wary glance. If Noah follows up asking the same questions I just did, Maxwell will see our conversation in an entirely different light. It's better he thinks my dad was covering for the competition. For now.

"Well, now, y'all enjoy Austin while you're here. And do me a favor." He drops a heavy hand on Noah's shoulder. "Be gentle on this guy. He's a good one." With a wink my way, Maxwell strolls down the hall, whistling the entire way.

"Gracie . . ."

I gather my things. "Just think, you wanted to leave me at home with Cyclops."

"What did you tell Maxwell?" There's a warning in his tone.

"I told him nothing. He told me everything." I quietly fill him in.

Noah heaves a sigh. One of relief. He was afraid of what role the boisterous lawyer might have played in my father's death. Just like he's afraid of what role his mother might have played.

In Maxwell's case, though, the only thing he's guilty of is buying the setup.

"So, what did your uncle say?"

He shakes his head. "He needs time to sort through everything and decide the best way to proceed. Basically, he said that knowing something and proving it are two different things."

"So he admitted that he knew about it?"

Noah frowns. "About what?"

"About how my dad had video evidence of Mantis stealing money at that drug bust."

"No, he . . . he had no idea." His frown grows deeper. "Why would you think that?"

I study Noah intently, searching for hints that he's covering for his uncle. A downward cast, fidgeting, switching topics quickly . . . Noah's a terrible liar and, now that I'm getting to know him, I'm easily able to spot when he's lying or hiding things. After all, I've had plenty of practice over the last few days.

But in those pretty blue eyes, I see only confusion.

Silas didn't tell him that he already knew.

The question is, why?

CHAPTER 34

Noah

"But it's good, right? That Betsy didn't turn up in that database?"

"I guess. It means she hasn't been arrested for anything."

"So what can we find out here?" Gracie's shrewd green eyes scan the stark white interior of the Texas State Health Services office as we wait our turn. Thankfully it was quiet today, with only three people ahead of us in line, paperwork clutched within their grasps.

"Any certificates filed with her name and date of birth. Marriage, a childbirth . . . death."

Gracie's jaw tightens over that last word. It's the only sign that she's at all perturbed. She's preparing herself for that possibility. Or, maybe at this point, inevitability.

So am I. But searching for Gracie's aunt is helping to keep my mind off other pressing issues.

Namely, why would Silas lie to me about the video and that drug bust?

But did he *really* lie? I've been playing the conversation over in my head. He never said he wasn't aware of the bust or the video. I assumed he wasn't. There must be some explanation for it.

Still . . . I saw the look on Gracie's face when she told me and, in her mind, Silas's name has been added to a long list of people who screwed over Abraham, people she doesn't trust.

The clerk waves me up.

"Do me a favor and hang back," I whisper to Gracie and then

head for the counter, plastering on a fake smile. "How's my favorite Health Services employee?"

Chelsea's hazel eyes are filled with sympathy. "Hey, Noah. How are you doin'?" she asks in that soft Southern twang.

I shrug. "You know . . ."

She takes in my T-shirt. I'm usually in a button-down and tie when I come down here. "You back to work?"

"Still easing in."

Her gaze flickers over my shoulder and hardens slightly. "Can I help you?"

"I'm with him." Gracie's voice carries that typical cool, indifferent tone.

I stifle my groan. Chelsea has never been subtle about her interest in me. She isn't my type, but she's sweet, and having a clerk here who will rush my requests has made me a god among my coworkers. Bringing another girl here—especially one that looks like Gracie—was a dumb move on my part. Not that Gracie gave me much choice.

"This is my cousin," I lie. "She's visiting from out of town."

"Oh! Cousin. Of course." Chelsea tucks a strand of golden-brown hair behind her ear, the relief on her face unmistakable.

"Fourth cousin, twice removed. We could legally marry." Gracie ropes her arm around my back, sending my blood racing.

I do my best to ignore her touch and slip forward the piece of paper. "Can you check these names against your records?"

With another fleeting glance Gracie's way, Chelsea accepts the slip of paper. "Give me a few minutes, okay?"

I wait until she's out of earshot. "Fourth cousins, twice removed? Is that a real thing?"

"I have no idea, but the look on her face was totally worth it." Gracie's arm slips away, and I miss it instantly.

"These kinds of searches normally cost money and take days, if not weeks. And she knows I'm not here for work. This information isn't available to just anyone. She's doing us a huge favor."

"She's not doing *me* the favor," Gracie mutters, studying her fingernails.

And it clicks. I can't help my grin at even the possibility.

She looks up in time to catch it. "What?"

"Nothing. Just, if I didn't know better, I'd say you were jealous." I brace myself for a punch or a kick.

She lets out a derisive snort instead. "Whatever. I'll be in the restroom." She wanders away, but not before I catch the flush of her cheeks.

"There's no Betsy or Elizabeth Richards in the system with that birth date, or even that birth year."

"And you checked Nesbitt, too, right?" Gracie asks, citing Betsy's father Brian's last name.

"I checked them all," Chelsea explains with an overly sweet smile.

Gracie's face crumples with disappointment.

Chelsea turns her attention back to me. "This isn't a bad thing. It means she's alive, right?"

"Or she died in another state."

"Well . . . I could put in a call for you with the national registry office. It'll take a bit to hear back, though."

I was hoping she'd offer that, and that I wouldn't have to ask. "Thanks, Chelsea. You're the best."

She grins, flirtier this time. "Don't you know it. See you soon?"

"Definitely." I trail Gracie out, keeping my forced smile on until I'm past the doors. "Don't worry, we still have plenty of places to check. Real estate records, voter records, the DMV, the IRS . . ."

"How long will that take?"

"A while," I admit reluctantly. *Weeks. Months.*

"Aren't there any cute girls you can bat your eyelashes at to speed that up?" she mutters sourly, walking ahead of me, her hips swinging with each step.

I struggle to smother my smile. "You hungry yet? We could grab food and then, I don't know, drive around Austin and—"

"Track down this Mantis asshole?"

A flashback of those hard, beady eyes hits me and Dina's plea to keep Gracie safe, to not let her get herself into trouble by being her usual bullheaded self, fills my head. "How about we do the opposite and stay far away from him?"

"Fine," she mutters reluctantly. She purses her lips. "Do you remember where my house was?"

"Yeah, why?"

"Because *maybe* there's a chance my dad hid this video there and it somehow got missed."

"Gracie, it's been fourteen years! There's no way—"

"It's worth checking!" She throws her arms out to the sides. "What the hell *else* do we have to do anyway?"

"Well . . . I could turn the heat on in the pool and—"

"*Really*, Noah? Let's take a break from figuring out who murdered my dad and go *swimming*?"

I heave a sigh and mutter, "Yeah, that's what I thought."

CHAPTER 35

Commander Jackie Marshall

April 25, 2003

"Alright, Gary Bird. Time to go inside!" I holler, grasping the young dandelion by its base to give it a good yank. This time next week, our front garden will be overgrown with them again.

"It's *Larry* Bird, Mom," Noah corrects with annoyance. "And it's Friday."

"And too late for bouncing balls. Respect the neighbors."

"Yes, ma'am." He tucks his basketball under his gangly arm and trudges up the pathway. At eleven years old, he's just inches shy of meeting me in height.

"You spendin' the night, Jenson?"

"If that's okay with you, ma'am."

I give Jenson's ginger hair a muss. "You know you're always welcome. Go on, now."

"Yes, ma'am," they chirp in unison.

But Noah lags behind, a frown zagging across his forehead.

"What's the matter?"

"Did Abe say if he was gonna stop by tonight?"

My stomach knots at the mention of Abe's name. I haven't talked to him since he came here looking to tear my head off. "He's workin' tonight."

"Oh, okay." He looks so crestfallen, it makes my chest ache. "He hasn't been around much."

"I promise you, he's just been busy with work."

"What's got him so busy all of a sudden?"

"A special project," I lie quickly. If "project" means lurking around every slum in Austin, looking for his prostitute sister-in-law. "You go on. You have a friend waitin'."

"Yes, ma'am."

I leave a peck on his cheek. "And just because it's Friday night don't mean y'all can be playin' that Nintendo 'til the sun rises."

With a sheepish grin—because that's exactly what those two boys will do, and then they'll sleep half the day away—he trudges down the hall.

I suck back the last mouthful of whiskey from my glass and welcome the familiar burn. It's too tempting to go for a refill, especially after how hard these last few weeks have been. I decide there's no harm in one more.

I'm turning to go inside when headlights catch my attention. A car pulls into our driveway. I know it's not Blair; he's in Denver at a sales conference. For a split second, I hold out hope that it's Abe, coming to tell me that he gets my side of things, that he sees what a difficult position I was put in.

That hope is dashed quickly enough, though, as Mantis steps out of the driver's seat.

"Wonderful," I mutter, wishing I had that refill already so I could suck it back. I need a drink to deal with this asshole. And after that latest big bust—coincidentally, at the same motel I followed Betsy to—he's strutting around like Canning's prize peacock. "What do you want?"

"That's how you greet visitors?" The porch steps creak under his weight.

"When they arrive uninvited on my doorstep and their name is Dwayne . . ."

"We need to talk."

"About that God-awful cologne you're wearing? Seriously, it should be banned from production."

He flashes me a cold smile. "Wilkes has been shooting his mouth off, making accusations he shouldn't be making."

Dread slides through my limbs, even as I steel my expression, not wanting to give my panic away. "Shooting his mouth off about what?"

Mantis drops his voice. "What he *thinks* he saw at the Lucky Nine bust last week."

I let out the softest exhale of relief. This isn't about Abe and me. "And what does he *think* he saw?"

"Nothing that he should be nosing around the evidence logs and then questioning me about."

There's only one reason I can think of for Abe to be doing either of those things—Mantis and his guys didn't turn something over. I don't have to ask what. This bust is the topic of the week around the department. I doubt I'm the only one who wondered why there was no money mentioned in the haul, along with the drugs and guns. With a bust like that, there's *always* money.

But everyone knows that dirt-bag dealer is guilty and deserves to be behind bars, so even though people might be wondering, no one's saying it out loud.

No one except Abe, it seems. Because he *always* does the right thing.

If Abe is nosing around and has said something to Mantis, then he's likely going to bring it forward, and if he goes to Internal Affairs with this, it'll be hard to ignore his accusations. And if it gets out in the press that Canning's star drug hounds are pocketing drug money?

The department's reputation will be smeared, Canning's valiant war on drugs in this city will be tarnished, and his drug task force will be dismantled. All of their busts may come into question.

In the end, who would win besides a bunch of criminals?

Mantis knows all this as well as I do, which is why he's on my doorstep, rattled.

"What the hell was he doing at that dive anyway? I thought him and his wife were solid."

Realization hits and I close my eyes, a fresh wave of guilt washing over me. "He was lookin' for someone." *You and your shitty luck,*

Abe, for being in the wrong place at the wrong time. "Dammit, Dwayne, why the hell would you think I can get you out of your mess?"

"*My* mess? What, you think your *best friend* can stir up shit and some of that shit won't land on you? Come on, Marshall . . ." He lets out a derisive snort. "If you can't keep one cop quiet for the good of this department, Canning won't be so quick to tap your shoulder for that assistant chief spot. Yeah, I know Canning wants a female. He needs to check off that box and get those diversity crybabies off his ass."

I grit my teeth. Of course Mantis would assume that's why Canning wants me there. That it's not because I'm good enough to be assistant chief—and maybe chief, one day. "Abe and I aren't exactly on good terms."

"Why?" Mantis's already beady eyes narrow even further. "What'd you do?"

"Who says *I* did anything?"

"Because Boy Scout never does anything wrong."

My ears catch Noah's voice, calling to me from inside the house. "Get outta here. We shouldn't even be having this conversation."

"You need to shut him the hell up."

"Or what?"

Mantis gets right into my face, looking ready to pick a fistfight with me. For just a second, I wonder if he'll follow through. I wouldn't put it past him. "Or someone else will."

Not until he's back in his car and peeling away can I release a shaky breath.

"Oh, Abe, what have you gone and started?" I mutter, heading back inside and straight for my bottle.

CHAPTER 36

Noah

"I'm sorry, miss. There wasn't *anything* that even remotely resembled a video or computer file or anything like that found, from what I know. And, as you can see, the renovations were extensive." The woman smiles kindly, though I sense her patience is waning as Gracie keeps pushing for a different answer. A possibility. A "yes, actually, there was a videotape found behind the drywall when we gutted the kitchen. I've kept it all these years. Here, let me get it for you!"

Wherever Abe hid this video, it definitely wasn't in this house.

"Thank you, ma'am. We appreciate your time. We'll let you get back to your lunch." I clasp Gracie's hand in mine and tug her away, feeling the woman's amber gaze on our backs as we take the narrow path down. It's the only part of the house that has remained the same. We drove up and down this street three times, in search of the small white bungalow that I remembered. It wasn't until I saw the carved porch door on the place to the left that I realized this modern two-story house was what we were looking for.

I expect Gracie to shake my hand off but she doesn't, allowing me to hold it all the way until we reach my SUV, not saying a single word of rebellion as I hold her door open, and then shut it behind her.

"Do you think they knew who lived here before they did?" Gracie's gaze drifts over the peaceful neighborhood as we drive. It's fifteen minutes from my house. It's not the nicest, but it has a certain charm.

"If they didn't, I'll bet they found out pretty quick. And we just gave them something to talk about with their neighbors." I spied a curtain or two drift as we pulled over in front of the house. And the lady three doors down, digging up her front flower bed, watched us curiously as we walked up the pathway.

"Good. Let them talk. Let everyone talk about Abraham Wilkes. Maybe they'll finally start questioning what they should have years ago," she mutters bitterly. "How could all these people buy that bullshit story?"

"Because they had no reason *not* to buy the bullshit story. Especially people who didn't know Abe from Adam."

Her plump lips curl with disgust. "Is it because my father was a *black* cop?"

"Plenty of people don't trust cops and it doesn't matter what color their skin is," I remind her.

"So you're telling me that if my father was white, people would have been as quick to write him off as a dirty cop?"

"I can't tell you that, Gracie, because you and I both know there are dumb-ass people out there who think the color of your skin decides how you're going to be. I wish it weren't true, but it is, especially in Texas. Hell, there's plenty of people who think *women* shouldn't be cops. I never could figure out how my mom landed that job." I turn onto Congress Avenue and head for Austin's downtown core. I should at least *try* to take Silas's advice and show Gracie around. "But what matters is that whatever evidence was collected and presented to the chief made Abe look unequivocally guilty, white or black. We need to focus on that."

"Fine. Did you ask your uncle about getting the police report? The unsanitized one that actually tells us something?"

Dammit . . . "With everything else we talked about, I didn't get a chance to ask."

"I'm guessing he won't be in a rush to get it for us anyway, seeing as he lied about everything else."

"He didn't lie!"

"Oh, right. I'm sorry." She snorts derisively. "He just didn't tell the truth. I mean, it wouldn't look too good on him if word got out that he knew about the allegations my dad made against Mantis and did nothing."

I try to keep my voice calm. "There's got to be an explanation."

"Well, that's the only explanation I can come up with for how someone got away with murdering my father."

"Silas isn't like that."

"He doesn't look out for himself? Bullshit. Everyone's like that. *Everyone*." Gracie shifts her body to face the side window, settling her gaze on the passing buildings as I weave through Austin's streets, her hands balled into tight fists of frustration.

I can't blame her for being suspicious. But is she including me in that "everyone"? Does she think I've been looking out for *myself* all this time? Because the only person I've been trying to protect has been my mother.

A wave of guilt washes over me. I need to tell her about Klein, before she finds out on her own and shuts me out, permanently.

It takes several blocks to work up my nerve. "Listen, Gracie, there's something important I need you to know—"

"We're being followed."

At first I'm sure I've misheard. "What?" I check my rearview mirror. "Where?"

"That gray car."

"The Civic?" I relax a bit.

"When you took that last right turn, it cut off two cars to follow us. And I saw it parked outside the DA's office."

"You probably saw twenty gray Civics parked there. They're *everywhere*, Gracie."

"Yeah, but this one had a *hundred* tree air fresheners dangling from the rearview mirror. It reminded me of my nan's car. She'd do the same, to try and mask the smell of cigarettes." She squishes her nose in disgust.

"You're being paranoid."

She folds her arms in that haughty way. "Fine. Prove me wrong."

Three turns later, I realize that I can't, and my scalp begins to prickle with unease.

All I can make out are two forms in the front, likely male. Who the hell could be following us? And what do they want? "Do me a favor and write down the plate number if you can catch it."

"And then what are we gonna do? Lead them home?" Her gaze flitters between her side-view mirror and the keyboard on her phone, her brow tight with concentration.

I see the sign up ahead. "I have an idea."

CHAPTER 37

Grace

The UT campus is crawling with students, book bags slung over their shoulders as they travel between classes. Plenty of others are scattered over the parklike setting, hiding beneath the shade of trees or lying on their backs on grassy patches, tuning out the world and soaking in the afternoon sun with either a book or music pumping through earphones.

"You went here?"

"Best years of my life." Noah pauses to step behind me, making room for a group of girls to pass while, at the same time, covertly scanning the area around us.

We pulled into the parking lot and watched the gray Civic coast past, the visor strategically positioned to hide the driver from view. All either of us could make out was a faded blue T-shirt and a white man's biceps, and then they were gone.

"What about you? Have you ever thought about going to college?"

I burst out laughing.

"What? You've never even thought about it?"

"No. I mean, I've *thought* about it, but . . ."

"But . . . ?" Again he shifts to the side to allow others to pass, this time setting a hand on the small of my back, steering me toward an elaborate fountain up ahead.

It takes me a moment to remember what we were talking about, his touch distracting. "But that's it. I've *thought* about it." Noah doesn't get it.

My school guidance counselor, Ms. Bracken, didn't get it either. I remember sitting across from her in her office my senior year. She was holding out a stack of college pamphlets and application forms, thinking she would change my life with a simple conversation. While my grades were far from Ivy League–worthy, she was sure I could get into one of the local community college programs if I applied.

I smiled and accepted the brochures, stuffing them in my backpack. I even let myself indulge in the idea of filling out a form that night. And then I came home to find the needles strewn on the coffee table. Before that it had been all pills.

"I guess I've learned to live more day by day."

"It's good to set goals for yourself."

"Trying to keep my mother alive and pay our bills are goals."

Noah's face falls in that guilty way it always does when he's reminded how different our upbringings were. "Well, now you can start thinking about your future."

My future. That's not a phrase that was tossed around much when I was growing up. My mom was too busy stuck in the past, and holding me there with her.

"Over here." He leads me to a retaining wall, and I admire his measured strides, his sleek movements. I take a seat next to him, and try to focus on our surroundings rather than him.

"Wow, now *that*'s a fountain." I've never seen anything like the elaborate sculpture beside us, of horses charging from the water, ridden by what I'd call mermen, guarded over by soldiers and a goddess. The entire piece is surrounded by a massive pool of water to feed into the jetting sprays.

Noah doesn't answer, his gaze searching faces.

"Do you think we lost them?"

"I hope so. I don't know what the hell they want." With a heavy sigh, he begins fumbling with the leather band around his wrist. His thoughts are elsewhere.

And I remember that I'm not the only one troubled by everything we've learned today, so far.

"I saw a sign for a lake back there," I offer, trying to distract him from his brooding.

"Lady Bird?"

"Sure. Tell me about it."

He closes his eyes and tips his head back to face the sky. "It's actually a reservoir from the Colorado River. You can rent kayaks and boats, and all sorts of things. And the Congress Avenue Bridge is there too. Every night in the summer, you can watch over a million bats fly out from their nests underneath it."

"That'd be . . . cool?" I cringe at the thought.

"It is, actually. If you're around, we'll go see it."

If I'm around. That's months away. Does he mean still in Austin? Or living in his house, with him?

How long will I be here? It all depends on whether I'd have a reason to stay. My mother will be in rehab for at least one month. Ideally, three, though I can't let Noah pay for more.

"I agree, the bats are cool," a male voice says suddenly. I was so busy staring at Noah's handsome profile that I didn't notice the man take the spot on the other side of me. He could pass for a student, albeit an older one, in his worn jeans and faded blue Houston Texans T-shirt.

I'm about to turn my back to the stranger, to overtly dismiss him for listening in on our conversation, when I hear a soft "fuck" slip out under Noah's breath.

The guy leans over to rest his elbows on his knees, his steely gray eyes shifting from Noah to me, and then back to Noah, amusement on his face. "How was your drive back from Tucson?"

Noah doesn't answer. He doesn't look the least bit pleased.

The guy studies me through a shrewd gaze. I'd put him in his early thirties. He's decidedly attractive—his jaw hard, his nose sharp, his blond hair holding a wave. There's a twinkle in his eye, and I can't tell if it's borne of arrogance or mischief, but I *can* tell that this guy is probably used to getting whatever he wants where females are concerned.

"Who the hell are you and why are you following us?"

"So you did see me." He smiles easily, highlighting the small cut and bruising on his bottom lip.

"Hard not to notice such a terrible tailing job. *Who are you?*"

"Special Agent Kristian Klein. I work with the FBI." He holds out a hand.

I simply glare at it. "Bullshit. You guys don't creep around in Honda Civics and faded jeans."

"You'd be surprised what we do." Suddenly there's a badge in Kristian's hand, the golden eagle unmistakable and, just as quickly and smoothly, it's gone again. "Ask Noah, if you don't believe me."

"You said forty-eight hours," Noah grumbles by way of response.

Klein shrugs. "I also said I was bad with telling time."

"Wait, when did you two talk?"

"Where's Tareen?" Noah searches the grounds around us.

"He's on the other side of the bush, listening while making sure no one else is listening."

"How fucking clandestine of you."

"So, which one of you spotted me?"

Noah nods to me.

"Nicely done, Grace Richards. Or are you going by Wilkes again, now that you're back in Texas?"

"Okay, what *the hell* is going on?" How does the FBI know my name? And why does Noah know this guy? And forty-eight hours to what?

"I'm trying to figure out what happened to Abraham Wilkes and I'd love some help. I was hoping Noah here would tell me what he knows."

I frown with realization. "Does this mean that the FBI is looking into my dad's case?"

Klein leans forward and peers across to Noah. "Wow. You actually didn't tell her."

"Tell me *what*?" I demand, glaring at Noah as Klein casually taunts him.

Noah heaves a sigh, his face drawn with misery. "Klein is the guy who came to your mom's hospital room. He came because my mom called him the night she died and told him that Abe had been set up. He was outside of our motel in Tucson on Saturday night."

"And you weren't going to tell me?" I hiss, my rage flaring.

He holds his hands up. "I was *just* about to when you noticed the car following us, I swear."

"I don't believe you." Again. Noah was withholding from me *again*. I turn my back to him, to face Agent Klein. "What do you know?"

He shrugs nonchalantly. "A bit. But first, I'm curious about what *you* know, Gracie."

"It's Grace. And I'll tell you everything. Every last detail."

A smile of satisfaction fills his handsome face. "That's what I was hoping for."

Klein snaps his notepad shut. "We'll be by to collect that evidence."

"And the picture of Betsy, right?"

"Give me all the names and birth dates that she may be going under and I'll see what my people can find out." His cool gaze drifts to Noah, who has been quiet, aside from a nod here or a grunt of agreement there. "For what it's worth, I don't think you had anything to do with your mother's death. I deserved this." His gestures at his lip. "And I get why you covered for your mom with the cops in your statement. I'm not out to get you for that. But if I find out that you're lying to me about anything—"

"Gracie's told you everything we know about Abe's death," Noah says, his gaze locked on the agent's.

"I believe you. Well . . . I believe *her*." Kristian stands, and I see how tall he is. He's lankier than Noah, but he has definition to his body. He gestures toward a man who suddenly appears next to him. "This is Agent Tareen."

The dark-haired man nods once toward me, his near-black eyes skating over Noah with indifference, before handing Klein a letter-sized envelope.

“Have you seen the police report on your father?”

“No. I need to request it . . .” Wherever it is you request police reports. I’m not going to rely on Noah or Silas to get it for me.

“Don’t bother. It’s the one meant for the public. You won’t find anything in it of any use.” He scrawls something across the front of the envelope and then passes it to me. “Here’s the real one.”

Noah’s mouth drops open. “How did you get that?”

“A courier showed up at my house the morning after your mother died. *She* sent it to me. How she got hold of it, I don’t know, but she *was* the chief, so I’m sure it wasn’t too hard.”

The envelope in my hand feels like a brick. Is this truly it? Is this the tale of my father’s supposed fall from saint to criminal?

The report that’s full of lies?

“Why are you giving this to me?”

“Because you won’t get it any other way. And after what you’ve been through, especially with your mother”—pity flashes across his face—“you deserve to see it. *And* because this case isn’t going to be easy to solve. I need all the help I can get. So take a read. See if anything jumps out at you.”

I slide the stack of papers out and see my dad’s name across the top. A strange feeling sweeps through me. “So you *are* investigating my dad’s death.” Klein hasn’t actually admitted it yet.

“Yes, ma’am. We’ll be in touch soon,” he drawls in a fake Texas twang. The two FBI agents stroll away, no one around us the wiser.

“Gracie, I—”

“When are you going to stop lying to me, Noah?” My voice cracks on his name, which only makes me more upset with him.

“I didn’t lie! I just . . . Klein blindsided me in Tucson. He played that message and . . . hearing her voice brought me right back to that fucking *horrible* night.” Noah swallows hard. “And then he basically accused me of killing her.”

Mixed in with my anger is unexpected sympathy. “Is that why you punched him?” It would probably take accusing Noah of murdering his own mother for his temper to erupt like that.

Noah nods. "I wanted to talk to Maxwell and Silas first, and I knew you wouldn't be willing to wait. I'm sorry." He settles those earnest eyes on me.

I'm forced to turn away from them before my anger melts. He's right; I wouldn't have been. I would have demanded we talk to Klein right away. Because why shouldn't we? "And let me guess: your uncle told you not to tell the FBI anything?"

He chews his bottom lip, delaying an answer. Giving me the answer I need. "It's all a moot point, now that you've told Klein everything."

"You're right, and I'm glad I did, because I have this police report and the FBI on my side, and I'm going to clear my dad's name. Something you obviously don't care that much about doing. But it's all going to come out eventually." I jump off the ledge and march in the direction of the parking lot, hugging the report to my chest.

Everyone keeps saying that this was an open-and-shut case. But there has to be something in these pages. Something that, if you knew the whole story—or at least what we now know about my dad and Mantis—would let you see it for what it actually is: proof of my father's innocence.

CHAPTER 38

Noah

"Gracie, I'm so—"

"Don't." Her tone is sharp. A warning.

I try another angle. "That report looks long. I'll help you go through it."

"So you can figure out how to sabotage the investigation?" she hisses, her eyes glued to the pages within her grip.

"I'm not—"

"Noah! Just . . ." She shakes her head, her rage filling my SUV with palpable tension. "Just *don't*."

I press my lips firmly together. Boy, does she have a temper to rival anyone's, and she is fucking pissed with me. I can't blame her. There's no point saying another word, not until she calms down.

If she ever calms down.

We're silent as we drive along a side street, minutes away from my house, my mind caught in inappropriate ways to beg for her forgiveness—*so* not the right time to be thinking about *that*—when the wail of a police siren sounds behind us.

"Are you speeding?" Gracie frowns at my odometer, forgetting her anger for the moment.

I check my dash. "No." That's usually what I get pulled over for, and I've been pulled over a few times over the years. They caught me on a rolling stop in a school zone once, too. Royally chewed me out for that. Since then, I wait an extra two beats at stop signs, so that's not the reason either.

"Will they let you off? You know, because of your mom?"

"I guess we'll see." I've never name-dropped; I've never needed to. The APD somehow always put two and two together and let me off with a warning. Except for that one guy, who either didn't clue in or didn't care and wrote me a ticket. Mom made that one go away, though she did it with a heavy warning that it would be the first and last time she stepped in.

Every single time I've seen those bright blue lights flashing in my rearview mirror, I've known exactly why.

This time around, though, I don't have a clue what I've done. All I *do* know is that no one's going to fix any tickets for me.

With a sigh, I pull over. "Maybe my taillight is busted." Plausible, and yet I can't help the unease that's sliding down my spine.

I feel Gracie's worried eyes burning a hole into the side of my face as I quietly watch the unmarked cruiser coast up behind me, the blare of the lights bright even in the midday sun.

"Don't say anything . . . about anything. *Please.*"

"Don't worry about that," she mutters. I get the impression Gracie generally doesn't like dealing with the police.

Opening my window, I rest my hands visibly on the top of my steering wheel and watch the side-view mirror as the officer climbs out of the driver's seat.

"Holy shit."

"What is it?" Gracie glances over her shoulder to spy through the rear window. Her eyes widen. "Is that—"

"Yeah." We didn't have to track down Mantis, after all.

He found us.

"This can't be a coincidence." What the hell is the head of Internal Affairs doing, pulling us over?

"Coincidence or not, I finally get to meet this piece of shit in person." I hear the challenge in her voice.

"Gracie . . ."

"He killed my father!" she hisses.

"Which would make him capable of murder. Besides, we don't

have proof. You need to play it cool. Don't let on about what we know. And don't aggravate him," I add in a low whisper, as Mantis slows and stoops on approach, trying to see inside. My windows are tinted, though.

"Hello, sir." I force a smile when he stops a foot away from my door.

"Please remove your sunglasses." The deep, grating voice I remember from the night my mother died sounds wooden now.

"Yes, sir." I slide them to my head and squint against the bright sun as I peer up at his hard face. Growing up around cops and having a high-ranking one for a mother, I have a healthy respect for police, but I'm also comfortable around them.

Mantis, though, made me uneasy even when I didn't know anything about him. Now . . . every muscle in my body feels tense.

He stoops to settle a shrewd gaze on Gracie and I catch a whiff of cheap cologne.

"What have I been pulled over for, Officer?"

"Is this your vehicle?"

"Yes, sir. Do you want to see the paperwork?"

"Just your license for now."

I fish my license out of my wallet and hand it to him.

"What are you up to today, Noah Marshall?" Is he playing dumb too? There's no way he hasn't made the connection between my name and the late chief. He saw me on the front porch less than two weeks ago, my hands covered in blood, for fuck's sake.

"Errands."

A ghost of a smirk touches his thin lips. "This your friend?" He nods toward Gracie.

"Yes, sir."

"What's your name, miss?"

"Grace."

"How old are you?"

A frown flickers over her brow. "Twenty. Why?"

"Let me see some ID."

After a glance my way, she reaches into her purse.

"Slowly!" he barks.

At first she freezes altogether, and then she moves cautiously, sliding her license out of her wallet and handing it to me, to pass along. I hear her teeth crack against each other, and I can't tell if it's because she's pissed or scared. Maybe both.

His beady eyes drift over the console to the envelope, holding the SIU report that sits on her lap, to the backseat. "You don't mind if I have a look in your car, do you?"

He asks it so smoothly. It's the oldest trick in the book, according to my mom—getting permission to search a car when you don't have cause. What is he up to?

His brows lift, waiting for my answer.

"I do mind. I'm not consenting to that."

"Do you have something to hide?"

"No, sir. I'm just not consenting to you searching my car."

By the stare he's leveling me with, I won't be winning any prizes from him today. "Do you have weapons?"

"I have a handgun locked in a safety box under the seat. I have a permit for it." Is the switchblade in Gracie's purse five or six inches? Because six is illegal in Texas. *Shit.*

He glances around himself, and then backs away. "Step out of the vehicle. Both of you."

Fuck. "What is this about?"

"Now!"

"Do what he says; don't give him cause," I softly warn Gracie, before easing myself out. That may be what he's looking for. Though, if what we suspect of him is true, he's perfectly capable of making up shit to haul us in.

"Stand over there." He points to the curb and I promptly listen, finding my place next to Gracie, my fingertips trailing lightly against her thigh. A reminder that I'm here, and I won't let anything happen to her.

Mantis eyes Gracie before shifting his attention back to me, studying our licenses for several long moments, allowing me to study him, in his dress pants and a button-down shirt. His gun is strapped to his body by a holster.

"Miss Richards, what are you doing in Texas?"

"Visiting my friend."

"*He's* your friend?"

"Yes."

His gaze slides down Gracie's body in a way that makes my fists clench. "How long will you be in Texas?"

"Depends." Her jaw tenses.

"On?" He watches her intently and I see it as a dare.

Please don't do it, Gracie.

Another beat passes and then she plasters on the widest—fakest—smile I've ever seen touch her face. "On how long it takes for Noah to admit he has feelings for me. I mean, I keep dropping these major hints, but he hasn't picked up on them yet. Are guys normally this thick-skulled or did I just pick an especially dumb one to chase after?"

I don't know whether to laugh or groan.

Mantis turns his attention back to my ID in his hand, not answering her question, and, by the way his square jaw tenses, not happy that she's toying with him. "Any relation to Chief Marshall?"

Will hearing that name—that title—ever *not* feel like a sucker punch to my gut again? "She was my mother." *And you damn well know that, you son of a bitch.*

"Sorry to hear what happened."

"Thanks." This is the point where an APD officer would hand me back my ID and tell me I'm free to go.

"Such a shame she couldn't hack it."

I grit my teeth against the urge to defend her. He's trying to provoke me.

"Women aren't meant to take on big roles. They don't have what it takes."

Gracie's nostrils flare in that way they do when she's about to lose her temper and spout off all kinds of things that will get us into trouble—I've experienced it enough to see it coming.

"Are we free to go?" I ask, before she has a chance.

"You're free to go when I tell you you're free to go." His gaze shifts to Gracie. "You know, you look an awful lot like an old friend of mine. Abe Wilkes. Ever heard of him?"

She doesn't look *anything* like Abe.

Gracie lifts her chin in defiance. "He was my father."

"Really . . ." His brow pops a beat too late to make the surprise believable. "Small world."

"So . . . you were *friends*?" She spits that word out like it tastes bad.

"We went way back. He was a decent guy. Good ballplayer."

"I'll take your word for it. Someone murdered him and set him up before I got to know him."

"Jesus Christ," slips out under my breath, but neither of them is paying attention to me.

Mantis stares her down. "That's not how I remember the story playing out."

"And were you there?" Gracie's returning gaze is just as scrutinizing.

"I wasn't."

She mock frowns. "Are you sure?"

"Gracie . . ." I mutter, but it's too late.

"Are you accusing me of something?"

"Should I be?"

I reach for her hand, gripping it tightly.

"You're definitely Abe Wilkes's girl. Ballsy, just like he was." He sucks on his bottom lip for a moment. "We received a tip that a vehicle matching your description may be transporting illegal substances. Please step aside while I search it."

"That's bullshit. You're not even in uniform!" Gracie snarls.

"Turn around. Now!" he barks, making for his holster.

I instinctively step forward, pushing Gracie behind me with my arm. This has gone on long enough. "You're the head of Internal Affairs, Mantis. You didn't get any tip and I don't know what you're trying to do, but you won't get away with it."

"You wouldn't believe what I can get away with." He grins viciously. "Are you saying that you're resisting?"

A cruiser slows to a stop on the street beside us then, and the window slides down.

"Everything good here?" Boyd calls out. The sound of his familiar voice is both a relief and a stinging reminder. I haven't seen him since my mom's funeral.

Mantis's hand shifts away from his gun. His gaze hasn't left Gracie, but his expression has turned sour. "Just letting them off with a warning," he hollers, thrusting our licenses back into our hands. "Enjoy your visit to Texas, Gracie May." He marches back to his car, a waft of that off-putting cologne trailing behind him.

I release a lung's worth of air.

"How're you doing, Noah?" Boyd says, genuine sympathy clouding his face. His partner sits quietly beside him.

"I've been better."

"Sorry I haven't called. I keep meaning to, but the kids, you know . . ."

"Yeah, of course." It's weird to think that Boyd is only one year older than me and he's already married with two kids, and another one on the way.

Boyd watches as the unmarked cruiser pulls a quick U-turn and speeds off in the opposite direction. "What was that about?"

"Nothing you want to get involved in," I mutter, glancing over to Gracie, whose face has taken on a pallid color. "Are you okay?"

"No one but my dad called me Gracie May. My middle name isn't even on this." She holds up her driver's license in her shaky hands.

"He was trying to rattle you."

"Too bad for him it didn't work." She lets out a derisive snort and nods toward Boyd. "Maybe you *should* tell him. He *is* a witness to Mantis's bullshit."

"And what happened the last time a cop witnessed Mantis's bullshit?" I remind her with a knowing look.

"Hey!" Boyd frowns. "Seriously. What the hell is going on?"

I sigh. "How well do you know Dwayne Mantis?"

"Just from playing ball. He's a tough son of a bitch." His eyes narrow. "Why are you asking?" Silas wasn't wrong when he mocked the blue wall of silence, that night with Canning.

Maybe I should be wary of Boyd, too, given that he was standing on my porch with Mantis.

But I also know that Boyd's exactly the kind of person you want behind a gun and a badge. He's what my mother would call a Steady Eddie. He's not chasing after stars and high-profile promotions. He's not a commando, itching to kick in doors and bust heads. He's just a reliable beat cop who likes to keep the peace, who's always going to be a reliable beat cop who likes to keep the peace.

Which is why I don't want to get him involved in this, because that was definitely a warning from Mantis.

A warning that he knows why Gracie's here, and he doesn't like it.

Boyd's radio begins chirping a series of codes. He pauses to listen. "We've gotta get to this. I'll catch up with you later." He throws on his lights and siren and they speed away.

"So much for our witness." Gracie's voice has a wobble to it.

"He'll loop back later."

"Sure he will." She doesn't believe that for a second. "How did Mantis find out why I'm here, anyway?"

"How should I know?"

"Only one person knows, besides the feds."

Yeah. My uncle. "What are you getting at?"

She shakes her head. "Stop being naïve." She climbs back into the passenger seat, slamming the door behind her.

I'm panting by the time I reach my quiet cul-de-sac. This is fucking pathetic. Take a couple weeks off of running and I'm ready to collapse after a mile. The only thing that kept me going was the vision of Gracie at the finish line.

Well, more accurately, barricaded with Cyclops in her bedroom, ignoring me, absorbed by the police report that Klein gave her.

Klein's her hero.

Me? I'm the asshole who didn't tell her about him in the first place. She hasn't said two words to me since we got home, and I deserve it. Still, I'd take the screaming and knife-wielding over the silent treatment.

I'd sure as hell take it over this heavy feeling that I've screwed up with Gracie one too many times.

She hasn't come right out and said it—because she isn't talking to me—but it's obvious she thinks Silas is in cahoots with Mantis. Maybe she should start by blaming the FBI. I mean, it's just as ridiculous an idea as pointing the finger at my uncle.

My feet feel like lead blocks as I climb the front steps of my porch and step into the house.

A thump comes from above me.

"Gracie?" I call out.

Another thump sounds, followed by a slam.

"Gracie!"

No response.

I didn't set the alarm when I left.

Icy dread begins coursing through my veins as I take the stairs up, two at a time.

Gracie's not in her room.

I find her in my mother's office, furiously scribbling on a blank sheet of computer paper. "How is there not one single working pen in this entire place!" She whips a dud toward the trash can, missing it completely. It joins the array already scattered over the carpeted floor.

"Jesus Christ!" My breathing is ragged with relief as I lean back against the door.

She frowns. "What's wrong with *you*?"

"Nothing. I thought . . . nothing." I silently vow to keep the alarm set at all times. Better yet, I won't leave Gracie alone again.

She finds another pen under a pile of magazines. "Ha!" she exclaims, as it leaves a streak of blue ink on a cover. She storms past me with it and a highlighter, Cyclops trotting behind her all the way to her room, his tail wagging excitedly.

"Did you find something?"

She yanks the cap off the yellow highlighter using her teeth and sets to drawing a box around half a page before thrusting the page at me.

I scan the paragraph in the section. "It's a statement from one of the motel guests." I frown. "Who saw nothing."

"Look harder!" Gracie urges, scribbling the highlighter over a name.

Holy shit. "Mantis was canvassing witnesses."

"Not *just* canvassing witnesses." She yanks another page off the bed and holds it up. It's a list of the team of investigators. Mantis's name is near the top. Gracie's lips twist with a smug smile of satisfaction. "Why would a special Narcotics squad cop be part of a homicide investigation?"

"Good question. I guess he could have volunteered. Or maybe they were short-staffed, or—"

"He got himself onto that team because he wanted to cover his tracks."

"Right," I agree. It would give Mantis access to potential witnesses and evidence. It would also give him the chance to ensure there were no witnesses or evidence pointing to him. I scan the rest of the list. "I don't recognize these names. We can look them up, though."

As if remembering that she's angry with me, Gracie smoothly lifts the page from my fingertips and settles herself onto her bed, cross-legged. Ignoring me once again.

"That's a *long* report."

"It is."

"It's going to take you *all night* to go through it alone."

She waves a dismissive hand toward the nightstand. "I made coffee."

"The two of us could get through it faster. We both want the truth, Gracie."

She considers that, her sharp green eyes finally lifting to meet mine. "Yeah, fine," she mutters, reluctantly.

I should stop now and just be thankful she's not itching to skin me alive anymore, but I can't bite my tongue hard enough. "I'm sorry I didn't tell you about Klein. If I could do it over again, I would have gone and woken you up and brought you downstairs to talk to him that same night."

She presses her lips together. And then sighs. "I get why you didn't tell me. I don't like it, but I get it."

"Please say you don't hate me." I offer her my best contrite face.

She rolls her eyes. "Stop that."

"Stop what?"

"Stop looking at me like *that*."

I smile. "I can't help it."

She averts her gaze, but I spot the corners of her mouth curve slightly. "Did you tell your uncle that we talked to the FBI?" There's a challenge in her voice.

"No." Silas called me while I was on my run. I didn't pick up. "He'll hear about it soon enough." I sound indifferent, but in reality I'm dreading that conversation. "All that matters is clearing Abe's name and finding the person responsible. Or people," I quietly add, knowing that could include my mother. "No more withholding information. No more worrying about anything except doing the right thing. We count on each other. We tell each other everything, right away. Deal?"

She exhales heavily. "Deal."

"Okay then." Gracie's forgiven me. All feels right, even though it's far from it.

"So . . . were you going to shower first?" Her nose twitches with exaggeration, but then she laughs, breaking the last of the tension.

"Yeah. Do you think you can control yourself for the next ten minutes? Or should I lock the bathroom door?" I tease. Knowing that I'm *really* pushing my luck here.

"Leave it wide open for all I care." She feigns indifference, but I catch the way her gaze flitters over my body, the way her throat bobs with a hard swallow, the way her cheeks flush.

"Okay, I needed to make sure. Remember, you did pick an especially dumb one to chase aft—" I duck just in time to avoid the pillow that she launches at my head.

CHAPTER 39

Commander Jackie Marshall

April 26, 2003

I watch the cigarette smoke curl out my driver's-side window and sail into the night sky. It's been an hour of sitting and waiting.

Finally, I spot Abe's familiar stride. He weaves through the cars, heading toward his white sedan. It's parked where he always parks—under the third light post on the south side. I swear, I could set my watch by that man's predictability.

"Abe!" I step out of my car.

He sees me and his face hardens. He doesn't stop.

"Come on, wait up a minute!" I cut him off at his door before he has a chance to open it, his hand gripping the handle.

"What do you want, Jackie?"

"Where you goin'?"

"*Where am I going?*" His brows climb halfway up his forehead and I brace myself for an earful. "Where do you *think* I'm going? To drive around the slums and sit in motel parking lots and bribe hookers for information, thanks to you! Now get outta my way."

The Abe I know would never have talked to me like this, but I can't say much. I deserve it.

"Mantis showed up at my house the other night." I glance around to make sure no one's within earshot. It's late, and the shift change came and went. The staff parking lot is full of cars and not much else at this point. Still, I drop my voice. "You need to stop stirrin' up that pot you've stuck your spoon into."

"Unbelievable." Abe starts to laugh, but it's not his usual hearty, boisterous laugh. It's full of bitterness. "You protecting Mantis too?"

"I'm protecting *you*. You know you can't go around threatening him!"

"Why? Because he's Canning's dog?"

"Because he has the temper of a rattlesnake that's been stepped on! Lord only knows what he'll do if you get him cornered." There are enough stories floating around about Mantis—sending opponents off sports fields in stretchers, putting a guy in a hospital after a bar brawl, complaints of excessive use of force, from criminals, mind you—to make any smart person wary of that guy.

"Then he shouldn't have stolen that money."

I knew it. "They're getting drugs and bad people off the streets, even if Mantis has a crooked way of doing it. I'm telling you, Abe, leave it alone. For everyone's sake, but especially your own." I don't know how I can warn him any more clearly than that.

"When did you get like this? You weren't always like this. I guess that assistant chief's star is just too damn tempting, isn't it?" He shakes his head, his chocolate eyes alight with anger. "If he's done it once, he's done it a hundred times. It's wrong. I can't turn a blind eye to that. Now if you'll move . . ." He opens his door, forcing me back. "I won't get to put my baby girl to bed—again—thanks to you."

I barely find time to step out of the way before he's speeding away.

CHAPTER 40

Grace

The first thing I'm aware of when I awake is the smell of soap.

The second is the feel of a broad chest against my cheek and an arm coiled around my body. It takes my brain several seconds to register the fact that I'm curled up against Noah in my bed, and another few to remember why.

We must have drifted off, going through each line of my dad's report with a fine-tooth comb. Pages are now scattered beneath our slumbering bodies. Others have slipped to the floor during the night.

I lie frozen for a moment, relishing the warmth of Noah's strong, hard body, the heat radiating through his thin cotton T-shirt. My palm is flat against the curves of his chest, and it feels even better than I imagined, enough to make my blood race through my limbs and my heart pound.

Just days ago, he was no one. An assumed drug dealer who faced the brunt of my rage. Then, he was a guy I didn't remember, the son of a woman whom my mother despised. Now . . . he's the only real person I can count on in my life.

True, he's deceived and outright lied to me plenty, and yet my anger with him melted almost instantly last night. I want to hate him for protecting his mother, for listening to his uncle, but I can't. I can't blame him for hoping that there's some grand explanation for her involvement, just like I can't blame him for giving everyone he cares for the benefit of the doubt.

Slowly, I shift my head so I can look up at his face. It's exactly as

I imagined it—boyish and peaceful in slumber, his brown eyelashes a thick fringe. And that jaw . . . My fingertips beg to slide across the layer of stubble covering it.

When exactly did I start having *these* feelings for Noah? Sure, he was attractive, even when I thought he was my mom's drug dealer. And I've admired him more than once from afar. But lying in bed next to him, my thoughts are on what those soft, full lips would feel like against mine, and on how he'd react if he woke up to find me pressed against him.

When was the last time I trusted *anyone* the way I seem to trust Noah almost instinctively, no matter how many times he's given me reason not to?

I never have.

Because I've never met a guy like him.

Noah is a genuinely good guy, trying to do the right thing, while protecting the people he cares for. Mom said that's how Dad was.

What worries me is what happened to Dad because he was trying to do the right thing.

Cyclops stands with a deep stretch from the spot where he made himself comfortable for the night—the pile of decorative pillows that I tossed to the floor—and trots over to the doorway, his tail wagging.

He lets out a high-pitched bark of protest.

I quietly curse the mutt as Noah's chest heaves with a deep, awakening breath. His eyelids begin to flutter and the sharp jut in his neck bobs with his hard swallow. Still, I don't move, hoping he'll drift back asleep.

Cyclops lets out a second high-pitched bark. I can't ignore him any longer. He may have been domesticated once, but he's a stray now. That he's even doing the decent thing by not lifting his leg on the furniture is a miracle.

I move to slide off Noah.

His arm tightens around me instantly, locking me in place. He doesn't say anything, but he doesn't need to—I can feel his heart begin to race. I catch his brilliant blue but sleepy eyes settled on me.

"Did you sleep okay?" he asks, his voice grating so deeply that I feel it in my chest.

I consider throwing back my usual sarcastic quip. Then I decide against it, because it'd be a lie and we agreed not to lie to each other. "Better than I have in a while," I admit. "Even on a bed of paper."

He groans. "I meant to gather it up before going to my room, but I must have fallen asleep reading."

"We can find it all easily enough. I highlighted everything important." The pages summarizing the interview with my mother, and how she couldn't explain the stacks of money and bags of cocaine and marijuana that turned up in the search warrant execution, taped to the backs and underside of their bedroom furniture. Nor could she explain why my dad left the house that night, other than to say that he had received a phone call and told her he had to go to work.

What was glaringly obvious wasn't what was in the report, but what *wasn't* in it. There was no mention of my dad's unaccounted-for Colt .45, or his custom-made holster. No mention of my mom's claims about a suspicious video. And not a single word about him acting as witness to a police corruption crime, which we know Silas—an ADA at the time—was aware of. So many minor details were documented—the times and dates that my father lied to my mother about working, with confirmation that he was not on the clock—and yet none of the facts that may have helped build reasonable doubt. Did they simply exclude them, assuming they weren't important? Or did Mantis make sure they never made it into the report?

Noah sighs as his fingers drag back and forth against my shoulder.

This is getting too intimate. I *should* pull away, and yet I stay, frozen against him. "How'd *you* sleep?"

"Great. Actually, I might still be asleep."

I frown. "Why do you say that?"

His warm breath skates across my forehead. "Because you're being nice to me."

I've never been shy, and yet I'm unable to look him in the eye again. "Don't get used to it." Meanwhile my body betrays me, pressing into his, reveling in his strength and warmth and protection.

"Hey."

I sense the air between us shifting, a heady anticipation swelling. "What?"

His hand pushes against my chin, lifting it until our eyes meet again.

He says nothing, but he doesn't need to. Everything he *doesn't* say is clear. The hard swallow, the shaky inhale, the way his fingers curl around locks of my hair, while sweeping them off my forehead.

The way he leans in, painstakingly slowly.

His lips graze against mine in a timid way, as if he's afraid of my response. Not until the second pass, when he presses a little harder, when he stalls there for a little longer, does it actually feel like a real kiss.

Not until the third pass do I meet his mouth with mine, reveling in the way our lips fit against each other in an unhurried, sensual dance, as his arm around me tightens, as his body coils into mine, his other hand finding my hip. His thumb grazes against my pelvic bone.

I could stop this.

Given what this FBI investigation might uncover about his mother and what she did to my father, I *should* stop this before it gets more complicated.

And yet my fingers claw their way up his chest, memorizing the feel of him, unable to stop myself.

Because nothing has felt more right than having Noah back in my life.

I'm so enthralled by his touch, his feel, his taste, that it takes a moment for the sound of a stream of liquid hitting the carpet to register. When it finally does, I'm breaking free and bolting upright in bed.

"*No!* Bad dog!"

"Where do you keep these?" I hold up the bottle of vinegar and rubber gloves.

"Under the sink is fine," Noah says absently, his hands clasped behind his neck in a morning stretch that hasn't quite finished, the hem of his T-shirt lifted to show a glimpse of his taut belly and the dark trail of hair.

He doesn't notice me admiring his body, his gaze locked on the backyard where the sun crawls over the horizon of trees. "He's a real asshole of a dog."

"It's our fault. He was telling us he had to go and we . . . weren't listening." I feel my cheeks flush.

"Yeah, but the way he was lookin' at us while he was doing it, through that squinty little eye of his, I could almost hear him saying 'fuck y'all!' "

I chuckle at the exaggerated Texas twang in Noah's voice. "It's going to take a while for him to get used to domesticated life. He's used to living under trailers."

"He was outside when he did all *that*." Noah waves a hand at the torn-up flower beds and overturned planters that we came home to yesterday—one of them resting at the bottom of the pool.

"Told you we shouldn't leave him alone here. He doesn't like being confined."

"Looks pretty damn happy to me," Noah mumbles, reaching over to hit a button on the coffeemaker.

I peer out the kitchen window in time to see my newfound pet charge a flock of those noisy iridescent blue-black birds, his jaws snapping with excitement. They squawk in protest as they scatter. "What are those birds, anyway?"

"Grackles."

I grimace. "Sounds like something out of the underworld."

He hands me a steaming cup of coffee—black, just how I like it. "Your dog left an underworld bird on the doormat last night. Headless."

"A present for you," I tease, inhaling the comforting aroma before taking my first sip.

Noah's gaze travels down my bare legs. He grins.

"What?"

Stooping over, Noah slowly drags a fingertip along my thigh, beginning just above my knee and moving upward. My skin sprouts gooseflesh instantly. "You weren't kidding when you said you highlighted everything important."

I look down to see wobbly yellow lines from my highlighter all over my legs. And arms. And my new crisp white T-shirt. I groan. "I must have been rolling on it all night! Dammit!"

"I should have capped it," he apologizes, as if this is his fault. "We can buy you more clothes today."

"I can't afford it."

"I've got money—"

"No." He's already been generous enough.

Noah studies me as if deciding whether it's worth the argument. "You're about the same size as my mom was. There's a whole room full of clothes upstairs. Take whatever you want."

Jackie Marshall's clothes? "Wouldn't that be . . . weird?"

"They're just clothes. She doesn't need them anymore." He heaps a spoonful of sugar into his coffee and heaves a sigh, the kind that tells me talking about his mother—even her clothes—isn't as easy as he's making it sound. "Seriously, take what you want. Your mom will fit into some of it, too. We can bring whatever you think she may like when we go to visit her."

We're going to visit her? "Thanks. I'll . . . see." The idea of pillaging a dead woman's closet doesn't sit well with me, but he's right. They're just clothes, and she doesn't need them. I, on the other hand, covered in streaks of fluorescent yellow, do. I savor another mouthful of coffee. "What time is it?"

"Eight."

I groan. "When did we fall asleep, anyway?"

"I don't know. Three? Four?" Noah's eyes are heavily lined by bags.

"No wonder I'm so tired."

He steps into me, and reaches up to push a wayward curl off my forehead, before leaning in to plant a gentle kiss against my lips.

"So, is *this* how it's going to be between us from now on?" I roll my eyes mockingly, trying to cover for the fact that my hands are trembling.

"It's dreadful, isn't it?" He grins against my mouth. "Why don't you go back to bed? We have nowhere we need to be."

As much as that idea—with Noah lying next to me—appeals . . . "We're going to The Lucky Nine today, remember? We talked about it last night."

He furrows his brow. "We did?"

"No. But we *are* going."

"Okay." A pained expression flashes across his face. "If you really want to."

"I do. And then we're going to find this Heath Dunn guy." My dad's partner at the time of his death.

"And why are we going to see him?"

"Because he told investigators that my dad had been taking shady phone calls. We need to know more."

"Of course we do." Noah doesn't look too thrilled at that idea. "I told my mom's secretary that I'd pick up a box of things from the station. We can ask her to look Dunn up while we're there."

"Perfect."

His gaze drifts down to my mouth, settling there. "Yeah . . . perfect," he whispers absently.

I take a step back, out of his reach, as my lower belly is flooded with warmth, because I know where this is headed. "Go! Hurry up and get dressed. This motel is about a half hour away, so we—"

The doorbell rings.

He groans and throws his head back, his Adam's apple jutting out. Long since a favorite male body part of mine, my fingertips itch to slide along the sharp curve.

"Jenson again?"

"No, he rings three times, like the impatient asshole that he is." Noah heads for the door, and I trail behind, admiring the curves of his muscular back and shoulders.

He peeks through the side panel of glass. "Speaking of assholes . . ." He unlocks and yanks open the door.

"Rise and shine, campers." Kristian's flat tone doesn't match his words. He takes a sip of his coffee, his eyes doing a quick head-to-toe of my stained T-shirt and shorts from yesterday. He's swapped his student garb for a pair of tan chinos and a white button-down. Still not how I imagined an FBI agent to look.

Neither is showing up on our doorstep holding a tray of coffees. Presumably, for Noah and me.

"What are you doing here?" Noah doesn't bother to hide his annoyance as he scans the street.

"I told you I was coming." He nods behind him to a man who *does* fit my mental image of an FBI agent, wearing a navy jacket marked by the letters *FBI*. He's leaning against one of two cars parked at the end of the driveway, talking on his phone. A large rectangular case sits by his feet. "That's my evidence guy."

"Right. Give me a minute. Gracie . . ." Noah lowers his voice, his hand coasting over my hip as he edges past me, adding, "Don't invite them in." He heads for the safe in the pantry, where we've locked up everything.

"So, Gracie—" Kristian begins.

"It's Grace."

"Oh . . . I see." He smirks.

"You see what?"

"*He's* the only one who's allowed to call you Gracie." His tone is dripping with insinuation.

My cheeks flame. I don't even notice when Noah calls me that anymore. "How about I worry about what Noah calls me, and you worry about why Dwayne Mantis pulled us over and threatened us yesterday." I recap the five terrifying minutes, unease settling in once again. There was something about that guy—the way he moved, or the way he looked down at me, or simply the fact that I suspect him of murder and I'm clearly on his radar—that instantly put me on edge.

Exactly what Mantis wants.

By the time I'm done recounting the bizarre move by Mantis, all hints of humor are gone from Kristian's handsome face. "Well, if he didn't know you suspected him before, he does now."

"Good—maybe he'll do something stupid."

"Pulling you over was pretty dumb."

"You know what *wasn't* dumb on his part? Getting himself on the investigation team for my father's death."

Kristian gives me a crisp nod of approval. "So you've read the report already."

"Front to back. And that's not all we noticed." I tell him about my mom's statement, about the lack of video or my father's missing gun being mentioned. "Shouldn't those details have been included in there? It should have raised doubt, shouldn't it? At least the missing gun should have."

He watches me curiously, but offers no opinion as he leans against the door frame.

Finally, I can't take it anymore. "So? What do you think?"

Those scrutinizing eyes flicker behind me before boring into my face. "I take you for a smart girl. Do you trust Jackie Marshall's son?" he asks, his voice too low to carry down the hall.

"Yes. I do."

"Really? Because I wouldn't. Not *completely*."

I fold my arms over my chest. "But you think I should trust *you*, right? Why? Because you flashed a badge and then showed up here with coffees, playing the nice guy?"

"Touché." He holds out the tray of Starbucks.

I ignore the offering. "Why shouldn't I trust Noah?"

Klein sets the tray down on the entry table beside the door. "For starters, he lied to the police in his statement. And then he lied to the FBI."

"To protect his mother."

"Who believed that her best friend was murdered and did nothing except leave me a drunken phone message shortly before shooting herself and sending her son across two states with a bag of circumspect money. Why would he protect a woman like that?"

"Because she's his *mother*." Though I've caught myself asking that same question. "Besides, none of that has anything to do with Noah."

Kristian raps his fingertips across the door frame, the beat slow and precise. "Have you noticed how close he is to his uncle?"

"He's lucky to have family." Even if I'm not a fan of that family right now. "What's your point?"

Kristian pauses as if reconsidering his next words. "If Dwayne Mantis set up and killed your father, or had him killed, he'd need help. The kind that usually comes from above." He waits a few beats for me to process that. "Your father had a reputation for being a regular Boy Scout, so the evidence against him would have had to be overwhelming for people to buy it. I'm talking not a shred of doubt. That report? If it was missing key information to allude to another theory, I'm guessing it was because someone made sure it wasn't included."

"Yeah. Mantis."

Kristian's doubtful expression suggests otherwise.

"*Who* then? The guy who wrote the report?" I hesitate. "Jackie Marshall?"

"The chief at the time, George Canning . . . Did you know he and Silas Reid go way back? I'm talking *way* back. Did Noah tell you that?"

No. "Why do you assume Noah knows?"

I get a casual shrug in response.

Kristian's right—I *am* a smart girl, and I can peg what kind of guy he is—the kind that plays on people's vulnerabilities to get under their skin and, inevitably, get what he wants. He wants me doubting Noah. I just don't know why.

I glance over my shoulder to see the hallway still clear. "Stop talking in riddles. What are you getting at?"

"Canning has a lot of influence in this city. More than most politicians. Dig deep enough into how the mayor got elected, how the city manager was chosen, and you'll find Canning's name come up.

People like that set warning bells off inside my head, especially when everyone loves them. And the public *loves* Canning. They think he's the best damn police chief this city has ever had. Hell, they're about to give him a bronze statue. Do you know why that is?" Kristian arches an eyebrow. "He fought against gangs and drug crimes and got results."

"And that's bad how?"

"Because he did it by using guys like Mantis—guys who don't have issues breaking rules along the way to get what they want. Guys whose moral compasses are skewed."

"How do you know Mantis is like that?"

"A hunch."

I sense it's more than a hunch, but I also sense that I'm not going to get an honest answer. "And you think Canning knew what kind of person Mantis is?"

"Do you *really* think someone stays chief for that long by being oblivious?"

I ignore his condescending tone while I quickly fit pieces together in my head. "So you think the chief knew my dad was innocent."

"Maybe. What I *know* is that Jackie Marshall thought your dad was innocent. And I also know that Canning's approval of her is the reason she made chief. And I also know that if a story about Canning's super-cop stealing money in a drug bust ever got out, Canning's legacy to this city would be different. I doubt he'd be getting a bronze statue."

"So the former chief of police had reason to want my father dead."

"Or at least to look dishonest and untrustworthy."

Holy shit. What if Klein is right? What if Mantis killed my father with the chief of police's protection? "So are you going to ask him?"

"Who, Canning?" Kristian chuckles. "You don't let a suspect know that they're a suspect until you've already caught them. You don't show your cards too soon."

The opposite of what I did with Mantis. I couldn't contain that spark of rage, couldn't keep my big mouth shut. I showed my cards. Hell, I didn't just show my cards. I held them up, face out, and let Mantis get a good, long look at them.

"Canning's got connections from all angles to help protect him. One of them happens to be the district attorney of Travis County."

My curiosity outweighs my apprehension. "So you think Noah's uncle will protect Canning?"

"I think he already has." He leans forward, dropping his voice to a whisper. "Noah may be a good guy, but unless you're one thousand percent sure that he's going to choose you over his mother and his uncle, I wouldn't get too caught up in whatever's going on between you two. I'd spend my time keeping an eye and ear out for anything important."

"Is that a warning?" What does Klein know that he's not telling me?

"That's good advice. Take it."

Noah strolls down the hall then, the gym bag dangling from his fingers. "I wrote down all the names that Betsy might be going by, and her birth date. We've already checked for arrest and death records." He holds out the envelope, his tidy writing scrawled across the front of it. "The gun holster is inside the bag."

"Thank you for your cooperation, Noah . . . *finally*. Bill will take care of collecting this. I take it your fingerprints are all over the holster?"

Noah nods. "And the money."

"He'll make note of that. And as soon as you're done with him, you two need to head to our office to give your official statements. The address is on my business card, but just in case you lost it . . ." He produces a card from his wallet and hands it to me. "Do not pass go. Do not collect two hundred dollars. No? Too young to appreciate that joke? Fine. Get there right away. This is now an active federal investigation. You are not to discuss this with anyone, including the district attorney." He levels Noah with a look of warning. "If I find out that you have, I'll nail you with obstruction. Anything else I need to know?"

"Dwayne Mantis pulled us over yesterday and—" Noah begins.

"Gracie's filled me in already. Sorry—*Grace.* I'd stay away from him, if I were you."

No worries there. "I need that picture of my aunt back when you're done. It's the only one we have of her."

Sympathy flashes across Kristian's face, so fast that I wonder if I imagined it. "I'll make sure of it."

"Better let you get to it, then." Noah has one hand on the door, looking ready to slam it in Kristian's face. I'm not used to this sharper side of him. It's nice to know he has one, and even nicer to know he's never felt the need to use it on me, no matter how abrasive I've been toward him.

Even if Kristian is just doing his job, I can't help but feel like he's doing me a personal favor. Maybe I should be nicer to him. "Thanks for the coffee."

Noah watches Kristian through narrowed eyes as the FBI agent strolls down the steps and path, stopping to talk with Bill.

"You really don't like him."

"He rubs me the wrong way," he admits, a brooding frown creasing his forehead.

"At least he's smart enough to bring the expensive coffee when it's this early."

"He's trying to convince us that he's a good guy." Noah smirks, echoing my earlier accusation as he collects the tray, handing me mine.

"And you don't think he is?"

"He could be," he admits reluctantly. "But I have this gut feeling that he's after more than just Mantis's head."

I hesitate. "Like whose? The chief?"

"There *is* no chief. Well, there's the interim, but he wouldn't be after him."

"No, I mean the one who was chief when my dad died," I say as casually as I can.

"Who, Canning?" Noah seems to think on that. "Maybe. I don't know how far he'll get with that. Everyone loves that guy."

Not everyone. Not Klein. "Have you met him?"

"He was at Silas's when I went for dinner last week." Noah shrugs. "He seems like a good guy. You know, one of those people who throws out an open invitation to his ranch and means it."

"He actually did that? Invited you out?"

"Yeah . . ." He frowns. "Why?"

If I repeat what Kristian said about Canning's motives for wanting my dad gone, will Noah then go and tell his uncle? And, if his uncle is as good friends with Canning as Kristian suggested, will he warn Canning that Kristian is on to him? *"You don't let a suspect know that they're a suspect until you've already caught them."*

Then why the hell would Kristian tell me in the first place? He knows there's something going on between Noah and me, so he has to also assume I'd tell Noah about this. Is he testing me?

I can't figure that guy out. It's like I'm playing a game with him, where the stakes are high but I don't know the rules.

"Gracie?"

"No reason. So, where is this FBI office? Is The Lucky Nine on the way?" Or Paradise Lane, as the motel is now called.

"Not really . . ."

I take a sip of my coffee, peering up at him with my best attempt at begging eyes. "Can it be?"

He grins. "Maybe. But you heard Klein. He said—"

"Do not pass go." I shrug. "We're not. We're passing a seedy hooker motel."

Noah rolls his eyes. "Fine. We'll stop." He points at Kristian's car as it pulls away. "And, for the record, I do *not* trust him."

"Yeah, there's a lot of that going around," I mumble under my breath as Bill the FBI evidence guy climbs the steps.

The vibrant feel of Austin's downtown is long gone by the time we spot the green neon sign that towers over Paradise Lane, advertising daily, weekly, and monthly rates. The shady motel is located on the far outskirts of Austin's lower-class suburbs, past the plain strip malls and sketchy chain gas stations, beside a freeway where a steady stream of cars buzzes by, off to other parts of Texas.

Noah turns into the parking lot, his SUV dipping and jumping over the uneven pavement and potholes. Ahead of us are three long beige buildings, positioned in a *U* shape—aptly named Building One, Building Two, and Building Three, according to the signs. Each is lined with dirty pea-soup-green room doors.

It feels as oppressive as The Hollow.

"You *sure* you want to do this?" he asks gently, pulling into a spot near the reception lobby.

"I *have* to. Don't you feel like we have to?" I scan the door numbers. I can't see Room 116 from here.

Noah's gaze drifts over the sparsely filled parking lot. "It's weird, isn't it? That he died *here*."

"Of all places." I climb out of the SUV. "Do you think they'll let us into the room?"

"Depends on how good you are at talking," a familiar voice calls out from behind me, making me jump.

"Don't you have people to see?" I snap as Kristian saunters toward us. How did we miss his sedan?

"I was going to say the same thing to you." His steely eyes lock on Noah, whose glare looks sharp enough to pierce skin. "What are you two doing here?"

"I wanted to see the place where my father died. We're heading in to give our statements right after this."

"And what do you hope to get out of it?"

"Closure." Is that even possible? I doubt it—not until I see Mantis, and anyone else who was involved, punished. "What are *you* doing here?"

Klein's brow quirks. "Investigating a murder . . . remember?"

"Where's Tareen?" Noah asks, looking around.

"On his way. Come on." He begins heading for the lobby door, warning over his shoulder, "Let me do the talking."

"Good luck with that," Noah murmurs under his breath, a smug smirk curling his lips.

We follow him inside, Noah behind me, his hand on the small of my back, as usual. I can't believe it used to bother me. I get it now—it's a protective gesture, and not in the "Gracie can't take care of herself" way, but an "if someone's going to get hurt, I won't let it be her" way.

The lobby is cramped and depressing, the blinds covering the front window soiled with years of dust and bent from prying fingertips. The low hum of voices from the ancient TV competes with the constant rattle of a vending machine in the corner. It looks like they've attempted to update the space, laying new green faux-marble linoleum tiles down over the old beige ones. But they didn't cut the pieces properly, and the beige is still visible along the walls.

There's a staleness to the air that I can't pinpoint—a combination of burnt coffee, musty cardboard, and tobacco, lingering from years gone by when it was acceptable for a receptionist to check you in while puffing on a cigarette.

Not that a place like this would be too worried about respecting laws even now.

Kristian sets his elbows on the front desk counter and leans, causing the entire unit to shift. He either doesn't notice or doesn't care, his focus on the heavyset woman working behind the counter, a crime thriller in her hands. "Miss Glorya Ruiz!" he says in a cheerful voice.

She closes her book and eyes him like I would eye anyone who came here—suspiciously. "You can read name badges. Good for you."

"How long have you worked here, Glorya?"

"Nine years. Why?" There's a challenge in her tone.

"Just curious."

"You gonna waste my time or get a room?" She glances over at me, then at Noah standing behind me. "I figure she ain't cheap, but I'm not givin' you no deal for sweet-talkin' me."

Glorya thinks I'm a hooker. An expensive one, but a hooker all the same.

I open my mouth to blast her, but Noah's arm curls around my waist. He pulls me back against him and leans in to whisper, so close to my ear that his lips graze my lobe, "Let him handle this."

Even in the sordid setting, the intimate contact sends a thrill down my spine. I instinctively sink into his body.

"So, Glorya . . . do you remember that big shooting here?"

She flashes a wicked smile that highlights all her missing teeth. "Darling, which one? There's been a few over the years."

"May third, 2003. An off-duty police officer was shot. It was a big deal. The owner changed the motel's name not long after that. Too much bad press, I guess."

"Right. I might've heard about that one."

"What'd you hear?"

She gives him a flat look. "That a cop got shot."

"In Room 116, right?"

She shrugs. "Sure. Why not."

"Listen, I was wondering if we could take a quick look in there."

"If it's available." She glances over at the key rack where the room keys hang. They clearly haven't upgraded . . . anything. "It's available."

"Great! We'll only be—"

"That's forty bucks for the two-hour rate."

"The *two-hour* rate?" I blurt out. "Is that a thing?"

"It's a forty-dollar *thing*." Now Glorya's treating me to that same stare.

Kristian leans forward, folding his hands in a pleading way. "Her dad was the cop. She hasn't been back to Austin since, and it would mean a lot to her if you'd let us step inside the room for five minutes, so she could get closure."

Kristian's words seem to melt the cynical layer from that woman's ice-cold heart. She reaches for the keys and slaps them on the counter, her eyes flickering to me, a touch softer. "End of Building One. You got five minutes."

"Thank you, Glorya. Hey, any chance there's someone on staff that would have been working here back then? You know, housekeeping, maintenance . . . security . . ."

Glorya settles onto her stool with a huff and, reaching for the worn paperback, continues reading from her marked page.

Ignoring us.

"Thanks for your time. I'll be right back with that key." Kristian waves for us to follow him out the door.

"Why didn't you flash your badge? Isn't this what it's for?" I ask.

"People in places like this tend to say less around badges, not more." He leads us down a covered walkway past a row of rooms. One of those ugly pea-soup-green doors pops open and a man steps out, adjusting his tie as he pulls the door shut. But not before I catch a glimpse of the woman inside, nude and tangled in sheets, a cigarette perched between her lips as she shuffles a wad of cash.

The man ducks his head and scoots past to his black sedan, avoiding my stare. Of the ten cars in the parking lot, five of them are shiny, newish models. Nothing too luxurious—no Audis or BMWs—but decent cars, all the same. Cars driven by people who could probably afford better hotel rooms than this, if they weren't here to pay for the services of a modestly priced prostitute.

"Come on, Gracie." Noah gently guides me forward to the far end of the building, where Kristian stands in front of an open door.

My breath catches as I take in the gold-plated number—*116*.

We step inside and the temperature instantly drops. At least, it feels cooler. If I didn't know this was *the* room where my dad died, would I have the same reaction? Would this strange hollowness, coupled with a swell of anger, stir?

"Definitely not the Ritz," Kristian murmurs, his hands resting on his hips as he takes in the room: one queen bed and a dresser, a basic kitchenette and, next to it, I presume a bathroom.

I scrunch my nose. "It smells like feet in here." And cigarettes. I'm not surprised, given the ashtray that sits right beside the "no smoking" plaque by the bed.

Kristian wanders in, squatting to peer at the floor near the window, dragging his finger along the thin burgundy carpet.

"What are you doing?"

"This seam, here. Do you see it?"

I frown. The carpet is dark and the lighting is poor, so it's hard to spot the line at first. "What about it?"

"Looks like the owner was too cheap to re-carpet the room, so he just cut away where it was stained and glued down a remnant piece."

My stomach drops as I stare at the spot with new understanding. The report said Hernandez was found by the window. The carpet would have been stained by his blood. "You really think this is from fourteen years ago?"

"There've been no reports of incidents in this room since." Klein stands and walks over to the opposite side of the bed, his stride purposeful. He runs his toe along another seam in the rug—another new piece to replace a section of blood-soaked carpet. "This is where they found Wilkes."

Wilkes. My father. Oddly, it doesn't sound strange to hear him referred to by his last name. Maybe that's because he's little more than a painful memory to me.

I take a deep breath, and try to imagine the man I know from pictures and a foggy recollection lying there.

"Coroner's report said he died quickly. Three bullets to his chest." Kristian smooths his hand over a layer of beige-striped wallpaper that's begun to separate on the wall behind the bed's headboard.

Quickly isn't instantly.

Noah's hand settles on my shoulder, the pad of his thumb rubbing over my collarbone affectionately. "You okay?"

"I'm fine." I swallow the growing lump in my throat and take in the dingy room again, wondering what it would have been like to die here. Wondering about those last few moments, as blood seeped into his lungs, as his heart gave way. What does "dying quickly" feel like? Does it *really* feel quick? Or are those last moments agonizingly long, as you play out all the things you won't get to say, won't get to experience, all the regrets?

What were my father's last thoughts about? My mother? Me? Noah?

"What are you looking for, exactly?" Noah asks, not hiding his impatience.

"Anything interesting," Kristian says in that flat way of his, where he makes everything sound boring when it's anything but.

"Do you have any theories?" Noah pushes.

"One."

Noah's jaw hardens as he waits for the evasive FBI agent to elaborate.

"The simplest, most obvious one," Kristian says after a pause. "There was a third person in this room, who pulled the trigger on one or both of Wilkes and Hernandez."

"Great. Now you just have to prove that, with no evidence." Noah folds his arms over his chest and waits quietly for an explanation.

A smirk touches Kristian's lips as he runs his hand over that strip of wallpaper again. "Do me a favor, Grace, and go stand over there, on the other side of the bed. Pretend you're Hernandez."

As much as I don't want to be playing the role of the dead drug dealer, I follow his instructions and wander over to stand where the carpet was patched.

"Take a look at the wall. What do you see?"

I squint. "Ducks?"

"Swans, actually. But look closely. What do you notice?"

I eye the expanse of ugly beige for a long moment before I notice a seam line, much like the one on Kristian's side. "This piece looks newer. Not as dirty." The strip of wallpaper runs about three feet wide, from floor to ceiling, just behind the nightstand.

"Right. It's the same over here." Kristian waves a hand in front of him. "If the motel owners cut out chunks of bloody carpet instead of just replacing it all, how much do you want to bet they also slapped remnant paper overtop blood splatter to save themselves the effort and money of re-wallpapering everything?"

"But . . . wait." I frown as I try to recall the crime scene notes, riffling through the pages of the report that I brought with me. "It says here that the blood splatter was on *that* wall." I point to the wall directly behind Kristian, which divides the bedroom area from the bathroom. "And on the window."

"You're right. That's what it says. And it would line up with the story that Wilkes and Hernandez took each other down, standing on either side of this bed."

"But . . ." Noah pushes.

"Hernandez took one bullet in the head, killing him instantly. That means he would have had to pull the trigger first. Right?"

I glance at Noah to see him nod.

"Let's suppose the report is right for a sec. Hernandez is standing over there when he shoots Wilkes three times in the chest. Wilkes goes down, but before he does, he manages to fire off a round that kills Hernandez where he stands, over there." He points at me. "The bullet goes right through Hernandez. Into his forehead and out the back of his skull at a hundred-and-eighty-degree angle, based on the coroner's report."

"That means Abe would have had to be standing," Noah murmurs.

"Right. A guy gets shot three times in the chest and manages to lift his gun to shoot a guy head-on? Not impossible, but it's definitely worth questioning. But what's more interesting is the old news footage I found from that night. There was nothing on that window. No blood, from what I can see, and definitely no bullet hole."

"So you're saying there's false evidence in the report?" Noah's brow is tight with concentration.

"Well, let's try another scenario. Wilkes and Hernandez are standing in the same place. Hernandez shoots Wilkes three times. Wilkes hits *this* wall," Kristian falls backward to hit the strip of wallpaper that was replaced, "and then, just before going down, shoots Hernandez in the head."

"But if that strip of wallpaper behind Gracie is hiding splatter from Hernandez, then . . ." Recognition fills Noah's face. "Abe couldn't have shot Hernandez." Noah takes long backward strides to the opposite side of Klein. He raises his hand like a mock gun. "Someone would have had to be standing over here to shoot Abe. And then shoot Hernandez from over here." He shifts over to the other side of the bed, closer to me.

There *had* to be a third person involved.

"Mantis," I say automatically.

"Maybe," Kristian agrees. "Turns out Luiz Hernandez was one of the APD's informants, so it's plausible that they knew each other."

"And the room was rented out to Hernandez, right? He could have opened the door and invited Mantis right on in," Noah murmurs. "Mantis probably shot Hernandez to keep him quiet."

"And made him the scapegoat," Kristian adds.

"Look at you two, getting along over murder theories." I eye the cut-out carpet patches and strips of wallpaper with renewed interest. "How can we trust *anything* that's in the report, then?"

Kristian's phone chirps with a message. He disappears out the door.

"I'll give him one thing: he hasn't wasted time looking into this," I murmur.

"Yeah, he's a real superstar." Noah's voice drips with sarcasm. He studies the spot where my dad died for a long moment, a troubled look on his face.

"What are you thinking?"

He hesitates. "That Silas said he looked over every piece of evidence. He should have noticed this."

I bite my tongue. Noah doesn't need to hear my accusations right now.

Silence lingers in the dingy motel room for a long moment.

"I'll be outside." He turns and strolls out the door.

I wait a beat longer. Long enough to close my eyes and try to recall something about my father. Anything. That laugh that Noah mentioned the other day, that infectious booming sound. "We won't let them get away with this," I whisper into the empty room, before finally leaving.

I find Noah and Kristian around the corner.

" . . . it'd be easy enough." Noah leads us along the path. Room 116 is on the end of Building One and there's a walkway between it and Building Two, which runs perpendicular. The walkway ends at the back, where there's nothing but Dumpsters and open space and, beyond that, a commuter parking lot for the highway.

"He could have ducked out and come this way. Made the 9-1-1 call from that parking lot." Kristian stops at the rusty chain-link fence that separates the properties, hidden from view. Grabbing hold of it, he gives it a tug. The one side comes clean off the pole. "Any bets that's been busted for at least fourteen years?"

"Did they even check?"

"Without the evidence files, we'll never know." Kristian's hands settle on his hips as he does a slow circle, his brow tight. With frustration or thought, I can't tell.

"Do you believe that evidence was 'accidentally incinerated'?" I ask.

He doesn't miss a beat. "Not a chance."

"Is that you being suspicious or do you have actual proof?" Noah levels him with an even gaze.

If Kristian's irritated by Noah's constant testing, he doesn't let on. He does, however, seem to weigh his words. "The team that investigated Abraham Wilkes's death was hand-selected by Chief George Canning. Mantis was one of them. Shawn Stapley was another. Canning pulled the two of them from their drug squad duties temporarily, to work this case for him.

"Nine months later, Stapley got hurt on duty and ended up assigned to administrative work. Guess where?" He pauses for a second. "The evidence room. He was the one who 'accidentally' sent the case to the incinerator."

The pieces are all starting to fit together nicely.

"And no one questioned this?" My voice carries through the near-vacant parking lot.

"Why would they? New system in place . . . horrible glitch . . ."

"Because they had no reason to question it," I mutter.

"I think someone started building a case against your dad before anyone crossed that motel-room threshold." Kristian's voice is a touch softer. "Why else would they execute a search warrant on his house less than twenty-four hours after he was shot?"

"Holy shit," Noah whispers under his breath. Realization dawns on his face.

Kristian studies him. "Care to enlighten?"

Noah sighs. "Canning said that right before Abe died, Mantis told him about a tip from an informant that an APD officer was dealing drugs. I'll bet Mantis started setting Abe up with the chief as soon as he knew Abe wanted to bust him."

"So you know Canning personally?" Behind that veiled flat look, I can see Kristian's thoughts swirling.

"No, not really. He was at my uncle's for dinner. We talked about Abe's case a bit."

Kristian's knowing gaze passes over me, his eyebrow arching. I see the unspoken accusation there. *See, Grace? Canning and Silas, like two peas in a pod.*

I ignore it. "Okay, so Canning picked Mantis and this Shawn Stapley guy to investigate. But what about the others?"

"You mean the two officers who work in Internal Affairs under Mantis? The ones who were recently investigated for falsifying evidence?" Amusement touches his lips. "I wouldn't count on them for honesty, either."

"Weren't they cleared?" Noah asks.

"They were. By Chief Marshall." Kristian begins walking away.

"Hey! Where are you going?"

"To go visit the lovely Glorya again." He holds up a business card between two fingers. "I want her to be able to call me when she hears anything."

I snort. "Because she's been *so* cooperative."

"We'll see if she changes her tune when I show her my badge and hand her the warrant we just got to tear apart this room."

So that's why he was here in the first place . . . "Do you actually think you'll find anything?"

"You two need to get to my office," Klein says, ignoring my question. "Give your name to security and Agent Proby will get you started. I'll be there as soon as I get my team settled here." He waves at Agent Tareen, who just stepped out of his car, holding papers in the air as if in confirmation. Beside him an unmarked white van has pulled up.

"If nothing else, he's efficient," Noah mumbles, digging change out of his pocket as he heads for the vending machine. "Do you want anything?"

"A Coke. Please."

After sliding the coins into the slot and stabbing at the button with his finger several times, he frowns at the machine, then smacks it. "Damn thing ate my money."

"Are you surprised?"

Noah's phone rings, distracting him. He looks at the screen and then, shaking his head to himself, hits a button, sending the call to voicemail. He's done that twice already today. My guess is he's avoiding his uncle.

"You all right?"

He squeezes the bridge of his nose between his fingers. "Yeah, I just . . . Let's get this statement thing over with." His phone rings again and he swears under his breath.

"Who is it?"

Surprise flashes across his face when he checks the screen again. "Pool company. Give me a sec?"

While he answers, I let my gaze drift over the three buildings. It's quiet here, not a soul milling around. Not many want to be caught loitering in a place like this.

If each block has sixteen rooms—which looks about right—then there are forty-eight rooms in total. And even if some of those rooms weren't rented that night, some of them had to be. How many people might have seen a third person duck out of 116?

How many of them did Mantis scare into not talking?

We don't have a list of contacts to track them down. Kristian's right—we don't have much.

From the corner of my eye, I catch a curtain shift in Room 201. It's the last room in Building Two, the room that sits kitty-corner to 116. A wiry old man stands in the window, his skin a dark chocolate, his hair frizzy and going gray at the tips. He's wearing brown trousers and a rumpled button-down shirt that hangs open to reveal the dirt-smeared white tank top beneath, and he's simply standing there.

Staring intently at me, not a flicker of a twitch, or a smile. He could pass for a mannequin.

A chill runs down my spine.

"Come on, let's go," Noah calls out. "That was the pool-cleaning guy. Cyclops decided he's a guard dog now and tried to bite him. He said he'd come back later this afternoon as long as we get Cy inside."

I glance back at the window of Room 201.

The man is gone.

CHAPTER 41

Noah

I stretch my cramped hands as I check the clock on the wall of the small room, empty save for a table and two chairs. Giving my statement took over two hours. "Can I go?"

"Yes, sir. Miss Richards is waiting for you," Agent Proby says.

"Thank you, ma'am."

"Uh-huh." I get a tight smile in return from the middle-aged blonde woman.

Gracie greets me in the hallway with a wide smile, and my feet falter. She's happy and hopeful, and I get it. Finally, someone—and not just *someone*, but the FBI—is working to clear Abe's name.

I smile back, even with this ever-looming dread that hangs over me. Because the flip side to all this is that it may not be all sunshine and roses for my family. I still don't know how my mother was involved in what happened to Abe, though—thankfully—she wasn't part of this Canning-picked investigation team. And Silas . . . I'm beginning to wonder what exactly he knows.

Gracie's smile wavers. "What's wrong?"

"Nothing. I'm famished. Let's get the hell out of here." Roping a loose arm around her waist, I pull her to me. We begin walking down the hall.

Agent Proby trails behind to escort us out. "Agent Klein will be in contact with you if he needs clarification," she says, nodding to the guard.

I let Gracie go ahead of me through security.

She comes to an abrupt stop, and I bump into her. "What's—" My words cut off as I see the problem—Dwayne Mantis is standing on the other side.

My adrenaline instantly begins racing through my veins.

He hasn't noticed us yet, his head down, busy checking his gun and other belongings with the guard. An older, bearded man in a gray suit stands next to him, and two other men trail closely behind. One of them looks vaguely familiar, though I can't place him.

Gracie's body has gone rigid.

I drop my voice to a whisper, settling my hand gently on her hip. "Let's slide out of here before—"

"Mr. Mantis!" Klein exclaims from behind us, pulling Mantis's attention up.

Those beady eyes flicker past us, searching for the source of the voice, but quickly fly back to lock on Gracie.

"Thank you for coming in on short notice." Klein grins as if completely oblivious to the choking tension in the lobby.

If there's one thing I've learned about Klein, he's anything but oblivious. The bastard timed this perfectly. He wants to unsettle Mantis and, unfortunately, he doesn't care what it does to us in the process.

Finally, Mantis peels that fierce gaze away from Gracie. "Anything to help the feds with a case," he says calmly.

Klein nods to the man in the suit. "And you are . . ."

"My lawyer, Sid DeHavelin," Mantis answers for him.

"Lawyer?" Klein mock-frowns. "To answer questions about an old case? Why would you think you need a lawyer?"

Mantis grins, showing off a row of perfectly straight, albeit stubby teeth. "Sid insisted."

"Alright. I mean, it's your dime, but waste of money if you ask me. Mr. Stapley, I'm guessing he's here to waste your money too?" Klein says to the man towering behind Mantis.

Klein is questioning Shawn Stapley, too.

Gracie and I exchange glances.

What pretenses did they come in on, I wonder.

Klein throws a casual wave to us. "Hey, thanks for the help, kids. It's a wonder what you can dig up, even after all these years, isn't it? We'll be in touch soon."

The prick. He's toying with them. If it weren't at the risk of Gracie's safety, I'd applaud him. I want to punch him in the face again. I settle for spearing him with a glare instead.

He ignores it, holding an arm out in invitation.

Mantis and Stapley pass through the metal detectors with their lawyers close behind.

Klein frowns at Stapley. "You okay, man?"

"Yeah, why?" Stapley's voice is so smooth and melodious next to Mantis's. And it's filled with wariness.

"That looks like blood." Klein nods toward Stapley's leg, where a dark spot seeps through his khaki pants at his calf.

"Oh, that." He brushes it off with a dismissive wave and a chuckle. "Got into a fight with a garden rake in the shed. It won."

Klein grimaces, and I can't tell if he's genuinely sympathetic or it's all part of the act.

Meanwhile, Mantis walks with a slow, easy swagger, his hands tucked casually in his pockets, like he's got nothing to hide, not a worry in the world. But before he disappears behind the door, he looks over his shoulder at us.

At Gracie.

His eyes narrow in challenge.

"I *am* just like my father, you son of a bitch," she growls, too low for anyone but me to hear.

I loop my arm around hers and guide her out before she starts screaming profanities.

"We didn't need that . . . or that . . . *Five* lemons?" Gracie dangles the fruit in the air in front of her before stuffing it into the fridge drawer. "We can't possibly eat all this, Noah."

"You'd be surprised how much I can eat." I grin, patting my belly. I'm starved, my appetite having come back with a vengeance.

She groans, fishing out the bag of avocados. "You said you don't eat these. *Why* would you buy them then?"

"Because I thought *you* wanted them?" I say slowly, warily.

"I hate avocados!"

I don't know whether to be amused or annoyed. "Well, if you'd tell me what you want instead of playing your little game, I wouldn't have had to guess." I don't think I've ever been more confused in a grocery store than I was today, trailing behind Gracie in the local HEB, watching her fondle fruits and vegetables before quietly putting them back on the shelf. What else was I supposed to do besides scoop them up and put them in the cart?

"It wasn't a game. It's . . ." Her voice trails off with a sigh of exasperation.

"It's what?" I toss Cyclops a dog bone as I rifle through the bags on the counter, looking for a quick snack. She's right. The two of us can't eat all this. We shouldn't have gone shopping while I was hungry.

"It's stupid. It's just something I do when I go grocery shopping." Her cheeks flush.

I settle on an apple, giving it a rinse as I watch her pointedly, waiting for her to explain.

"We couldn't afford fresh stuff. When I was younger, I'd watch people squeeze avocados and check tomatoes and peppers for bruises, before picking the best ones to put in their cart. So I started pretending I was doing the same thing.

"Then we'd head over to the canned goods aisles, to buy whatever was on sale. Sometimes, when no one was looking, my nan would 'accidentally' knock an expensive can off the shelf with her elbow, just so it'd dent, 'cause you can get a discount on dented cans."

"So you *never* had fresh food?"

"A special treat, here or there. On my birthday and for Christmas. Nan would buy those little Christmas oranges—"

"Clementines?"

"Yeah, those. And a frozen turkey, that she'd bake. Just a small one. But we mostly ate canned tuna. Or Spam. Have you ever eaten Spam?"

"Can't say I have." I hide my cringe by biting a chunk out of my apple. My mom likened Spam to the canned dog food we'd feed Jake.

Gracie smiles, but it's bittersweet. "Yeah, I'm not surprised. I'll bet the grocery stores around this neighborhood don't stock a lot of it. Anyway, like I said. It's stupid."

"No it's not." I reach over to give her slender forearm what I hope is a comforting rub. I let my hand linger there for a long moment, the feel of her silky skin against mine too hard to resist. Thoughts of this morning—of her warm, soft body in my arms, of her pliable lips opening for me—flood my mind and set my heart racing.

But the mood has shifted since this morning, in those brief, intimate moments where there was just her and me. Klein invaded, and then we went to The Lucky Nine and the stark reality of why Gracie's here in the first place came crashing back. I haven't had the nerve to kiss her again.

I've thought about it a hundred times, though.

And just the thought of Gracie struggling to pay her bills or having to eat canned meat, or living next to a lowlife like that Sims guy, ever again has me panicking. "Hey, so I was thinking, you should move back to Texas."

She frowns as she pulls away from me—from my touch—to unload more groceries. "Why?"

"Because I have this big house to myself. Why not stay here? You don't have to pay rent. You could get a job, and save your money."

"You're not obligated to pay for what others have done to us, Noah," she says quietly. She leans over to stuff meat into drawers in the fridge, giving me a view I could sit here and appreciate for days.

"That's not why I'm doing this," I insist.

She seems to consider it. "Is it even a good idea?"

"Why wouldn't it be?"

"Because of—" She cuts herself off, her brow furrowing. "Things are getting complicated."

Complicated because of what's happening between us? This thing that's come out of nowhere, and yet has probably been here all along? At least, it has on my end.

Or complicated with the investigation? With what Silas might know, what he may be lying about?

A soft, shaky sigh sails from her full lips. "Let's see if Kristian can clear my dad's name, first. Okay?"

Kristian. Not Agent Klein. Or Klein. She's calling the FBI agent by his first name.

I grit my teeth and nod.

"Where should I put this?" She hoists the hefty watermelon up.

"In the pantry. Here, let me." I reach for it, but she sidesteps me.

"I've got it." Cradling it in one arm like a football, she struggles to open the door off the side of the kitchen and then disappears inside. A moment later, there's a holler of, "God, Noah! There's enough food in here to feed a family for a year! Why did we even go shopping?"

I give Cyclops a rough pat and then let him outside before heading into the long, narrow room, giving the dangling chain a yank to flood the space with dull light. "See? Another reason to stay in Austin. I need you to keep me in check."

She rolls her eyes. "I don't know where you want this thing."

I slip the watermelon from her grasp, my hand skimming across the flat of her stomach in the process. She inhales sharply, the slight feminine sound rushing blood straight to my groin as I set the fruit on a shelf. "Come on . . . How will I survive without you giving me grief?" I say it with a smile, so she knows I'm teasing.

She slides on a mask of calm indifference. "Hey, I didn't give you grief for paying a fool's price for that thing. And there's no way you're going to finish it before it goes bad."

"Actually, it's all on you. I'm deathly allergic to all melons."

Her mouth hangs open. "Why the hell would you buy it!" she exclaims, smacking my arm.

I shrug, and then smile sheepishly. "You seemed interested."

"In the ridiculous size of it, yeah." She shakes her head. "You're right. You *do* need me here to give you grief." Her throat bobs with a hard swallow, all lightheartedness vanishing. "And I need you because you're the only one who won't let me down."

"But, I *have*. I didn't tell—"

"No, Noah." Her green eyes flitter over my features, stalling on my mouth. "Since you showed up on my doorstep, you have been there for me, *every* step of the way, whether I deserved it or not. You are everything I could possibly have asked for." Her face twists with a grimace, as if that's not a good thing.

The pantry seemed narrow and cramped before. Now I can't get close enough to her, fast enough. She's small next to me, and I'm afraid of overwhelming her as my hands settle on her hips, and her head tilts back to meet my eyes. "I'm not going anywhere. And we're not going to let that asshole Mantis, or anyone who's responsible, get away with this, I swear it."

She sighs softly, and I revel in the feel of her breath caressing my skin. "You can't promise that, Noah. What if we find out something about your mother—"

"Then she's guilty, and I'll make sure everyone knows it." As much as that pains me to even say.

A fire smolders in her gaze. "And what if your mother isn't the only one close to you who did this?"

She doesn't have to say Silas's name. "Then that person will get what's coming to him, too." My stomach churns with the thought, but I steel myself against that vulnerability, instead filling my thoughts with Abe, with the emptiness I felt standing in that seedy motel room today, staring down at the spot where he took his last breaths.

Alone.

No doubt, spending those moments thinking of this girl standing in front of me, and how she would remember him. "Your dad . . . he *was* a good, honest man and he deserves for the world to know that." I push a wayward curl off her face. "And, even under the shitty circumstances, I can't tell you how glad I am that you're back in my life." I hesitate. "Even if you want it to be just as friends. There's no pressure here, Gracie. I'm here to stay, no matter what."

Her eyes settle on my mouth, her own lips parting. "Well, if friends is all *you* want, then—"

"No, it's not," I say, way too eagerly, and then grin, feeling my cheeks heat. *I want a hell of a lot more.*

A rare wave of shyness radiates from her, and yet she stretches to her tiptoes to trail her cool nose along the side of my neck. "You sure you want to deal with the likes of me? Some people say I'm difficult." There's a hint of something in her voice, something exposed. Like she actually may believe that I would second-guess my feelings, that I would decide that she's too much for me.

My face is buried in her mass of floral-scented curls, so she can't possibly see my mock frown, but maybe she can hear it in my voice. "Who would say that?"

"I don't know . . . crazy people?"

"Exactly. *I'm* not crazy. Are you crazy?" I mimic her words from that first day, remembering how I had to beg her to trust me. Now, those hands that wielded a switchblade are memorizing the feel of my chest. How things have changed.

Her responding chuckle is deep and throaty, sending shivers down my spine. "Sims would say I am."

I groan at the mention of that asshole. "You really know how to kill the mood."

"Did I kill the mood for you?"

I shudder against the feel of her tongue trailing along my skin where her nose just touched. And lose my ability to think altogether as her teeth graze my earlobe, at the sound of her shaky breath in my ear as she whispers, "Well, if you don't feel up to it, I'll just go and—"

I steal her words with my mouth, my hand slipping around the back of her neck to gain purchase as I kiss her, my fingers weaving into her hair. There's no hesitation on either of our parts this time, that tentative, sweet tempo of this morning replaced with something more fervent, more needy.

"Believe me, I'm *up* to it." My free hand travels down her arm, around her back, pulling her body flush against mine. Erasing any doubt she may have about how "up" to it I am.

Yet still, Gracie goads me. "Prove it," she purrs against my lips, nose to nose, eyes locked on mine. It's a challenge.

An invitation.

Maybe, permission.

Whatever it is, I greedily take it, my fingers testing the waistband of her shorts with a quick swipe before slipping beneath her T-shirt. Her breathing turns raspy as I memorize the ridges of her spine first, and then move my hand around to her flat, hard stomach.

Her own hands have found their place on my shoulders now, and they claw and tighten as my fingers venture upward to settle between the swell of her breasts, the lace of her bra itchy against my palm.

Her hands disappear from my shoulders and, a moment later, that lace material loosens, giving me access to her ample breasts. "Since you're taking your time . . ." She smirks, her fingertips returning to my body—to my chest this time—to softly drag over the ridges of muscle.

I've never been nervous with a girl, but with Gracie my gut is rolling with nerves as I push her bra aside and cup her breast, full and heavy within my palm. My thumb grazes against her peaked nipple, eliciting a soft gasp from her against my lips. I'm desperate to see Gracie naked, to trace every one of her curves with my fingers, my tongue.

Yet sudden, rare fear holds me back from making a move.

Fear that she'll change her mind on a whim, that I want this way more than she does; that, in the end, *I* won't be what she wants. I fight desperately to chase that fear away by pulling her mouth into mine, to kiss her like I'm convincing her that I *am* what she wants. All that she will *ever* want. I kiss her like I want her to pine over me. I kiss her like I want her to remember this moment in case we never have another chance.

She melts into my body, her hands sliding down to my stomach, hot skin pressed against hot skin, her thumbs teasing my belt line. I feel myself swelling more, and I grit my teeth against the wish that those nimble fingers would make quick work of my buckle and zipper and slide farther down.

Gripping her firm backside, I lift and carry her into a corner, pinning her to the wall with my hips. It gives me easier access to her body and I take it, lifting her shirt high enough to take one of her nipples in my mouth, the delicious scent of peach-scented body wash that lingers on her skin making me inhale deeply.

Gracie moans my name softly, tightening her thighs around my waist.

This is going too far, much too fast. If I take her to my bedroom, I already know I'll be inside her in minutes like some fool who can't control himself. So I stay put in these cramped quarters, instead sinking to my knees and maneuvering around, until I'm sitting on the floor with my back to the wall and Gracie is straddling my hips, her eyes wild with need.

"Gracie, I think we should slow down and . . ." My voice fails me as she peels her shirt over her head and shrugs her unfastened bra off, leaving me to gape at her naked breasts, heavy and heaving with each quick breath. I knew her body would be beautiful, but she's utterly perfect. "You're . . ." I can't even get the words out, admiring her bared top half while I run my hands up her muscular thighs, my finger slipping beneath the hem of her shorts. I manage to stop at her panty line, and it takes everything in me to not go farther, to not find out if she's in the same predicament as I am. And I am in a terrible predicament—I don't want to rush with her, and yet I'm about to explode, the anticipation too much.

Hooking my hands around the backs of her knees, I pull her body flush against me. "We're not doing this yet," I whisper against her lips, my arms folding around her body to hold her close to me.

"You *sure* about that?" Her voice is dripping with sarcasm.

I hiss as Gracie rolls her hips, pressing hard into me.

"I'm sorry, what did you say? I missed that last part," she murmurs, cocking her head in mock concern, grinding down on me again. And again, her hips rolling in an erotic dance, the swell of her breasts brushing against my chest.

I hadn't expected *this* version of Gracie—seductive, playful, forward.

Who am I kidding? I'm doomed to be a fool.

My head falls back against the wall and I close my eyes. "You wicked woman."

Gracie's delightful deep-bellied laughter answers, and she leans in to trace the edge of my neck with her tongue.

I groan as she pushes a hand down between us, to smooth over my length.

"What is that?"

"Uh . . . what do you mean?" That's a question I've never had a girl ask me before, in this particular situation.

Her ragged breathing slows. "No, I'm serious, Noah. It looks like . . . blood?"

Finally I realize she's intently focused on her fingertips, rubbing something between them. I follow her gaze to the hardwood floor beside us, to the dark crimson smear. It's definitely fresh blood.

"Did you cut yourself?" Gracie's hand begins prodding me as she searches.

"No. And that's a few hours old, at least." I can tell by the dark line that's formed around the original drop.

"Maybe Cyclops cut himself?"

"He was outside all day. Besides, the pantry door was closed."

Throwing her bra and shirt back on, she climbs off my lap and heads out to the kitchen, whistling for him. Meanwhile, a sinking suspicion begins to settle into my stomach.

I stand to get a better look at the floor. That's when I notice the second blood spot. And a third.

All surrounding my mother's safe.

Fumbling for my wallet, I fish out the safe combination. Careful not to smear the remaining blood spots, I quickly dial the numbers. I throw open the door.

Four guns still hang in their slots and, while I never counted the boxes of ammunition, it looks like they're all accounted for.

Everything seems normal.

That is, until I crouch down to inspect the bottom shelf more closely, and spot the brown lunch bag. It's crinkled with age and handling, and stuffed in a small gap between the ammo and the shelf, at the back.

Did I miss that before?

Did Silas miss it too?

Swallowing against my growing anxiety, I use the hem of my shirt to ease the bag out.

Inside is a handgun.

A Colt .45.

"Jesus Christ," I whisper, instantly aware. That's got to be Abe's gun. Has it been here all along?

Or did someone break in here today and plant it? If they did . . . *how?* No one has this combination except me.

Either way, someone was definitely in this house while we were out.

I grab my mom's Glock and, checking the chamber to make sure it's loaded, I charge for the backyard, hyperaware of the fact that the alarm was set when we left, which means that person circumvented the system. Someone with the equipment and the know-how to do it.

I find Gracie outside, talking to Mr. Stiles over the fence.

" . . . he was making one heck of a racket earlier."

"I'm sorry, sir. We didn't mean to be gone—"

"You can't leave dogs outside for hours, unattended!" my neighbor, with his hands on his hips, his gray hair mussed and standing on end, scolds Gracie.

"I know. I'm sorry," she apologizes in a placating voice that's so foreign to her. "He's normally a quiet dog."

I tuck the gun into the back of my pants and then ease in behind Gracie, settling my hands on her shoulders. Missing the feel of her hands on mine.

"He was barking because someone broke into my house," I explain.

Gracie tenses. "What?"

"A robbery!" Shock fills Mr. Stiles's weathered face, the thought of it happening in our peaceful neighborhood appalling. "But don't you have an alarm?"

"We do." And common, dumb criminals won't get past it. But seasoned cops with a history of sneaking in and threatening widowed women are another story. Still, for them to gain access to the safe . . .

"Well, I can't blame the little guy for all the noise, then." Stiles's gray eyes search out Cyclops. He frowns. "What's he got over there?"

"I don't think I want to know," I mutter, following Stiles's gaze to the far corner of the yard, where the dog is furiously digging in the garden. "Hey! Stop that!"

He peers up at me with a piece of tan-colored material dangling from his mouth.

"Come here, Cy!" Gracie calls.

He trots over obediently, dropping the strip in front of us.

"What *is* that?" Gracie lifts it in the air so we can all see it more closely.

One side of the material is hemmed while the other side was clearly torn. A spot of crimson stains it. "It looks like it could be from a pant leg!" Mr. Stiles chuckles. "Heck, I think your dog took a chunk out of the burglar!"

"Maybe right out of the guy's calf. I'll bet he's in pain, wherever he is."

Like possibly in a room with Klein, being questioned by the FBI.

Realization fills Gracie's face as she catches my drift.

Mr. Stiles's amusement vanishes abruptly. "You need to call the police, Noah. If there's a thief targeting homes in this neighborhood—"

"Yes, sir. We'll get right on that. Sorry again for the noise." I lead Gracie into the house, Cyclops trotting closely behind, his nose pressed to the floor.

"What do you think that asshole took?" she asks, her voice hard. She's furious, I realize. And here I was sure she'd be terrified.

"I don't know if he *took* anything." I show her the gun inside the brown bag. "It's a Colt .45."

Understanding fills her face. "Is it my dad's?"

"I'm guessing so . . . yeah."

"Are you saying Stapley put that in there?"

"Someone did."

"But . . ." She frowns. "It's a gun safe. People aren't supposed to be able to open them. How did he get in there?"

"I don't know." *Did he* actually get into it? Or did he simply try?

Did I miss seeing the bag in the first place?

It's as if she can read my mind. "Maybe your mom had it all this time." Accusation doses her words as her gaze wanders the pantry shelves aimlessly, as if searching for an answer among the cans and supplies.

Cyclops starts barking wildly from upstairs.

Gracie and I exchange looks.

Was Stapley alone in this? Is someone *still* in the house?

Seizing the Glock in my hands, I head for the stairs, my heart thumping in my chest. "Stay here," I whisper, taking the steps quietly.

The stairs creak behind me. Not a surprise, Gracie isn't listening.

I hesitate for a moment, wondering if I'm an idiot, if we should get out of the house and call the cops.

And then I keep going.

Cyclops's howls of protest are coming from my mother's room. We find him at the dresser, standing on his hind legs, his front paws pressed against the drawers. Seeing us, he drops to his haunches, his tail wagging furiously.

"What is it, Cy?" Gracie murmurs, edging past me.

He barks in answer, excited.

With a wary look over her shoulder at me, she slowly slides open the top drawer and begins sifting through my mother's things with a delicate hand. "I don't know what you want me to see, buddy . . . It's all the same stuff I saw yester—" Her voice cuts off.

"What?" I edge in next to her, to see the small packet nestled in my mother's T-shirts. "What is that?"

"My guess is cocaine."

"*Cocaine?*" Why the hell would Stapley bother putting drugs in my mother's drawer?

Gracie looks up at me. "That wasn't in here yesterday. I went through this drawer for clothes and it was *not* here yesterday."

A curse slips out from under my breath as I look around the room. A murder victim's gun, drugs . . . "What the hell are they up to?"

Gracie's gaze follows mine. "If I didn't know better, I'd say they're doing the same thing to your mom that they did to my dad—planting things to make her look guilty." Her mouth twists with a bitter smile as she points to Cyclops, who's busy sniffing around my mother's bed frame. "They didn't expect to contend with *him*."

I slide my phone out of my pocket. "We need to call the cops."

"No! Wait."

"Gracie, we need to report this. It needs to be on record. That blood is evidence."

"Yeah, but Stapley and Mantis *are* the cops."

"Two dirty ones out of thousands of good ones." I see where she's going with this as soon as the words leave my mouth. "But Mantis heads Internal Affairs."

"You heard him yesterday. He said 'you wouldn't believe the kinds of things I can get away with.'" She pauses to give me a knowing look. "What if he can make Stapley get away with doing this? Do you want to risk that?" Gracie slides her phone out and starts punching in numbers.

CHAPTER 42

Officer Abraham Wilkes

April 28, 2003

"Just doing my usual rounds!" I holler from my open window, sounding more chipper than I feel. I left Gracie at home with Dina, with big, fat tears rolling down her chubby cheeks. She doesn't understand why Daddy's out so much lately, why he can't stay home and play.

Isaac tosses the window squeegee into the bucket of suds behind him, sending dirty water onto the sidewalk around it. He slowly heads toward me, wiping his hands with a rag hanging from his back pocket. "I was wonderin' if I'd see you today."

"Anything new to report?"

"No, sir." Isaac's soulful brown eyes skate over the near-empty parking lot. "It's been awful quiet here since that excitement the other day."

I sigh with disappointment. How long before I should give up and accept that Betsy's gone for good? That it was a fluke that I ran into her in the first place, and I will never find her again?

Maybe Jackie's right and Betsy doesn't want to be found. But from the way she looked up at me, those green eyes—twins of Dina's—wide with a mixture of fear, panic, and relief, I can't believe that.

"Best be on my way, then." I have another few local spots to stop by.

"Now wait up a minute." Isaac comes up close—close enough that I can smell the sweat lingering on his skin—to rest an elbow on the hood of my car. "Those police officers that came stormin' in here . . . you know 'em?"

"I know them."

"You friends with 'em?"

"No, sir. I wouldn't call them friends." Sure, we've played ball together; we've gone out for celebratory beers after a game. But friends? Hell no, especially not now.

"So if they were doin' somethin' they shouldn't be doin' . . ."

Understanding settles onto my shoulders. "What did you see, Isaac?"

"The question isn't what *I* saw. It's what *you* saw." Isaac stoops over to meet me face to face. "And what you're doin' about it."

He saw Mantis take the money; that much is obvious. He also knows that I saw Mantis take the money. I sigh. "It's complicated." "Doing something" means saying something—to my supervisors, to Internal Affairs, to the chief. I read the news; I'm no idiot. Right or wrong, speaking up against a fellow officer is never without consequences. Threats, retaliation, suspensions. The kind of consequences that can make life for me on the force impossible.

"Well, I have something that might help *un*complicate it." Isaac reaches into his pocket.

CHAPTER 43

Noah

"Who knew you'd be a good drug hound," I murmur, scratching Cyclops between his tattered ears before sinking into the living room couch. An FBI evidence tech strolls past, peeling gloves from his hands on his way out the door.

"*I* knew." Gracie's eyes twinkle. "Last year, Sims was on his stomach one night, searching under his trailer, cursing and threatening to kill the bastard when he finds out who was stealing from him. I was coming home from work a week later and I saw Cyclops tear out from under the Simses' trailer with a bag of weed in his mouth. It had this long piece of duct tape attached to it, all torn up by Cyclops's teeth. I guess Sims was taping weed to the underside." She chuckles. "I followed him across the road, and watched him dig a hole and bury it."

"I take it you didn't enlighten Sims?"

"Hell no!" She grins. "It was way more fun knowing that idiot was getting robbed by a one-eyed dog."

Klein charges down the stairs then and into the living room, cutting off our laughter. "We haven't found anything else so far, but we'll keep looking."

"You checked the office? And my room?" A few drawers were sitting open a crack, enough to flag that someone might have been in there.

"Yup. Nothing." He flips open his notepad, his eyes on Gracie. "Why don't you give me a rundown again . . . You got home around two fifteen p.m. You were in the pantry . . ."

"Putting away groceries," I answer, noting Gracie's cheeks flushing. "Gracie noticed a spot of blood on the floor." I run through the next few moments again, Gracie finding her composure quickly enough to fill in a word here and there.

"And there were no signs that anyone was still in the house when you came home?"

I shudder at the thought. "No, sir."

A loud knock sounds on the front door.

"You expecting someone?" Klein nods toward Tareen, who's been floating around, to answer it.

"Actually, I am, but he doesn't usually knock," I mutter, checking my phone. Silas has been calling me all day, leaving messages. I can't talk to him right now, not when I'm too busy wondering how he could swear up and down that Abe was guilty despite *knowing* about the video and Abe's plans to out Mantis; despite the evidence we saw today that clearly shows a third person was in that room.

A moment later, Tareen returns with Boyd and his partner in tow, a worried look on Boyd's face.

"Hey, Marshall. Is everything okay?"

I shrug. "Somebody broke in."

"Dang. That sucks." He looks between me and Gracie, and then to Klein, and Bill the evidence guy, who trots down the steps carrying a plastic bag with the cocaine in it, and I can see the questions churning. *Why would the feds be here? Why didn't Noah call the APD?*

What trouble has Noah gotten himself into?

God only knows what the neighbors will think, with FBI agents outside only two weeks after the last circus at this address. Reporters will be here soon enough, fishing for information.

"Can we help you with something, Officer?" Klein asks in that calm, even voice that sounds so goddamn arrogant.

Boyd stands a little taller as he faces Klein, his demeanor shifting instantly from longtime friend to cop-on-duty. "We were on patrol and saw the activity outside. I know there's protocol, but if the APD can be of assistance—"

"Thanks. I'll let you know." Klein cuts him off abruptly, disappearing into the kitchen to make a call.

"Does this have anything to do with that run-in with Mantis?" Boyd asks.

"Why would you think that?" Gracie fires back, that hard, naturally suspicious side of her making its appearance.

"Because I'm no idiot, and nothing about what I saw yesterday looked normal," he answers evenly.

I sigh. "Gracie, this is Boyd; Boyd, . . ." I gesture between the two of them, making fast introductions.

"So?" Boyd folds his arms across his chest.

"It might. It's . . . a long story."

"Do you need help, Noah?" His thick brows rise in question.

"We need you to tell the truth about what you saw yesterday," Gracie answers for me, her tone challenging.

Boyd studies her for a long moment. "We can do one better. Our dash cam was running when we approached you. We caught that exchange on video. At least, from our viewpoint. Would that help?"

I don't think Gracie was expecting that answer. "Yeah." She clears her throat. "It would. Thanks."

"What would help Noah?" a loud voice calls from the entryway.

My body tenses. *It's about time he gave up on the phone.*

"You can't be in here," Tareen begins, moving toward Silas, his arm out as if to usher him outside.

As if that would stop Silas. "I *can* and *will* be in here. I'm the district attorney of Travis County and that is my nephew." He limps farther into the living room. "And I demand to know what's going on."

Silas tosses his phone onto the kitchen table, rubbing the bridge of his nose. He looks like he hasn't slept in days. And his face is visibly thinner. "He's refusing to give his DNA without a court order, and the judge won't issue one until we give sufficient reason to believe it was Stapley in this house."

"Surprise, surprise . . ." Klein mutters, his steely gaze set on the backyard. "That's fine. His blood isn't going anywhere."

"Tell him he should probably get a tetanus shot. Maybe one for rabies, too." Gracie smirks, tossing Cyclops a strawberry.

"You haven't had that dog vaccinated?" Silas glares at me. As if that's *my* fault.

I don't know what's been going on behind the scenes, but per typical Silas, within fifteen minutes of stepping in here, he gained approval from Klein's higher-ups to involve the APD in the break-in investigation and has smoothly inserted himself into the middle of it.

Now, Boyd and his partner are canvassing the neighborhood for potential witnesses, the APD has Stapley in an interrogation room, and Silas is getting regular updates from the acting police chief.

Of course, Stapley is feeding the APD the same bullshit excuse I heard him give Klein earlier—he caught his leg on a rake. Before the meeting with the FBI, he was home, cleaning up the yard. His wife can vouch for him.

Klein is right, though; there's nothing Stapley can do to hide the blood that courses through his veins. It's only a matter of time before they have him.

Silas drums his fingertips across the table. A tic of his when he's frustrated. It's because Klein is being Klein—closed off, talking in riddles, unwilling to tell Silas what he wants to know. "So, is it safe to say that Lieutenant Stapley is a person of interest in the Abraham Wilkes murder investigation? I presume that's why Noah would have called the FBI instead of the APD for a break-in. Though I'm not sure why you guys wouldn't have called for APD assistance."

Gracie and I exchange a glance. Silas knows there is an official investigation. I have to assume he's also figured out that we've told Klein everything.

"Sure. I think that's safe to say," Klein answers in his laid-back, "nothing really matters" tone, his arms folded across his chest.

Uncomfortable silence hangs for a few beats, before Silas shifts his attention back to me.

"Did you find anything on Grace's aunt in the arrest records, Noah?"

"No, sir. Nothing in the death and marriage records, either."

"And the FBI is looking for her too. Right?" Gracie peers at Kristian, expectantly.

"We will be. We're tight on resources at the moment."

Gracie's disapproving huff says she doesn't like that answer.

"Relax. It shouldn't take too long using facial recognition software, with that picture you gave me. If she's alive, we'll get a hit eventually."

"You have a picture of her?" Silas asks.

"Just one. My mom had it in her things."

Silas frowns in thought. "Agent Klein, why don't you let the APD help with tracking Betsy down so you can focus on your case? I'll make sure it's a priority for them. Or, at the very least, they can check out the leads you come up with."

Klein regards him curiously. "Thanks for the offer. I'll let you know."

The kitchen chair creaks as Silas leans back against it. "Hey, if we can give Dina Wilkes back her sister . . . it should be a priority. It's the least we can do." It's the first semi-civil exchange between these two since Silas walked through the door.

And everything about it sounds *off*.

One of the FBI evidence collectors pops his head in to say they're wrapping up.

Boyd trails in right behind them.

"Got anything?" Silas asks.

"Yes, sir. A lady on the other side of the park noticed a dark blue pickup truck parked on the street during the time frame of the break-in." They're not calling it "theft." As far as anyone can tell, nothing was taken. "She also noticed a tall, white male walking across from this side, in a hurry."

"So you're thinking Stapley parked over there, came through the park, and used the gate in the back to get through?"

"Yes, sir," Boyd says.

"And do we know what Stapley drives?"

"A navy-blue Ford F10, sir."

Silas smiles with grim satisfaction. "God bless idiots. What was he thinking, driving here in broad daylight to break into the late chief's house?"

"I'm guessing he wasn't expecting a vicious guard dog lying in wait," Klein muses. "But the bigger question is, why would he want to plant cocaine and a gun in Jackie Marshall's house?" A gun last registered to Abraham Wilkes, they've confirmed.

"You mean, besides trying to frame Jackie Marshall with my father's death to cover his own tracks? His and Mantis's?" Gracie's lips twist bitterly.

A faint smile flitters across Klein's face, saying that's the conclusion he's come to as well. It vanishes almost instantly. "And we're sure that gun wasn't in there before?"

"I don't recall checking that shelf thoroughly, no," Silas begins. "It *could* have been—"

"No, that gun was not in there," I say with firm resolution.

Silas's brow raises. "I don't recall you checking that thoroughly, either."

"I did. And besides, it would make no sense for her to put a bag of money and the gun holster in that hole under the floorboards, and not the gun."

"I have to agree with you on that," Klein murmurs.

But it then begs another question. "How did Stapley get the combination to the safe?" Because no one broke into it.

"I don't know, son. I can't figure it out either." Silas's brow furrows with worry as he watches Cyclops, standing outside the door, staring in at us.

"Just think, if this little guy hadn't bitten him, you wouldn't even know that someone had broken in here," Klein offers mildly.

"Too bad Cy wasn't around when Stapley pulled this shit at *my* house fourteen years ago," Gracie mumbles.

"You think Stapley was the one who broke into your house to threaten your mother?" Silas asks her, but quickly turns to Klein. "Is *that* what the FBI suspects? That Stapley planted evidence in Abraham Wilkes's house to make him appear guilty?"

Klein shrugs. "That's one theory."

Silas raps his fingers against the table's surface in a rushed drumbeat, waiting for Klein to elaborate.

And Boyd's watching this entire exchange quietly from the entryway, probably wondering what the hell kind of mess I've gotten myself into.

Finally, Silas gives up on an answer from Klein. "I'll bet there's blood in his truck. We can match it against what the FBI has collected here. Officer, are you on shift tonight?"

"For a few more hours," Boyd says.

"I want a car patrolling this street the entire night, y'all hear? The entire night." Silas's phone rings then. His hand flies to answer it.

While he's occupied on a call, Klein begins moving for the door. "How about you two try and stay out of trouble for a minute." He's speaking to the both of us, but his eyes are locked on Gracie, as usual, and he doesn't even bother to hide it. A cord of tension rises inside of me. *Fucking guy.* He's got to be at least ten years older than her, maybe even fifteen.

"What'd you get out of Mantis and Stapley today, anyway?" Gracie asks. Can she tell that he's attracted to her? Does she care?

"Exactly what I expected to get," he answers cryptically, glancing at Silas. "If anything else comes up, you call *me* first, *got* it?"

"I will," she promises. "And thanks for coming today."

He flashes that arrogant smirk and my fist aches with the memory of hitting that jaw. "Yes, ma'am. *Any*time."

"What?" Silas exclaims into the phone, distracting all of us. "But that press conference was . . . Right *now*?" He waves at the small flatscreen mounted on the wall in the kitchen. "Noah . . . quick! Fox 7!"

I grab the remote and quickly flip through, until Chief Canning's round face appears. He's standing on the steps outside the police station, with reporters' microphones poised to catch his words. ". . . Officer Abraham Wilkes, who was shot and killed on May third, 2003, was previously alleged to have been participatin' in illegal activities outside his role as a police officer. However, new evidence has come to light today that would indicate Wilkes was *not* engaged in any sort of illegal activity and was in fact the target of the premeditated crime of murder." Canning speaks slowly and clearly into the microphone as all of us—Klein included—cling to his words. "The APD and FBI are working jointly to understand exactly what transpired that night just shy of fourteen years ago. I cannot speak to the new evidence or to possible suspects, but if Officer Abraham Wilkes was the victim of this horrible crime . . ." He pauses, his brow furrowing as if he's in pain. "Well, let's make sure this city remembers Abe for what he truly was—a good and honorable police officer. No more questions." He walks away from the microphone.

"Is this for real?" I glance from Silas to Klein, and back to Silas, looking for answers.

Klein's expression betrays nothing.

Silas is rubbing his forehead furiously.

Meanwhile, Gracie's face is full of shock. "Did he just clear my dad's name to the public?"

"Not exactly, but—"

"This is . . ." Her eyes begin to well. "I need to call my mother." She darts outside.

"What the hell was that, Silas?" Why would Canning—a *retired* police chief—be doing a press conference on an old murder case, without any conclusive findings, at the beginning of the investigation that the FBI is leading?

"Apparently, he was talking to the press about the coming ceremony and a reporter started asking him about Abraham. Someone must have tipped off the media. Probably after the FBI taped off that motel room today. That kind of thing does tend to raise questions." Silas shoots an accusatory look at Klein.

"He could have brushed them off."

"Yes, he could have, but . . . it happened under George's watch. He'd want to be the one to take responsibility, to make it right."

"So he obviously knows what we've learned."

"Well, if you had picked up your damn phone at all today, you'd know that I went to Canning last night and told him everything you told me."

"Everything?"

"Everything."

"And?"

"What do you mean '*and*'?" He flings a hand at the television. "You just saw 'and'! We've both been on the phone with everyone and their brother all day. If any APD officers were involved in this, Canning will personally have their heads mounted on a spike!"

I look to Klein, baffled. "So, Abe's case is now a joint investigation between the APD and FBI?" *And the retired chief,* apparently?

"Sure sounds like it, doesn't it?" If Klein's bothered, he doesn't let on, sharing a whispered word with another FBI tech before focusing on the backyard to where Gracie sits on the lounger, speaking to someone—I assume Dina—her free hand waving excitedly, her face filled with a lightness that I haven't seen before. He exits out the French doors to the back.

Silas's dark gaze trails after him. "He's the one you punched?"

"Yes, sir."

A faint smile of satisfaction flickers over Silas's face. "I'll make sure his superiors speak with him. Help him understand what collaboration means." The smile is followed by a frown of disapproval, as Silas's gaze drifts over the yard. "Your mother would be upset if she saw this."

I sigh. Leave it to Silas to give me grief about gardens at a time like this. "Cyclops did some rearranging. Don't worry, I'll fix it all." It's a good thing he hasn't seen the mound of dirt at the bottom of the pool.

"Yes. That's an interesting pet."

I chuckle. "He's starting to grow on me, actually."

"He definitely earned his keep today." Silas shakes his head. "In all your twenty-five years, Noah, you have *never* shown me anything but the utmost respect. Until today."

I avert my gaze.

"I called you five times and you couldn't answer? Couldn't call back?"

"I'm sorry."

"Why? Because you were too busy getting the FBI involved, after I *specifically* told you to *wait*?"

"I had no choice." I tell him how Klein tailed and then ambushed us. "As if I had any right to ask Gracie to wait."

"No, I suppose not." He shakes his head. "I don't like the way these guys are operating. Haven't been able to get much out of anyone, all day. I can appreciate why they'd be tight-lipped, though, especially given Dwayne Mantis's position, and the fact that they don't have much of anything that's concrete." He runs his hands over his face. "But I can't help you if you keep secrets from me."

"And what about the secrets you're keeping from me?" I struggle to steel my spine as I confront my uncle. "You knew about that video, didn't you? And about Abe going after Mantis for stealing the money."

He chews the inside of his cheek in thought, his finger tracing the grain of the wood on the table's surface. And every second I wait for his answer, my anxiety grows. "I did. And when you came to me yesterday, to tell me all this . . . I thought I was going to lose my breakfast right there in my office. Because I did know about it and I wrote it off as a lie fourteen years ago. If I'd believed it, I would have brought it forward as part of the investigation into his death."

"What do you mean *if* you believed it? What the hell did you believe, then?" I can't help my accusatory tone.

"The same damn thing as Harvey Maxwell! That it was all a part of this elaborate lie Abe was living, another fiber in the wool he'd pulled over everyone's eyes."

"Why on earth would he do that?"

"For the same reason he was lying to his wife for weeks about his whereabouts!"

"He was searching for her sister!"

Silas throws his hands in the air in an act of surrender. "I didn't know that! *No one* knew anything about this Betsy girl! Dina didn't even know! Why lie to her about it? If he'd told her the truth, then he would have had an alibi."

I level him with a look. "*Mom* knew about Betsy."

"Well, she didn't tell me." His voice is bitter. "And I looked through the evidence they found on his computer and in his house. There was nothing there. So I figured there was never anything there to begin with. Had Dina come to me about this man who'd threatened her . . ." He lets his words drift.

"Is this why Mom blamed herself for Abe dying? Does this have something to do with Dina's sister? Does Betsy have something to do with the fallout between Abe and her?"

His throat bobs with his swallow as he gazes at the chair my mother was sitting in that night. I had been preparing to warn anyone who made for it today—not *that* chair; don't sit in *that* chair—but no one even came close. "I wish I knew, Noah, but she never told me. Apparently there's a lot she didn't tell me. Your mom . . . she was different after Abe died."

"That's when she started drinking."

"It wasn't just the drinking. She became closed off. To everyone, myself included. She got that promotion to assistant chief not long after and she became so focused on her career, nothing else seemed to matter. She wasn't the same. I figured it had to do with Abe—with him not being the man she thought he was." He sighs. "All I know is that with the overwhelming evidence in front of us, we were all left to believe the obvious answer."

Yes. The evidence. "We went to the motel today, Silas. And there had to be a third person in that room."

"Maybe there was. But it isn't as conclusive as what *he* made you think." Silas throws a casual hand toward the back, where Klein paces around Gracie, a lit cigarette in his hand. "That guy was still a kid stealing his daddy's beer and feeling up his girlfriend in the back of a car while I was standing in that motel room, surrounded by dead bodies and blood and drugs and a million hard questions. If there were people in that investigation working to erase fingerprints, to make Abe look guilty . . . well, that means everything was questionable, then, doesn't it?"

"You can't rule his theory out, though."

"His theory is the backbone of this investigation, now, for what it's worth, without any hard evidence."

"Thanks to Stapley."

Silas shakes his head in disbelief. "If Abe was murdered by those two, they will be punished to the full extent of the law." He sounds resolute, and yet his expression shows only worry. "But we may have to be satisfied with simply clearing Abe's name with reasonable doubt and moving on with our lives."

"I know that."

"Make sure that girl out there knows that. You don't want her following in her mother's footsteps."

"She's the strongest person I've ever met. Gracie would never become that."

"Let's hope not."

"Dina says she's just like Abe. Except, you know . . . a girl." A girl who has me ensnared in her spell.

"Yes, I've noticed." I feel Silas's shrewd gaze on me.

Can he tell I'm falling hard for Abe's daughter?

I clear my throat. "I may need a loan for Dina's rehab. Just until Mom's insurance—"

"Judy'll call to sort that out. She can send a payment to the rehab center first thing tomorrow."

I sigh with relief. "Thanks, Silas."

"Don't mention it. I'm *always* here for you. Don't ever doubt that."

It's true. He always has been. And I was a dick today. "I'm sorry. I should have just picked up the phone and told you about Klein yesterday. This whole thing is . . . it's making me crazy."

"I told you it would, son. It's done that to all of us." His eyes wander outside, to where Gracie sits, his face suddenly grim as if burdened with a thousand unspoken worries. "For what it's worth, she didn't deserve this. None of them did."

"At least now maybe we'll get justice for Abe."

He stands and pats my shoulder. "Yes, sir. Justice."

CHAPTER 44

Grace

The elevator music finally cuts out. "Grace?"

I pause for a moment, absorbing the sound of my mother's voice, clear and strong, even after only a few sober days. What will a few *months* without drugs coursing through her veins do? Will I actually get my mother back? Do I dare hope?

"Hello? Grace?"

"Mom." Unexpected tears start rolling down my cheeks. I feel like I'm in a daze.

"What's wrong?" she asks, panicked.

"Nothing. Everything's great. You wouldn't believe what just happened." I tell her about Canning's press conference. By the time I'm done, she's sobbing into the phone.

"You can't be serious. Is this a joke?"

"I am! I mean, no, it's not a joke." I quickly explain the last several days.

"The FBI? Did Silas call them?"

"No, actually we have Jackie Marshall to thank for that. They were already investigating by the time we got here."

The door to the kitchen opens and Kristian steps out, sauntering over to me with that casual swagger of his.

"The man who came to your hospital room was an FBI agent. His name was Kristian Klein." I watch as Kristian pulls a cigarette pack out of his back pocket. I had no idea he even smoked. I wonder if he's allowed to light up in the backyard of a crime scene. Something tells me he'd do it with or without permission.

"Klein . . ." my mom repeats, and I can picture her brow furrowing. "That *does* sound familiar."

I doubt it, but I'll let her hold on to that. "You don't need to be afraid, Mom. No one's coming to Tucson to get you."

"And what about you? You're there in Austin, right in the thick of things."

"I'll be fine." I left out the part about Mantis pulling us over. Details she doesn't need to know. "Besides, I have Noah here to protect me. And Cyclops."

Klein paces aimlessly around the yard, puffing on his cigarette. Listening to my every word. On impulse, I toss the tennis ball, aiming it to fly a foot or so in front of his face, just close enough to startle him. I get nothing but a raised brow in response.

My mom chuckles. It's a soft, nostalgic melody. "I knew that dog would bite someone eventually. Glad he made it count."

"So . . . How's Desert Oaks?"

"It's okay," she admits grudgingly. "They're awful strict, though."

"You're surprised?"

"No, I guess not. But does the FBI need me there? I could come. I could—"

"No, you need to stay in rehab. You're still detoxing, Mom. You won't be credible as a heroin addict and you need to be credible. For Dad."

"Yes. Of course. I just . . . I want to help."

"I'm sure they'll want to come out to speak to you at some point."

"I'll tell them everything I remember."

Everything you should have told them fourteen years ago, that bitter voice inside my head chirps. I push it aside. What's done is done.

"Oh! I remembered something! That's what I wanted to tell you. About that guy who broke into the house. I mean, it's not really anything, but I thought you should know. It probably won't help—"

"What is it?"

"The man, he was wearing that awful cologne that some of the customers at Aunt Chilada's used to wear. It's called Brut, I think. And he wore so much of it, like he spilled a bottle on his clothes."

Familiarity washes over me.

"I don't know if it helps, but—"

"It does help. Call me if you remember anything else."

Kristian's curious gaze flickers to me.

"Any news on Betsy?" She sounds hopeful.

"Not yet, but they're looking. We'll find her soon." I sound more hopeful than I feel. But that's what my mother needs—hope.

"How's Noah, by the way?"

"He's good." *I think.* I can see him through the glass, his elbows resting on his knees, talking to his uncle. His expression heavy. "Listen, the FBI agent is here to talk to me. I've got to go."

"Okay." There's a pause. "I love you, Grace."

My voice gets caught in my throat. It's been so long since she's said those words out loud. Years. Long enough that I was sure she'd forgotten their meaning.

I don't know how to accept them yet.

"I'll phone when I know more." I end the call and look to Kristian, who's pretending to study the gate that leads out the back of the property, to the treed park directly behind us. The one that we think Stapley used to make a quick escape. "Did you need something? Or do you just like to listen in on personal calls?" I mentally scold myself for being snarky with him. Kristian is one of the good guys, even if he can be a real ass.

If my tone bothers him, he doesn't let on, leaning down to put his cigarette out on a stone. "I actually do like listening in on personal calls. You learn a lot."

"And what did you learn just now?"

"Nothing I didn't already know."

I roll my eyes as he settles down onto the end of my lounge chair without asking. "How is she?" His voice is suddenly soft with sympathy.

"A thousand times better than when you saw her last."

"Yeah, she was . . . not good." He has a square jaw and it tenses now as his thoughts drift somewhere. To my mother, perhaps, a collection of frail bones lying in that hospital bed, barely lucid. Probably raving mad. "So what did she remember about that night?"

I tell him about the cologne. "I don't think it was Stapley who broke in and threatened her. I'm betting it was Mantis."

"Maybe. I had a headache by the time I left the interrogation room today." So casual, so unfazed by everything. He nods toward the kitchen. "Wasn't that something, back there?"

"That's a loaded question if I've ever heard one."

He purses his lips, as if considering his words. "Stapley and Mantis are trying to set Jackie up to take the fall for your dad."

"Didn't we already come to that conclusion?"

"They named her today. In the interview. Similar stories, about Jackie and Abe having a huge fight. Apparently Abe had something on her. They didn't know what, but they got the impression it was big. Something that could get her into a lot of trouble."

"My mother said as much." About the huge fight, anyway. "So what are you saying? That Jackie had motive to kill my father?"

"That's what they made it out to sound like." Klein's eyes wander over the pool, stalling at the planter sitting at the bottom. The pool guy never did make it back to clean it this afternoon, what with the FBI crawling all over the house.

"Then why didn't that come up in their investigation, seeing as they were the special investigators for his death?"

"My thoughts exactly." Kristian smiles knowingly. "They also said that Jackie was there, at The Lucky Nine, the night your dad died."

"So what if she was? We know *they're* guilty. Jackie didn't kill my father." I can't believe I'm actually defending that woman.

"I think they're both guilty," Kristian agrees. "But that doesn't mean Jackie isn't, too."

I steal another glance at Noah, his face drawn and serious as his uncle chatters on, likely giving him grief. *Hopefully* giving a valid explanation for his silence about the video all these years. Silas has been nothing but helpful since he charged through the front door today, even if that help was uninvited and unwanted by the likes of Kristian.

Still, I don't know how I feel about Silas. He unsettles me. It's probably because from the moment I met him at the DA's office, I knew he wasn't happy about me being in Texas. That usually makes for bad first impressions.

Maybe, once this case is resolved, I'll get a chance to see another side of him, the side that Noah knows, trusts, and loves.

"If we hadn't found those drops of blood, would Stapley have gotten away with this?"

"Probably. And it wouldn't have looked good for Jackie, having Wilkes's gun locked up in her safe. You don't mind, do you?" Kristian slides another cigarette out of his pocket and lights it before getting my answer.

He can smoke a crack pipe for all I care, as long I'm getting information from him about my father's case.

"Did you find anything in that motel room yet?" I ask, changing gears.

"Dried blood behind the strips of wallpaper, like I expected. We'll have to test it. See if we can get a match. Thanks for that, by the way." He nods to my arm, where a specialist drew blood earlier, at the FBI office. A familial sample to compare DNA markers against. The next best thing to having my dad's blood, they said. I want to help, but still, it feels strange to know that federal agents now have my DNA on record.

"And if it does match?"

For the first time, Kristian's face shows signs of concern, of doubt. "We have a long way to go before we have *anything* to tie a person to your father's death, Grace. *If* we ever do."

"I know that," I admit grudgingly. I'll never accept it, though.

His mood shifts again, and he's back to his typical indifferent self. "Who knows, though? Mantis pulling you two over yesterday was one thing. But what Stapley did today was stupid and reckless, and that tells me he's worried." He studies the lit end of his cigarette for a long moment, the ember glowing like a firefly in the dusk. "I like it when guilty people are worried. They make a lot of fucking dumb mistakes, and that's how I nail them."

I hug myself against the evening chill. "At least now *everyone* thinks my dad was innocent."

"Right . . . That was quite a show Canning put on."

"It works for me. And for my dad."

"It'll probably work for Canning, too, that arrogant son of a bitch."

Pot and kettle. "You still think he's behind this?" Maybe my judgment is clouded by his words on the TV not long ago, by the way Canning seems so vested in clearing my father's name, because I don't see it.

"If I were him and I were involved in this? I'd be looking for a way to clear your dad's name to get you off my back, while making sure someone other than my star guys take the fall. Someone who can't defend themself anymore."

"Jackie Marshall."

"Jackie Marshall." He takes a long puff of his cigarette and a tendril of smoke curls out his lips. "That spectacle on the news back there? That wasn't for your father. That was for Canning. He figured he'd get out ahead of this and put himself in the public eye as the man who uncovered the scandal. That's what he wants the public to remember. My boss's boss has been fielding calls from everyone right up to the governor of Texas since this morning, demanding the APD be involved in the investigation. Who do you think was behind that?"

"Canning?"

"Canning."

"Wouldn't it be better for him to stay far away from this?"

"If there's anyone who knows how to kick a hornet's nest and not get stung, I'm guessing it's him."

Kristian's painting quite the picture of George Canning. I'm wondering how accurate it is, or if this agent is just the most suspicious man I've ever met. The Canning I saw on TV—ruddy-faced and grandfatherly; a man who'd pull off a Santa Claus suit better than most—doesn't look like a master manipulator. Maybe that's his angle, though. What is this George Canning *really* like?

I'd love to find out.

Another thought strikes me; a worry. "Isn't it a bad idea to have the APD involved, given who Mantis is?" I'd think the head of Internal Affairs is connected.

Klein smirks. "Depends who you ask."

I groan. "God, you are infuriating! Why do you even bother telling me anything?"

"Imagine what I'm *not* telling you." Kristian puts his cigarette out on the patio stone. "How old are you again?"

"Way too young for you," I throw back without missing a beat. I'm not oblivious—I've caught the looks he has cast my way. I've also caught the glares he's earned from Noah because of them. Noah's jealous of the FBI agent. That shouldn't make me giddy.

It *shouldn't*, but it does.

Kristian chuckles. "Have you ever thought about a career in law enforcement?"

"What? No!" That was unexpected.

He stands, stretching his arms over his head. "You're sharp. You've got the right head for this kind of thing. Who knows? You may want to follow in your father's footsteps."

"So I can be murdered and framed, too? No thanks," I mutter dryly.

His gaze drifts over the fence line again. "Austin's my home. I grew up here, before I went away to college. In 'a good part' of Austin. That's what my mom calls it. A place where you can borrow a cup of sugar from your neighbor when you run out. Where your kids can run up and down the sidewalk. No random home invasions, but you lock your doors all the same.

"One night I was in the kitchen, getting something to eat. It was late. And I saw Mr. Monroe—the same neighbor who'd had us over for a barbecue the week before—beating the hell out of his wife in their backyard. Like a man possessed, like he wanted to kill her.

"So I called the cops and then I hopped over that fence and threw myself at him, trying to stop him before he did something to her that the doctors couldn't fix. But Mr. Monroe was tipping the scales at two-fifty, at least, and I was a scrawny sixteen-year-old . . . I got banged up. Might have ended worse, had the cops not shown up so quickly." Kristian's steely eyes flicker over to me. "One of the officers was your dad."

My stomach tightens. "You're lying."

"I've never forgotten him, or that night. It was . . . messy. I got a little community award for it a few months later, and your dad was there on his day off, front and center. He came up to me afterward and said that if I was going to be doing the police's work, I should think about putting on muscle and becoming an actual cop. And then he told me to trust my gut, no matter what anyone else might say; that helping someone in need is *never* a mistake." A sad smile touches Kristian's face. "It was about a year later when his death hit the news." Silence lingers for a long moment. "That whole thing? It never sat right in my gut."

I desperately want to believe his story. "Why are you only telling me this now?"

He simply shrugs. And begins moving toward the gate leading to the front yard.

"Hey! How come you joined the FBI instead of the APD?"

"The badge is shinier. Make sure your guard dog is on alert. And that Noah's *extra* close." He winks.

I shake my head as I watch the cagey agent stroll away.

Wondering what else he hasn't told me yet.

"What are you reading?"

I look up from the iPad to see Noah standing in the doorway of my room, his hands resting on the door frame above his head, his sculpted biceps and his long, lean torso all the more noticeable.

"A sixteen-year-old Kristian." He wasn't lying, after all. There's an Austin newspaper article from 2002, showing a gangly but still handsome teenaged version of him accepting a medal from the mayor for saving the life of one Mrs. Sara Monroe. "He knew my dad."

Noah's face fills with surprise. And a hint of jealousy.

A selfish thrill courses through my veins before I'm able to tamp it down.

"See? They mention my dad in here." I show Noah the article and quietly watch him read, his bottom lip pulled between his teeth. *My* bottom lip was in that exact spot only hours ago.

Heat floods my core. If I hadn't touched the floor, if I hadn't felt something wet against my fingertip . . . I shudder at the thought of Stapley's blood on me. It's an effective way to temper these illicit thoughts I'm having about the guy standing four feet away from me right now, though. The intense ones that are becoming impossible to ignore, even with the threat of dirty cops looming over us.

Am I crazy for getting this involved with Noah right now? Am I setting myself up for guaranteed heartache? We're in the middle of investigating my father's murder and there's a good chance that his mother played a part in it.

Noah was right, earlier. We need to take things slow.

I clear my throat. "So, what did Boyd say?"

Noah sets the iPad on the nightstand. "They'll have a car patrolling the street all night. He'll be there off-duty if he has to be. Stapley's still being held and Mantis isn't stupid enough to come here. What would be the point?"

"That doesn't bring me much comfort."

"Yeah, me neither." Noah turns to test the doorknob, giving me his back. That gun is tucked into his jeans again. While I don't have a lot of experience around guns, Noah seems confident in handling it.

"This lock is broken."

"Yeah, I noticed."

"You'll need to stay in my room tonight. With me. I'd feel better having you right there."

Oh God. And there goes my heart, pounding inside my chest again, with thoughts of where this night might lead. Where I want it to lead, if I'm being honest.

So much for taking things slow.

"What was this one for?" I tap the gold trophy closest to me.

"Regionals. I was ten."

"And this one?" I eye the plaque next to it.

"I can't remember. 'Most improved player,' I think?"

I let my gaze drift over the array of medals and trophies that line the metal shelf on the wall. A thin layer of dust coats everything. Someone kept them clean over the years. Just not in recent months.

I carefully lift one from 1999 and study it. "Is this the one you were holding in that picture?"

I sense Noah coming up behind me. "Yeah. That was my first trophy, ever."

"It looked a lot bigger back then."

"It's the same size." He reaches around to cup the small gold statuette within his large, strong hand, his fingers entwining with mine. "*I* just got a lot bigger."

And I can feel his size, towering over me from behind, his body radiating heat.

My breathing grows ragged.

I clear the huskiness from my throat. "Where's Cyclops?"

Noah settles the trophy back on the shelf and then wanders over to the doorway. He chuckles. "Looks like he's ready for guard duty. He's lying in front of the stairs. Probably the best place for him. He'll warn us if anyone gets past the alarm again." Shutting the door, he turns the lock.

Why am I suddenly so nervous? Why is the air in the room suddenly so dense?

"Is that loaded?" I nod toward the gun sitting on the nightstand, trying to distract myself, even as I steal glimpses of Noah—of his body clad in only a T-shirt and shorts; of his smooth stride as he walks toward the gun; of the muscles in his arms as they cord when he picks it up, to check it.

"Yes, ma'am. I'll leave it right here for the night, within easy reach for me." He sets it down. "You know, once they're done with your dad's Colt, maybe they'd be willing to give it back to you."

To me? "I've never fired a gun." To be honest, the idea of them has always made me edgy.

His brow raises in curiosity as his gaze drifts over my bare legs. "You want to upgrade from the switchblade?"

I smirk. "Only if you teach me how to use it."

"I'll take you out to the range where my mother taught me," he promises.

"Deal." My heart stutters as I crawl into the double bed—too small for the two of us—and take my place on the far end near the wall.

With a flick of Noah's wrist, the lamp is shut off, the room thrown into darkness save for the glimmer of streetlights from beyond the blinds. It's just enough light for me to watch him reach over his head and yank off his T-shirt, then kick off his shorts. Exposing that hard body, molded by hours of effort, now covered in nothing but a pair of boxer briefs that sit dangerously low on his hips.

My shaky breath fills the quiet room as he settles in beside me, the bed sinking under his weight.

I've been with guys before, I remind myself.

And I've already seen Noah naked. Unintentionally, but all the same . . . And I slept against that chest—clothed—last night. And I climbed onto that lap, just this afternoon.

It's as if he can read my mind. Stretching his arm across, he wordlessly beckons me to him, to take over the same position that I woke up to this morning. I happily slither into it, pushing aside the warning voices in the back of my mind. The ones that have lingered, a soft hiss in my conscience, reminding me of the possible pitfalls ahead, given our history.

"I doubt either of us is going to sleep much tonight," he murmurs, drawing sloppy circles against my bare shoulder with one hand, while his other brushes my wild mane of hair back, tucking it under his chin. "I mean, because of paranoia."

"Right. *That's* why." I note the growing ridge in the front of his briefs and chuckle.

Noah's responding laugh vibrates deep within my chest.

And then suddenly he's rolling me onto my back. Even in the dimness, I can see the brilliant blue of his eyes as he hovers over me, his hand sweeping away the stray curls from my face.

"No matter what happens, whatever we find out . . . we will *always* have each other, right?" he asks.

"No matter what." Just the thought of not having Noah within reach tomorrow, next week, next year, causes an unbearable emptiness in my heart.

He's changed my life.

And with that realization, all my reservations about letting this—us—happen melt away.

CHAPTER 45

Officer Abraham Wilkes

April 29, 2003

"Wilkes, I need a minute." Mantis appears out of nowhere, marching toward my car.

"Sorry, don't have one." I need to change my parking spot, starting tomorrow.

I unlock my door, but Mantis blocks it with his stocky body before I'm able to yank it open.

"Make one." There's a sharpness in his tone that instantly puts me on high alert. "I want to make sure you're clear that you were mistaken about what you think you saw the other night."

"Was I?" A low, bitter chuckle sails from my lips.

Mantis's eyes narrow. "Don't be a fucking moron. This fight you're picking isn't worth it."

"I'm not picking any fights."

"Good, 'cause you won't get anywhere with it."

"Then why are you even here, Dwayne? You worried?" Everything about him—his stance, his expression, his voice—tells me why he's here: to issue an ultimatum, a warning.

An unspoken threat.

He takes two steps back, scanning the parking lot. There's no one within earshot, from what I can see. "I *am* worried. About you tanking your career for a lowlife drug dealer."

"I'll worry about my career. You worry about yours. Along with your freedom." I climb into my car and crank my engine. I pull out, slowing just long enough to open my window and holler, "Oh, hey, Mantis, by the way . . . I have proof."

I wish I could record the look on his face in my rearview mirror as I speed off.

CHAPTER 46

Noah

"*Noah . . .*" a female voice croons seductively.

"*Noah . . .*"

"Noah." A hand paws my face, and I realize I'm not dreaming. Gracie's calling my name.

"Yeah?" My voice carries with it a heavy morning scratch.

"Can you let Cyclops out? *Please?*" she mumbles into the pillow.

I frown, forcing my head to one side, to see him curled up by the door, fast asleep. I let him in around three a.m. while up to use the bathroom. He hasn't moved from that spot. "He's not asking."

"He needs to go outside and kill all those damn birds."

The bed shakes with my hearty laugh. I reach over to smooth my hand over her arm. "*That's* what you woke me up for?"

"They're torturing me. I'm *so* tired." She hugs the sheets to her chest but they cascade down, over her hip, exposing her slender, naked back to me. That back that I admired last night, as she positioned herself on the bed before me, as I gripped her curvy hips tight within my hands.

However I imagined Gracie might feel—against her, inside her?

I was wrong.

She felt a thousand times better.

Just thinking about it now . . . I'm instantly hard.

I roll onto my side to fit snugly against her back, her bare skin silky and warm and so inviting. "You shouldn't have stayed up so late, then." I burrow my face into the back of her neck to kiss her, her wild, soft curls tickling my cheek. The smell of her skin is intoxicating to me.

"You wouldn't stop bothering me."

"Is that what you call it?" With a swift tug, I yank the sheet away from her tight grip, sliding it down to expose her. "Am I bothering you now?"

"Very much. You're a menace."

Pushing against her shoulder gently until she rolls onto her back, toward me, I take in those beautiful breasts, visible in the morning light. "A menace?"

Her lips twitch as she hides her smile.

But she's unable to stifle the soft gasp as I lean down to take a peaked nipple into my mouth. I grin as gooseflesh erupts over her skin.

The shrill sound of my phone ringing cuts into the moment. "I'm ignoring that."

"It could be Kristian."

"Then I'm *definitely* ignoring that." Bastard probably knew what he was about to interrupt as he was dialing.

She climbs over me to check the screen on my phone. "It's your uncle."

"I'll call him later."

"It could be about my dad's case."

"I'll call him back in ten." I doubt I'll need even half that long.

She grabs the phone and, hitting the answer button, shoves it against my ear.

His voice, full of energy, is too much for me this morning. "You've learned how to answer your phone again."

"Yeah," I mutter. I can't even manage a "yes, sir."

"No issues last night, I assume?"

"None."

"Good. Canning wants you and Gracie to pay him a visit today."

I'm instantly wary. "For what?"

"What do you mean, for what? To talk about Abe's case."

"I'm not sure if—"

"If Gracie wants any hope of bringing Mantis to justice, believe me, George is the best ally you could ask for. He's expecting you for an early lunch. Eleven o'clock."

I glance at the clock. "Where does he live again?"

"McDade. I'll send you the address. Don't be late."

"Yes, sir." I hang up with a groan.

"Where are we going?" Gracie asks, still draped over me, her green eyes flaring with excitement as she gazes down at me.

"Canning invited us out for lunch." *Invited* may not be the right word. "He wants to talk about your dad's case."

Instant suspicion fills Gracie's gaze. She hesitates. "Kristian thinks Canning might be involved in this cover-up."

"*Kristian* thinks the stray cat six doors down might be involved," I mutter, though I shouldn't be surprised by the agent's suspicion. I wondered the same thing. "When did he tell you that?"

"Last night." Her fingertips skate over my chest, outlining my muscles. "I want to meet Canning. See what he has to say. Then I can decide for myself."

"If Klein thinks Canning is involved, then we shouldn't be going out there."

"We *have* to. If we don't, he'll be suspicious. He can't know that Kristian suspects him."

I sigh. She's right. Still, if that's the case, then bringing Gracie out there to meet him is probably a *bad* idea. "He's going to see through you in five seconds flat."

"What are you implying?"

I give her a pointed look, only to earn a scathing glare in return. "Maybe you should call Klein, then, and let him know." Let *him* tell her it's a bad idea and earn her wrath.

"So he can tell us to not go?" She scoffs.

Exactly.

"So . . . when are we leaving?"

I sigh. "Within the hour."

"I need to shower." She peels herself off me. "Come on, get up."

"I *am* up." I chuckle.

Gracie peers over her shoulder at me, her intense gaze trailing the length of my body, studying me like a cat studies its prized mouse. She bites her bottom lip and I swell in response.

I don't think she expects me to move as fast as I do, because she lets out a playful squeal as I reach for her, flipping her onto her back, and fit my body to settle between her thighs.

"How much does a police chief make, anyway?" Gracie mutters, staring up at the impressive gateway that we pass underneath; stone pillars hold up an ironwork archway with a metal sign that reads "Three Lakes Ranch."

"Not *this* much." We coast up the winding path, in awe of the sprawling two-story rectangular house ahead of us, an inviting row of blue rocking chairs set out on the porch to overlook the lake in front. Beyond the house and to the left is a barn designed to match the house. Horses graze off to the side.

"Do you trust Canning?"

"I don't know if I trust anyone, anymore," I admit. "Except you."

I feel her eyes on my profile and it instantly brings me back to this morning, to her body pressed against me, her heart pounding in her chest, her breathing fast and heavy. Her skin slick in all the right places.

Not the time to be thinking about that.

I throw my Cherokee in park. "Remember, Gracie . . ."

She rolls her eyes. "Do you honestly think he doesn't already know that the FBI suspects him?"

"Maybe he does. But if he doesn't, he's not going to find out from us." I climb out of the driver's seat.

Two sheepdogs come galloping around the house, and a moment later, the screen door creaks open and George Canning steps out, smoothing his button-down shirt over a round, hard belly. The loud thwack it makes when it releases to slam shut echoes, earning a few horse neighs from nearby.

"He looks so . . . *harmless*." Gracie eyes him as we meet around the front of the truck, a potted plant for Dolores within her grasp.

Canning eases down the front stairs and makes his way toward us at a leisurely pace, but I sense the extra time isn't so much on account of his slowness with age as it is his chance to do some assessing of his own, his shrewd, calculating gaze never leaving us. "I'm so glad you came!" He sticks a hand out.

"Thank you for the invitation, sir."

"And this lovely young lady must be Grace Wilkes. Wait, it's something else now?"

"Richards."

"Right." The corners of his eyes crinkle with his smile. "My, you've grown up! You look like the perfect mix of your parents, don't you?"

"I guess?" Gracie says in an even voice.

"Why of course you do! I remember your mother, at the funeral. Pretty little thing." His brow tightens. "Silas told me about her affliction. I hope she's finally on the mend."

Affliction. That's a polite term for it.

Gracie offers a tight smile. "We have a long road ahead, but she's doing better."

I slip my hand over Gracie's back, a gesture of comfort.

The move doesn't go unnoticed by Canning's ever-watchful eyes.

"So, how are you likin' Austin, Grace?"

"It's been . . . eventful so far."

He chuckles. "I'll bet. And you." He turns to me. "Sounds like you've been doing a bit of drivin'."

"Yes, sir."

His eyes flash to Gracie, and then back to me, a knowing twinkle in them. "Come on. Dolores has been busy in the kitchen all mornin'."

"We hope she didn't go to any trouble on our account."

He waves it off. "Heavens no, son! No trouble at all. Dolores lives for feedin' folk until their bellies are ready to explode. I'm living proof." He pats his round belly.

We trail him along the stone walkway that wraps around the house, Gracie walking so close to me that her arm nudges my side with almost every step. "You have a beautiful home," she finally offers, her overly polite voice sounding so foreign that I can't help but grin at her.

I get an elbow to the ribs in return.

Canning chuckles in that easy way of his. "Oh, this is my wife's house. I just take up space here."

We round the corner to the back, where three young children clamber over a play set.

"Hope y'all don't mind the noise, but we're watching the young'ns. My sons and their wives are down in Louisiana with our thoroughbreds. They live just over there." George waves a hand toward what I assume is his property—rolling hills and trees as far as the eye can see, along with two imposing houses, one to the far left, the other to the far right.

"You have a lot of land," Gracie notes.

He leads us to a covered seating area with plush wicker furniture. "Yes, ma'am. It's been in Dolores's family for generations. We had a house in Austin for some years, 'til it was time to move out here full-time. Her great-granddaddy was big into racin'. Her daddy was hopin' I'd follow suit, and I might have, had the city stopped beggin' me to stay on. My sons, though, they got the racin' gene in their blood, so they run the show. I'm here for the pretty view."

The back porch door creaks. "George! Why didn't you tell me they were here!" Dolores—who looks every bit the well-bred Southern woman, right down to the paisley apron that covers her white silk blouse and creamy pleated pants—strolls through the sliding door carrying a silver tray. "Noah! It's so nice to see you again. And so soon!"

"Good day, ma'am." I push the chairs aside to make room for her to set the tray down. It holds a pitcher of sweet tea and three already-filled glasses, along with a small basket covered in a tea towel. "We brought you pansies. Thought you might like them for your windowsill."

"Well, how thoughtful of you. That Jackie sure did raise you right."

I gesture toward Gracie to make introductions.

"It's *so* nice to meet you. Why, aren't you just the most stunning little thing!"

I brace myself for Gracie's coarse response to being called a "little thing."

"Likewise, ma'am." The genuine smile plastered across Gracie's mesmerizing face has me breathing a sigh of relief.

"Call me Dolores. Welcome to our home. I was bakin' biscuits for the children, so they're just hot from the oven." She pulls the tea towel off the bowl to reveal the golden, round treats. Canning reaches for one and she promptly smacks his hand away. "George Archibald Canning! Now you heard what the doctor said about your diet!"

"I heard it. I just wasn't payin' no heed to it," he grumbles, leaning back into his chair, looking properly chastised.

"My homemade marmalade is there, too. I've made a chicken casserole for lunch and it's coolin' from the oven. I just need to scoot up the road for some milk, because we're fresh out and the grandbabies won't drink water. I know, they're spoiled. I'll be ten minutes at most. George, would you be a doll and keep your eyes on them? If they come lookin' for food, send the little vultures into the kitchen. There's a plate waiting for them on the counter. Make sure they wash their hands first!"

"Yes, ma'am. Would you mind droppin' the books on my desk at the library? They're due back tomorrow. Lord knows I can't be turnin' them in late."

"Certainly, dear." She chuckles, patting his shoulder. "Two years ago, Miss Olivia Cane working behind the desk gave this man a good talkin'-down for returning a book late and he's been afraid to miss a due date ever since!"

"I deserved it, too." He watches his wife until she disappears into the house with nothing but adoration in his eyes.

"Does Miss Olivia Cane know who you are?" I ask, half in jest.

"Oh heck, she knows. I reckon that old woman's been workin' at the library for as long as I've been alive. She remembers me when I was as little as them out there on that swing set. Badge or no badge, she don't care. What's right is right in her book." He chuckles. "I respect that. I live by it, the best I can. Goodness, we need some butter for those biscuits. I'll be right back." He heaves himself out of his chair and heads for the door, slowing long enough to add, "Mind them, will ya? Make sure they don't kill each other." He doesn't wait for our answer before stepping inside, the screen door slapping against the frame.

Gracie's brow furrows.

"What's the matter?" I ask, handing her a glass.

"He isn't at all what I expected."

"What'd you expect?"

"Someone who seems like he might have set up my dad," she whispers, as if unhappy with the alternative. She may have stepped onto this property with a backbone full of suspicion, but whatever country charm Dolores and George Canning are dishing out, she can't seem to help but lap up. "I don't see it. I think you're right about Kristian being suspicious of everyone."

"Police chiefs are always under fire for what goes on in their department," I say, echoing Silas's words from last week as I place a biscuit on her plate. "I'll bet you've never had a home-baked biscuit before." I help myself to two, heaping on the marmalade by the spoonful.

Gracie shakes her head at me. "How do you eat so much and stay so . . ." Her gaze rolls over my chest as her words trail off.

"Handsome? Muscular? Fit?" I grin as I suck a glob of the sticky orange jam from my thumb.

"I was going to say 'scrawny.' " She grins, her eyes flashing to the giggling kids.

"Here we go! Give this a quick minute to soften up." George reappears with a small plate, a thick slab of butter sitting in the middle of it. "And if Dolores asks y'all, I didn't have so much as a sliver." The wicker chair crackles under his weight. "So? How's your uncle doin', Noah? I had him runnin' ragged last night. But he's always doin' fine, even when he's not. The man thrives on chaos."

"He seemed in good spirits this morning."

"Silas and I have been friends for going on forty years." George slices off a sizeable chunk of butter for his biscuit. "I was a patrolman and he was a public defender, and we were at odds from the start. He was tryin' to get a reduced sentence for this young punk I busted for drunk and disorderly. Somehow, we ended up figurin' out that we'd rather be on the same side of things. Sometimes it feels like we've gone to war together, for all the battles over the years." Canning drops a dollop of marmalade on his butter-laden biscuit. "So, that was quite the doozy I dropped on the city last night, wasn't it?"

"It was definitely unexpected," I say slowly, stealing a glance Gracie's way.

"But in the best way." She adds, "I never thought I'd hear those words."

"It's the least I can do. When Silas filled me in . . ." His brow furrows deeply. "Sometimes the devil gets ahold of good people and they lose their way. I thought that's what happened to your daddy. Everything pointed to that. But turns out I had the wool pulled over my eyes, just like everyone else. And I'll be damned if I allow whoever's responsible to get away with this."

He takes a long sip of his sweet tea before setting his glass down with a loud thunk. "I didn't know Abraham well. Not like I knew Jackie. But it only took five minutes of reviewing his employee file to be utterly flabbergasted. The man was a saint on paper. I've had to rid myself of a few officers who didn't fit the mold over my years, but I'd like to think I have a keen eye for certain . . . personalities. The corruptible kind. There were no hints with Abraham. Nothing to make me say that I could have seen that comin'."

"All the more reason to have believed he didn't do it," Gracie says carefully.

"You are right, there, Miss Wilkes. Sorry—*Richards.*" He sighs. "I put my best, most trustworthy cops on it. Never in a million years did I think . . ." His voice drifts off. "I don't know what that says about me, how easily I was had. I'm sure my critics will have a field day with it." He waves it away. "None of that matters, though. What matters is gettin' to the bottom of this. And making sure you and your mother get some sort of compensation for it."

Gracie frowns, confused. "Compensation?"

"You'd best believe it. If I have my way, you and your mother won't have to be worryin' about money for a *long* time. Why, look at you, sweet thing." He chuckles, taking in Gracie's surprised face. "Most folk these days are just itchin' to lawyer up and ring every last penny out that they can. But you haven't even thought of suin'. I have to say, I like that."

Neither did I, I'll admit. But he's right. Gracie and Dina may have one hell of a winnable lawsuit against the APD. Not that it'll bring Abe back, but at least it will help them finally move forward.

First, though, we need to find out—and prove—what really happened. "So you believe that Mantis and Stapley set Abe up?" I ask.

"The theory is definitely a concerning one, I'll agree. But after all this, I'm afraid to believe anything unless I have 'see it with my own eyes' irrefutable proof."

"You mean the video."

"Well, that would certainly lend credibility to this theory about Mantis's motive. Lord knows where that thing is, though. Your uncle swears up and down that he had asked the tech guys to search Abraham's computer for it and there was nothin' there. Unless the tech guys were in on this, too." He snorts, but there's no amusement on his face.

"They didn't find it. Not if Mantis was still looking for it, the night he broke into our house and threatened my mom," Grace says.

"Right." Canning frowns. "That's what the feds are thinking? It was Mantis?"

I throw Gracie the fastest warning glance I can manage, not wanting Canning to see it.

"That's what *I'm* thinking," she says smoothly.

"And what makes you say that?"

"Just my gut, for whatever that's worth." She takes a large bite of the biscuit and chews slowly, her face giving nothing away. She can play ambivalent much better than I gave her credit for.

"I think the best next move is to retrace Abraham's steps as much as we can in those last few days. If that video wasn't in his house or on his person, then he must have hidden it somewhere where he figured it would be safe. Noah, you may be the key here. You might be the only one old enough and clearheaded enough to remember anything." Canning's brow furrows deeply. "Silas said you saw him the day he died. Did he say anything strange to you? Anything at all?"

"No, sir . . ." I shake my head, picking through my brain. It's all a foggy recollection, though. Hell, I was only eleven. "He came by to talk to my mom, out back, but I didn't hear them. And then he asked me if I wanted to go to a Spurs game with him that weekend. That was it."

"Hmm. After fourteen years, we might have to assume that video was lost." He shakes his head. "But enough about the nitty-gritty details for now. I wanted you both here today so I could personally tell you how sorry I am. And I won't let it go unpunished."

"I appreciate that." Gracie offers him a smile.

One of the children starts crying, having tumbled off the slide.

"Excuse me for a sec." Canning eases himself out of his chair and leaves the veranda. Just a loving grandfather, checking on his grandchildren.

Gracie's hopeful eyes watching his every move.

In less than a minute, all three are climbing again, their childish laughter carrying in the warm breeze.

"Hang back here, just a second, son." Canning throws a small wave toward Gracie, who's a few steps ahead, her hands full of leftover biscuits and casserole, courtesy of Dolores. "Hope you don't mind—I need to borrow Noah. We'll be in touch soon, though, ya hear?"

With a smile and a nod, Gracie keeps going, heading toward the lake beside the driveway, where the early afternoon sun beats down and those massive sheepdogs laze.

"Do good by that girl, Noah. She's had it rough."

"Yes, sir. She sure has."

"I don't have a lot of hope for how this case will turn out, but if we can at least give Abraham the clean name he deserves, it should make her and Dina happy, don't you think?"

"It's definitely a start. Especially if we can get Dina the help she needs." True to Silas's word, I've already received a phone call from Desert Oaks, notifying me that Dina's rehab has been covered for the next two months. I know Judy and Silas have been smart with their money, but that has to have set them back.

"You need to help her move on, so this doesn't fester."

"Yes, sir. I'll try."

"Good. I'm glad she has you." He drops a heavy hand on my shoulder. "Help her focus on her future, not the past."

My head bobs up and down.

"Best to just let sleeping dogs lie. They're less likely to bite."

The hairs on the back of my neck spike. "Pardon me?"

He frowns with confusion.

"What you just said . . ."

"'Let sleeping dogs lie'?" He chuckles. "Oh, that's just an expression. You never heard it?"

"Yeah. I have. It's just . . . not in a bit," I force myself to finish, my mouth going dry.

"Well, it's nothing you young folk ever say."

"No, sir. It's not." *"He always liked that saying, every time I pushed him. Every time I told him they were up to no good."*

A curious look flashes in Canning's eyes and I force a smile. "I'm gonna take Gracie home now. Try to get her mind off things."

He raises his brows. "I'll bet. Y'all keep in touch. And come straight to me if you remember anything about Abraham, about that visit he paid. Anything at all."

"Sure thing." I feel his gaze on my back as I walk, pacing my steps so I don't seem in a rush. Meanwhile, my mind races with understanding.

Gracie sees me coming and, with one last pat for the dogs, heads for the SUV. "Not that we need *more* food, but that was nice of Dolores, to pack this care package for us," she murmurs, opening the paper bag and inhaling deeply.

Cranking my engine, I tap my horn as we pull out, making sure my wave and smile are as big as possible.

Gracie follows suit. "I feel guilty for ever letting Kristian convince me that—"

"Canning knew." My voice wobbles.

"What? He just told you that?"

"Not intentionally."

Let sleeping dogs lie.

My mom knew Mantis was corrupt. She must have brought it up with Canning and Canning must have told her to leave it alone, to stay quiet. Let his "hounds" be. Let them keep busting drug dealers for the city, even if it meant they might be pocketing money on the side while doing it.

Let them be, or they might retaliate.

Like they did with Abe.

My teeth gnash against each other. "That son of a bitch knew that Mantis was corrupt, all along."

CHAPTER 47

Commander Jackie Marshall

April 30, 2003

Canning waves me in, pointing a weathered hand toward a chair, a receiver pressed against his ear.

He still has the silver-framed picture of Wyatt Canning at his police academy graduation sitting on his desk. I feel a twinge of sadness in my gut, looking into those honest, baby-blue eyes. Wyatt was a good guy. What happened to him was plain tragic. Worse is the fact that it's gone unsolved. Not even Canning's prized hounds have been able to unearth so much as a rumor, after all these years.

"I want to know how the hell that scumbag made it back out onto the streets. He's a drug dealer!" Canning's face is turning beet red as he chews someone out. The man's going to give himself a heart attack if he doesn't learn how to contain his frustration. "I won't let my department get dragged through the gutter because you couldn't make this stick, Ross. That little girl? Her death is on you, and I'll make sure every last voter knows it. I can't wait to see the back of your head. Thank God Reid has the balls to do what needs to be done."

It's not hard to piece together what's going on here. Canning's tearing a new one into our current DA, Dylan Ross. He's had it with Ross and thinks my brother will be just what the department, and the city, needs.

Let's hope the election goes our way.

Canning slams down the phone. "God dammit!"

"The drive-by in MLK?"

"That little girl was five years old! Just sittin' in her kitchen, eatin' her cornflakes—" He inhales sharply. "That scumbag should have been behind bars, not allowed to drive around, shootin' up neighborhoods, killin' kids right in front of their mothers." He heaves a sigh, releasing his anger. "What's goin' on, Jackie?"

I hesitate.

"Is it about that *thing* from the other night? Because you know you did right by—"

"No. I'm not here to talk about *that*." I want to forget that night ever happened.

He frowns. "Then what? Is it your son?"

"No, Noah's great."

"Then what is it? Ashley said it was urgent."

How the hell do I bring this up? I guess I just come out and say it. "Mantis was seen taking a bag of cash from that Lucky Nine motel bust."

"What?"

"Mantis was seen—"

"I heard ya." Canning's face remains frozen for a long moment as he processes this. "Who saw him?"

"Abe Wilkes, sir. He was at the motel, searching for his sister-in-law." I give him a knowing look.

Canning leans back in his chair, scowling at the door. A shadow shifts past it. Canning's assistant, no doubt. "He must be mistaken about what he saw."

"He's not mistaken." Lowering my voice, I tell Canning everything. By the time I'm done, he looks ready for that heart attack.

"It's probably better for everyone involved that you get IA involved right away. If Abe comes forward with this—"

"IA?" Canning's frown deepens. "No one's going to IA about this."

"But—"

"Think of the big picture, here, Jackie. Think of what will happen if this gets out."

"Yes, sir. I'm certainly afraid of that." All the goodwill we work hard to build in the community? It'll all be undone, buried under a thick layer of public distrust, thanks to one dirty cop.

"If this story leaks, this drug dealer will be back out on the street, catering to gangbangers who shoot up houses with little girls and boys in them. Why would we risk that? Over some cash?"

"Yes, sir. But—"

"Sometimes we have to do things that don't sit well with our conscience, because it's for the greater good."

"I'm well aware of that, as you know, sir." I give him a pointed look.

"And that's what being a real leader is about. If you want any hope of replacing me one day, you will help Wilkes see that."

"I don't think he can be swayed. At least, not by me. I'm the devil reincarnate, as far as he's concerned."

Canning's gaze flickers over the framed picture of his son for a moment, before meeting my eyes. "*Everyone* can be swayed."

CHAPTER 48

Officer Abraham Wilkes

May 2, 2003

"Hey, babe." I lean over the couch to plant a kiss on Dina's lips. "Sorry I missed soccer tonight."

"Did you catch the bad guys?" She peers up at me with those stunning green eyes, the ones she's blessed our daughter with. She's not happy about all the extra hours lately, but she's never openly given me grief about it.

That's why lying to her about what I'm doing is especially shitty. But I'd rather lie than tell her the whole truth. At least, for now.

"Not yet. Did she go down easy?"

Dina shrugs. "She's *your* daughter. Stubborn to the bone."

I chuckle.

"I'll bet she's still holding on to that book."

"Did you do the gruff voice?"

"'Not like Daddy does it,'" Dina mimics Gracie's childish timbre. "Hey, did you come home at all tonight?"

I frown. "No. Why?"

A worried look flickers over her face. "Just a feeling I had, is all. Like someone had been in here."

"The doors were locked?"

"Yeah."

"Anything missing?"

"Not from what I can see. I don't know . . . it was a weird vibe. It's probably just me, being home alone so much. Maybe we should get a dog," she admits reluctantly, and then rolls her eyes at my wide grin. I've been trying to convince her to get one for years, with no luck. "You know, Gracie saw this mangy little thing at the park and tried to bring it home with us." It sounds like an accusation. "I told her that Noah wouldn't come over anymore if we brought a stray home."

"He'd get over it soon enough." As soon as he saw how much Gracie loved having a dog.

Dina levels me with a look. "We are *not* bringing home a stray."

"They need love, too." I lean down to kiss her again. "Gonna grab a shower. See you in bed soon?"

I get a coy smile in return, and it's enough to make me rush.

But Dina's words linger in my mind, long after her naked body lies still beside me. Enough that I find myself wandering through the house in the middle of the night, checking the locks and drawers, seeing if anything looks out of place.

I find nothing.

And yet my unease lingers.

May 3, 2003

"A head of romaine, right?" I call out over my shoulder, heading for my car.

"Please."

"Daddy, wait! I wanna come to the store with you!" Gracie comes tearing down the steps, stopping to adjust the Velcro on her bright pink sneakers before rushing the rest of the way.

Dina and I share a knowing look. Gracie hasn't left my side all morning. "I'll be back in fifteen." I give one of Gracie's curly pigtails a light yank and then open the car door.

I freeze when I spot a black duffel bag sitting on the backseat. I don't have to open it to guess what it is.

"You know what, Gracie May? I just remembered. I have to stop at the station today and—"

"No!" She begins to pout. "I wanna come with you!"

"You can't today. Next time, I promise."

"But, Daddy! I want to—"

"No, Gracie," I say with a rare firm voice, before she resorts to a full-blown tantrum in the middle of the sidewalk. I soften it with a promise to get ice cream later.

With a huff and tears in her eyes, she trudges back up the stairs and buries her face in Dina's legs.

"I'm sorry," I mouth, nearly flinching at the look of displeasure on Dina's face. "It'll be more like an hour."

CHAPTER 49

Grace

Noah slides in from behind to hover over my shoulder as I toss a handful of peppers into a bowl. His skin is slick with sweat, but I don't mind. Actually, I find it appealing.

"Is Jenson still here?" I left them outside, playing one-on-one in the driveway.

"Gone home." I can't help the slight tremble as he leans in to kiss the side of my neck, his hands hot against my hips. "Is there enough for me, too?"

"There's plenty. This fool I know bought way too much of everything."

I feel his lips curve into a smile. "Lucky for me. I'm *starving*."

"Didn't you eat half a cow an hour ago?" I glance at the oven clock to confirm when Jenson showed up with a bag of burgers. Noah ate his and most of mine.

"What's your point?"

"I don't understand where you put it all."

"I burn it. Playing ball, running . . . doing *other* things."

I glance up in time to catch Noah's eyes dipping into my tank top. He grins at me and heat floods through my body instantly. It's been three days since I woke up tangled in his bedsheets, and we've spent most of that time holed up in that room, distracting ourselves while we wait for the FBI and APD to nail Mantis and Stapley.

Noah has made the frustrating wait bearable.

I sniff teasingly. "You need a shower."

"I *do* need a shower." Strong hands pull me backward.

"Uh-uh. No way. I'm not drying my hair *again* today."

"Then don't."

"Are you . . . did you forget what happens?"

His deep chuckles tell me he hasn't forgotten the untamed clown's wig that I woke up with this morning, after I shared a shower with him last night.

"You're such a jerk."

"Come on . . . You can wear one of those things to keep it dry."

"A *shower cap*?" I cringe at the mental image of a gorgeous, naked Noah and me, in my pink plastic cap. Having sex. I turn to give him a playful shove away, but he's no longer paying attention to me, distracted by the TV.

Canning's on the news again.

I dive for the remote to turn up the volume.

"We have what we'd call 'persons of interest,'" Canning says. "Though, I'm fairly confident two of them will be cleared of all wrongdoing."

I frown. "Who's he talking about? Mantis and Stapley?"

"I don't know. But look at him, pretending to be innocent." Noah's teeth grind, his jaw so tense. "He shouldn't be up there. Towle's the acting chief. Why the hell is he up there!"

"There's nothing we can do about it. You heard Kristian." I called him the second we turned out of Canning's driveway yesterday. Aside from an "I told you so" and a sharp warning to not say a word about it to anyone including the DA, he confirmed what we already know—that "sleeping dogs" gets us nowhere.

"Confidential sources have confirmed that these persons of interest are APD officers. Can you comment?" a voice in the crowd says.

"I cannot. Next question."

"Is there any connection between Chief Jackie Marshall's suicide and the uncovering of this new evidence behind Abraham Wilkes's death?"

Noah's back stiffens.

"I can confirm that Chief Marshall's death led to law enforcement discovering new evidence."

"Did Chief Marshall have knowledge about Abraham Wilkes's death that she did not make public?"

"She did."

"Son of a bitch," Noah mutters.

"Was Chief Marshall involved in Abraham Wilkes's death?"

"Involved?" Canning seems to mull that over. "I'd say there certainly have been questions raised, yes, sir."

"That *son of a bitch*!" Noah roars, looking ready to tear the flat-screen from the wall. "He's trying to throw her under the damn bus!"

I bite my tongue before I say something insensitive. Before I point out that nothing Canning said was a lie. Technically, *all* of it was true. Because Noah's also right—Canning is trying to focus the attention on Jackie. He wants her pinned with my father's murder. Kristian warned as much.

"Do you want me to phone Kris—"

"What the hell is *he* going to do?" Noah snaps, then pinches the bridge of his nose. "I'm sorry. I didn't mean to yell at you."

I reach for him, smoothing a hand over his back, his shirt damp beneath my palm, the tension coursing through him palpable.

"This can't happen. They need to arrest and charge Mantis and Stapley, and be done with it, so we can all move on."

"We're a long way from that happening." And it's not looking promising. The APD got a warrant on Stapley's truck and pulled blood samples that matched what was found in the pantry. They have him on breaking and entering, though he's claiming he's being set up. And there are no fingerprints anywhere—on the safe or the gun—to prove otherwise.

The only thing that ties him to the house without a doubt is three drops of blood.

"We need to find that video," Noah says with grim determination.

Easier said than done. "He didn't give it to either of our moms, and he didn't give it to you or me, so who else could have it? Who did he trust?"

"No one." Noah leans against the wall, his gaze settling on the lights overhead, his thoughts visibly drifting into the past.

"Are you *sure* he didn't give it to your mom that day? Maybe she destroyed it."

"Why destroy that, but keep the gun holster and the money?"

"Yeah, you're right." I sigh. "Well, he didn't give it to me. Not unless he hid it in one of my toys, but that'd be stupid. I was six. Six-year-olds break and lose their toys all the time."

"Right . . ." Several long beats pass. And then a whisper of "holy shit!" slips from him. Noah peers down at me, his eyes wide with realization. "I think I know where it is."

CHAPTER 50

Officer Abraham Wilkes

May 3, 2003

The duffel bag lands at Jackie's feet with a thump.

She dusts the soil from her hands. "What is this?"

"The ninety-eight thousand bucks that Mantis stole. He broke into my car last night and left it in the backseat. I sat in a remote parking lot for the past hour, counting it, curious what that asshole was giving up in his attempt to buy me off. Did he come up with the idea? Or did you put him up to this?"

She looks down at it with new understanding, and sighs. "I'd never even bother suggesting it to him, Abe. I know you too well. But why on earth would you bring it here?"

"Because I'm not stupid enough to get caught with it. Here's *your* chance to do the right thing." I turn to leave.

"Wait!" She steps over the bag and moves closer to me. "Maybe it's not a bad idea that you take it. Just think how much good you could do with it."

"Have you lost your damn mind, woman?"

"All I'm saying is, this way Mantis isn't richer for it, and that drug dealer goes to jail. Everyone wins. You could give it to charity. You always say you wished the department did that with the drug money seized."

"Mantis is corrupt and he needs to be stopped."

"Abe . . . let this go. Please." She hesitates. "Canning will never let anything come of this."

"How do you know that?" The careful look on her face answers me. "You've already gone to him about it."

"Your career will be finished. Don't throw it all away."

Screw that. "Well, Canning won't be able to stop this, because I have a video."

Jackie's face pales. "What? How?"

"Doesn't matter how. All that matters is that I have Mantis stealing a bag of money from a bust and I'm going to make sure it's put to good use."

I leave Jackie in the garden, gaping at my back.

A sullen Noah trudges down the stairs, pieces of his trophy in each hand. "I knocked it off the shelf," he mutters, and then pushes past me.

I quell my rage at Jackie for Noah's sake. "Hold up. What are you doing?"

"Throwing it out. It's trash now."

"This is your first one!" I take the pieces from his hand. "No way are you throwing this out. We can fix this. Go on, get me the Krazy Glue. I think it's in your mom's junk drawer."

He trots off to fetch the tube, while I study the pieces.

And note the hollow square base, about three inches in diameter.

CHAPTER 51

Noah

My hands are sweating as I wedge the end of a flat-head screwdriver into the base of the trophy. I tap the handle with a hammer, working away where the dried gobs of glue still exist. Gracie hovers over my shoulder, not saying a word.

After four tries, the base splits off.

I hold up the square case, showing a round disc inside, my heart pounding in my chest.

I can't believe it's been here all this time.

"A miniature DVD, maybe?" It's about three inches in diameter. Grabbing my phone, I type in the code printed on the front to see what Google returns. "It's for a camcorder."

"My dad recorded the bust with a camcorder?"

"I guess so." I hesitate. "We should call Klein."

We both look at the disc in my hand and then at each other.

"It's not working. I'm going to kill that—"

"Relax. It's reading the disc." The guy from the computer store promised this special adapter would work, and he seemed to know what he was talking about.

Gracie huffs from her spot in the desk chair, frantically drumming her fingers next to the mouse, as I hover over her.

The drive screen finally pops up. With a few quick clicks, the Lucky Nine motel appears.

"Oh my God. This is actually it!" she exclaims.

The sun has just set, and the last traces of pink and purple are on the verge of being eaten up by a night sky. Half of the green neon sign that Dina mentioned flickers in the top right of the screen, enough to identify the place for what it was if we hadn't already been there.

The camera angle is low and the filming is steady, I note, as a car suddenly peels into the lot and parks. Not ten seconds later, an SUV races in and our suspects pile out. Neither of us utters a single word for the next few minutes, our eyes glued to the swirl of shouting orders and aimed guns on the screen as Canning's drug hounds—Mantis at the helm—arrest the wiry man.

We both inhale sharply as a black duffel bag goes smoothly sailing into the passenger-side window of the police vehicle.

Gracie grins up at me. A bitter but victorious grin. Probably the same grin Dina saw on Abe's face that night she walked into the office and caught him watching this video.

"Let's replay it. See what else we can find." I reset it to the beginning and we watch again. "Holy shit. Look there." I tap on the white Cavalier parked across from where the bust is happening. Only the front half of it shows on the screen, but it's enough. I recognize that car. And the lone figure in the driver's seat.

My chest tightens. "That's your dad."

Gracie's face pales slightly as she quietly studies her father. He's sitting still, watching Mantis and the others. Her eyes don't move from him the entire time, and when the video ends, she resets it to play again.

"Who's he talking to? Who's that man?" She jabs the computer screen. A wiry black man is standing next to Abe's open window at the beginning, but he steps out of the frame quickly. She rewinds it three more times, trying to glean more. But the man never gives us his face.

"My dad's *in* the video," she says suddenly. "That means he wasn't recording Mantis. Someone else was. Someone standing over *here*." She taps the bottom of the screen, her brow pinched with thought.

"Not standing. Sitting," I add. "This angle is too low for someone to be standing." And too steady for someone to be holding the camera, I'm thinking.

"Wouldn't Mantis have noticed someone taping them?"

"He didn't notice Abe there," I counter, but she's right. I find it hard to believe the cops wouldn't notice someone out in the open, pointing a camcorder at them.

"Unless the person recording this wasn't out in the open." She pauses the video and points to the edge of the screen on the left. "This is 116." Realization fills her face. "I think I know where this video was taken from. Come on, we've got to go there." She nearly knocks me over in her mad dash out of the chair.

"Hold up a sec." I grab my phone and, resetting the video yet again, begin making a copy.

CHAPTER 52

Grace

"This place comes alive at night, doesn't it . . ." Noah murmurs, his blue eyes rolling over the row of cars parked on either side of the lot. A few people linger outside—leaning against windowsills while puffing on cigarettes; pacing along the shadowy sidewalks, their phones pressed to their ear. From somewhere within, a television blares the news and raucous laughter carries, serving as an ill mask to the other, more carnal sounds that thin walls can't keep in.

"I'm ready when you are." I hit send on the text to Kristian, telling him to meet us here and why. I'm assuming that he'll come and fast, once he watches the video Noah just forwarded to him.

"Hold on." Noah reaches over, his sinewy arm sliding between my legs to find the gun box from beneath my seat. I watch quietly while he fits it into his ankle holster, adjusting his jeans to fit over the top. "With what's been going on lately—"

"The hookers are scary, I get it." I climb out of my seat with a smile, not feeling as brave as I let on, because I know that Noah's not thinking about the blonde girl up ahead, in her skimpy black dress and her crimson lips. And I know he's not too worried about the two guys down by the corner of buildings Two and Three, who are doing a terrible job of hiding the exchange of some weekend recreational drugs for money.

It's the dirty cops who have gotten away with corruption and murder for fourteen years that have him strapping a gun to his body anytime we leave the house.

The ones who probably would have gotten away with it for the rest of their lives, had it not been for us.

I meet up with Noah at the front of his Cherokee. "How fast will Kristian get here, do you think?"

"Pretty damn fast." He loops an arm around my waist and holds me close as we walk along the sidewalk of Building One, both our gazes on the exact spot where the drug bust went down.

And where my father watched.

He was barely a shadow in the camera, and yet my heart filled with longing all the same. So many years stolen from me, all because my father was a good man, driven to do the right thing.

I push that ache aside. "It had to be taken from over here." I hold up my phone, the video open and paused, and keep going—past Room 116, which is dark inside and, I'm assuming, in no shape for rental after the FBI tore it apart—until I've found the exact angle, at the window of Room 201. "It was taken from here."

Noah steps in beside me to survey the angle. "Lower . . ." He takes my phone and crouches down, until my phone very nearly sits on the windowsill. "Here. The camera had to be sitting on the sill. Maybe on the inside. That's why it was so steady. That's why Mantis didn't notice it."

"So, someone renting *this* room that night just happened to have a camcorder, and just happened to tape the bust?"

"Having a video camera in a place like this isn't the surprising part." Noah gives me a knowing look. "But you're right, something doesn't add up. How'd your dad get it?"

I stand. "Maybe whoever was renting here knew that my father was a—" I let out a yelp of surprise when I look up to find that same man from the other day standing in the window, his face inches away from the glass.

Staring at me.

Noah stands to his full height and levels the guy with his own stare, one full of warning.

But the man—I'm guessing in his late sixties—doesn't seem the least bit fazed.

"He was here that first day we came, when Klein was here," I whisper, my gaze drifting over the wiry, old black man. He's wearing the same brown trousers and rumpled shirt that he was wearing that day as well.

And . . .

"Oh my God." I restart the video from my phone.

He's wearing basically the same thing as the mysterious man talking to my father was wearing.

"Noah . . . this man was there that night." I hold my phone to the glass, to where the man can see it clearly.

Chocolate-brown eyes shift to the screen, watching for two . . . three . . . four beats, before drifting back to me. And then he nods ever so subtly, almost to himself, and vanishes into the darkness of the room.

I'm about to slam my fist on the door when it opens.

"Who are you?"

He inhales deeply through his nostrils. "My name is Isaac. And you are Gracie May Wilkes."

Hearing my full name roll off the tongue of this man—a complete stranger—makes my stomach flip. "How do you know that?"

"Because your father told me." He jerks his head, indicating that we should follow him.

With a look back at Noah, we trail the old man into the motel room. His apartment, it would seem, based on the everyday clutter. The standard furniture has been replaced with a twin bed in the corner, a worn brown Barcalounger across from a contrastingly new small flat-screen TV, and a small table with two chairs, currently housing stacks of newspapers. Magazines sit on a side table, and dirty dishes are piled neatly by the sink. The air is stale, a faint scent of body odor lingering.

"I wondered when you'd find your way here." Isaac moves slowly as he clears the papers away to allow us a place to sit.

"You knew Abraham Wilkes?" Noah asks for me, because I can't seem to form words.

"I talked to him here and there. He was comin' here every day, lookin' for someone—"

"Betsy." I finally find my tongue. "He was looking for her."

"Lookin'. But not findin'. He'd just missed her by a few days, if I recall."

"She was staying *here*?"

"Yes, ma'am. She was here. And then she was gone. Kept an eye out for her, but . . . never saw hair nor hide of her again."

"Did you take the video of the drug bust?"

"I did. Right from that very spot over there. But it seems you've already figured that out." He sighs as he eases himself into his lounge chair. "I'd been having trouble with vandals bustin' into that vending machine. I wanted to catch 'em red-handed and I needed one of those things to do it. What do you call them again? Those . . ." His hand waves aimlessly in front of himself, as if the answer is in the air.

"A camcorder?"

"Camcorder. Yes. Can't keep up with all this technology." He chuckles as my gaze roams the room again, to the flat screen, and the laptop on the corner desk. "That's all my son's doing. He brings this stuff over for me every once in a while. God only knows which trucks they fall out the back from, but I don't ask questions anymore. Anyway, he brought one of those fancy new camcorders and set it up right over there, by the window. Stacked some books to get it the right height. Taught me how to turn it on before I went to bed, and that was that.

"Well, I was tinkering with it over dinner and I guess I set it to record earlier than usual. I went out to do a few last jobs for the day. That's when I ran into your dad, out in the parking lot. And then the cavalry came in after that guy. Didn't realize I'd caught the whole thing on tape until later that night when I went to turn it on, only to find it already running. And I sure didn't realize exactly what I'd caught until I replayed it." He waggles his brow. "So I did what I thought was right, and I gave the video to your dad, the next time he came 'round."

"When was that?" Noah asks.

"A few days before he died."

I share a glance with Noah. "Have you watched the news lately?"

Isaac leans forward, resting his bony elbows on his knees, leveling me with those wise eyes. "Girl, I've known your daddy was innocent from the night he died."

Something in his tone makes my heart flip. "How?"

"Because he was set up." He says it so matter-of-factly.

"And how do you know that?" I ask, my voice barely a whisper. "Did you see someone do it?" Did Mantis scare him from speaking?

But Isaac says nothing, heaving himself out of his chair to mosey over to the corner of the room. Digging out a screwdriver from his tool belt, he eases himself down onto one knee and unfastens the air exchange panel from the wall. He reaches in and pulls out a jump drive.

"I did one better. I *recorded* someone doing it."

CHAPTER 53

Officer Abraham Wilkes

May 3, 2003

"You the cop who's been lookin' for that girl?" The woman's abrasive tone fills my ear.

"Yes, ma'am. Do you have information?"

"Saw her goin' into Room 116 at The Lucky Nine tonight. About an hour ago. Better hurry if you want to catch her." The line goes dead.

And my heart starts racing.

"Babe? It's late. Who was that?" Dina calls from the living room.

It's so tempting to finally tell her. But what if this caller is wrong? Or what if Betsy's already gone? What if I've missed her again? Dina's such an emotional woman, and she's had an especially hard time of this whole thing. It would crush her, if I came home empty-handed.

"Work. I've gotta run out for a bit. I'll be back soon." It's a twenty-minute drive out to The Lucky Nine from here. If Betsy's just there for a client, and she's already been there an hour . . . I've got to hurry.

I'm pulling my Colt .45 out of the safe when Dina comes into the office, hugging herself, a frown of disappointment marring her beautiful face. "Shouldn't you be taking your police gun instead?"

"Not when I have this *amazing* holster that my lovely wife had made for me." I force a smile as I fasten it. "I'm just going out to check on something. I won't be long."

Her frown hasn't faded yet, though. "Why don't you ever wear your uniform for these extra hours?"

"It's better if I don't."

"Is it undercover work?"

"Something like that." The lies are tasting worse each day. Fortunately, Dina hasn't figured out yet that I'm feeding her bullshit.

I'll come clean the second I've brought Betsy home to us.

I give her a kiss. "See you in a bit."

The motel parking lot is especially quiet tonight, I note as I make my way along the sidewalk, eyeing the door numbers until I get to the last one in the block.

The lights are on inside.

My adrenaline races through my veins. A small voice in the back of my head keeps asking me if maybe I want to phone for police backup, but I push it aside. I just want to get Betsy away from this once and for all.

Pulling my badge and gun out, I rap my knuckles against the door.

Someone opens it.

I ignore protocol and push right in. "I'm looking for Betsy. Where is she?"

The guy inside, a lanky punk with sagging pants and gang tattoos decorating his skin, takes several steps backward. "Don't know who you're talking about."

My gaze drifts over the bed, to where a small navy gym bag sits open, just wide enough to show me glimpses of the cocaine and weed parcels inside. Several bundles of cash sit piled over the tacky bedspread.

Shit. What the hell have I walked into?

The toilet flushes from inside the bathroom.

"Hands up, where I can see them!" I warn the guy standing in front of me. He complies without a word, as I wait for the person in the bathroom to emerge.

Mantis strolls out and comes to a dead stop. "Wilkes! What the hell are you doing here?"

"I got a tip that my sister-in-law was here. You?" I stare pointedly at the bed.

Mantis sighs. "Wilkes, this is Hernandez. An informant." He gestures to the guy. "I'm working on a setup, and he's the guy who's gonna help me pull it off." He juts his chin out. "Wanna stop pointing that fucking thing at me?"

I holster my gun. "So there was no blonde girl here in the past hour?"

"Blonde girl? There hasn't been no one but *this* ugly asshole here all night," Hernandez confirms, chuckling as he wanders over to the window to peek out. "Yo, how much longer? It's not good for my cover, with you and *him* showin' up at the door. Never know who's watching."

I turn to leave, my feet weighed down with disappointment.

"So, how are you gonna spend that money?" Mantis asks, humor in his rough voice. "Some jewelry for that pretty wife?"

"What money?" I spit out. "You talkin' about the bag you left in my car last night? The bag you're trying to buy me off with?" A bitter laugh escapes me. "I dropped that shit off with Marshall today. You want your money back, you'll have to go and get it from her."

He bares his stubby teeth in a sneer. "Yeah . . . I told him it'd be a waste of time. That you wouldn't be shut up so easily."

"Told who?"

"Who do you think? The guy that's gonna make sure your whining goes nowhere."

Realization sinks in. I should have known. The chief is the one who commissioned this brat pack. He's the one who told Mantis to try and buy me off.

"And you know why he's gonna cover for me?" Mantis lifts a bag of cocaine. "Because I get this shit off Austin's streets, and that's all Canning cares about. That's all *you* should care about. Not some scumbag's rights. As soon as they start dealing drugs to kids, they don't get rights!"

I glance over to Hernandez, who's watching with a mixture of curiosity and wariness. If he has any street smarts, he's probably already figured out that there's more going on here than whatever Mantis has roped him into.

"How old's your little Gracie now? Six?" Mantis asks.

"Don't you say my daughter's name again. Ever," I growl, charging at him.

He holds his hands up in the air in surrender, taking several steps back and around me, toward the door. "Relax. Just tryin' to make a point. I'm getting this stuff off the streets for your daughter."

"And I'm glad for that. But that doesn't mean *this* stuff"—I sidestep around him to reach for a wad of cash, and hold it up—"should be lining your pockets."

He gives a lazy shrug. "It was one time."

"Bullshit." The way he took that money—with smooth movements and such ease—he's done it plenty. "Your mattress is probably lined with cash."

"Funny, someone might say the same about you."

"No, sir. I don't think so."

"You sure about that?" A wicked gleam shines in his beady eyes.

Wariness sinks in. "What have you done?"

"Where's this proof that you've got?" he asks quietly, ignoring my question.

"Nowhere you'll ever find it. What did you do, Mantis?" I repeat through gritted teeth.

"What I needed to, to make sure no one ever believes a word you've said."

The call . . . the drugs . . . the cash . . . Jesus Christ. This is a setup. Mantis is setting me up. I need to get out of here. I need to—

Unbearable pain rips through my chest, sending my body backward, into the wall. In the next second I'm on my knees. I manage to look up, to see Mantis aiming his gun at a shocked Hernandez. I didn't even see him pull it out. When did he pull it out?

Hernandez is shouting something, but I can't make out the words over the agony.

Another blast sounds, just as my face collides with the dirty, thin carpet. I can see Hernandez's boots from beneath the bed.

And then I can see more of him, as his body hits the floor on the other side.

Everything begins to dim, as my lungs pull for air that won't come, as the burning fire in my chest begins to dull.

My eyelids shutter.

Behind them, I see Gracie May's big, beautiful green eyes.

I feel her tiny arms wrapping around my neck.

I hear her sweet laughter.

CHAPTER 54

Noah

Gracie and I huddle around Isaac's laptop and watch as, twenty seconds after four gunshots go off, a single figure ducks out of Room 116. The person locks the door and smoothly strolls down the narrow path between the buildings, toward the parking lot.

Glancing ever so briefly at the room perpendicular to 116.

Not noticing the camcorder perched inside the motel room window.

The camera that captured his face beneath a baseball cap for that split second.

Long enough to identify him.

"Holy shit," I whisper.

Beside me, Gracie's body is stiff with tension.

"I usually like to watch a little bit of late-night news," Isaac says, from his chair. He didn't bother to watch the video with us, which makes me think he's watched it plenty. "But that night I was already in bed, and not fast enough getting out of it when those gunshots went off. Lucky for me. Otherwise I'd have been standing in that window. That fella and me would have met eye to eye. He'd have known that I had him pegged."

"Why didn't you give this video to the cops!" Gracie's voice cracks with frustration.

"You just keep watching, there." Isaac shifts the curtain to peer out at the parking lot.

She shakes her head with frustration, but refocuses her attention on the screen, as we wait.

Barely a minute later, we get our answer. The same SUV from the Lucky Nine drug bust—or something similar—speeds into the parking lot, lights flashing.

Mantis and Stapley jump out and move straight for Room 116 to kick in the door.

Two minutes later a police cruiser comes racing in. Stapley meets them at the threshold, holding them back with a raised hand and some words.

"Let me guess: that's where he's telling them that Canning has ordered that no one step inside," I mutter. What a perfect cover for Mantis.

A second and third police cruiser roll in.

And suddenly the video cuts out.

"I wanted to see what my little camera had caught, so I went back a bit. When I saw your daddy walk into that room and not walk back out . . . I had a damn good idea about exactly what I'd caught."

Gracie's body was already tense by the time we watched Abe stroll up to 116 to push into the room, badge and gun in hand. Because Isaac's recording started twenty-five minutes before, when Mantis appeared. We watched him hand cash and a phone to a hooker who'd ducked out of a room and was heading toward her car. She made a call.

A call, I'm betting, to Abe, on the phone found on Hernandez.

It'd take about twenty minutes to get to The Lucky Nine from Abe's old house. Twenty-five by the time Abe said goodbye to Dina and collected his Colt .45 from his safe.

Mantis sent that hooker scurrying away at a fast pace, the fear in her face telling me his words were laced with sharp warning. And then Mantis, his hand laden with a small navy-blue gym bag, knocked on 116. Someone opened the door; Mantis went in and didn't come out until after the gunshots were fired.

He was the only person who ever came out.

"I recognized that cop. He was the same one that night of the bust, tossin' that bag into his car window. I gave your daddy that recording and he was gonna do something about it. I ain't stupid. I could see what was goin' on," Isaac mutters. "And then that cop comes knockin' on my door with a pad of paper, looking for witnesses?" He scoffs. "More like to shut up witnesses. I wasn't about to give him that video. So I shook my head and said, 'No, sir. I didn't see a thing. Have yourself a good night, sir.' I figured I'd wait for someone else to come around, someone I could trust, before I turned over that video." He pauses. "No one else came."

"But you *knew* my father was innocent and you sat on this for *fourteen years*?" Gracie cries out, tears in her eyes.

"And I also knew he was dead, and nothing would be bringing him back. Besides, I like my body *not* riddled with bullet holes, thank you very much." Isaac says that with confidence, but he averts his gaze to the floor. I sense a hint of shame hiding beneath that exterior. "Like I said, I was waitin' for the right person to come by, askin'. And you finally came."

Gracie's phone rings. Two seconds into her conversation, I can tell it's Kristian on the other end. He's here and he's looking for us.

"We can take this, right?" I hold up the jump drive.

"You can take that. You can take the original DVD, too. I've got that one in a safety deposit box at the bank. You never can be too careful, 'specially around here."

My eyes roam over the small room again. "So you've lived here for . . ."

"Goin' on twenty years. What can I say? I lead a simple life. Do my own thing. People don't bother me and I don't bother them, and that's how I like it." A hard knock sounds on the door and Isaac lifts the curtain to peek past. His face twists with displeasure. "Well, there he is again."

Gracie opens the door and Klein strolls in, closely followed by Tareen.

"I see you've met the owner of this fine establishment," Klein says, giving Isaac a once-over.

My mouth drops open. *Owner?*

Klein shakes his head at the old man. "Don't know nothing about nothing, hey?"

"I suddenly remembered somethin'."

Klein jabs a finger toward Isaac, his aloof mask cracking to show irritation. "I'm going to nail you for obstruction of—"

"Kristian! Forget that!" Gracie snaps, smacking his arm to gain his attention. "He has a video of the night my father died. We have proof. We have Mantis!"

Klein's threats die on his lips as they curl into that arrogant smile. But behind it, I see satisfaction. And relief.

"Well, what are you waiting for? Let's see it."

Silas hits the power button on the television to shut off the latest news, throwing the kitchen into silence. "That's enough about that." He pushes his half-eaten breakfast of eggs and bacon away and rubs his weary face. These past couple of weeks have aged him five years. He looks like he hasn't slept in days, and he probably hasn't, not with the media frenzy that's taken over after the FBI arrested Mantis and Stapley, with charges for everything from murder, to conspiracy to commit murder, to a dozen other crimes.

Abe's story has grabbed statewide attention. We've had to sequester ourselves inside the house to avoid persistent reporters camped outside, hoping to talk to Chief Jackie Marshall's son.

Wait until they discover that Abraham Wilkes's daughter is with me.

"Well, if there's one good thing that's come from all of this, it's that your mother isn't anywhere on that video," Silas mutters.

"But we still don't know why she had that bag of money and Abe's holster." I thought I'd feel more relief once Mantis and Stapley were caught. But this disquiet persists.

"Have the FBI told you anything?"

"Nothing." Klein's shut us out completely and, from the sounds of it, the FBI is no longer collaborating with the APD. If they ever really were to begin with.

"Well, maybe Mantis or Stapley can fill in some gaps."

Gracie tosses a treat to Cyclops. "I wouldn't trust any explanation those two give."

Silas drums the table with his fingers. "What about the search for Gracie's aunt?"

"They had a lead the other day, but it turned out to be false." It was painful, watching the hope bloom on Gracie's face, only to have it crumble.

Silas pats my hand and then, with a heavy sigh, stands. "I best be getting into the office. You need to stay away from there for the time being. It's a zoo. We're getting grilled from every direction. We'll talk about your return to work once this all settles."

"Yes, sir." I couldn't imagine going back to work right now; my head is still swimming with unanswered questions.

With a nod toward Gracie, Silas limps down the hall and out the front door.

"What if they get off?" She turns green eyes toward me and I see the fear in them. "What if they find some loophole, or mistake, or some way to make that video inadmissible?"

I settle a hand on the back of Gracie's neck. It's taut with tension, just like mine.

"You can't think like that."

"That's all I've been able to think," she admits.

I believe it. Her thoughts have been fourteen years away these past two days. I've woken up to catch her curled up in a ball with her phone in her hand, playing and replaying those few brief moments over and over again, of Abe strolling up to the door of Room 116 and pounding on it.

She took the video in Isaac's room, when we were replaying the original with Klein. That clip was all she was able to get before Klein caught her and demanded she stop. But he didn't make her erase it. He knew why she wanted those few seconds. Why she needed it.

Both of us have been struggling with our private worries and, while Gracie has much to be relieved about, nothing is for certain.

"So?" I try to rub those worries away with my fingers. "What do you want to do today? The pool's finally clean. We could—"

"—track down my dad's old partner. That Dunn guy."

I wasn't expecting that, but I see thoughts forming in Gracie's gaze.

"If my dad saw Betsy, I'm thinking it was while he was on shift. I mean, she was a prostitute. How *else* would he run into her?"

"You're probably right." And finding Betsy might shed light on why my mom and Abe were fighting before he died.

She pauses and then, with a slight smirk, says, "Of course I'm right."

I grin. There's the girl I know. "But what about the reporters outside?"

"Run them over."

I roll my eyes.

"Come on . . ." She leans forward to slide her hand along my thigh. "It'll be fun. Didn't you say you had to go to the police station anyway?"

"Yeah. For my mom's things. I wouldn't call that fun."

"No . . . but coming back here after will be." Her fingers crawl along the edge of my belt.

I haven't seen this playful, flirty side of Gracie in two days. Blood flows straight to my groin. "You're trying to manipulate me."

"Is it working?"

"Grab your purse. And your sunglasses." I take in that wild mane of hair. "And something to tame *that*."

She fires off an obscene gesture, but it's coupled with a grin.

CHAPTER 55

Grace

"*That's* your mother's secretary?" I murmur as we approach the desk and the raven-haired beauty behind it.

"Her name's Ashley Sheridan. And fair warning, she likes to flirt with me, but she's harmless."

"Everyone seems to like flirting with you, don't they?"

He flashes his boyish grin, awareness in those blue eyes. Like he knows that watching other women fawn over him slides under my skin in a teeth-gritting way. "Be nice," he scolds teasingly before we're within earshot.

"Give me a sec, darlin'," Ashley Sheridan croons in a heavy Mississippi lilt, lifting a finger to signal for us to wait while she finishes up a phone call.

"Sure thing, ma'am." He shows her that thousand-watt smile, and I have to turn away to hide my eye roll.

The moment she hangs up the phone, Miss Ashley Sheridan is on her feet, stretching her arms—toned from hours of lifting weights—around his neck. "Noah! So glad to see you!" she exclaims, the corners of her eyes crinkling with her smile. Though, behind that exterior façade, I see the same sympathy for him that I've seen in every familiar face Noah passed on the way here. "I was just fixin' to grab a bite down the street." Her purse dangles from her shoulder, emphasizing the fact that she was literally about to leave.

"I'm sorry for taking so long, ma'am—"

"Now what did I tell you about callin' me 'ma'am'! I know it's the

Southern way, but gosh, I never did like it. Makes me feel so *old.*" She slides her hands up and down Noah's arms in what some might call innocent affection. But the way they slow over his muscular biceps, her clawed fingertips clinging just a touch, *harmless* isn't a word I'd use to describe this woman.

I bite my tongue before I remind her that she's old enough to be Noah's mother.

"No, ma'am. I mean, Miss Sheridan. I'm sorry; we've been busy."

"Yes, we've all heard." She tsks. "This business with Dwayne Mantis! Can you believe it? It's been a mad house here with reporters and the like."

Noah gestures to me. "This is Gracie Richards, by the way."

"Wilkes." I hold my hand out.

She takes it, her hazel eyes flashing with a fresh wave of sympathy. "Well now, you poor thing. My condolences. I hope you and your mama can finally find some peace."

"So do I." Not only does everyone know about my father's case; thanks to the media, they also know about the aftereffects. I called Desert Oaks and warned them that reporters might come fishing for information. So far, though, the super-sleuths haven't tracked her down there.

Ashley turns back to Noah. "I've got Jackie's things ready to go, right here." She hauls out a document box from beneath her desk with a huff, her arms straining under the weight as she drops it onto the desk. "It's mainly the contents of her drawers, along with a few things she kept in her office safe that we deemed personal."

"I appreciate it."

"Uh-huh. You know I'll help you whenever I can, Noah. I respected your mother so much. It's such a shame."

"Have they announced your new boss yet?"

"Not yet, but I'm hearing it'll be Jim Towle, which would be fantastic. He should have been the automatic pick to begin with if you ask me, but then Canning had to start meddlin'. To think, we almost had a murderer for a chief!"

Noah frowns. "What do you mean?"

"Canning was pushin' for Mantis to be chief! And when you got George Canning's backing, you're basically a shoo-in, right?" She starts hunting through her purse.

"You're kidding."

"I'm not. Praise God that didn't come to pass." She leans forward, as if to share a secret. "Your mama'd be rolling in her grave if that man replaced her."

Noah pauses, and in his eyes I see that curious glimmer I've come to recognize. "How do you know? Did she say something to you about Mantis?"

"Oh, you sweet boy," she chuckles. "I managed her calendar, her emails. Heck, I made her doctor's appointments for womanly things. I know a lot. Except of course what she was thinkin' of doin' to herself." A flash of pain skitters across her eyes. "She couldn't stand that man. Used to call him a Neanderthal behind his back. Not long before she passed, she came right out and called him a lyin' criminal bastard to his face, then kicked him straight outta her office."

"Do you have any idea why?"

Ashley shakes her head. "*Probably* something to do with Canning wanting her to appoint Mantis assistant chief, and her telling Canning it'd be a cold day in hell before she did that."

"How did Canning take that?"

"As well as to be expected, which is not well at all. But your mama wasn't one to bite her tongue too hard. And she also couldn't stand Canning, so it only made things worse."

Noah looks like Ashley slapped him across the face. "She and Canning weren't friends?"

"They were friendly at the very start, sure. But not after Canning started trying to intervene in everything, tellin' her what she could and couldn't do. He acted like he had puppet strings attached to her. I swear that man will be tryin' to run this department from six feet underground!" She pulls out a lipstick from her purse. "Those two were like oil and water. Jackie stopped takin' his calls and that made him so dang mad. You know, he was in here, arguin' with her on the very day she died?"

Noah's face has gone from baffled to wary. "Do you know what about?"

"I don't know. Something about a girl. Jackie said she had big regrets and she was going to do right by that girl for once."

Noah's face pales. "Did she say the name Betsy?"

"I didn't catch names, I'm sorry. Anyway, I don't want to rush you out, but I've got plans and I need to go powder my nose."

"Wait! Could you find someone for us?" I blurt out, nudging Noah in the thigh.

"Yeah, actually, there's one other *really* quick favor I have to ask of you, if you would be so kind." Noah winces an apology and, dammit, he looks even more attractive. "I'm looking to track down an Officer Heath Dunn."

"What division?"

"He would have been working in street patrol fourteen years ago. He was Abraham's partner."

"Fourteen years ago, huh?" She gives Noah a look—one that says she's doing him a huge favor and he'd better remember it—before picking up the receiver, her perfect, long nails clacking against the buttons as she calls someone. Two minutes later, Ashley "don't call me ma'am because it makes me feel old in front of your strapping young self" Sheridan has our answer.

"Heath Dunn retired ten years ago. Best place to find him is Dunn's, down on—"

"Red River, yeah. I know it. Great barbecue."

"Isn't it, though? I've been down there a few times. Go figure—I didn't realize one of ours owns it. Anyway, that's the best place for y'all to find him."

"You're a lifesaver, Miss Sheridan."

With a gentle pat against her desk, Noah steers me toward the exit, his free hand settling against the small of my back while his other arm hugs the hefty box.

"What are you thinking?" I murmur, noting the way Noah's lips press into a firm line.

"Well, for one thing, George Canning was on a plane to Italy the night my mother died. Seems weird that he'd come to her office and have a fight with her the day he's flying across the world, but to each their own." He glances over his shoulder. "But, when I had dinner at my uncle's that night, Canning made it sound like my mom and him were good friends right up until the end."

"We already know he's a lying bastard."

"Right. Well, I think they might have been fighting about Betsy." Noah speeds up two steps to grab the door handle, holding it open for me. "Which means Canning knew about her."

"Your mom said she was going to do right by her. What does that mean?"

The worry on Noah's face tells me he's wondering the same thing.

CHAPTER 56

Noah

Gracie pokes the sausage with her fork, her brow furrowed deeply.

"What's the matter?"

"Aside from the heart attack I'm gonna have later?"

"Coming from the girl who would live off bacon."

"There are *three* different types of meat on my plate and it's not even noon."

I gesture at the tiny white ramekins. "And green beans. And potato salad."

"Honestly, how much meat do you Texans eat in one sitting?"

I grin. "Careful. You're a Texan, too."

She rolls her eyes, but I can see the smile in them. She's poking fun for the sake of poking fun. "And what is this *thing* they brought my food on?" She gestures at the silver tray.

"What's wrong with that? It gives you more eating room."

"So do troughs." She glances around us, at the rows of worn wood tables laid out with easy-wipe red-and-white-checkered tablecloths. "It's quiet in here."

"It's early for lunch." And empty, save for one other couple in the far corner. But it'll fill up fast. Dunn's BBQ is casual and comfortable, and like most other barbecue places I've been to—wooden walls, and plenty of napkin dispensers and condiment trays.

"So is this what people do in Texas? Sidle up to a tray and eat enough animal flesh to give them the meat sweats?"

I burst out laughing. "Shut up and eat." Stabbing my fork into a hunk of brisket from her plate, I hold it up to her mouth, half expecting her to swat my hand away. With teasing eyes locked on mine, she opens just enough to scrape her teeth along the metal tines as she bites it off.

She chews slowly.

"Well?"

I get an indifferent shrug in response—because she'll never admit that she was wrong—and then she wastes no time stabbing her own fork into another hunk, readying it. "So, is this like one of those big dreams for a Texan? Owning a barbecue joint? Are you going to tell me that you want to own one someday?"

"It is for Heath Dunn." It probably beats patrolling the streets of Austin.

"Do you think we'll see him today?"

"I hope so. At least we'll know who to look for." There's a bulletin board on the wall by the door, first thing customers see as they step in. It's a place to advertise events at Dunn's—bands, charity fundraisers, sports teams that Dunn's sponsors. Heath Dunn—a tall graying man—is prominently photographed in several of the notices.

I watch the busy street and the restaurant for signs of him while Gracie works her way through the range of sausage, brisket, and ribs on her platter, not saying a word in between mouthfuls. Barely taking a breath.

I can't help it anymore. "You gonna at least try a vegetable?"

"Shut up."

I grin. "Not so bad after all, huh?"

The corner of her mouth quirks as she reaches for her phone. "I just remembered, I promised my mom I'd call today."

"Go on, then," I say, watching her quietly. Despite the hell Dina put Gracie through, I think they'll be able to mend those fences just fine. I'm glad for that, because there's no way I'm letting either of them disappear from my life ever again. They're family, even if Gracie kicks me to the curb one day.

Gracie's scrolling through her contact list when I spot a tall man strolling down the sidewalk toward the front door, a newspaper tucked under his arm and a broad cowboy hat covering his balding head.

"Hold up a second on that call."

She follows my line of sight, and we watch as Heath Dunn greets the hostess with a smile and a tip of his hat.

"That's definitely him." For all the hipsters and trendy side of Austin, Dunn could blend in at any Texas rodeo, right down to his starched Wrangler jeans, the silver buckle on his belt, and his round-tipped cowboy boots.

Dunn and the hostess make small talk for a few moments before a guy—the manager, I'm guessing—interrupts them, holding up a clipboard.

"I need five minutes. Just give me five minutes, 'kay?" Dunn waves him off and begins marching through the restaurant, toward us, his focus intent on a hallway at the other end.

I wipe my hands on my napkin and stand. "Mr. Dunn?"

He slows, his gray eyes instantly sizing me up, the same way my mom would size up approaching strangers.

"Hi, sir. I'm Noah Marshall, Chief Jackie Marshall's son." I hold out a hand.

Recognition washes over his face as he accepts it. "Yes, sir. My condolences—such a shame. How are y'all doin' today?"

"Pretty good."

"You and your girlfriend here enjoy whatever you want, on the house. Now, if you'll excuse me—"

"Actually, I was hoping we could get a few minutes of your time?"

He's already pulling away, stepping toward the door. "Sorry, son. I'm up to my eyeballs with paperwork and the like. Maybe you can come in another day and—"

"It's about my father, Abraham Wilkes." Somehow, even with Dunn towering over her small seated frame, Gracie manages to level him with a gaze that stops him in his tracks.

He struggles to maintain a neutral expression. With the faintest sigh, and then a lightning-quick glance around him, Dunn settles into the spare seat beside her. "You're Gracie?"

It's her turn to look surprised. "You remember my name?"

Dunn chuckles softly. "You don't spend day in and day out in a car with a man who won't stop talking about his daughter and *not* remember her name." He pauses and glances over at me. "You, too. He went on about the both of you."

"How long were you partners for?" Gracie asks.

"Three years." He frowns. "How'd y'all find me, anyway?"

"*Dunn*'s BBQ? Voted best barbecue in Austin last year?" I smile. "You're not exactly hard to track down."

He grins. "I guess not."

"Gracie's barely taken a breath, she's so busy gobbling up your food." I ignore her eye roll.

"Listen . . ." He heaves a sigh. "I'm sorry that I ever gave my statement. I can't help but feel it helped with making Abraham look guilty. I still don't know what all those phone calls were that he kept getting, but I should have known it wasn't anything wrong. It was Abe, after all."

"We think the phone calls had to do with this girl." I pull out my phone. "Do you by chance remember seeing her?" I show him the shot I took of Betsy's picture.

His murky gray eyes sit on Betsy's face for far too long to be mistaken for simple consideration. He's carefully weighing what to say. "Who is she?"

"Her name is Betsy. She's my mother's little sister," Gracie says, watching him closely. She's picked up on his hesitation too. "She was a runaway, and we think she got pulled into prostitution by a trafficking ring. My father must have seen her in Austin, because he was looking for her in the weeks before he died. We think that's why he went to the Lucky Nine motel the night he was killed."

"Jesus Christ . . ." Dunn's gaze drifts past me, out the window, his jaw tightening.

"You remember her, don't you? You saw her? When? What happened?"

"Gracie." I give her a warning look. She's going on the offensive, and with that posture, getting people to talk—especially cops—might not get us far.

"Maybe it's best we leave this alone."

She looks at him in disbelief. And then she erupts. "Fine!" Gracie pushes her tray forward, as if done with her meal. "We'll tell the FBI to come and talk to you. Maybe here, in front of all your customers. Maybe I'll call the newspapers, too," she throws in almost as an afterthought. "Let's help you get the kind of PR your 'Best Barbecue in Austin' restaurant deserves."

"You don't wanna be doin' that," Dunn warns, his jaw clenched.

"Then you'd better start talking."

He glances around us—again. His face is a grim mask as he gestures for Gracie to sit back down. "Dispatch sent us out to a hotel one night; I can't remember the name of it. Decent enough place. They'd gotten an anonymous call about prostitution, possibly with a minor. So we went." He hesitates. "The man at the door said he was on a date and brought out the girl's ID. Your father insisted that the girl come to the door to make sure the ID matched. When she finally did, Abe lost it. He was ready to arrest the guy and haul her out of there."

I exchange a surprised glance with Gracie. "So Abe definitely recognized her?"

"He seemed to."

"And it was this girl?"

"I believe it was."

"And then what?" Gracie pushes.

Dunn takes a deep breath, his eyes flickering to me. "And then Jackie Marshall showed up and dismissed us. Said she'd handle it from there. My guess is the man called her as soon as we knocked on the door. It took him a good while to come to the door in the first place, using the shower as an excuse to stall having to answer. And then he kept checkin' the hall, as if waitin' for someone. Anyway,

Wilkes wasn't happy. But your mom, she tore my notes right out of my book and sent me to the car. Wilkes came out five minutes later, hoppin' mad. He radioed in that all was clear, and then we left for a robbery call."

My stomach drops in that way it does when you realize you've gotten caught for screwing up. Only *I* didn't screw up. But it sounds like my mom did. "You guys left a fifteen-year-old human trafficking victim there?"

"No. We followed a superior officer's orders. If that girl got left there, it's on Jackie Marshall," he says carefully, but I see the guilt in his eyes.

Gracie's brow furrows. I'm sure she's filling in the blanks with what we learned from Dina already, and Dunn's account of that night fits well with everything, except the one thing we both know of Abe—that he wouldn't leave Betsy in a hotel room, not even because of an order from a superior officer.

My mother must have found some way to compel Abe to leave.

But the bigger question is, why the hell would my mother interfere like that in the first place?

Holy shit. "She was protecting the guy in the room."

"That would be my guess. But you'd have to ask her." His words dig exactly where he means them to—deep into my chest.

"Who was he?" Gracie pushes.

Dunn wipes away at some salt on the table with his hand, his eyes downcast. "He never produced his identification. He made up some lousy story about it being lost."

Gracie's jaw tightens with frustration. "What did he look like?"

"White guy. That's all I remember." He pauses for a moment. "Red hair, I think. Sorry, that's all I know." Dunn eases out of the chair. "Y'all enjoy your meal."

Gracie's eyes narrow. "Was he a cop?"

Dunn's shoulders tense. Whatever cooperation he was showing us has gone out the window. "You listen here, miss . . ." He leans in, his hand gripping the back of Gracie's wooden chair, his anger poorly veiled, though he manages to keep his voice low. "I'm tired of hearin' the kinds of accusations thrown around about the APD. I hear 'em *all day long*. Lazy cop this, dirty cop that. There are a lot of mighty fine police officers in this city who risk their lives day in, day out so y'all can stroll down the streets in peace. Just because Dwayne Mantis was a rotten apple in the bushel basket doesn't give people the right to turn our integrity into the punch line of a joke."

Our server shows up then, oblivious to the choking tension around us. "Can I get y'all a refill on your sweet teas?"

Dunn stands abruptly and, with a deep inhale, manages to slough his anger away. "Jillian, you make sure these two get whatever they want on the house. Their parents were both fine officers." With that, Dunn marches for his office.

"What the hell, Noah!" Gracie hisses the second our server is gone.

I pick at a piece of sausage, a lump swelling in my throat. I have no answer for her.

How could my mother do that to Abe? To Dina? To Gracie? To fifteen-year-old Betsy? They were family and she chose a *friend*—some 'white guy, red hair' friend—over them.

All I can do is shake my head as I pick through my memories, trying to place this person. The only white guy with red hair I know is Jenson, and he was eleven at the time. "I guess now we know what our parents were fighting over," I mutter.

"You realize what this means, don't you?" Gracie's words escape her slowly, her mind still trying to make sense of this. "My dad was out searching for Betsy when he witnessed that bust at The Lucky Nine, and because he witnessed that bust, he got himself into that mess with Mantis. And because of that, he died."

And the reason he was out looking for Betsy in the first place is because my mother made him leave her in that hotel room.

"What I let happen . . . I may as well have pulled the trigger."

Now I know what she meant.

Basically, Abe died because of what my mother did that night.

And the only way she could see to "do right" by it all was to put a gun to her temple.

"What do you say we order in pizza?" I holler, knowing my voice will carry through the open window to the backyard.

"You're kidding me, right?"

"I'm not, actually . . ." I mutter, standing in front of the open fridge, patting my grumbling stomach while I eye the still-full shelves. Nothing looks appetizing.

With a sigh, I find an apple, along with a strip of beef jerky, and I wander through the French doors. Gracie propels herself through the water with ease, her normally wild hair soaked and stretching halfway down her back.

Cyclops comes trotting up to me, eyeing the beef. "Go find a squirrel or something." I take a bite off the end, ignoring him and watching Gracie swim to the edge of the pool, to rest lean arms on the side.

"You know that's his, right?"

"I wouldn't necessarily call it 'his.' "

A whimper sounds and I look down to see him licking his lips. "Begging doesn't suit you." It actually does, with that one eye. He looks downright pathetic.

"I bring those home from work for him once a week. He loves them."

"Well, I love them, too—ow!" I yelp, as Cyclops snatches the strip right out from my lowered hand. He scampers away with it between his jaws. "You little . . ."

Gracie's deep bellow of laughter carries through the warm spring air, erasing my annoyance instantly. How long has it been since anyone's laughed like *that* back here? At least fourteen years.

The beautiful sound dies slowly on her lips. "Why are you looking at me like that?"

"Because you laugh just like your dad did."

Her jaw hardens slightly. "Sometimes it makes me angry, that you remember so much about him and I can't even picture his face."

I make my way toward the edge of the pool. "I'll tell you everything I remember."

After a moment, she nods. Her gaze drifts over my T-shirt and shorts. "Not swimming?"

"Nah, don't feel like it."

"The water's warm," she taunts.

"Liar. Your lips are blue." We've been in a cold spell these past few days. I turned the pool heater up, but it'll take hours to get to a comfortable temperature.

"Huh."

Here we go. " 'Huh' . . . what?"

She shrugs. "Nothing. Just didn't take you for a giant baby." She casts off from the side using her legs. "I think I saw a blanket in the living room. You should go and swaddle yourself before—" She squeals as I charge toward her, diving into the cool water fully dressed, the shock of the temperature oddly refreshing on my muscles.

A curse slides from my lips as I surface, gooseflesh instantly covering my arms.

"Give it a minute," she warns, adding on a quiet, "wuss."

Coasting over to the shallow end, I quickly peel off my T-shirt and toss it off to the side before diving back under.

Gracie stretches out and floats on her back along the surface of the water, her gaze drifting somewhere unseen above us, into the sky.

It gives me ample opportunity to admire her flat stomach and the swell of her breasts and her hips while I quietly tread water, trying to warm up. The girl has curves like I've never seen, so full and solid, they're almost cartoonish.

She clears her throat and I realize she's caught me checking her out.

"Do you think if my dad hadn't died and your mom hadn't . . . *you know* . . . we would've been friends?"

"As opposed to what we are now?"

She sighs with exasperation. "You know what I mean."

Do I? Exactly what *are* we now? "I'd probably be like an older brother to you," I finally say.

Horror flashes across Gracie's face and it makes me laugh. But it also makes my heart race.

I dive in to glide beneath her, my back pushing against hers, making her lose her balance and fold into the water.

When she surfaces, she's sputtering water. "You're definitely . . . annoying enough . . . to be my brother!" She splashes me in the face.

I slide my hand around her waist and guide her to the edge of the pool. "Sorry, I didn't think you'd go right under." I wait, studying her intoxicating face until she quiets down, reveling in the feel of her silky skin beneath my fingers. It sends my adrenaline pumping through my veins.

She turns her green gaze onto me, and I brace myself for a tongue-lashing. I'm caught off guard when she leans in and presses her lips against mine in a quick, firm kiss. "You know that I don't blame you for any of this, right?"

Her words bring my mind swerving back to the thoughts I'm desperately trying to avoid.

What happened that night, with Abe and my mother squaring off in front of a hotel room that held Betsy and some white guy with red hair?

Tension courses through my body. "Every time I think about it . . ." We told Silas and Klein what Dunn revealed. Klein was indifferent to it. His focus is all on Abraham's murder, not delivering a bittersweet family reunion. Meanwhile, Silas's face paled two shades, and he cursed under his breath three times before rifling through the liquor cabinet to pour himself a bourbon from a bottle my mom kept just for him.

He's been taking a lot of heat over Abe's case, being the ADA during that time. I can only imagine what it'll be like if what my mom did—knowingly leaving a fifteen-year-old trafficking victim in a hotel room with a john—gets out to the media.

Who was my mom protecting? Who did she throw her friendship with Abe away for?

I've spent two days going through every photo album of my mother's, looking for every red-haired white guy. I even called up Ashley Sheridan and made her list every red-haired guy on the force that my mom might have known. The list is short, and not promising.

I've come to the conclusion that Dunn is either mistaken . . . or he's lying.

And if that's the case, why?

Gracie squirms within my grasp, turning around to face me. She wraps her legs around my hips and her arms around my neck and whispers, "Don't think about it. At least for now. Think about me instead. About this . . ." She leans in, covering my mouth with hers in a slow, teasing kiss.

My hands instinctively slide down to grip her hips, my fingers playfully tugging on the strings of her bikini bottoms. The backyard is private enough. Besides, I heard the neighbor's car pull away not long ago. We don't even have to go inside—

Cyclops goes tearing past us, his barks wild as he charges for the gate to the front yard.

Klein's face appears. He frowns at the dog from the safety of the other side. "You want to call Cujo off?"

"Not really," I growl, adjusting myself as Gracie pulls away. She climbs out using the pool steps and heads for the towel draped over a chair, giving both me and Kristian ample time to check out her body.

And that asshole isn't even bothering to hide the fact that he's getting a good look.

Gracie whistles and Cyclops trots over immediately, keeping his wary eye on our guest as Klein lets himself through the gate. He looks more official today, in a button-down shirt and black chinos.

"You couldn't call?"

"Where's the fun in that?" Klein smirks. He knows exactly what was about to happen. But the amusement slides off his face abruptly. "You two need to get dressed and come with me. We'll take my car."

Unease sets in. "Why?"

"Because we've found Betsy."

CHAPTER 57

Grace

"Hold on a sec," Noah says, staying Kristian and Agent Tareen's hands on their door handles. We sit quietly in the backseat of the dark FBI sedan and watch the woman in the front garden, inspecting a flowering bush. Her wide-brimmed hat hides her face, but the fitted shorts and T-shirt show off a young, fit body. "Is she the gardener? Or nanny?"

Klein smirks. "No, she lives here with her husband."

"And you are one hundred percent positive this is her?"

"More like ninety-five. But we can close that gap quickly by going up there and asking her."

Noah shakes his head, unconvinced. He's had that same skeptical look since we turned into this neighborhood of sprawling houses and huge properties and manicured lawns, one of the wealthiest in Austin according to him. "Gracie? What do you think?"

I think that my mom's necklace is going to cut into the palm of my hand if I don't stop squeezing it so tight. "There's only one way to be sure." Wouldn't it be something—a sexually abused girl from a trailer park who was picked up by a human trafficking ring, now living in this mansion where she quietly plucks weeds? Seemingly at peace.

Noah sighs. "If you guys are wrong, this is going to be a really fucking awkward conversation, isn't it?"

"Maybe we don't lead with 'were you a prostitute'?"

My heart is racing as I step out of the car to follow the two FBI agents up the interlocked path, Noah at my side.

"Mrs. Mandy Wheeler?" Kristian calls out.

Mandy Wheeler?

The woman turns, her platinum-blonde bob peeking out from beneath the rim of her hat. "We don't accept door-to-door solicitation," she responds in a crisp tone. Cool green eyes drift over us, stalling on me for a moment. They're even lighter than mine.

And they definitely look familiar.

"We're not here to sell anything, ma'am." Kristian pulls out his FBI badge.

Wariness creeps into her features. She glances around to the neighbors on both sides. "What is this in regards to, then?"

"Are you Elizabeth Richards, originally from Tucson, Arizona?"

"No." Her face pales a few shades.

She's lying.

"Your mom's name was Peggy Richards," I hear myself say in a shaky voice. "Your father was Brian. You had an older sister named Dina, and she married Abraham Wilkes. They had a daughter together, named Grace. That's me. I'm Grace."

"How did you . . ." Her whispered words drift as her wide and teary eyes flitter between us.

Kristian opens the file folder tucked under his arm and holds up a mug shot of a woman with long, scraggly blonde hair in an orange jumpsuit. "You assumed the name of Mandy Hawkins. You served ninety days in Beaumont for prostitution charges in 2007 after—"

"Okay." She stops him with a raised hand, her face pinched.

I hold my breath, afraid she's going to tell us to go away, to never come back. That she doesn't care about me or my mom, or what happened to my dad. "I was wondering if this day would ever come." She doesn't look at all happy about the fact that it has.

I have so many questions. About what happened to her; about

what she knows of my father, and what happened to him. But right now, one seems to outweigh all the rest.

"Why didn't you come home?"

"It's been forever since I've heard that name, 'Betsy.'" She sets glasses of water on the island countertop in front of us.

All I can do is stare at her.

I can't believe we've found my mom's sister. My aunt. The girl who ran away from home, who my dad tried so hard to find.

Who my dad *died* trying to find.

She definitely has the Richards eyes. She has the same face shape, same jaw as my mother, too—wide and angular. The rest of her features are daintier than my mom's, though.

I see my nan in her, too. In her looks as well as in her mannerisms. The way she'll stare intensely at you for a few seconds and then glance away, as if she can't bear the connection for one more second.

She doesn't smile much, just like Nan didn't smile much. Or, at least, her smiles are tight and reserved, and she lets out a small huff right before she lets you see them. Also like Nan.

And she's been wiping that same spot on the counter with a cloth for several minutes now, just like Nan used to do.

She clears her voice. "I saw the news. How's Dina?"

"In rehab. We're hoping it'll stick this time."

She nods. "Was there something you needed from me? Or . . ."

I open my mouth to explain, but I don't know where to start. And both Kristian and Agent Tareen have been uncharacteristically quiet so far.

"It's a bit of a story, ma'am," Noah says, reaching over to place his hand on my knee. An offer of reassurance. He's not used to seeing me so flustered.

"I have a bit of time." She pauses to take a long sip of her drink, her hand trembling slightly. "Who are you, exactly?"

"Noah Marshall, ma'am. My mother was Chief Jackie Marshall."

That earns a flash of surprise in Betsy's eyes, followed by softness. "I'm sorry about what happened to her."

Noah simply nods.

Betsy's gaze turns to Kristian, hardening a touch. He *is* the one who produced her mug-shot photo, after all, and it's clear she'd rather keep that part of her past buried. "And you two are the FBI agents investigating Abraham's death, I take it?"

"Yes, ma'am. And we have some questions for you." Kristian flashes an easy smile.

After a moment, Betsy—Mandy—nods. "Go ahead."

"In April of 2003, Wilkes and his partner went to an Austin area hotel on a prostitution call. Abraham recognized the girl in the room. Were you that girl?"

"Yes." A frown flickers over Betsy's face. "It'd been years since Abe saw me last. Still, I saw it in his eyes, the moment it clicked."

"Do you know the man you were with?"

She shakes her head. "My . . . handler drove me out to this quiet hotel. It was nicer than the ones I'd usually end up in. He gave me the room number, and I went in."

"Do you remember any names?"

"No, but it was probably John, or Don. Or Bill." She chuckles. "None of them give their real names."

Agent Tareen is jotting down notes on a pad of paper while Klein questions. "What do you remember about that night?"

"Enough," she says quietly. "We heard a knock on the door about twenty minutes after I got there. The man checked the peephole and then he panicked, and started the shower right away. He told me to get in the bathroom. So I did."

"And then he answered the door?"

She shakes her head. "No. The bathroom door was open a crack, and I heard him talking on the phone, telling someone that there were cops at the door, and to get them off his back right away. *Then* he answered the door."

Noah and I share a look. He must have called Jackie. "And you didn't hear him say any names on the phone?"

She shakes her head. "We'd done a line of coke ten minutes before. I was trying to keep it together, and I was scared I was going to get busted. I heard the cops saying that someone from the hotel reported suspected prostitution with an underage girl in the room. He denied it. One of the cops kept saying, 'Sorry to bother you, sir,' and 'It was definitely a mistake, sir,' but the other insisted to see my ID and for me to come to the door. That's when he told them I was in the bathroom and they'd have to wait a few minutes and allow me the privacy of closing the door so I could get dressed.

"He came and got me. Made me drink a lot of water, hoping that would clear my head. He reminded me what to say—that we were on a date and to deny anything else."

"Did it seem like he was stalling?"

"Yeah, definitely. He kept checking his watch. Finally the cops started pounding on the door, demanding he open it. He made me get my ID. He asked how old it said I was."

"How old were you?"

She swallows hard. "I'd just turned fifteen."

"And do you think he knew you were that young?"

She twists her lips. "The guys that like young girls . . . you can tell. Besides, whoever he was on the phone with, he told them I was underage."

The sleazy bastard knew alright.

"And his ID?"

"He hid it in the inside pocket of his messenger bag." She frowns. "But they weren't asking for his. It seemed like they already knew who he was."

I share a glance with Noah, to see he's realized the same thing—Dunn lied to us.

"He told me to hang back while he dealt with the cops. But the one cop insisted that if I didn't come to the door, they'd arrest us both. So I came. I didn't recognize Abe at first, but I was scared all the same. I didn't want to get in trouble with Damien. That was my . . . well, I guess you could say he owned me," she adds quietly.

"And then what happened?"

"Another cop showed up then—a woman—and told them she'd take over. The one cop took off fast, like he didn't want to be within a hundred miles of that doorstep. But Abe started to argue with her. My client made me go back inside while he talked to her and then she left, too. The guy threw cash on the table and told me to go. So, I met my driver by one of the side doors. Ricky. That was his name. He was waiting in the parking lot. He saw the cop cars coming in, and grilled me a bit about it after."

"And that was it?"

She shakes her head. "A cop tailed us out of the parking lot. It was the female cop. She followed us all the way to the motel I was staying at. Somehow Ricky didn't notice."

"Do you remember what she looked like?" Noah asks, too calmly.

"Pretty. Short blonde hair and these piercing blue eyes." Betsy stares at Noah for a long moment before averting her gaze. I can't tell if she's made the connection. "She came to the room we were staying in, and told Damien to get me out of town right away or we'd both end up in jail. And then she left."

Noah's hand tenses on my knee.

"Damien was furious. He thought I was working with the police, which didn't make much sense, but he was a paranoid guy. He beat me real bad that night, and then threw me into the back of his car and took me to Houston."

"Did you ever see Abraham Wilkes again?" Klein asks.

She shakes her head. "Give me a sec?" She disappears through a door on the other side of the kitchen, the glimpse of a heavy wooden desk telling me it's an office. A moment later, she returns and lays a business card down on the counter, the edges worn and torn, looking like it had been folded and crumpled a hundred times.

"Abe left me at that hotel that night and I convinced myself it was because he didn't care what happened to me, just like everyone else. But one day, months later, I crossed paths with a girl I knew and she handed that to me. She said the cop had been going around, showing people my picture and passing out his card. She didn't tell him that she knew me, but she held on to it in the chance she'd see me again. In that world, you never were sure if you'd see someone again." She smiles sadly. "I've held on to that card all these years, to remind myself that even in my darkest days, someone did care."

This is as good a time as any. I lay the charm necklace next to the card. "My mother never took this off."

Betsy's eyes gloss over as she paws at her neck, empty of jewelry. "Damien took my half. He didn't want anything that could identify me."

"People cared, Betsy."

She swallows hard. "I called the number on the card, but it was disconnected. I didn't know he had died until much later. I didn't know much of what was going on back then at all. They shuttled us from one city to another. Someone was always with us or nearby, watching. Making sure we did as we were told, reminding us what would happen if we didn't. They'd make us do lines of coke, and then bring us to hotel rooms to work. That's how I usually found out where I was—a flyer in a hotel room. All I knew back then was that if I did what Damien asked, I'd get my next fix and he wouldn't hurt me."

"Where's this Damien guy now?" I ask through gritted teeth. Because I want to kill him.

"He went to jail. He could still be there. Or maybe he's dead." She sounds hopeful about that.

"What else do you remember about that client?" Kristian asks, pulling the conversation back to that night.

She tops up our glasses with water, her eyes glued to the pitcher. "He was like all of them. Middle-aged. Married, with kids."

"What did he look like?"

"Forties . . . but a lot of gray hair. Fairly fit."

"Was his natural hair red-colored?"

She frowns, in thought. "No, I don't remember him being a redhead."

"Any idea what he did for a living?" Klein asks.

"We didn't talk much." Her cheeks flush.

"Right. Just . . . anything at all. Guys like to blow off steam, talk about things they shouldn't talk about with girls who only pretend to listen."

Betsy chews her cheek in thought. "No. I'm sorry. He was nice, if that helps. Some of them were . . . not nice." She runs the tap to rinse out her glass, only to fill it back up with water from the pitcher again. "How's my . . . how's Peggy?"

"Nan died about five years ago of a heart attack."

She presses her lips together and nods quietly.

I can't help but ask. "Why didn't you come back? We were still in Tucson. Still in The Hollow."

She buys herself time, finishing her drink. "Did your mom tell you about my dad?"

"I just found out. Nan kicked him out right after you ran away. Did you know that?"

She shakes her head. "Once I left, I never looked back. It's a hard thing, you know, to get the guts to go to your mom and tell her what your dad's been doing to you when she's out late at night. And when she tells you that you're making things up . . ." Her eyes begin to glisten. "I hated her so much for that. Hated them both. Couldn't wait to get away. And then I met Damien. He was older and attractive and doted on me. He bought me things and drove me everywhere, told me how beautiful I was and how much he loved me. He's the one who put the idea in my head to leave. I mean, I'd thought of it plenty, but I was barely fourteen. I had nowhere to go. So when he said he'd take care of me, it was an easy decision. I packed my backpack, wrote a letter, and left. Met him a few blocks away."

"My dad drove to Tucson, and came looking for you."

"I'm not surprised." Her bottom lip wobbles. "We headed to California for a bit, down near LA. It was exciting. No curfews, no rules, no school. Just partying in different people's houses every night. Damien started feeding me alcohol and drugs. A joint here, a pill there." She hesitates. "Then one day his friend came over and told me how pretty I was and that he wanted to sleep with me. Damien told him it was okay, that he could. He convinced me to do it, that he'd love me more for it. I was fourteen. I was stupid. And I just wanted to be loved."

"You're not alone. That's how most girls get pulled into this. These guys know who to target," Kristian says softly.

She smiles appreciatively at him. "And then it happened again with another friend, and then another, until I started to wonder if they were really his friends. Finally I told him that I didn't want to be with anyone but him. He got *so* angry. He hit me a few times. I was scared that he'd dump me. Can you believe that? That's what I was worried about." Betsy's face pinches, like admitting all this is painful. "I'm not sure when I actually figured out that Damien was selling me."

"Why didn't you run, then? You could have come back."

"To what? A father that . . ." She doesn't bother to finish.

"Still . . . all these years later. What happened to you?"

"When Damien was arrested, I had this brief glimpse of freedom." She laughs bitterly. "It lasted all of an hour, and then this other guy took over me and two other girls. His name was Naseer, and he taught me just how good Damien had actually treated me. He got me hooked on cheap smack and locked me in rooms for twelve hours, letting a parade of guys come through and use me. He'd beat me, too. I mean, Damien hit me, but not like Naseer did, not on a daily basis.

"He told me that he knew where I was from and that I was disgusting, that my family would never take me back. He convinced me that he'd find me and hurt me if I ever tried to go. I believed him. I was scared. So I kept turning tricks, until one day I got busted by an undercover cop down in San Antonio and thrown in jail. And it was the best thing that ever happened to me. I got away from Naseer, from the life, and got clean in the inmate drug rehab program."

"Does your husband know about all this?" Noah asks softly.

Her eyes drift to a framed wedding portrait on the wall and a small smile touches her lips. "He was my lawyer. His firm did pro bono work and I was assigned to him. He started checking in on me, while I was in jail, to make sure I was getting all the help I needed. And after I got out, he helped me get a job and a place to live. One thing led to another. I still can't believe that he would ever want to marry me."

The man in the portrait is at least ten years older than her, his hair sparse on top, his chin sporting sagging skin. Next to Betsy—beaming and beautiful in an elegant white lace gown, her golden-blonde hair cascading over her shoulders—anyone would say the opposite is true.

"No one but Gale knows about my past. We lied to his family and our friends about how we met. While he may be open-minded, others aren't, especially not in this neighborhood."

"So, this man . . . are you sure there isn't anything else you can remember about him?" Kristian pushes, once again giving her just enough time to prattle before gently reining her back in.

She shakes her head. "I'm sorry I can't be of more help." There's a pause. "But what does that night have to do with Abe's death?"

"We're not entirely sure yet." He sets his card out next to my father's. "If you think of anything else, please give me a call." His steely gray gaze shifts to me. "Ready?"

"I . . . uh . . ." Now that we've found my aunt, I don't want to leave. But I guess that's the appropriate thing to do. Betsy will need time to process all this. I can't blame her. She was picking weeds from her garden when we showed up, dragging with us a past that she hoped was dead and buried.

Betsy pulls a pad of paper from the fridge and scribbles down a phone number. "You know where I live. Here is my number." She presses the page into my hand. "Please call me. And tell your mom I said hello." She hesitates. "Maybe I could contact her, when she's better."

"She'd love that."

"And maybe you could come over again another day, if you're staying in Austin? It'd be nice . . . to have family of my own again." Betsy gives me one of those small, tight-lipped smiles.

"I will. I'm not going anywhere." I absently reach for Noah, my fingers grazing his bicep. He's definitely stuck with me now.

It isn't until we reach the massive two-story foyer that Betsy suddenly exclaims, "Wait! I do . . . yes, I do remember something." She frowns, as if she's trying to grasp a thought that's flittering just out of reach in her memories. "The man . . . he walked with a limp."

CHAPTER 58

Commander Jackie Marshall

May 4, 2003

I climb over the police tape and march forward into a circus show of flashing lights and people.

The last time I was at this seedy motel, it was to get Betsy out of Austin.

Now . . . I don't know what the hell is going on, but I got woken up by a call from dispatch to tell me that an officer's been shot and I needed to get out here.

Silas steps into my path.

That son of a bitch . . . I have nothing to say to him. I try to skirt him, but he grabs my arm. "Hold up, Jackie." His eyes flash around us, checking to see who's watching. "You can't go in there."

"The hell I can't!" I try to shake his arm off me, but he squeezes tighter.

"Canning's orders. Only a special team is allowed in there right now. They're making me wait outside too, and *I'm* the damn DA!"

"You are *not* the DA, yet," I grit through my teeth, adding quietly, "and you *never* will be if anyone finds out what you *really* are." It was all I could do to keep from vomiting, walking up to that hotel room two weeks ago to find Abe facing off with none other than my *brother*, in a hotel room with a *prostitute*.

My by-the-book, righteous, this-side-of-the-law big brother. And not just any prostitute. A fifteen-year-old.

A fifteen-year-old who also happened to be Dina's half-sister.

"God damn it, Jackie! I made a mistake! Don't you dare act like you've never made one!" He tugs me farther back, into the shadows, away from prying ears. "She said she was twenty-one! I didn't know how old she really was, and I sure as hell didn't know *who* she was."

"Oh come on! One look at that girl and I knew she had to be related to Dina."

"Well, yes. She was a striking girl, but—"

I make a sound of disgust. "The fact that you'd cheat on Judy with a hooker! It would kill that sweet woman if she ever found out."

Silas holds his hands up in surrender. "You're right. That's why Judy can never find out. My kids can never find out. It was a mistake. I made a terrible mistake."

"And just how many 'mistakes' have you made?" I glare at him, daring him to lie to me.

He hesitates. "Twice. And only once with someone under eighteen."

"How the hell would you know! You thought Betsy was twenty-one!"

"I'm never going to do it again, I swear, Jackie. It's been difficult at home lately, and with work . . . I just needed to get some—"

"Oh, I know what you needed to get," I spit out. "What *I* had to do that night . . . You cost me one of my very best friends, Silas! Worse, I had to chase that girl away so you could protect your precious job and reputation."

"Don't pretend you weren't helping yourself out, too." He has the nerve to look smug.

"You are right about that." I jab him in the chest with my finger. "Your 'mistake' could have cost me my future, something I've worked my tail off for. But to be honest? I was worried about what this would do to your family. To my son." That boy thinks the sun rises and sets by his uncle.

The only other man he might adore more is the one I just betrayed.

"I'm going to regret covering for you every damn day for as long as I live."

Silas flinches. "I didn't mean to—"

"I don't want to hear it. If I *ever* catch you with a girl again, I will *not* bail you out."

"I promise, I—"

"And don't fool yourself into believing you're outta the woods yet. The only reason Abe hasn't said a word is because he's protecting Dina, but if he finds Betsy, this will come out, eventually. And it will ruin *all* of us." I turn to leave.

Silas grabs hold of my arm again. "Abe won't be looking for Betsy anymore," he says softly.

CHAPTER 59

Noah

Klein eases the car into a parking spot. "Let's go."

I grit my teeth against the urge to tell him to go fuck himself, to take me home, to give me back my goddamn phone so I can call Silas and ask him why Klein showed Betsy a picture of Silas and Betsy said, yeah, that looks like the guy she was with that night in the hotel room.

Couple that with the limp, and the fact that my mother was protecting someone that night—someone who she'd put ahead of Abe—and I don't have to ask Silas anything, because deep down, I already know.

I just can't believe it.

And so I numbly climb out of the FBI sedan. Unable to meet Gracie's gaze, feeling as if I might heave my stomach's contents on the sidewalk.

I'm trapped in a never-ending nightmare that keeps getting worse.

"What is this place?" Gracie asks as we follow Kristian down a narrow path of what appears to be a condo complex, either side walled by six feet of brick and canopied by mature, leafy trees. Behind the walls are pint-sized backyards.

Tareen trails us through one of the small black gates and past a door, closing it behind him to seal us in.

"It's an agency rental," Klein finally explains. "Sometimes we use it as a safe house. Right now we're using it for our case."

"Against Mantis and Stapley?" Gracie's gaze takes in the honeyed wood and dove-gray walls. There isn't much in the way of furnishings—a black leather couch, a flat-screen TV, built-in shelves peppered with books, a teapot on the stove in a masculine-looking kitchen of dark wood and stainless-steel appliances. One abstract painting on the wall directly ahead of me.

I feel Klein's eyes boring into me. "No. Our case against Silas Reid."

The air leaves my lungs.

"We've been investigating him for five months," Tareen offers, ducking past us and disappearing into a room.

It dawns on me. "You were after someone else," I mumble. "That's what my mother said in that message. 'Since you're so hell-bent on arresting someone' . . . or something like that."

Klein heads to the fridge, stocked with soda cans and water bottles. He holds up a Coke in offer and when Gracie nods, tosses it to her. Gesturing to the couch, he takes a seat in the chair across from it. The sound of his soda can cracking open carries through the quiet condo, as we wait for an explanation.

"Last November, we were contacted by Amy Bivens."

I frown. "My uncle's secretary?"

"Ex-secretary. He'd fired her earlier that week. Anyway, she claimed that she overheard an alarming private phone conversation that made her think Silas Reid was looking for a prostitute for himself. An underage one."

"He wouldn't be dumb enough to do that over the phone," I counter.

Gracie's face twists with disgust. I can't tell if it's at my uncle. Or at me, for defending him.

Klein goes on, ignoring my protest. "Bivens didn't go to the APD for *obvious* reasons. We thought it might be a case of a disgruntled employee, but she had the date and the name of a hotel in Houston where he was to meet her. So, we decided to look into it." He pauses for what feels like forever. "Security footage caught a girl coming to his hotel room."

I squeeze my eyes shut. *This can't be real. This can't be real . . .*

"She was dressed to not raise suspicion, in jeans and a T-shirt. But she stayed for an hour, before being picked up out front by a car with fake plates. We couldn't get a good look at her face. This girl was a dead end, but we knew we had a case. So we started listening in on his personal and home phones."

Gracie makes a sound. "You like listening in on conversations," she murmurs, as if echoing something Klein may have said. They share a knowing smile. A private exchange between them that I don't understand, and I don't like.

Klein rests his elbows on his knees. "After six weeks of nothing, I decided to do a bit of fishing. So I went to Jackie Marshall."

Tareen reemerges, bringing a laptop with him.

"I'd had a few run-ins with her in the past and we got along well enough. Figured I'd see if she knew her brother had a thing for underage prostitutes."

"That couldn't have gone well," Gracie mutters under her breath.

"It got me kicked out of her office." Klein chuckles, but the humor doesn't reach his eyes. "But it also ended up being a break for us, because that night Jackie phoned her brother and asked him why the hell the feds were coming to her about him and his proclivities." He waggles his eyebrows. "Jackie knew. Or at least, she knew it had happened before. She was pissed. She asked him if he'd had any intention of keeping his promise, after Betsy."

Gracie's eyes widen. "She named Betsy? *You* already knew about Betsy?" Her voice drips with accusation.

"We knew of a girl named Betsy. We had no idea who she was."

"Wait, when was this?" I interrupt.

"January, by this point."

I do the quick math. That was around the time my mother started drinking heavily again.

"He promised me he didn't know her age. He promised he'd never do it again."

"Jesus Christ." Her rambles were a mess of truths; the "he" wasn't just one person. It was Mantis, and Canning. And Silas. "He" told her he thought she was of age and she believed him. "She thought it was an honest mistake with Betsy." Silas being with a prostitute would be shameful, but my mom was the type of woman to forgive a male for satisfying that need.

But if that need involved a fifteen-year-old girl?

Her actions that night let Silas go free of his crime. But he lied to her and did it again, because she protected him.

That would have eaten her up.

"That's not all we got that night. Silas made references to an APD internal investigation on Mantis and his guys that 'needed to go away.' It was clear this was coming from someone else, through Silas to Jackie, but no names were mentioned."

"Canning," Gracie says.

"That'd be my first guess. That's when we broadened our investigation to include your mother."

Fuck. "Did she know about it?"

"Eventually . . . when we caught a heated phone exchange between her and Canning about how she found Abraham Wilkes's gun holster buried in a ziplock bag in her garden. She accused Dwayne Mantis of putting it there; some sort of scare tactic to make sure she'd clear him of any wrongdoing in the current investigation."

I glare at Klein, only to get a weak, "sorry, I couldn't tell you sooner" shrug.

"She flat-out told Canning that Mantis was guilty and she was going to make sure he was punished. And then two days later, she cleared him."

My stomach turns. *God, Mom, what did you get yourself involved in?*

"That's when I went back in and started putting pressure on her." Klein shakes his head. "I worked on her for weeks. I knew I could open a case on Mantis and probably dig up enough to bust him, with or without her help, but I wanted Reid. And I needed her for that." He nods toward Tareen, who hits a key on the laptop.

My mother's drunken voice fills the room. It's that same voice message that Klein played for me, that night in Tucson. I close my eyes, the wave of anguish that floods me not quite as shocking as it was the first time around. But painful, nonetheless.

" *. . . I don't know exactly how Mantis did it, but I know he killed Abe. Look into him. Look into how Dwayne Mantis murdered a good man. You do that and I'll give you my brother on a silver platter. I'll at least do that much for Betsy.*"

My eyes fly open.

"I didn't play you the entire message before," Klein admits without a hint of regret. "I couldn't jeopardize the case. We needed you talking to your uncle, feeding him information about Dina and Gracie, and what they knew."

With a flick of his wrist, Tareen plays another clip.

"*Money.*"

"*Yes. Money.*"

"*How much are we talking about here?*"

"*Enough to raise eyebrows.*"

I feel my face burn as my recorded voice fills the room, in that same way it does when you've done something wrong and you've gotten caught. "That's how you knew about the bag of money."

"And that you were in Tucson, and at which motel."

"Jesus Christ." I grip my forehead in my palms. My head feels like it's going to explode. "But wouldn't Silas have worried that you had tapped his phones?" Wouldn't Klein questioning my mother make him paranoid?

Klein smirks. "He was too arrogant to be worried. He told your mother we had nothing on him, and that no judge would issue a warrant based on nothing."

I believe that. "What else have you guys heard?"

They share a glance.

"Conversations between Canning and Reid that implicate them both in the setup of Abraham Wilkes, as well as a half dozen other crimes. But probably not enough to nail him for what he did to Betsy, and other young girls."

"But you have Betsy's testimony now," Gracie argues, adding bitterly, "and Heath Dunn's, if he'd stop lying long enough to admit that he recognized the future district attorney."

"My money's on her refusing to testify, even if she wants to help. She has a new life now, and she doesn't want people to know who she was," Tareen says.

"Besides, there are too many ways to poke holes in her story. It was fourteen years ago, she was high, she couldn't definitively ID him . . . We need a slam-dunk." Klein levels me with a look. "And you can do that for us, if you're willing." He hesitates, as if somewhere deep down under that callous exterior of his, he has a conscience. Or maybe he's just using my conscience against me. "For Abe."

"Of course Noah's willing," Gracie blurts out, answering for me. She turns to me and in her green eyes, I see my options—help the FBI put my uncle in jail for life and destroy the only family I have left.

Or lose her forever.

CHAPTER 60

Grace

He's awake.

I can tell by the rhythm of his breathing, by the rigid feel of his body against mine.

He's awake, just as I'm still awake, quietly hanging in this state of limbo as I wait for him to commit. To make a choice.

To make the right choice, the one that will see his uncle face punishment for his crimes.

And cause his dead mother's name to be dragged through the mud.

Now I know what Klein meant when he told me to be careful, to not get in too deep with Noah, unless I was 1,000 percent sure that he would choose me over his mother, and his uncle.

He predicted that Noah might be lying in bed next to me one day, deciding whom to protect.

Whom to disappoint.

Whom to betray.

We all know who Jackie chose. Her brother . . . herself. She chose wrong.

But will Noah make the same mistake?

CHAPTER 61

Commander Jackie Marshall

May 6, 2003

I watch Canning make his way around the pool to where I sit in my lounge chair, under my lilac tree. He's swaying with his steps.

Or maybe *I'm* swaying.

I reach down to grab the bottle of whiskey and top up my glass.

"Jackie." Canning drags over a chair to place it next to me.

"I heard they found things in Abe's house." I'm not going to bother with pretenses.

"Yes, ma'am. I don't know what to tell you, except I'm sorry. I know he was a good friend."

"There's no way Abe was dealing drugs." Just like I know there's a reason for Mantis and Stapley being placed on this unorthodox "special" investigative team, and there's a reason that crime scene was shut down like a vault, nobody in, nobody out.

"It's not lookin' good for him."

"That's because you have Mantis on the case. *Mantis!*" I hiss. "The very same guy who Abe was about to bury for stealing money!"

"Mantis is as shocked about this as anyone else."

"Yeah, I'll bet." I let out a derisive snort. "Was he shocked when Abe refused to keep the bag of money he found in his car? The bribe from Mantis, to shut him up?" .

Canning's brow furrows in thought. "Did Wilkes say that Mantis handed him a bag of money?"

"No, Mantis left it there for Abe to find."

"So Abe didn't see who left this bag."

"No, but . . ." I sigh. *God damn it.*

"Is there an accusation you'd like to make, Jackie? Something you can actually *prove* beyond a reasonable doubt? Something that will sound plausible, next to the concrete case they're building for Abe's corruption as we speak?" Canning looks at me through shrewd eyes. "Think carefully. Think about what it could mean to your career. To your family's happiness." He leans in as far as his round belly will allow him, to say in a voice so low that only I can hear, "Because the way I see it, *nothing good* will come of you falling on your sword for Abraham Wilkes." Then, in a more placating tone, "You warned him, didn't you? You told him about the greater good, about sometimes making choices that sacrifice the few to help the many. But it sounds like Abraham chose to help the few. Mainly, to help himself."

But didn't I help myself, too? What I did to Betsy, I did it for my family—for my brother, for his sweet wife and kids, for my darling Noah who adores Silas—but I also did it for myself. Because in those few minutes by that door, in that drive out to The Lucky Nine, the only solution I could think of was the one where *my* family, *my* life, *my* ambitions were safe.

"You want to play in the big boys' yard, you need to follow the rules." Canning reaches into his pocket and pulls out a silver star.

The one that would make me assistant chief.

"Why don't you hang on to that for now, until this investigation is over. We can pin it to your collar and make it official." He drops the star into my palm and then heaves himself out of his chair. "Slow down on the drink, will ya? Or you won't remember anything we talked about."

Exactly what he'd play on, should I dare ever repeat it.

"Oh, by the way . . . do you know what happened to that bag of money that Abe *claimed* Mantis left in his car?" He says it so casually, as if it's an afterthought. I know it's anything but. It's evidence, to a story that Canning doesn't want to get out.

I meet his inquisitive stare. "I burned it."

He nods to himself. "See? People like you and me . . . this city needs us." He leaves me sitting under that lilac tree, with a silver star in my palm.

The points gouging into my flesh.

CHAPTER 62

Noah

"Noah!" My aunt Judy is known for giving fierce hugs, despite her tiny stature. Normally, I love them.

Tonight . . . I grab her hands, gripping them tight until I'm sure the urge to rope her arms around my wooden body has passed.

"How are you doing?" She frowns, peering up at me. "You don't look well."

Because I feel like I'm three seconds away from vomiting all over her pink slippers. "I must be coming down with something."

"It's going around. Silas came home early today, looking dreadful."

I swallow my anxiety. "Where is he, anyway?"

"Where he always is. Hiding in there." She waves a hand toward the office. "I can't get him to take a day off. Would you like some tea?"

"No thank you, ma'am."

"Alright. You let me know if you need anything else. I'll be over here, planning our trip to Italy this fall." Excitement flashes across her face as she heads back to her seat at the island, her laptop out in front of her.

This must be what it feels like to take a harpoon to the gut.

I'm sorry, I mouth, and then I head down the hall.

I find Silas seated at his desk, his chair turned so he can stare out the window. He doesn't seem to notice me come in.

I clear my throat roughly.

"Noah. Hi. I didn't know you were coming over." His voice is flat, weary.

"I wasn't planning on it." I wander over to the chair closest to him and take a seat, avoiding his gaze for as long as possible.

He reaches for his drink. "Want some?"

"No thank you." I drop the "sir." That's a sign of respect, of manners. Silas doesn't deserve either.

If he notices, he doesn't say anything. "I was thinking we should talk about your return to work. Things should calm down in another week or so, and it'd be good for you to be there. Put this all behind you."

How does he do that? How does he sit there, drinking his bourbon, pretending to be this man he's not? How has he pretended for these last fourteen years?

"The FBI found Betsy," I blurt out.

"Oh? Are they sure it's her? They had that false—"

"It's her. We went to see her."

"I see." He takes his time, polishing off the rest of his glass. Would I even notice that stalling tactic if I didn't know what he was hiding? "Well, at least Grace will have family in her life. And Dina will—"

"I know what happened that night at the hotel, with Abe. What Mom did. What *you* did."

I ready myself for his denials, for the way he can so quickly divert, so smoothly lie—he's proved to me time and time again, from that first night on the front porch after Mom died, that he is a true master of deception.

But instead, he simply takes another long sip.

"This is why you didn't want me talking to Gracie or Dina, or the feds. You were afraid we'd stumble on the truth. How could you do this, Silas!"

"We never wanted you to know. I never . . . I was trying to protect you." He sinks back into his chair. Is that relief I see in his eyes? In the way his body slouches? Relief that his secret is *finally* out?

Having Klein tell me my uncle's basically a pedophile is one thing. But hearing it from my uncle's own lips . . . "It doesn't matter whether I found out or not. The fact is you did it!" I explode, my eyes burning. "She was *fifteen*!"

"I . . . she told me she was old enough," he says feebly. Unconvincingly.

"And you never did it again? You never broke your promise to Mom that you'd never do it again? You didn't *lie* to her about that?"

He averts his gaze to his desk's surface. "Sometimes I just *need* . . ." His voice trails off. He finishes off softly with, "I just need." He knows it's wrong.

Rage flares inside me. "And what? You saw Abe and Dunn through that peephole and decided to dial up my mother? Drag her into this mess to save the day for you?"

"It would have been as much her mess as it was mine, if this got out," he mutters. "But no, I called Canning. *He* called your mother, sent her there."

It takes me a moment to get my bearings. "George Canning knew that you were with an underage prostitute and he ordered my mom there to get Abe and Dunn to leave?"

Silas pours himself another drink. "Canning wanted me in the DA seat, no matter what. If I'd known that he'd hang this over my head every single time I disagreed with him on a case he wanted dropped, or a charge he wanted laid, maybe I would have reconsidered it. Maybe I would have taken my licks.

"I told him it was a bad idea to call her, but he said Jackie was the most motivated to have this blow over for everyone's sake. That she was the only person Abe would listen to. That was before we knew who the girl was. It was just . . . any other cops and none of this would have happened."

"You mean Abe wouldn't have ended up dead."

He squeezes his eyes shut. "I never wanted Abe dead. But then he had to go toe-to-toe with Mantis. Your mother tried to talk him out of it. She warned him that Mantis had made a threat." Silas shakes his head. "Canning wanted me in that DA seat and Mantis chasing down drug dealers, and he is one damn determined man. Abe was not earning any points with him."

My heart starts racing. "What are you saying? That *Canning* was behind Abe's death?"

Silas fills his glass again, like he's a man on a mission to black out, and soon. "I don't know that he went as far as to spell it out to Mantis. But I know he told Mantis to leave that bag of money in Abe's car, see if Abe would be fool enough to bite." He chuckles. "When Canning came looking for it, your mother told him she'd burned the money. Boy was he mad when he found out she'd squirreled it away instead." He sighs. "And he's likely the one who told Mantis about Abe's search for Betsy. That's how Mantis lured Abe to the Lucky Nine." Another long sip. "And he *certainly* made sure the whole mess was all wrapped up with shiny paper and a pretty bow, to hide the ugly underneath."

Silence hangs. "How many girls, Silas?"

He sets his jaw, and my heart speeds up, thinking he's going to shut down.

"Three. I was weak only three times."

I cringe as mental images flash through my mind. "Including Betsy?"

"Four," he corrects softly.

I sway as I struggle to stand and head for the door, unable to bear this for one more second. "It's over for you."

"That damn federal agent." Silas's voice turns bitter, his tongue loose from drink. "Did he blackmail her? I'll bet he did. I'll bet that's why she called me up that night. She told me the feds had found out about her making the IA investigation against Mantis go away."

Jesus. He knew about that too? Every word out of Silas's mouth since stepping onto the porch the night my mother died has been a complete lie.

"She was unhinged, rambling about Betsy. This is all his fault. The bastard had managed to spin your mother into such a web of anxiety that she'd drink herself into passing out on her kitchen table, with a damn gun lying next to her head. He's a bastard, through and through . . ."

Silas's voice drifts into the background as I process what he's just said. "Wait. Why would you say she was passed out on the table?"

"What?" He pauses as if to replay his own words in his head, a flicker of something in his eyes.

"You said she was passed out on the kitchen table with a 'damn gun lying next to her head.'"

"Oh. Just . . . I assumed that's what happened." He tries to brush it off with a wave, but I hear the rare stumble in his words; I see the flash of panic, the way he holds his breath.

And the one piece that's been missing this entire time—that one glaring piece I couldn't see, because there's no way I could possibly imagine this version of the truth—falls into place.

"My mother didn't kill herself, did she?"

And with those words, that realization, an overwhelming wave of relief weakens my knees.

Racing fast behind it is a wave of paralyzing shock. Because if my mom didn't kill herself, it means someone slipped into the kitchen while I was in the shower and, finding her passed out on the table, put the gun into her hand and pulled the trigger.

Someone who knew the alarm's code by heart.

Someone who had a lot to lose if my unhinged mother came clean to the feds about what she knew.

My mother phoned Klein that night to make a deal. She had no intention of killing herself. And she wasn't saying I'd be "just fine" after she shot herself. She was saying I'd be able to handle the backlash that came once I learned the mountain of poisonous truth that had been hidden from me. She hid that money from everyone—especially Silas—because she knew what it represented, and she wanted it going to Dina and Gracie, though she wasn't brave enough to hand it over herself and risk answering questions.

"Silas . . ." Hot tears roll down my cheeks, my voice barely audible.

"I just wanted to talk some sense into her. That's why I drove there that night. To talk some sense into her. I don't know what came over me. The gun was there and she sounded so sure on the phone. I don't . . ." He shakes his head, his words drifting.

I start backing away. I can't believe this is happening. I can't believe I'm hearing this.

"She was going to ruin so many lives, including yours. I don't know what came over me in that moment, but I couldn't let her do that. I couldn't lose everything. I couldn't spend my life in prison. But this . . . if I had any idea what it would feel like, to carry this guilt, day in, day out . . ."

His increasingly pronounced limp, the dark rings under his eyes from countless sleepless nights . . . it's not because my mother killed herself.

It's because *he* killed her.

"But, I don't . . . I bolted out of the shower . . ." How did he get away?

"I heard you coming," he confirms. "You called out to her, and then your feet were pounding down the stairs, just as I closed the door behind me. I thought you would have heard the alarm activating. I thought someone might notice me pulling away in my car. And when the cruiser rolled down our driveway that night, I was sure I'd be leaving in handcuffs."

"You *are* going to be in handcuffs, soon."

"Am I not already?" He pauses, his eyes glossy—from emotion or bourbon, I can't tell. "They wired you, didn't they?"

"Right here." I tap the sunglasses that sit atop my head. The tiny device is attached to the arm.

He nods, more to himself. "I'm not going to prison, Noah."

"I don't see how you're going to avoid it. You can't argue your way out of this one." My voice sounds hollow as I reach for the door.

"She was right. She said this would ruin all of us." He smiles sadly at me. "Take care of your aunt for me, and your cousins."

I steel my jaw. "I will, but I won't do it on your behalf. We'll all be just fine without you." I pull the office door shut behind me and walk woodenly toward the foyer, in a fog.

Aunt Judy suddenly appears in my path. Her mouth is moving but my mind isn't fully grasping anything. "Noah, are you okay?" I think she says.

This time I do hug her, wrapping my arms around her tiny body, wishing I could protect her from all that's to come.

"It'll get better, I promise," she murmurs, squeezing me tight. She thinks this is about my mother. And it is, in a way.

But we *will* be just fine. I'll make sure of it.

A gunshot blasts behind us.

CHAPTER 63

Grace

"You're sure she's coming?" My mom tucks strands of her freshly cut and styled hair behind her ear. The blonde highlights make her look younger.

I sigh, my gaze on the path that winds through the cactus garden at Desert Oaks. "Yes, for the third time." If there's one thing I've learned about Betsy in the two months since we found her, it's that she wants family as much as we do. Neither of them has been patient about waiting, but both agreed it was the best choice, for my mother's recovery.

She waves at one of her friends who passes by—Coral, I think—and then fumbles with the sleeves of her cardigan, pulling them down to cover the needle marks still visible along her forearms. She's dressed far too warmly for June in Tucson, even in the shade. "You're sure I look fine?"

"You look great, Mom." She's put on at least ten pounds. Her gums are no longer puffy, her eyes no longer hollow. She's beginning to look like the woman she once was.

Cyclops comes around the bend first, trotting on his leash with his head held high, like some prized poodle. Next to him is Betsy, in a lemon-yellow dress that reminds me of the fifties—prim and proper, and representing everything that her past is not. I've noticed Betsy's wardrobe is full of modest, feminine clothing.

Tears begin to roll down my mom's cheeks as she sees her little sister for the first time in fifteen years. A sister she had convinced herself for so long was likely dead. Betsy, also, struggles to keep her emotions in check. They have much to catch up on, and many years to make up for.

But my eyes are for the guy walking alongside Betsy, standing tall and strong, allowing the joy in the moment to touch his features, even when I know he hides a mountain of sorrow beneath that smile.

The past two months have been nothing short of triumphant for my dad's case. Between the video of that night from Isaac, Silas's recorded confession, and whatever they've pulled from the wiretaps on the phone surveillance, Kristian is feeling confident that they'll have enough to put away not only Mantis and Stapley but Canning, too, despite the old chief's venomous denials. That bronze statue of Canning? Austin's decided it has no place anywhere in this city. It's sitting in some warehouse, likely waiting to be destroyed.

But on the other side of the coin are the ugly facts that have surfaced. The painful revelations about his mother and uncle that keep Noah restless at night, things that he'll have to live with for the rest of his life.

I know what that feels like, and yet I don't. I was so young when I lost my father. It's easier to move on with life when you don't quite realize all that you've lost. And, while my mother and Nan may have cocooned me in lies for years, they also served as buffers to hard truths.

But Noah has no buffer. There is no one protecting him from the pain tied to this scandal. We've been hiding out in Betsy's house for weeks, avoiding reporters who press him for the story about how his uncle murdered his mother. That story will come out in due time and, when it does, they'll learn exactly to what lengths Jackie Marshall went in her climb to become chief.

That truth hounds him; I can see the pain in his eyes, in the way he carries the weight upon those broad shoulders.

And yet, still, he is here for me, for my mother, for Betsy. Smiling wide. Genuinely happy for us. Maybe he's here to right his mother's wrongs, or maybe it's because he has nowhere else to go. All I do know is that since the moment that gunshot sounded, he could have made so many different choices. He could have not asked questions; he could have decided that the potentially dark secrets were better left buried. He could have never come to find me, to save my mom. He could have simply continued on with his life, coping over time with the pain of his mother's "suicide," with his Uncle Silas as his closest family member. But he chose differently. And for that, I will be his buffer. I will stand by his side, in the hard weeks and months, and years, to come. I will challenge anyone who dares claim that he is anything but a good, honest man.

I leave the park bench where my mother sits and go to Noah, to rope my arms around his waist and melt into his chest.

It rises and falls with his deep sigh.

And then his arms tighten around me.

ACKNOWLEDGMENTS

I set out to write a book that combined an intense suspense story with a genuine and deep-rooted romance. I can say with certainty that *Keep Her Safe* is unlike any other that I've written, but I hope you have enjoyed it all the same. It turned out much darker than I anticipated. You've made it to the bittersweet end, and you might not feel warm and fuzzy right now. I have a remedy for that: (re)read *Until It Fades*.

I did a lot of research for this book, but I also made a lot of stuff up, so don't be baffled by the fact that Congress Avenue exists but that Travis County's DA office doesn't have a cherry-red kitchenette, or that there isn't a St. Bart's in Tucson. I chose Austin, Texas, because I love the city and I've always wanted to set a story there. Much of the corruption and scandal in *Keep Her Safe* is inspired by true-life stories I found while scouring the news and then twisted to suit my needs, but none of it is based on Austin or its police department. This story is not a reflection of my opinion of the police department there. In fact, I believe there are many, many Abraham Wilkeses working to protect communities every day. Alas, *Keep Her Safe* focuses on the few rotten apples.

This was a beast of a story to write. I have many people to mention, and not much space to mention them (as I've gone *way* over my word count). Thank you . . .

To some very helpful readers who I reached out to for general information—Vilma Gonzalez, Krista Kelly Iverson, Clemencia Salinas Ramirez, and Heather Self.

To Sandra Cortez, for helping me get the Spanish dialogue and some of the Texas-specific stuff right.

To Jennifer Wiers Severino, for letting me bounce around ideas and strategize this wild plot.

To Amélie, Sarah, and Tami, I'll say it again . . . the very best readers and Facebook group admins a person could ask for. Thank you for *always* being excited to read my latest books.

To Stacey Donaghy of Donaghy Literary Group, for being there whenever I need you, whether it be for a ramble, a rant, or a good laugh.

To Sarah Cantin, for your patience and willingness to read the many ugly drafts of this story before it came together.

To Judith Curr and the team at Atria Books: Suzanne Donahue, Albert Tang, Jonathan Bush, Jackie Jou, Lisa Wolff, Alysha Bullock, Ariele Fredman, Rachel Brenner, Lisa Keim, and Haley Weaver, for taking my words and putting them into the hands of my readers.

To my husband and my girls, this book was a year and a half of late nights, missed beach days, and a lot of frustration. Thank you for being in my corner through all of it.